And

Laughter

Fell from

the Sky

And Laughter Fell from the Sky

JYOTSNA SREENIVASAN

wm

WILLIAM MORROW
An Imprint of HarperCollins*Publishers*

AND LAUGHTER FELL FROM THE SKY. Copyright © 2012 by Jyotsna Sreenivasan. All rights reserved. Printed in the United States of America. No part of this book may be used or reproduced in any manner whatsoever without written permission except in the case of brief quotations embodied in critical articles and reviews. For information address HarperCollins Publishers, 10 East 53rd Street, New York, NY 10022.

HarperCollins books may be purchased for educational, business, or sales promotional use. For information please write: Special Markets Department, HarperCollins Publishers, 10 East 53rd Street, New York, NY 10022.

FIRST EDITION

Designed by Diahann Sturge

Library of Congress Cataloging-in-Publication Data has been applied for.

ISBN 978-0-06-210576-9

12 13 14 15 16   OV/RRD   10 9 8 7 6 5 4 3 2 1

And Laughter Fell from the Sky

1

On a humid Friday afternoon in August, twenty-four-year-old Abhay Setty sat cross-legged on the grass in front of the Fox and Hound restaurant and bar in the tired college town of Kent, Ohio. He took occasional bites of a floppy slice of pizza while writing in a little notebook balanced on one knee. Next to him on the grass was a stack of books, the top one open, at which he occasionally glanced as he wrote. He didn't want to be inside the noisy, dim bar, and Kent seemed not to have heard of outdoor dining. A steady stream of cars drove past on the five-lane highway. Across the highway, at the entrance to campus, was a metal archway, spelling out KENT STATE UNIVERSITY in blue letters. The campus itself was quiet. It was happy hour time, which to Abhay was a misnomer, because it seemed the saddest part of the day. The air was heavy and still.

A gleam of light at the corner of his eye caused him to look up from his notebook. A gold Lexus crossed the intersection and turned into the Starbucks parking lot. A young woman in a tan pantsuit stepped out of the car, slammed the door, and stood scanning the air around her, as though not sure what to do next.

He blinked with recognition. Rasika? His friend Pramod's older sister? She was the last person he expected to see in Kent. They'd both gone to college at Kent State, but she'd graduated three years ago. She lived with her parents in Fairlawn, a wealthy suburb of Akron. He hadn't seen her since she'd graduated from college. She worked in banking, last he'd heard. Why would she bother to drive all the way across Akron to show up in Kent?

For a second he wondered whether to stay out of sight so she wouldn't notice him. Maybe she was meeting someone. But she looked lost, standing there on the street corner—not like someone who had plans. He closed his notebook, stood up, and waved his arms above his head. "Rasika!"

She turned toward the sound of his voice. Even from across the street he could see that she was still breathtakingly beautiful. She was tall and slim. Her skin was a creamy tan, and her black, thick hair was combed neatly into a gold barrette at the base of her neck.

"Rasika!" he shouted again.

She spotted him and waved back.

Abhay stood there and enjoyed the spectacle of her crossing the street and strolling over to him in her sleek pumps and trim work attire. A silky melon-colored blouse peeked from her suit jacket. There was nothing remarkable about the way she walked, except she was perfectly aligned without seeming to make the effort, her head floating on her neck, her shoulders floating over her hips. She looked completely out of place in this university town where no one bothered to dress up.

"You're back in town!" She stopped beside him and gave him a brilliant smile. Normally, Abhay liked natural women, yet on Rasika, the tinge of red on her lips, the twinkle of diamonds in her ears, and the faint scent of a floral perfume all worked together to create a stunning whole. She took her sunglasses off using the balls of her fingers, to keep her manicured nails out of the way, and raised her arched eyebrows. "My mom mentioned that you were home."

"I guess my mom told all her friends." He suddenly felt awkward and sloppy, standing next to this elegant woman. He bent down to pick up his paper plate of pizza, and in the process dropped his pen. He kneeled down, closed the book he'd been reading—an orange-covered volume titled *Peak Oil Survival*—gathered up his things, and stuffed them all into his backpack.

"Your mother really missed you," Rasika said.

"Yeah." He stood back up, flushed. "That's one reason I came home. To see her."

"I could never do what you did—go somewhere my parents didn't approve of, and stay there for so long. My mother would be so worried, and I can't even imagine what my father would do. He'd probably feel ill because he missed me so much."

"Sounds like your parents are really dependent on you."

"It makes my dad happy to have me around." She slipped her jacket off, folded it neatly over her arm, and plucked at the front of her sleeveless blouse. "God, it's still muggy, and it's after five."

Abhay dragged his eyes away from her bare shoulders. Rasika scratched her neck delicately with her glossy pink fingernails. The sun glared off the red and white Papa John's pizza sign across the side street. They heard a shout, and a sound of breaking glass, probably from one of the frat houses down the street.

"What're you doing in Kent, anyway?" he asked.

"I just wanted to get away." She adjusted the handle of her purse on her shoulder.

"From what? Your high-paying job? Your parents who love you too much?"

"From everything."

"So you came to Kent to be bohemian or something?" He

laughed, trying to be casual at seeing her again. He wasn't even sure what emotions he was trying to hide.

Behind her on the highway the light changed to green, and an old, dented Mustang from the 1970s lumbered by, its paint scratched and faded.

"Why is that funny?" she asked. "You grew up in Kent, so it's normal for you. I'm in Fairlawn, so Kent is different from my normal life. For you, maybe all of Ohio is too bourgeois."

He was surprised she'd used, or even knew, that word. He couldn't read her expression, and felt himself growing hot. Why was he baiting her? They weren't kids anymore. He used to be best friends with her younger brother Pramod. Rasika was a year older, but Pramod was always threatening to skip a grade and catch up to her. Abhay and Pramod had loved teasing Rasika: tripping her up with math puzzles, asking her silly riddles. He'd been amazed at her stupidity. She'd never seemed to catch on.

Now he wondered if she really was dense, or if she'd just enjoyed seeing them collapse into giggles. They were such geeks back then. He hadn't even realized she was beautiful until he was in college. Rasika probably still thought of him as Pramod's little friend.

"So, were you planning to go in?" She waved her sunglasses at the front door of the Fox and Hound. The place was built with heavy tan brick, steep roofline, and few windows: a suburban American version of an old English tavern.

"I need to get home."

"Come on. It's my treat." Rasika stepped toward the doorway.

He didn't want to reveal his poverty. He'd signed on with a temp agency, and his first paycheck was a week away. His mother had slipped him a twenty before he left the house this evening, and after buying the pizza, he was down to seventeen dollars and some coins, which needed to last until his paycheck.

"I'm not hungry," he lied.

"Just sit with me, then. I don't feel like being alone right now."

He hesitated. She smiled at him. "Why not?" he said, and held the door open for her.

At the hostess stand, Rasika stood very still and tall.

"What're you looking at?" he whispered.

"Those girls over there."

He followed her glance to a nearby table. Two young women in tank tops sat with two muscled guys, one wearing a Cleveland Cavaliers cap. One girl, whose black scoop-neck shirt showed a lot of cleavage, had a wide, red-splotched face and a large nose. Her eyes crinkled almost shut whenever she smiled.

"That girl in the black thinks she's beautiful," Rasika said.

"How can you tell?"

"She's giggling with those guys and running her hands through her hair."

"Yeah?" Abhay noticed the girl did keep fluffing up the top of her long hair and letting it fall to the other side. The boys seemed transfixed.

"The way you present yourself is so important," Rasika said. "Why doesn't that girl wear some makeup? At least a light concealing cream."

"She's captivating them despite being ugly," Abhay observed.

Rasika narrowed her eyes at the girl. "Yeah. Maybe."

As the hostess led them to their table, Abhay followed Rasika and enjoyed watching her hips move as she walked. They were seated at a booth near a window overlooking the parking lot. The hostess slid a basket of popcorn onto the table.

"What would you say about my looks?" As soon as he asked this, he regretted it. He didn't really want to hear that he was too short, or not muscular enough, to suit her taste.

She settled her purse, a firm bag with tan and brown checks, squarely on the bench next to her, as though it were another guest.

"You're really very handsome." Her gaze was more scientific than admiring. "Strong jawline. Straight nose. Beautiful eyes. You're short but fit, and your shoulders are broad. Why not make the most of it? It's like you're trying to hide your good looks with that tie-dyed T-shirt, and that little pigtail, or whatever it is. How hard could it be to get a decent haircut and wear a real shirt?"

He put his hand up to his head and stroked the tiny braided pigtail at the nape of his neck. He was pleased with her positive opinion. "Aren't you worried about insulting me?" he asked, to cover up his pleasure.

"You asked. Plus, you're an old pal. You don't take me seriously."

The waiter, a tall blond man, deposited two glasses of ice water on the table.

"So, how're you doing?" Abhay changed the subject. "How's life?"

"Good." She raked a strand of hair off her forehead with her perfect fingernails.

"You work at a bank, right?"

"I'm a junior commercial loan officer with Ohio West Bank."

"I guess you make a decent amount of money." He opened his menu as a way to take his eyes off her.

"Everyone thinks I'm rolling in cash because I work at a bank, but banking salaries aren't that high. If I were smarter, I'd've become a doctor or a software engineer. But I'm doing OK. I have plenty of money to spend on myself." She put her elbows on the table, intertwined her fingers, and set her chin on the shelf of her hands.

"You live with your parents, so that saves money."

"That's what a good Indian girl is supposed to do, right? Why bother getting my own place when my job is so close to my parents' house?"

The pictures of nachos, potato skins, and cheddar cheese soup made his mouth water. The piece of pizza had just whetted his appetite. Although she had offered to pay, he'd rather be hungry than sponge off Rasika. He closed his menu and grabbed a handful of popcorn. "So your life is settled."

She took her elbows off the table and sat back. "Of course not. I'm not married. Hopefully soon." She rubbed a palm over her forearm. "Someone's coming to see me tomorrow."

"You mean, someone your parents have invited?"

She nodded and held out a hand to examine her fingernails.

"You want an arranged marriage?"

"Of course."

"You don't seem terribly excited."

"Well, I am." She tugged up the shoulders of her blouse, although it wasn't low-cut at all.

"Why would you want that kind of marriage?"

"It's the next step in my life. I don't want to be unconventional, like you."

"Having an arranged marriage is not exactly conventional in the U.S."

"Come on, Abhay. It's expected in my family. Your family, too. You know that."

"You want to be conventional within the context of your unique, unconventional situation."

"Whatever."

"You're an Indian-American woman at the beginning of a new millennium. You're in a unique situation. There's no convention for you to fit into. You have to *create* yourself."

Rasika shook her head. "I just need to do what my parents want me to do, and everything'll be fine."

"So you feel the need to fit into their image of who you're supposed to be?"

Rasika rolled her eyes. "You don't understand, Abhay."

The waiter approached them, and Abhay pushed his menu to the edge of the table. "I'm fine."

"I'm going to have some wine," Rasika said.

Abhay decided it would be awkward to sit here watching Rasika drink. "I'll have a beer," he told the waiter. He'd just be extra frugal for the rest of the week.

When the drinks arrived, Rasika licked the edge of her wineglass. "I learned it on the Internet. You lick the edge of your glass before taking a sip, and you don't leave a lipstick print." She giggled, and he saw a glimpse of her younger self, Pramod's silly sister.

"So, an eligible bachelor is coming to visit." He raised one eyebrow. He had mastered this art when he was a child, in order to annoy his mother, and it still sometimes came in handy.

"He's related somehow to my father's cousin's wife, so that's how we found out about him. I liked his photo, and he liked mine, we talked, and we invited him to visit."

"Are you happy about it?"

"My parents are happy." She picked up one kernel of popcorn with the tips of her fingers and shook it slightly, as though to remove any impurities before eating it. "They think I'm getting too old to be single."

"You're, what, twenty-five?"

"My horoscope says I should get married before twenty-six."

"And when will that be?"

"January." She gazed up at the ceiling.

Her eyes were shaped like half-moons. To take his gaze away from her face, he lifted his mug of beer and took a long swallow. "You don't believe in horoscopes, do you? I mean, we're in the twenty-first century. It's 2007. Why bother with that kind of thing?"

She shrugged. "It's important to my parents."

"You seem ambivalent. Is that why you wanted to get away this evening? To think about things?"

"No. I'm not ambivalent."

Abhay twisted his thin leather bracelet, a souvenir from the commune, around his wrist. He wondered what she really wanted. He wondered if she even knew. "What's the guy like?"

"He has a bachelor's degree in computer software engineering and an MBA. He's from New Jersey, but he's willing to relocate here."

"Sounds like you're ready to hire him."

"Ha, ha. You know those are the kinds of things Indian parents care about."

"What about you? Have you actually spoken to him? Do you know anything about him?"

"Of course I've spoken to him. My parents have spoken to him and his parents. We've had the horoscopes matched. You know, the works." She ran a finger over the edge of her glass. "He's quite handsome." She smiled faintly. "He's tall, and he has a relaxed look. At least, that's what I got from his picture. I don't want to marry the usual Indian-American guy—short and scrawny, intellectually brilliant, and with no social skills. Someone who makes a lot of money but doesn't know how to spend it."

"You don't want to marry a nerd, in other words." Abhay wondered if Rasika put him in the category of the "usual Indian-American guy." Was he still a nerd? He was short but not scrawny. He prided himself on his intellectual brilliance, but he wasn't someone who would ever make a lot of money. "Listen. You don't have to go through with this. You can make your own decisions."

"I don't want to talk about it anymore. I don't know why I told you in the first place." She lifted her glass.

In the middle of the room, a waiter pushed three tables together. A dozen overweight, middle-aged people dragged out chairs, seated themselves, and started shouting out drink orders.

Rasika turned her shoulder against the noisy group and put her glass down. "Tell me about your—where you were." She brightened her face with a smile and held up both hands, as though ready to catch whatever he would tell her. "What was it like?"

What could he say about the last year of his life? That he'd learned to cook a meal for thirty people, make a straw-bale house, and endure hours of meetings in order to reach a consensus for any little thing? That he'd had what he assumed was his first long-term, serious relationship with a woman, and his assumption had proven false? That his illusions of the life he thought he was going to live had been shattered, and he had no idea what to do now?

"You lived on a kind of farm, right?" she asked. "Where was it again?"

"West Virginia. It was a commune."

"How could it be a commune? We're not a Communist country."

Usually, once he brought up this word, Indians turned away and asked him no more. His parents had only come to visit him once at Rising Star, during one of the "outreach days," when all community members were properly clothed. Abhay remembered this about Rasika: she'd ask questions where other people were not curious. Sometimes her questions made her seem slow, but at least she was interested.

"A commune's a group of unrelated people living together who share labor and resources," he said. "You can have a commune any-where."

"Don't you like having your own space and your own things?"

"We each had our own private room, where we slept and kept our personal stuff. But we shared everything else: cars, food, a ste-reo system, tools. Even clothes. There was a room where you could go and get something to wear."

"You went there to do research, right?" Rasika asked. "For your senior thesis?"

"I can't believe you remember that I did a senior thesis." Even his parents hadn't read his paper.

"I was impressed. I wasn't about to write a huge paper if I didn't have to. But we all know about your high grades and test scores."

Abhay knew that his intelligence was a topic of general conversation among his parents' circle of Indian friends. That was one of the things that bothered his dad—that everyone knew Abhay's grades were fantastic, and no one could understand how his parents had messed up by not making sure he studied sciences and went to medical school. "My thesis was on utopian communities. But I finished that before I graduated. I'm not writing anything now."

"Then why'd you go?"

"To live. I thought I'd like to live in a community like that."

"And you didn't?"

"It wasn't that simple," he said.

"What happened?"

"I liked the people." He tugged his ponytail. How to explain this in a way that made sense? "I thought I was going to love tilling the earth, building barns, and all that. At first I was exhausted. I figured I'd get used to that, and physically I did. But then I got bored. It was all physical labor and no intellectual stimulation. I kept trying to like it. But the harder I tried, the worse it became. Then I got angry. I started fighting with people." Abhay had never, until now, revealed to another person this humiliating end of his sojourn at the community. Somehow he felt OK talking to Rasika. He'd never realized before that she was a good listener. Anyway, he'd probably never see her again after this, so it didn't really matter what he told her.

"What were you angry about?" She was resting her chin in her hand. Her face was unclouded and clear. She didn't seem disturbed by his behavior.

"It was just—the place was so lacking. We had all these meetings at the commune, these interminable meetings about nothing, it seemed to me: whether we should eat honey or buy a new radio.

I couldn't stand it. And the incompetence of some people, how shoddy their work was. The kitchen was never completely clean. Once we all got a stomach bug, and I'm pretty sure it was because the dishes weren't properly sanitized. After that I tried to institute a protocol for cleaning the kitchen, and we had a bunch of long meetings about it, but finally people felt like they didn't want to be regimented and policed in that way." He shook his head.

"You got angry because the place wasn't as good as you thought it would be."

"Exactly. I know that sounds immature, but I realize that, all my life, I've gotten angry when people or situations aren't like I think they should be. So even after I got angry, I wanted to make the commune work. I felt like I was learning a lot about myself. I wanted to stay. I got assigned a coach to help me overcome my anger problem." He stopped talking. Rasika's eyes were still on him, and he could feel himself warming and opening up under her interested gaze. Should he tell her about his dream? He grasped his pen and began doodling a lightning bolt on his napkin.

"Why did you finally decide to leave?" she prompted. Two waiters approached the noisy table with drinks-laden trays.

"I had a dream where we were having one of our interminable meetings, and during this meeting we decided to kill ourselves." He raised his voice over the clatter of the waiters. "Group suicide for the sake of some ideal. I was confused about the purpose, I couldn't figure it out, but I didn't object. We were supposed to walk through a dark tunnel, and that was how it was done. I watched people walk through before me—men, women, even children. Then it was my turn. I hesitated. I wasn't sure if I should. I started asking questions. And the guy behind me said, 'You have to do it. We agreed.'"

Rasika nodded. "Sometimes I have weird dreams too. I just try to forget about them."

"For a long time, since I was a kid, I've used visions or dreams to make decisions. That's why I moved to Rising Star, because when I visited, I saw a kind of glow around almost every person at that place." He pushed away his lightning-bolt-covered napkin.

"So you left just because of that dream?"

"Sort of. I was also in a relationship. I thought we were pretty serious. Then I found out she was also sleeping with someone else—one of the men who, I thought, was married to a woman with a couple of kids." A waiter walked past with sizzling fajita trays, and the rich smell of grilled beef and onions wafted by. "I actually walked in on them one day in her room, and I confronted her, and she said it was my problem, that I needed to get over my jealousy. She threatened to bring it up at a meeting. I asked her to let me think about it first, and that night is when I had the dream. I left the next day."

She reached for his hand on the table and grasped it in hers. "That sounds really painful."

He squeezed her smooth fingers.

"You still think about her?" she asked.

"Sometimes. Mostly I feel angry, instead of sad."

The waiter set the bill in its tray on the table. While Rasika rummaged in her purse for her card, Abhay added several dollars to the tray. "For my beer," he said.

"Let me get the whole thing." She put her card on the tray.

"At least let me pay for the tip."

"Fine."

He folded his dollars and slipped them under his beer mug.

Once the waiter took away the bill, Rasika held the stem of her empty glass and slid it back and forth on the table. "What should we do tonight?"

"You want to hang out with me?"

"Sure. Let's do something different."

He wondered what she thought of as "different." He was still hungry and wished he could suggest they have dinner. "Let's go to the memorial," he said.

"What memorial?"

"You know. The one for the students who were killed in 1970."

"Oh. God. I hate it when people keep bringing up that old thing all the time."

"I hate it when people have that attitude. People think it's all ancient history, that the government could never again turn its guns on innocent young people. But it wasn't that long ago."

Rasika picked up her purse, scooted herself off the seat, and stood up. "OK, fine. Let's go." She gathered her jacket into her arms. "You can follow me in your car."

"I walked here."

"You *walked*? All the way from your mom and dad's house?"

"It's only a few miles. I donated my bike to the communal bike pool at Rising Star."

"Won't your parents let you use a car?"

"I'm trying to stay off fossil-fuel-based energy as much as possible."

She flung up her hands. "All right. I'll give you a ride."

"Why don't we walk? It's not that far, just up the hill behind the Auditorium Building." Then he looked down at her feet, encased in tan pumps with squarish high heels at least a few inches tall. "Can you walk in those things?"

"I can manage."

"Why do women wear shoes they can't walk in? It's like Chinese foot-binding or something, except you're doing it to yourself."

"They're cute shoes. It's not like I planned to climb a mountain today or anything."

Abhay stood up next to Rasika and realized her heels made him several inches shorter than she was. Now he'd be walking with a beautiful woman towering over him.

They stepped out into the sticky evening air. After the dim interior, the glare of the evening sun made Abhay blink for a moment. An overweight couple in shorts and flip-flops lumbered by, each holding thirty-two-ounce plastic cups filled with bubbly brown soda.

On the road in front of them, a shiny blue Hyundai was slowing, although it had a green light. The Hyundai pulled up to the curb and stopped. The passenger window descended. Rasika halted in her tracks, a stunned look on her face. Abhay saw the driver lean over to the passenger-side window. He recognized that face from somewhere: solemn, brown, somewhat large.

"Rasika! You need a ride?" the man shouted.

Rasika composed herself, smiled, and waved. "Oh, hi, Subhash!" She stepped briskly to the window and leaned over. Abhay couldn't hear what she said, but he saw her shake her head and point to the Starbucks parking lot, where her car was parked. Then the man got out of the car—right there at the intersection—and stepped onto the sidewalk. He was tall and verging on plump. He wore a sport coat that seemed a bit too large for him. He looked to be in his late twenties or early thirties. As they talked, the man seemed nervous: he patted his pants pocket several times, as though making sure his wallet was there. At one point he glanced at Abhay and gestured toward him. Rasika shook her head and laughed. She made no move to call Abhay over to introduce him. Finally, the man got back in the car and drove on. Rasika waited until the car was out of sight before rejoining Abhay.

"My cousin." She pulled a tissue from her purse and patted her upper lip. "I wish he hadn't seen you. I'm sure he'll tell my parents."

"I think I've met him before. Maybe at one of those Diwali events or something?"

"Probably." They waited on the curb for the light to turn green. "He and his parents moved here from India when I was in high school. Subhash's father is my dad's cousin. I guess they were close growing up, and when Subhash's dad lost his job in India, Appa wanted to help out, so he set Balu Uncle up with an insurance business in Cleveland. I forgot that Subhash is starting an office in Kent."

"Why does it matter if Subhash tells your parents that he saw you with me?"

A line of cars turned left in front of them. "He knows Viraj, because Viraj is related to his mother."

"And Viraj is . . ."

"The guy who's coming over tomorrow. It just looks bad for me to be seen with a man the day before I'm meeting the person I'm going to marry."

The light finally changed. They crossed the highway, skirting a rubbly pothole. "I still can't believe you're going through with an arranged marriage at all," Abhay said.

"This is the way Indians get married. It's always worked out fine."

"Yeah? What about Yashoda? You know her? Her parents took her to India right after college and got her married to some guy, and they brought him back to live with them. One big happy family, right? So she had a kid, and then the guy started shouting at Yashoda and her parents, and even hitting Yashoda. Right in their own house, their son-in-law was abusing their daughter. How awful is that?"

"That won't happen to me." They passed under the university archway and climbed up the sidewalk toward the Auditorium Building.

"How can you be sure?"

"Because. It just won't. I'll be fine."

"Haven't you found anyone on your own?"

"I've never tried. I don't date."

"That's not true. I used to see you with guys, all over campus."

On the lawn beside them, a group of students threw a football around. One girl fumbled with the ball, which came hopping onto the sidewalk at Rasika's feet. Without breaking her pace, she stepped over it and kept going. "No, you didn't."

"One time you were in the parking lot behind Olson Hall, kissing this really tall guy. He was practically lifting you off your feet. The two of you were so into it, you didn't even notice me walk by."

She picked up the pace, striding along dangerously on her heels. "You're obviously mistaken."

"And another time, you were playing footsie with some guy in the corner of the cafeteria."

She stopped in front of the white Auditorium Building. "I don't know what you're trying to prove." She flicked something off the jacket she was carrying. "If you're going to spread rumors about me, we may as well say good-bye now."

He stuffed his hands into his shorts pockets. The early evening sun glared behind her head, and he could barely see her face. "I haven't told anyone else," he said quietly.

She tilted her lips inward, as if to check the status of her lipstick. Then she started walking again. "Let's go see the memorial, at least."

2

Rasika and Abhay sat on the warm granite bench at the top of the grassy memorial slope, watching the students toss their football far down the hill, and listening to their shouts. On the ground in front of the bench, inscribed in granite slabs, were the words *Inquire, Learn,* and *Reflect.* To the right were four stone blocks representing the four students shot and killed thirty-seven years ago. The sky above them was a faded blue, and beyond the memorial, the branches of the trees going down the slope were still.

Rasika felt like she'd dropped the script of her life, and pages were blowing around and away from her. First of all, she had the bad luck of seeing Subhash. And tonight of all nights, how could Abhay have brought up all that crap about seeing her with men? She was already stressed by the idea of this weekend's performance: she'd have to be beautiful and charming to Viraj, demure and respectful to his parents, and compliant to her parents' wishes. She wanted to relax with company, and Abhay had seemed like a good candidate. He wasn't someone who would even care if she tried to impress him.

But there were certain things about her life she didn't want anyone to see right now. She didn't even want to look too closely herself. Why had she come to Kent today? Why hadn't she gone straight home, as she was supposed to do? Why had she invited Abhay to spend time with her?

She heard the melody of her phone, a maniacally fast version of "Heart and Soul." She dug it out of her purse, flipped it open, and saw Jill's number. "I have to take this call," Rasika apologized.

"Are you still at my house?" Jill asked.

Jill had been her cover since high school. Whenever Rasika went somewhere that she didn't want her parents to know about, she told them she was with Jill. "Yeah. Why?"

"Jared and I are going out for dinner."

"That's fine. If my mom calls you, just tell her I'm with you. Anyway, I've got my phone on. She shouldn't call you, plus I'm going home soon. Have a good night, I'll call you later." Rasika closed the phone. She probably shouldn't have bothered lying to her parents tonight. She hadn't planned to spend any time with a man, and Abhay wasn't anyone special. Still, she wanted to be absolutely safe on the day before such an important occasion.

She dropped her phone into her purse. "What're you planning to do, now that you're home?"

"I came home mostly because I didn't know what else to do, or where else to go. But once I got here, I realized it was a good opportunity to reconnect with my parents. As an adult."

"What do you mean?"

"Before I left for the commune, I was angry because they treated me like a kid. Even after I graduated from college, Mom tried to buy clothes for me, do my laundry, and tell me to eat my breakfast. Dad tried to get me to apply to law school or graduate school. They'd tell me what time to be home when—"

"All Indian parents are like that," Rasika interrupted.

"But why? That's what I want to find out. We had these personal development sessions at Rising Star, and I learned that any relationship is the product of all the people involved." Abhay drew a circle in the air with his forefinger. "I realized maybe my parents treated me like a kid because I acted like one. I either obeyed them, or rebelled against whatever they were saying."

"So how's it working now that you're home? Are they treating you like an adult?" Rasika sat very straight and silent, hands clasped in her lap, gazing out over the memorial hill. She had discovered some years ago that by making her body still, she could also quiet the thoughts racing around in her mind. The football-playing students had left. Leaves rustled softly around her in the slight breeze. There was no one else nearby.

"I'm not sure. Mom's gotten involved with some sort of pyramid marketing scheme, selling educational games through home parties."

"My mom mentioned that to me."

"She seems almost like a different person to me now. I mean, she seems happy. In a way. But she quit her job for this new thing."

"She used to work in your dad's department, right?"

"Yeah. She was the administrative assistant for the physics department. Now she's cut her hair—it's really short." He made a cap with his hands around his head. "And she wears these pantsuits. She used to wear knit pants and blouses."

"I really like your mom," Rasika said. "She's so gentle and sweet."

"She is, and I'm worried that this company is taking advantage of her."

"How's your dad?"

"The same. He was upset with me all through college because I couldn't pick a major and took five years to graduate, finally, with a degree in general studies. He wanted me to pick something lucrative, and I managed to drive him crazy by not choosing anything at all."

"Well, you're so smart. I'm sure it would drive any parent crazy to see their kid, who's been getting straight As since he was born, wander around completely lost like you did."

"Yeah. I can see that now."

"So how is he, now that you're home?"

Abhay laughed and shook his head. "He's still upset. I haven't done anything that would look decent on a résumé. In his opinion, at least."

Rasika felt like she was becoming too interested in Abhay. She wanted to keep herself clean and separate, ready to meet and merge with Viraj. She willed herself to think about something else. She chose one of her favorite subjects—the kind of engagement ring she would like—and concentrated on following her thoughts, trying not to pay too much attention to Abhay. "So you've decided to settle down at home?"

"I thought I'd hang out here for several months. Regroup. Earn some money. Figure out what to do next. Now that I'm here, I can see that I'll eventually need to get out to explore different parts of the country and figure out where I belong."

"Don't you feel like you belong here?"

"Not really. Do you? I mean, we ended up here more or less by chance. Our fathers got jobs here, and then they just stayed. We both ended up at Kent State because it's the closest four-year college. Plus, I got free tuition because my dad's a professor. There's nothing special about northeastern Ohio for our families. We could be anywhere, and our parents would want the same things. They'd want to keep doing their poojas and having their parties, while taking full advantage of the financial and shopping opportunities offered in the U.S. That's what all Indians are like."

Rasika's thoughts about the diamond ring ended abruptly. Was

Abhay right? Were her parents and their entire Indian community that shallow? "I don't think you can make a blanket statement like that about all Indians."

"Fair enough. But I'll say that for many of the Indians I know, the U.S. is just a place to get a high-paying job and buy stuff. That's the way it's been for my parents, at least, and I think for yours, too. They're just here on assignment; they run back to visit India every chance they get."

"We go to India almost every year," Rasika agreed.

"I went every three or four years when I was a kid until I finally put my foot down, right before my senior year in high school, and refused to waste my summers that way. I feel like I have no particular roots in India or in Ohio. I have no roots anywhere, and neither do you."

"That's so depressing. I can't believe that's true."

"Are your parents citizens?"

"Not yet. My mom almost became a citizen when I turned eighteen and went through the process, but then at the last minute she decided not to. She said she couldn't see any reason to go through the trouble. And for my dad, it's an emotional thing. He likes having an Indian passport."

"That's right. It's cultural loyalty. My parents aren't citizens yet either. What's holding them back? It's only because they don't really think of themselves as Americans. They don't want to vote. They don't want to get involved with the local community."

"We have our own community here. The Indian community."

"Exactly my point. Your parents probably have very few non-Indian friends, right?"

Rasika had to admit this was true. "So what? People of every culture prefer to hang out with others like them. Anyway, Ohio's not such a bad place. We have friends here, connections." Rasika felt like she was grasping at straws. She did want to stay in this area.

She wanted to be near the people who knew her and appreciated her high quality. The Indian community here valued her impeccable taste when it came to both Indian and Western clothes, gifts, and other social niceties. If she went elsewhere, would anyone even care about how special she was? She couldn't say this to Abhay. He would think she was vain. Not that she cared what he thought.

"In a way, it's good that I don't have any ties here," Abhay said. "I can choose to settle anywhere, and I certainly wouldn't choose this place. The only thing people seem to care about around here is building more shopping malls and parking lots. In other parts of the country, they're putting in bike lanes and creating more parks. I come back here and see more housing developments everywhere. They've ripped up perfectly good fields to put in more buildings, more pavement."

"Abhay, you're being kind of naive. People do need to shop. They need to live somewhere."

"They don't need to buy a bunch of stuff made by people working for slave wages in factories in China and Mexico. They don't need to buy a bunch of plastic that's going to break and go into a landfill." Abhay waved his arms as he talked, as though trying to foment some action out of the air.

Rasika laughed. "Do you think the world will ever be the way you want it to be?"

"I don't know." He looked at his toes, scratched his knee, and then gazed up into the sky. "I'm searching. I'm feeling kinda lost right now."

"I guess I feel closer to India because I was born there, and I didn't come here until I was eight."

"But you don't feel Indian anymore, do you?"

Rasika rubbed a palm over the tan skin of her forearm. She was Indian. She knew that. Yet she was also aware that, since she'd arrived in the U.S. in the third grade, her feeling of being Indian had grown more and more tenuous. "Once I get married, I'll feel completely Indian," she said.

"It sounds like you want to get married to find yourself."

"I'm not lost. Not like you."

He glanced at her for a moment, and then sat up straight and turned his face to the sky. She followed his gaze. High above them a pale moon had appeared in the blue evening sky. Rasika fixed her mind on the engagement ring again. She hoped Viraj hadn't gone and picked out the ring himself. She didn't necessarily care about a large diamond. She wanted one of high quality, very clear and sparkling. Some men—and she could certainly imagine Viraj in this category, given what she knew about him—just thought bigger was better. And what if his mother had bought the ring from an Indian jewelry store? It would be set in that bright yellow Indian gold, and it wouldn't be a high-quality stone. Diamonds mined in India generally weren't the highest quality. If Viraj had bought the ring already, she wondered how she could persuade him to do things her way, without coming across as spoiled or difficult.

"Have you already decided to marry this guy?" Abhay asked. "The one you're meeting tomorrow?"

"Yes," she said.

"Are you sure?"

"Of course," she said flatly. "I'm not going to turn him down after they've traveled all the way out here. My parents have wanted me to get married since I graduated from college. It's been hard to find someone that we all agree on. Now we've found him. It's time for me to get married, and he meets all my criteria. It's as simple as that."

"What kind of future do you want to have?" He was sitting sideways, one bent leg resting on the bench, looking at her intently. "What do you really want out of life?"

She wondered how to address Abhay's questions. She didn't

want to come out and tell Abhay her dearest wish, which was to impress people with her taste, beauty, and elegance. It would make it sound too crass to say it out loud.

She'd always been confident of her own high quality, as she liked to think of it, but it had sometimes been difficult to persuade others to see this. Growing up, some of the other kids just thought she was aloof. In high school, she stuck with classic clothes, mostly jeans and sweaters, and had avoided most of the fashion horrors other kids were embracing, such as extra-short baby doll dresses, and dirty flannel shirts, and baggy overalls (although one year she had gotten her hair cut in the popular bouncy, shaggy style of the character Rachel on *Friends*). Of course at that age she never flirted with boys. During her sophomore year, she'd made friends with Ashley Smith, the most popular girl in the school, a head cheerleader. Ashley had invited Rasika to a party one Saturday night. Rasika had worn a pretty sweater over her jeans, and had taken a box of chocolates for Ashley's mother. When she got to the house, the mother was nowhere to be seen. Neither was the father. The house was dark and milling with bodies, some of whom she recognized from high school. Pounding music filled every room. The focal point of the party was the keg of beer in the basement. Rasika retreated to the kitchen, where she left her chocolates on the table, called her father, and waited at the end of the driveway for him to pick her up.

After that, she hadn't made much effort to be friends with the popular girls at school. She'd mostly just kept to herself, and maintained her friends from elementary school. Her teachers loved her poise and good manners. As she grew older, in college and the work world, some of her peers came to appreciate her elegance and sophistication.

"I just want what most people want," she finally said to Abhay. "A nice place to live, a family. And we'll have that, Viraj and I." It sounded strange to couple his name with hers. She'd get used to it.

"What are you passionate about?"

She was passionate about—she didn't know. Besides inappropriate men, that is. Could a person be passionate about material objects? She loved beautiful things. Sometimes she wished she could have been a jeweler, but that wasn't a suitable career for her family. So instead, she had to deal with the idea of money, with numbers on a computer screen.

It was best, she felt, not to be passionate about anything. Passion had steered her into the arms of the wrong man enough times. She crossed her arms over her chest. Of course, she hoped she would feel passion for Viraj. That would be fitting.

"I'm trying to figure out how other people make decisions," Abhay said. "Do you feel drawn, or pulled, to do certain things? Is it an emotional decision, or an intellectual decision?"

She wanted to put an end to these questions, in a gracious way. She turned to him and raised her eyebrows. "I'm a pretty simple person, Abhay. I just want what most people want." She stood up, strolled a few steps away, and stopped with her back to him. She was aware that he was gazing at her, and that her slim figure made a pretty picture against the fading sky.

"I mean, I hope you're not doing this just out of obedience to your parents," Abhay said.

"I'm not. This is what I want to do." She was still facing away.

"Your parents want you to be happy. They think the way to make sure you're happy is to try to run your life for you. But you don't have to let them."

"You're one to talk. It's not like you've figured your life out." Rasika's phone sang again. She grabbed for her purse on the bench.

"I hate it when people are slaves to their phone," Abhay said.

"Let me just see who it is. My mother'll keep calling if I don't pick up."

Instead, Benito's name was on the screen. She shoved the phone to the bottom of her purse. Benito was her gym trainer—very sweet, very encouraging. He had been interested in her for months. She clutched the purse in her lap until the phone went silent, then set her purse on the bench again. "What were we talking about?"

"The fact that you're held captive by your phone."

"Before that."

"You were telling me that I haven't figured my life out."

"Right." She crossed her legs and leaned her knees toward Abhay. "Life's not so hard. Just pick something and do it. Get a job. Make some money. Get on with things."

"You sound like my dad," he said. "I thought I had figured it out. I thought I'd live and work at Rising Star all my life. I thought I'd experience a working-together feeling, but without the judgmental nature of traditional cultures. It didn't work for me."

The air was cooler now, and she slipped on her jacket. "You can't solve all the world's problems by yourself." Talking to Abhay made her appreciate her own life. She wanted to be ready for tomorrow, ready to meet her future husband. "What do you know about tennis?"

"Why?"

"Viraj is interested in tennis. I need to know the latest news."

"Why don't you ask him?"

"I don't want to appear completely clueless."

"So you want to pretend like you know all about tennis?"

"At least enough to ask a few intelligent questions."

"The U.S. Open is coming up."

"What should I ask him about that?"

"Ask who he thinks will win."

Rasika considered this. That might draw him out. Men always had opinions on the future results of sporting events. "What are some of the names of the players?"

"I don't know."

"Where's it going to be?"

"Somewhere in New York."

Her phone rang again. She dug it out of her purse. It was her mother this time. She turned off the phone and stood up. "I need to get home. I'll give you a ride to your house." She felt ready to face her real life now, after this little interlude with Abhay.

When Abhay got out of Rasika's car in front of his parents' ranch house, it was about seven o'clock. He saw his mother at the dining table behind the picture window. She had taken over the dining room to display her product samples. He pushed open the door, kicked off his sandals, and dropped his backpack inside the door.

The heavy, dark chairs and china cabinet took up all the air space in the small dining room. A few small, lonely photos arranged in no particular order hung on one wall: his grandparents, his graduation photo, his sister Seema's school picture. The china cabinet contained a haphazard collection of useless items too nice to throw away: cloth dolls and little wooden toys from India, a carved soapstone pen caddy someone had given him for a graduation present, various cutesy porcelain figures Mom had received from the "girls" she used to work with.

"Good time you had?" Mom gave him her new, practiced smile. She sat at the table, which was covered with a lace tablecloth under a clear plastic protective sheet. She was reading a book called *Unleash Your Selling Capacity* and jotting notes on a legal pad.

"I ran into Rasika." He pulled out a chair and sat down in front of a stack of educational game boxes. The cover of the top game showed two crudely drawn anthropomorphic animals with huge eyes, playing with a spinning dial with numbers on it.

"Rasika." Mom tapped her pen on her legal pad. "Her mother

I must call. Sujata said she will give name of someone to host sales party." She pointed her pen at Abhay. "Key to success is networking."

Growing up, Abhay had often wished his mother would find some interests of her own and stop meddling in his life. Yet he never imagined his steady, sensible mother would have been taken in by this company. He lifted one of the educational game boxes closer to him. "Mom, do you really know what you're getting into? How much did these samples cost, anyway?"

She thumped her palm on the table's plastic covering. "It is investment," she said. "In myself I must invest."

Abhay was glad his father wasn't around. He'd not only make fun of Mom's bad English—which was for some reason worse than that of most other Indians they knew, and certainly worse than his father's perfect speech—but also of her new sales talk.

Despite his mother's poor English, his parents always spoke English at home; they didn't actually share a common Indian language. Abhay's mother had grown up all over India, as her father was posted here and there for his government job. Her family had spoken an odd mixture of Telugu, Hindi, and English at home. His mother could get by in five or six languages, but according to his father, she had never learned any language properly. His father, in contrast, had grown up in Bangalore and had mastered a fluent, literary-quality Kannada (at least in his own opinion). To practice his English, he used to listen to speeches by Winston Churchill and Jawaharlal Nehru. Abhay's parents had not felt it necessary to teach him or his sister any Indian language.

"It's really difficult to make any money with these pyramid scheme things. It's a scam, Mom," Abhay said. "Only people at the top make anything. They get you to pay them for these samples, and then you're stuck. And when you do make a sale, everyone else above you gets a cut."

"I will not listen to negative talk. Anyone will make money who works hard."

"Why are you doing this, Mom? I thought you liked your job."

"I want to follow passion," Mom said.

"Your passion?" He'd never once heard his mother use this word. He'd been trying to prod Rasika into stating her passion, and here his own mother, who had a very nice path to follow, had suddenly found some crazy desire.

A door opened down the hallway, and they heard a faint, insistent drumbeat. His sister Seema listened, very quietly, to a rhythm and blues station from Cleveland. He was surprised at her musical choices. She was six years younger than him, eighteen—thin, shy, and almost friendless, as far as he could tell. While they were growing up, he hadn't paid much attention to her. But he knew her enough to notice she'd changed while he was away, becoming more odd and reclusive. Then the door closed again, and the house resumed its tomblike silence.

"Education is passion for me," Mom said. "Learning will be fun with the games. Look. They come with video. Kids will love video." Mom set the appropriate boxes in front of him as she spoke. "Letters . . . numbers . . . addition . . . spelling. Even geography."

"There are so many educational games out there already."

"These are different. Children will self-teach. Child watches video and learns to play. Game is self-correcting. See?" She opened a box and displayed the game board, cards, and playing pieces. "While mother is cooking, child will be learning."

"What kids need is more time with their parents, not more time watching a video."

"What you know about raising children? Anyway, parent can play with child. Very versatile these games."

She must have picked up these words—*self-correcting, versatile*—

at her sales meetings. Outside the dining room picture window their neighbor, Mrs. Tully, was taking an evening walk with a tiny terrier on a leash. Abhay had a crush on her daughter, Michelle, during high school. He could still picture her long, dark-blond hair. He'd sent her a "secret valentine" cupcake during the student council's fund-raiser and had asked her to several school dances. Michelle never spoke to him, not even when they were waiting for the school bus together at the corner.

"So, Mom—have you set up any parties yet?"

"Almost. This close I am." Mom held up two fingers a centimeter apart. "At least I think you will support." She set her pen down. "Seema is embarrassed because mother is trying something new. Your father does not want me to keep things in dining room. Where should I keep? Everyone else has own space. Your father has whole room for home office. I have no place. Kitchen is my place, yes? No more."

Abhay had no idea his mother had ever felt resentful of her role within the family.

"You said I should do this," Mom said. "Now even you are against."

"I suggested you get into a pyramid scheme?"

"You always said, 'Mom, don't let Dad push you. You are smart. Get life of your own.'" Without her fake smile, she looked more like the mother he remembered from his childhood. "So lonely I was, after you left. Your father was upset because you went to that place. You will never come back, I think. And then Linda at work said there is this company and invited me to meeting. Dad was against, but I remember what you told and I went."

Abhay did remember telling his mother, occasionally, not to let Dad get her down. Dad was ten years older and had a Ph.D. in physics, while Mom had only completed two years of college. Dad sometimes ridiculed her for her lack of understanding of investing, her lack of interest in current affairs, her confusion around scientific topics like electricity and bacteria and molecules.

"I want to show I can also do something important," she said.

"If it makes you happy, I guess I'm happy for you," he said.

His mother stood and started stacking the game boxes. "How is Rasika?"

"Fine. I guess she's meeting an eligible bachelor tomorrow."

His mother clicked her tongue. "I don't know. So well Sujata has done. Rasika is not at all smart, and look at her—making all money, driving around in Lexus car."

"I think Rasika is actually very smart, but for some reason she tries to hide it," Abhay suggested.

His mother waved away this reasoning. "Even Pramod, his test scores were not so good as yours, and now almost finished with medical school he is. What do we do wrong? Your sister stays in room all the time now. Your father is telling about medical school or engineering or computer science. Such high scores she got on SAT exam. But she will not talk. I only wish she will take more interest in appearance. I tell her, Seema, you must smile and speak nicely. My best I have tried."

Here was the mother he knew! "It's not your fault, Mom." How could he explain to her that his situation wasn't a tragedy? And that Rasika's situation was not necessarily a success?

She patted his arm. "At least you are home. Now you can go graduate school. Never too late it is. Try again if you don't succeed first time. Never give up. You talk to Dad about graduate school, OK? He went to sleep early today. Tomorrow you talk. He will advise you."

Abhay nodded. Maybe he ought to talk to his father, man to man.

"I put food away already," she apologized. "For some time I kept out. When you did not come, I put in fridge."

"That's OK, Mom."

"Can I heat something for you?"

"Don't worry about it."

"No worry." Mom bustled into the kitchen. He heard her open the fridge door. "Rice I have, and mixed vegetable kurma. And rotis. You like rotis with kurma." Her voice sounded hollow, coming from inside the fridge.

He didn't feel like having her serve him and hover around, asking questions. On the other hand, he was hungry. And he did want to reconnect with his mother. He followed her into the kitchen and served himself from the containers she was taking out of the fridge. While his plate was rotating in the microwave, his mother started drying and putting away the dishes in the drainer. He said, "Let me do that later. Sit down with me while I eat."

His mother seemed stunned by this invitation. She stood in the middle of the kitchen, towel still raised.

"Can I make you a cup of tea?" he asked.

"No, no." She laughed. "I will not drink tea now. Some water I will have." She ran the faucet and filled a glass for herself.

Once they were seated, Abhay scooped up some kurma with a piece of roti and asked, "How did you decide that you wanted to marry Dad?"

"Only eighteen I was when I got married. My parents said he is good man, so I said yes. Yogurt you want?"

"I'll get it later." He mixed a bit of rice with the vegetables. "How could you agree to marry him? You'd only met him a week before the wedding, and after the honeymoon he came back to this country. You didn't see him again for months, and then you got on an airplane and came here all by yourself to live with a stranger?"

"Our families are knowing each other. They are not strangers."

"You didn't know Dad."

"All marriages are happening like that only."

"What was it you wanted when you got married? Why did you get married at all?"

"It was expected. And I was—I feel proud that this man, so educated, handsome, coming from America, wants to marry me."

"So you wanted to marry him."

"Of course. My parents did not force. If I did not want, I could say no."

"What was it like when you came to Ohio?"

His mother paused. "It was hard. Before I come here, I think it is like a movie, or TV show—everyone dressed up so nice. Everything so clean and big. Then I come here, and it is so cold. Almost all year it is cold. The snow gets black and dirty. My English is bad, so I am shy to speak and make friends. Even with other Indians I feel shy sometimes. And your father—bad temper he has. I was not used to that."

"He'd yell at you?"

"He does not shout. He is quiet, but angry. He wants me to be smart. I am not. He wants me to cook all kind of dishes. I know only few at that time. So he thinks he married stupid girl."

"He said that to you?"

His mother nodded. Abhay was outraged. How could his father have treated his innocent mother so poorly? He ripped off a large piece of roti, used it to gather a pile of kurma, and chewed furiously. He saw, out of the corner of his eye, his mother wiping her eyes with her fingers. Once he'd swallowed, he asked softly,

"Did you ever regret marrying Dad?"

"Sometimes."

"Did you ever"—he hesitated to ask this—"did you ever think about leaving him?"

"My mother wanted me to try longer."

"You told her?" Abhay's eyebrows shot up.

"I wrote to her after few months. I said I want to come home."

"Did you tell Dad? Did he know?"

She shook her head. "My mother's advice I wanted first, before telling."

"If you had gone home, would you have gotten a divorce?" Abhay couldn't believe he was having this conversation with his mother.

His mother shrugged. "I don't know. I was not thinking. No one got divorce then. Divorce was always woman's fault. That is how society considered. No one would allow their son to marry divorced woman."

"You were so miserable," Abhay said slowly, "that you were going to risk returning to India and living as a single woman for the rest of your life, just to—"

His mother shook her head. "Too young I was. I did not think. My mother said, you stay one year, and then we will see. And then I start taking classes. Typing, bookkeeping. I meet friends. Then it was OK. I managed. You see, I found out his secret—when he is worried, he becomes angry. So, then I could say, what you are worried?"

"You figured him out," Abhay said. "Did you—do you think you loved him then?" Again, Abhay was surprised at his bold words.

His mother considered her water glass. "We do not worry about love all the time in Indian marriage. It is not all about love. He is my husband. I must help him by taking care of house and children, and by cooking food. And I am his wife. He must earn the money. He must take care of me. I felt—before, when I was just married—I think he does not like me. I think, he is angry at me. Then later, I saw that he is not angry at me. He is just angry. And then you were born. He was so proud to have son, and I am happy to have cute baby to play with." She smiled at him fondly and patted his hand. "Why you ask about all this long-ago things?"

"I want to know you as a person," he said. "Not just as my mother."

"Good boy you are." She patted his hand again. "About you he is also worried now. So he is angry. But I know you are smart. Finally, you will surprise him."

After his meal, Abhay shooed his mother out of the kitchen and put away the dishes in the drainer. Then he picked up his backpack from the dining room and trudged past the living room with its white carpeting and shiny white furniture, which no one ever sat on. It always looked cheaply furnished to him, although he knew it wasn't. Past the family room, which was equally depressing: the usual dirty-looking brown shag rug, the sagging brown furniture.

As he walked down the hallway, Seema's radio grew louder. Some sort of dance tune, sung in a high, cloying male voice almost drowned out by a synthesizer and that crashing, echoing drumbeat every R & B dance band seemed to want to use.

He knocked on her door.

"Who is it?"

"It's me. Abhay."

The radio switched off, and paper was shuffled. The door slid open a crack to reveal part of Seema's thin face, and her prominent nose.

"Yeah?" she whispered.

"Can I come in?"

"Why?"

He smelled cloves. Could she possibly be smoking clove cigarettes in her room? Yet it wasn't smoky. "Come on, Seema. I've hardly seen you since I've been home."

She disappeared from the door crack, and then the door opened just enough to admit him. The air was stuffy, despite the air-conditioning. This was the smallest bedroom in the house. It had been Seema's since she was a little girl, and she'd never wanted to move, to switch rooms with Dad's office, as Mom suggested.

The bed was made—Seema still used an old flowered spread—and there was none of the clutter one would expect in a teenaged girl's room, none of the clothes bursting out of the closet, or hair dryers and makeup and jewelry scattered everywhere. On top of her neat desk were a tiny radio, a stack of books, and a handmade journal from Rising Star, which he'd sent for her birthday. The walls were bare, except for an outdated calendar she'd had for years showing a photo of two big-eyed fluffy gray kittens.

Seema sat on her desk chair, which she had placed with its back to the desk, as though to guard her books. She crossed her arms over her chest and crossed her skinny legs around each other until one foot was behind the other ankle.

Abhay set his backpack on the bed and sat beside it. He rested his palms on his knees. "What's up?"

She shrugged.

"How's your summer been?"

"I took a class at Kent State." Without turning away from him, she reached behind her back, tugged open the pencil drawer, picked up something with her forefinger and thumb, and slipped it into her mouth. She started working at it, gnawing it and rolling it around with her tongue.

"What's that?" he asked.

"Clove. Want one?" She reached behind her back again.

He shook his head. "You just eat them plain?"

"Yeah." She pulled one out and held it on her palm. "They're like little nails. They're sweet at first, and then hot. So hot it hurts."

He didn't know what to say to this. He had noticed, at dinner, that Seema had taken to eating Indian pickled chilies with her rice. Mom warned her every evening—"Not so much, Seema." But Seema didn't listen. She ate almost nothing except white rice and hot chilies, as if she needed the intense sensation to balance out the blandness of her life.

"Are you looking forward to your first year at Kent State?" he asked.

"It'll be something to do."

"What're you taking?"

"General requirements. Calculus, English, world history, biology."

"I heard Dad's been bugging you about your college major. Don't let him get to you."

She put the second clove in her mouth.

"What are you thinking you'd like to study?"

She chewed her clove. "Medicine. Or engineering."

"Really?" He raised one eyebrow. "That's what you think you'd enjoy?"

"I don't really like anything else. Not enough to make Mom and Dad upset."

"Pretend Mom and Dad don't care. Then what would you do?"

She untwisted herself and sighed. "I don't know, Abhay." She looked like a rag draped on the chair.

"Remember, Seema. The whole world is open to you."

She rotated herself again, this time in the other direction. "I just want to pick something and get it over with. I don't want to leave things open and have to keep figuring it out, like you're having to do."

He'd thought he was setting a good example for her by trying to figure out what he really wanted to do, and the whole time she was trying to avoid ending up like him.

3

Amma. Be sure to use the toothbrush on your hair," Rasika shouted into her mother's bathroom on Saturday morning. She spoke in Tamil, except said the word *toothbrush* in English. The family was getting ready for Viraj and his parents, who were coming over for lunch. Rasika was proud of her mother's beauty, and she'd inherited Amma's high cheekbones and smooth skin. But her mother sometimes went too long before touching up her hair dye, and the gray showed through.

Rasika sat on her mother's bed in a plush pink robe, looking at her outfit choices. She'd already showered and washed her hair. She still wasn't sure what to wear. Amma wanted her to put on a sari and jewelry, as was appropriate for a traditional bride viewing, but Rasika felt a silk sari and gold jewelry were too much for a daytime event. In India the women wore their fancy clothes at any time of day, if the situation warranted. Still, Rasika felt odd, decking herself out for lunch. Also, Viraj might be put off by a sari. He didn't want to marry a traditional Indian girl, after all, but a modern Indian-American.

She considered the green salvar kameez with sprays of flowers embroidered over it; and a pale saffron salvar kameez printed lightly and tastefully in gold. She had chosen these with care at an Indian clothing store in a Cleveland suburb. So often, Indian clothes were made to show off fancy needlework or beadwork, and not for a good fit. She had to try on so many to find one that draped well and showed off her figure without being revealing.

Rasika looked around her parents' bedroom, which was one of her favorite rooms in their home. Like the rest of the house, it had just the right touches of Indian and Western decorations. The bed, dresser, and other furniture were sleek and modern, in a light maple finish. The bedspread and curtains were done in Indian textiles: a tan background with a pattern of lotuses. A few years ago Rasika had helped her parents redecorate this room, as well as the entire house. She'd had to use all her charm to get her father to pay for the makeover. He was mostly concerned about saving his money for retirement or to guard against every possible disaster. She hoped Viraj also enjoyed luxury and would feel comfortable allowing her to spend their money as she saw fit.

The bay window let in the morning light through the sheer curtains, and the king-size bed made the room very inviting. Rasika lay back on the bed and closed her eyes. She didn't want to think about Viraj any more. She didn't want to think about anything. Since yesterday, her mind had been full of Abhay, and she definitely wanted to forget about him. She loved to sleep, and she allowed her mind to lull and drift. She knew she ought to feel nervous. Instead, she felt tired despite the two cups of coffee she'd had.

The bathroom door opened. Rasika sat up.

Amma, wearing a robe, threw her dirty clothes into the bin in the closet and looked at the outfits Rasika had laid on the bed. "You won't wear a sari?"

"Should I?" Rasika asked.

"A sari is always appropriate. It is both traditional and modern." Amma opened a dresser drawer and lifted several saris folded in neat rectangular packages.

"If I wear a sari, Viraj might think I'm too old-fashioned." Although she was speaking in Tamil, as she normally did with her parents, she said the words *old-fashioned* in English. This was the way they spoke: her parents and relatives often mixed English words with their Tamil.

"Right now, you worry about impressing his parents. Viraj will see you are beautiful even in a sari. You can wear one of your own, or one of mine. Later this afternoon, when you and Viraj go out on your own, then you can wear whatever you like."

Rasika nodded and picked up the rectangular packages, looking for something light and cheerful. Amma was right. She couldn't go wrong by wearing a sari.

As she considered her choices, an unhappy thought struck her. "Is Appa going to wear a suit?" Her father was eager to see this marriage go through, and a suit at an informal at-home luncheon might broadcast this eagerness in an embarrassing way.

"I don't know what he will wear." Amma unfolded one of the saris so Rasika could see the glistening gold on the palloo.

"Tell him to wear one of his silk jubbas. It's summer. It's Saturday. We're having lunch at home."

"He does not like me to meddle with his clothes." Amma lifted petticoats and blouses out of a drawer.

Would Viraj allow her to "meddle" with his clothes? She hoped he would be open to her suggestions. Or, better yet—maybe he would have a fine fashion sense of his own.

"I don't want one with gold," Rasika said. "Maybe a printed silk." She leaned over the drawer to find something that wasn't so fussy.

"Why not gold? You are meeting your future husband. You

must get dressed up!" Amma displayed a bright red, heavy silk sari with a green plaid pattern and a wide gold border. It looked like a Christmas tree, or a winter scarf.

"I won't wear that one. It's too heavy and dark. I'll burn up in it."

"You will be in the air-conditioning. No one is asking you to go outside. We used to wear this Kanjeevaram silk all the time, for any festival or wedding. No one complained." Nevertheless, Amma refolded the sari and put it back in the drawer.

Rasika picked up a light green rectangle printed with water-colorlike flowers.

"That is too old." Amma grabbed it from her. "If you want something light, wear a Benares silk." She opened another red sari printed with paisleys and scrolls.

"You really want me to wear red," Rasika said.

"Red is festive. The astrologer said it's your lucky color."

"I don't want to look too gaudy."

"You won't have to look at it." Amma's eyes were wild with frustration. "We will all be looking at you. Who knows? Maybe red is Viraj's favorite color."

Rasika took the sari from her mother's hands and rubbed a layer of fabric between her fingers. It was thin and light. The gold embroidery was subtle. The color wasn't as bright as she'd originally thought, and she did look good in red.

Amma pulled out a red blouse to match and laid it on top of the sari. "I think this will fit you." She gave Rasika a red cotton petticoat. "Try it on, raja. Then we can select your jewelry. I will go and wake up Pramod. He must be ready. We want to show ourselves in the best light."

Amma left the room and closed the door. Rasika laid her robe on the bed and began dressing. She could hear her mother knocking and shouting at Pramod's door. Her mother had insisted that he come home from Cleveland Clinic Medical School especially for this bride-viewing. Pramod's presence was necessary to prove that her family produced not only beautiful young women, but also medical students with bright futures.

Viraj really was handsome. Rasika had been afraid his photo might have been altered to show him in a better light, but as soon as he stepped in the door, she could see he really did have the thick, wavy hair, the large, dark eyes, and the dazzling smile that appeared in his photo.

The entryway of the house was full of smiles, greetings, taking-off of shoes. Rasika stayed behind her parents—she didn't want to appear too forward, too pushy—but put on a high-wattage smile, so they wouldn't think she was shy. Pramod sat on the steps behind her, and while everyone else was occupied with greetings, she kicked him on the shin with her bare foot to persuade him to stand up, which he did.

The men reached across each other to shake hands all around, and the women pressed their palms together in namaskar. Viraj put his palms together to greet her mother, and Amma smiled with pleasure at this traditional greeting. As everyone made their way into the living room, Viraj held out his hand to Rasika. She put her hand in his, and their eyes met. His gaze was steady, almost businesslike. And then he turned his right hand palm up, so her hand was lying in it, and patted her hand. She was so startled by this strange gesture that she giggled. He smiled back, let go, and turned away to follow the others. She felt silly standing there, alone, in the entryway.

Amma appeared in the kitchen doorway. "Come and pass out the drinks," she stage-whispered. In the kitchen Rasika recovered her composure. She walked, smiling and balancing a tray of soda glasses, into the living room. When they'd renovated a few years ago Rasika had suggested her parents buy furniture with simple lines and bland colors, so as not to compete with the Indian rugs and decorations.

Everyone was dressed just right. Viraj's mother was wearing a sari as fancy as Rasika's mother's, so that was OK. Rasika had persuaded her father, in the armchair next to the sofa, to put aside his dark suit and wear a white silk jubba and dress pants. Pramod wore a jubba over jeans, and other than the fact that the back of his hair was still a little wet from his shower, he looked reasonably awake and involved.

Viraj's father was wearing slacks and a dress shirt. Viraj, at the other end of the room, sitting on a sofa next to his father, was in a pair of dress pants and a silky-looking light blue shirt. Nice, she thought. Dressy, but not too formal. She wished she wasn't wearing a sari. She'd left her hair loose and had worn makeup, so hopefully Viraj wouldn't think she was too traditional.

As she walked around the room offering fruit juice punch to everyone, she felt Viraj's gaze following her around the room. She glanced back at him, but instead of averting his eyes, he kept his gaze steady. It made her feel as though she were some kind of painting or artwork.

She was glad to see Appa looking happy. Or at least, appearing calm. His body was almost free of the tics he had when he was worried or stressed. Almost every evening after work, his eyes squeezed shut and open rapidly, and his shoulders twitched. Appa had wanted to be a surgeon, but these tics—something he had since birth—prevented him from having a steady enough hand, so he had settled for anesthesiology. Today even his hands, which often picked at his nails until the cuticles were bloody, were still, clasped together on one knee as he listened to Mr. Shankar.

After Rasika returned the tray to the kitchen and came back into the living room, the only empty seat was next to Viraj's mother, across the room from Viraj. Mrs. Shankar's graying hair was pulled into a simple ponytail, and she wore no makeup. Rasika put on a friendly smile and sat down. What could she talk about to this woman, who seemed so much more old-fashioned than her own mother?

She needn't have worried; Mrs. Shankar started speaking immediately. "Viraj's future is very bright," she said. "He will be in top management soon. He wants a girl who is able to keep up with him." She spoke in Tamil and said the words *top management* in English.

Rasika wondered if this meant he wanted a girl who would also be in top management? Or someone who would be able to comfortably mingle with other top management and their spouses? She glanced in Viraj's direction and found him still looking at her.

"He wants someone who knows how to keep a beautiful house, and to entertain," Mrs. Shankar said.

Rasika murmured her agreement.

"He is not interested in a girl who is too forward." Mrs. Shankar had a way of lifting her upper lip when she talked, which exposed her long front teeth and made her look like a rodent. "She must be able to adapt to his way of life. He was raised to be decent. He will treat his wife like a queen. But he will be her king. And she must know that."

Rasika's mother appeared at the doorway, a large apron over her sari. "Come and have lunch."

"Let me help." Mrs. Shankar stood up and wrapped the palloo of her sari around her shoulders.

"There is nothing to do." Amma led them into the dining room, which had been set, the previous night, with the best china. When Amma shopped for china a few years ago, Rasika had recommended a simple, starkly elegant pattern with a thin rim of platinum. Amma wanted something more decorated, and they had compromised on this pattern: still simple, but with a wider design in platinum, almost like a sari border. It was beautiful against the white tablecloth embroidered in a subtle cutwork design. Amma had ordered a fancy floral centerpiece, like something belonging on a bridal table: a large triangular spray of roses and ferns, with three white candles sticking up from the middle. There was hardly room for the platters of vaday and raw vegetables, and the jars of pickles and chutney pudi.

Rasika managed to place herself at the other end of the table from Viraj. She was reluctant to get too close to him. There would be plenty of time for closeness later on, she reasoned.

Amma appeared with a pot of rice and went around the table serving everyone, as was traditional in India.

"Why should you be serving us?" Mrs. Shankar stood up. "Let us all go into the kitchen and get our own food."

"No, no. This is the way I like to do it," Amma insisted. "Rasika will help me with the rest. Come on, Rasika."

In truth, Rasika had never seen her mother do this before. Amma's parties were always buffet style. Rasika followed her mother into the kitchen, where Amma handed her a pot of avial—vegetables in coconut sauce—and a serving spoon.

The talk droned on. The fathers were discussing Indian politics.

"The U.S. is finally paying attention to India," Appa said as Rasika spooned avial onto his plate.

The men were talking in English, maybe because Viraj didn't understand Tamil—he had never lived in India.

"Yes. Yes." Mr. Shankar nodded his long head, like a cow's head. She wasn't sure if he was agreeing with her father, or her offer of food. She served him.

"All these years, U.S. is sending the arms to Pakistan," Mr. Shankar said. "Now only they realize they must also pay attention to India. India is having high-tech boom. India is becoming economic superpower." He mixed his rice and avial into neat balls and popped them into this mouth.

Eating with fingers was traditional in India, yet it always looked awful to Rasika, especially at a beautiful table like this.

Viraj glanced from one older man to the other, nodding.

"Over thirty percent of India's population lives on less than one dollar a day," said Pramod, the lone liberal in the family. "If Mahatma Gandhi were alive now, I don't think he'd see India as economically successful."

"We are long past age of Mahatma Gandhi," Mr. Shankar said. "We are now in different era."

As soon as Rasika sat down, Mrs. Shankar, who was also eating with her fingers, said, "Viraj prefers vegetarian. He will eat meat outside, to be sociable. At home, no. He is not picky about food. He will eat Indian, Italian, Chinese, Mexican. Anything at all. But a good home-cooked South Indian meal is best for his digestion."

"Rasika is learning to cook South Indian food," Amma said.

Rasika smiled and nodded. Amma had been writing down recipes on index cards for Rasika and had already filled a whole box of them, but Rasika had not looked at even one.

"She helps me cook every day," Amma said.

This part was truer. Rasika sometimes cut vegetables for her mother.

As Rasika ate her rice and vegetables and dal neatly with a fork, she glanced once or twice in Viraj's direction. He seemed completely absorbed in his meal and in the conversation. Which was worse, his constant stare, or his obliviousness?

After lunch, as everyone made their way back to the living room, Rasika picked up plates and carried them into the kitchen where Amma lifted them out of her hand. "Go and change," she whispered. "I will clean up. You are going to the mall with him." Amma said the word *him* as though it were capitalized. "You can have your coffee there." Then, before Rasika left, Amma grasped her upper arm. "You let him drive," she said.

In the garage, Rasika pulled her car keys from her purse and held them out to Viraj. "Would you like to drive?"

He grabbed them from her hand. "Sure." He slipped behind the wheel and ran a palm over the leather seat. "Nice." He flicked his fingers at the GPS screen, and Rasika winced. "Your parents buy this for you?"

"I bought it myself," she said.

He raised his eyebrows. "I just asked. You don't need to get huffy about it."

She hadn't realized she was being "huffy."

The car whined as he backed out of the driveway with far more force than Rasika used, and she involuntarily pressed her right foot against the floor.

"Ohio's not a bad place." Viraj veered onto the main road from her parents' housing development. "I was in Cleveland a couple of years ago, to visit Deepti Auntie, but I've never been down in this area. It's more, I don't know, *modern* than I thought it would be. I guess, being from the East Coast, I pictured a lot of cornfields out here. But, your parents' house is really nice. Much nicer than I expected."

She wasn't sure what to say to this. "Make a left here," she said. "And then another left after we go under the highway."

"I guess real estate is a lot cheaper out here than in New Jersey. Still, I wasn't sure what to expect. I know Akron's got some major corporations, like Goodyear, right?"

"Here's where you want to make a left," she said.

"Goodyear's not a bad company, as far as I can tell, although I believe it used to be doing better than it is now."

"You just missed it," Rasika said.

"What? Why didn't you tell me? You have to give me some advance warning."

Rasika had him backtrack and this time was more insistent with her directions. "Sorry about that," she said.

"Don't worry about it," he said. "No one's perfect."

They hummed along the black roadway. "I think you'll find that I'm pretty easy to get along with," he continued. "I don't think you'll have any complaints. As I said on the phone, I don't have any bad habits. I do drink occasionally. Who doesn't? We can have a drink together every day after work, just to relax. I'm into enjoying myself. I don't know about your parents, but my parents have always worked really hard. And I've done that. It's gotten me to where I am now, and so I'm finally ready to enjoy things. I like the very best. I can afford it, so why not? I know what I want, and I go for it."

Rasika wondered if *she* was something he wanted, and was going for. They passed a Chevrolet dealership hung with streamers and displaying a large sign with blinking words: GET PRE-APPROVED IN SECONDS! "We need to make another left pretty soon," she said loudly.

"I'll be making a very good living, and I know you'll enjoy that. You're free to work until we have kids."

"A left is coming up," she repeated.

"After we have kids, you can stay home and enjoy yourself. You'll be busy enough taking charge of the house. I'm not saying you have to clean. We can hire all the help you want. My home should be my oasis. I have enough stress at work. I want a happy wife and happy children, and I'll be making enough money so we can have that. But if you're off working, then it's not going to jive."

"Here it is!" she shouted.

"Don't get so worked up." He swerved into the left lane. They heard a loud honk. "Hey, cool it," he said to the other driver.

Was this how everyone drove in New Jersey?

As soon as they stepped into the white interior of the mall, with the familiar stores around her, she felt calmer. "There's a coffee place down this way," she said. Her white beaded low-heeled sandals clicked smartly along the hard marble floor. She felt the eyes of other shoppers watching her. She and Viraj were already presenting a stylish image together. She had chosen to wear the pale saffron salvar kameez with a white clutch purse because they seemed summery. They passed upscale home furnishings, chic women's clothes, and adorable children's outfits. Each window held a picture of a happy and harmonious life. She always loved the feeling of knowing she could afford to buy almost anything she wanted. Not that she was a spendthrift. Sometimes she walked out of the mall without buying anything at all. Just looking, and knowing she could buy, was sometimes enough. As the wife of Viraj, her spending power would only increase.

"Not bad." Viraj surveyed the scene and nodded. "You've got some pretty decent stores out here."

The café was under a high dome of skylights, near a splashing fountain that made enough noise such that Rasika didn't feel the need to talk. As they stood in line she wondered if she should offer to pay for her coffee. Then she heard a burst of trumpets. Viraj pulled his cell phone from his pocket and glanced at the display screen. "I gotta take this," he said. She watched in disbelief as he stepped away from her. She smiled faintly, just in case anyone was watching. Could he be getting calls about work on a Saturday? And if it wasn't about work, what was possibly more important than being with his future wife?

She reached the counter, and Viraj was still out in the hallway. She stepped out of line and stood straight and tall at the entrance of the café, trying not to draw his or anyone's attention to herself. She wasn't going to be a nag.

Eventually he flipped his phone closed. When he saw her, he threw his arms in the air theatrically. "I thought you were holding our place in line!"

"I didn't know what you wanted to order," she said.

He shrugged. "Whatever. Come on."

When they sat down with their drinks (he had insisted on paying), she got ready to break out her question on the U.S. Open so they could have some light conversation before moving on to more serious topics, like the honeymoon destination.

Before she could speak, he said, "I'm impressed with your area. I really am." He peered at his cup, twisting it a quarter turn this way, and another quarter turn back. "But not impressed enough to move here. I know you prefer to stay in Ohio, but it's not going to work for me. I'm doing really well with my company, and you'll like New Jersey. Lots of Indian stuff, if you're into that—saris, jewelry, anything you want. There's nothing you can't get in New Jersey." He twisted his cup again and settled into his seat.

Rasika gripped her warm cup and sipped. Her hazelnut latte was too hot, and she felt a heavy pain in her chest. She closed her eyes and waited for the pain to pass. So, she would be moving to New Jersey. It would be okay. She could get a job there. She'd find new friends. And besides, soon she'd be busy running the household and having children.

"I've already bought a house," Viraj said. "I wanted to get married before doing a lot of decorating. I know that's what ladies enjoy. You have good taste. I can see that." He tilted his head back as he examined her outfit, and then patted her arm approvingly.

Rasika rubbed the raw, burned spot on her tongue against the roof of her mouth. She looked past Viraj and recognized a handsome Indian man in the walkway.

She stood up, knowing this was the wrong thing to do. "Abhay!" she called.

Abhay turned. "Hey, Rasika." He walked over and nodded at Viraj, who gave him a cold look.

"You got your hair cut," Rasika said. "Your ponytail's gone. And your clothes . . ." Abhay wore a purple button-down shirt with a subtle pattern of dark stripes.

"I'm a working stiff now," he said. "My first week temping, they let me get away with T-shirts. Now I gotta fit in with the crowd. Mom sent me to the mall to get some work clothes." He opened the giant white plastic bag he was carrying. "I'm hoping I can get away with some actual color, even in an office."

Rasika peeked in and saw a blue shirt, similar to the one he had on, and an olive green one with tiny flowers all over it. "Nice." She felt Viraj glaring at her.

"By the way," she said, "this is Viraj."

Abhay leaned over the table and held out a hand to Viraj, whose smile stiffened. He made no move to take Abhay's hand. He seemed to be grinding his teeth.

"Okay, well, I should go." Abhay held up his hand in a wave. "See you around."

"Bye," Rasika said. "Let's get together sometime." She was shocked at her own words, and as Abhay receded, she concentrated on her latte. Viraj was silent. After several seconds she stole a glance at him and saw his mouth contorting, as though he couldn't get the words out. She took a sip of coffee for something to do, but as soon as she swallowed, she felt it bubble up—the thing she was trying to keep hidden. It frothed and expanded until it burst, and she was laughing hysterically.

She turned away from Viraj and covered her mouth with her hands. She felt her face getting red and her whole body was shaking. She had to remember to close her mouth and swallow, so she wouldn't drool. It was completely inappropriate; everyone was probably staring at her. She pressed her palms to her belly and took a deep breath. On the exhale, it started again.

"I'm so sorry!" she squeaked.

He stood up. "Let's get out of here."

She stood up, too, and trailed behind him, helpless with giggling. By the time they got into the car, she had managed to calm down enough to keep a straight face. During the silent drive home, she tried not to think of how Viraj had looked after Abhay left, but of course she couldn't help it, and every time she did she felt hysterics coming on again. She dug her fingernails into her palm and that way managed to keep it down to a smile.

As soon as they were in the house, she fled upstairs and locked herself in her bedroom. She could hear what was going on downstairs—Viraj's loud insistence that they leave right away, and Amma's high-pitched worrying tones. She felt free behind her bedroom door, taking off her fancy clothes and jewelry. She put on her oldest, softest pair of jeans and her rattiest T-shirt. She stood in front of her dresser mirror and carefully wiped off every trace of makeup. The front door closed, her mother's footsteps ascended, and she steeled herself for the worst. She unlocked the door just before her mother turned the handle and came in.

She sat on her bed looking up contritely as Amma loomed over her. "What happened?"

"I'm sorry, Amma."

"He was very angry. What did you do?"

Rasika looked down at her feet, and then gazed around the room, as though looking for the answer to her mother's question.

"If you keep throwing away opportunities like this, you will never get properly married. Everyone in India has been scouring the planet for you. We have looked at so many pictures and biodata, and finally you agreed to meet this boy. Now we will have to start the whole process again. Your father is very upset. He can't even sit still. He is downstairs, pacing the floor."

Rasika felt terrible about increasing Appa's stress. She couldn't explain her actions. Viraj was everything she was looking for, everything her parents were trying to provide for her. Except . . .

"He wanted me to live in New Jersey," she mumbled. "I want to stay here."

"And for that you have ruined everything?" her mother screeched. "I came across the ocean with my husband. Did I cry to stay at home with my mother? A woman must follow her husband."

Rasika hated to hear her calm and cultured mother get frantic like this. "I'm sorry, Amma." She stood up and put her arms around her mother, nestling her head in her mother's neck.

Amma pushed her away. "You must grow up, Rasika." She sat down on the bed. Rasika sat beside her, draping her arms around her mother and resting her head on her mother's shoulder.

"Other Indian mothers want their children to live at home." Amma patted Rasika's hand. "All the other youngsters run away as soon as they can, to New York, Chicago, San Francisco. Abhay ran away to that crazy farm. Pramod has all of a sudden decided he wants to join the Peace Corps. Can you imagine? We are not sending him to medical school so he can go rot in some African country. But, you are staying at home. You are a good girl. I think maybe . . . I don't want to say you should leave. The girls in India stay at home, too, but when it is time to get married, they know they must follow their husbands. You cannot stay with us forever."

"I know," Rasika murmured. She wished she had better control over herself. What had made her stand up and call to Abhay? That's what started it all.

Amma pushed Rasika aside and stood up. "I don't know what we should do now. Your birthday is coming so soon. Maybe we should consider Subhash after all."

"What?"

"I never told you before, but Deepti Auntie mentioned a few months ago that Subhash would like to marry you."

"But—he's related to me!"

"Second-cousin marriage is acceptable, but your Appa thinks we should not marry you to such a close relative. Now since nothing else is working out, maybe we should reconsider. He is a good boy."

"Amma. I can't marry him. He's just so awkward. Did you know he's even changing his name to 'Sam,' so he can attract more American customers?"

"When did you find out about that?"

"The other day, I—" Rasika stopped. She didn't want to tell her mother about seeing Subhash when she'd been with Abhay.

"Many Indians change their names," Amma said. "He will still be 'Subhash' within the family. He will do very well for himself, I am sure. He is a hard worker, and very conscientious and polite. Maybe we should get your horoscopes matched, just in case."

Rasika started to panic. She pulled on her mother's arm, as she used to do when she was a child. "Amma, I can't marry him!" Rasika imagined a lifetime of trying to get Subhash to lose weight, floss his teeth, wear the right clothes, and acquire some social graces.

Amma shook off Rasika's grip. "I have been wanting to go through personal connections, but maybe we should consider these Internet sites. I will ask Pramod to look into this." Amma bustled into the hallway. "Pramod!" She started downstairs, shouting all the way. "Pramod! Come here. I have something for you to do."

Rasika closed the door and crawled under the sheets. She didn't want to think about anything right now. Her bed was one of her favorite places in the world. Since she'd been earning her own money, she'd dispensed with her mother's polyester-blend sheets and used only Egyptian cotton in the summer, and thick flannel in the winter. She also had a goose down duvet. The air-conditioning made her want to get really warm in bed. She allowed her mind to drift pleasantly. She didn't find it difficult to think of nothing, and never had trouble going to sleep.

4

So many different muffled sounds: the metallic whirr of the X-ray machine, the high-pitched whine of a tooth drill, the low murmur of the telephone. It was Monday morning, and Abhay was at a dentists' office—his first day of temping for a receptionist on maternity leave. The office was decorated in beige and gray, and smelled like an astringent mixure of dentist-office chemicals. Abhay sat at one end of a long gray counter, with the customer window in front of him. The office manager, Daloris, sat next to him.

"She wasn't due for three more weeks," Daloris was saying. "We were planning to have the person come in the day before and get trained. But she went into labor last night, so we'll have to do the best we can."

"He looks smart," Shavonne said. She was in charge of billing and sat down the counter from him, in front of the billing window. She smiled at him, and when he glanced back, she looked away. She had smooth dark brown skin, and her hair was done in an intricate braided maze. She wore a skirt that just grazed her knees when she sat.

Daloris cleared her throat. "Here's the list for today." She opened a large appointment calendar. "When patients come in, have them sign here." She reached through his window and patted a clipboard on the high counter.

As Abhay listened, he thought about the sad state of his life. How could Daloris and Shavonne be so cheerful, working here day after day? Shavonne had decorated her section of the counter with framed photos of two shaggy cats, a digital clock in the shape of an apple, and a giant mug with a cartoon hippo on it, which held pens. Wasn't it strange how women in all dentists' and doctors' offices had similar things on their desks? Did they learn this at school or something? *In order to work in a dentist's office, you must develop a liking for tasteless, useless items with which to decorate your work space.*

"When you get a chance," Daloris was saying, "you'll need to make reminder calls for upcoming appointments. If you don't get to it today, don't worry about it. Shavonne and I can help."

On the counter near him was a large vase filled with red roses. One of the dentists bought flowers every morning, and the receptionist (he, in this case) was to hand one to every woman patient as she left the office. Abhay objected silently to this sexism. What about the men? Surely they could also use some floral cheer after enduring a visit to the dentist.

Daloris went back to her office. Abhay began asking people to sign in. Between patients, he picked up the phone and made a few reminder calls. Fortunately, no one answered, but he felt ridiculous leaving his message: "This is the office of Doctors Harley, Tan, and Remerovsky, calling to remind you of your dentist appointment on Wednesday at nine-fifteen. If you are unable to make this appointment, please call us at your earliest convenience." Who cared? So if someone missed an appointment, they might get a cavity, or maybe some gingivitis. The whole thing was just so unimportant.

A patient appeared at Shavonne's window, a young white man in a business suit. As she ran his credit card through the machine, the man probed thoughtfully around his mouth with his tongue. When he walked past Abhay's window, Abhay tugged a rose from the vase and stood up. "Would you like a flower?" he called.

The man stopped. Abhay was sure he'd refuse, thereby confirming Abhay's opinion that most men in American society had cut themselves off from natural beauty. Not that this rose was particularly natural. It had probably been grown in a greenhouse and fed a diet of chemicals.

The man held out a pink hand. "Sure."

Shavonne leaped up, reached across Abhay, pulled open a drawer, and withdrew a paper towel, which she handed to the man to wrap around his dripping stem.

"It's for the *women*." Shavonne giggled after the man walked out clutching his rose. She leaned in front of Abhay again, lifted a pile of paper towels out of the drawer, and set them beside the vase.

"Men like flowers, too," Abhay said. Maybe things were changing, and even conventional young men were willing to embrace at least some of their femininity.

"He'll just give it to his girlfriend or his assistant." Shavonne sat back down at her section of the counter. "If you hand them out to everyone, you'll run out before the end of the day."

The frilly V-neck of Shavonne's blouse suggested what was underneath. She also wore a silver-colored cross with a lifelike figure of Jesus attached to it. He never understood why people wore jewelry depicting a tortured man.

"It doesn't seem fair that only the women get roses," he said.

She cocked her head at him dramatically. "You're not gay. Are you?"

He shook his head.

"Good." She looked at him suggestively. He glanced away. Why was it he was never particularly interested in the women who liked him? Shavonne was certainly cute, and she was shorter than him, too.

The morning wore on, occasionally enlivened by banter with Shavonne. At lunchtime he ate his sandwich, chips, and apple in the tiny employee kitchen. From his backpack he tugged out a stack of career books, opened one of them to a random page, and read about an exercise called "clustering your interests." The words swam on the page, and he thought about Rasika. She couldn't be interested in him. But why had she called out to him at the mall on Saturday? Why had she suggested they get together again? And in front of that stuffed shirt she was supposed to marry. Probably she was trying to give the guy a hint, and he, Abhay, happened to be convenient. She must not have meant anything by it.

Yet she'd seemed so happy to see him.

Even if she were interested, he ought to stay away from her. She probably voted Republican. Or worse, maybe she didn't bother to vote at all.

By Wednesday, Abhay felt like his brain would collapse from emptiness. He couldn't keep temping. During his lunch break he wandered around the building, looking for a pay phone. He finally found one near the bathroom at the gas station next door to the office. He called his temp agency supervisor and told her this would be his last week with the agency, because he'd found another job. "What will you be doing?" she asked, surprised. He said, "Uh. It involves, uh, books." Which was true. He planned to do a lot of reading in the coming weeks.

He put in another fifty cents and, before he could change his mind, called directory assistance, asked for Ohio West Bank's commercial loan office, and was connected. When the recorded voice said, "To use the company directory, spell the last name of the person you wish to reach," he spelled out *Subramanian* and was connected to Rasika's voice mail. He listened to her message—her voice seemed so distant and businesslike—heard the beep, and hung up. Then he felt cowardly, deposited yet another fifty cents, called again, and said into her voice mail, in what he hoped was a casual, cool voice, "Rasika. It's Abhay. Just wanted to catch up with you. Maybe we can get together on Friday. Give me a call." He left his parents' phone number.

He went back to the dentists' office, ate his lunch, and felt elated. Two more days of this, and he'd be free! The money he'd already earned could last him for weeks—months, even—depending on how careful he was. Of course, he didn't want to live at his parents' house for months. Would Rasika return his call? He tried to pretend he didn't care much one way or the other. He tried to pretend he was only calling her because he was newly back in town, and ought to reconnect with the few old acquaintances who were still here.

That evening he walked around the house and checked on Seema, his mother, and his father. No one was tying up the phone, and still it didn't ring.

Finally he felt so restless that he called up an old high school friend, Christopher Haldorson. He knew Chris's number by heart because Chris still lived with his parents. Abhay had been avoiding him—Chris hadn't progressed much since high school—but after all, Abhay himself was now living with his parents.

Chris invited him over. On the way, Abhay walked past their old high school. He stopped at the driveway and looked at the sprawling brick building set back on the lawn. The school was silent and still, now that it was summer. He remembered, as a senior, longing to get away from the school, and here he was again, living within a mile of it.

Chris's parents lived in a 1950s neighborhood of modest one-story houses. From the outside, Abhay could see the blue flickering light of the large-screen TV through the living room picture window. He knocked on the back door, as usual, and Chris let him into the kitchen, which was brightly lit and spotless.

"Adios!" Chris slapped him on the back. "How goes it?"

Abhay was startled to hear his high school nickname again. In ninth grade some kids noticed that his name, correctly pronounced "uh-bye," sounded like "good-bye," and started calling him "Adios." Apparently because he could pass for Hispanic, most kids thought this nickname was appropriate or hilarious or both, and it stuck.

Chris looked the same—tall, with dull tan hair—except that he'd gained some weight. As they headed down the hallway to Chris's room, they passed the dark living room, where Chris's parents were watching *Wheel of Fortune*.

"Mom, Dad, Adios is here," Chris called.

Mrs. Haldorson padded over in her fluffy bedroom slippers, with Mr. Haldorson behind her, leaning on a cane. She wrapped her arms around him in a tight hug. "Great to see you, honey." She turned him so he faced the lighted kitchen, and looked at him. "You haven't changed," she declared. "He's the same, isn't he, Steve?" she said to her husband.

Mr. Haldorson shifted his cane to his left hand and held out his right hand. "Good to see you," he said. He was a shorter, older version of Chris, and Abhay was startled by his apparent ill health. Mr. Haldorson had for years coached the baseball team at the high school.

Chris's room was even more crammed with stuff than it had been in high school. His double bed took up most of the floor space, but around it were stacks of cardboard boxes. In one corner was a desk with a computer. The desk was clean except for an upright rack of file folders. On a bookshelf next to the bed were displayed a variety of porcelain figurines—horses, dogs, cats, dancing ladies, praying children, a fat chef next to a wine barrel—all clean and free of dust. Abhay hadn't known that Chris collected figurines.

"What's with the boxes?" Abhay asked. "You moving out?"

"I sell stuff on eBay." He tossed his thick bangs out of his eyes, just as he used to do in high school.

"You make money that way?"

"Yeah. It's not bad. It's something we can do as a family."

"So your parents are involved, too?"

"Dad's on disability now. He's had a couple of strokes."

"I'm sorry to hear that," Abhay murmured.

"Yeah, it's been scary, but at least the house is paid off, so we're not desperate for cash. Mom and Dad scout out estate sales, and Mom's even set up a little sideline where we help people clean out all the junk in their house, and organize things, and in exchange we get to keep anything we want to sell. And Dad's an expert about old tools. But I'm the brains of the operation. You'd be amazed how much difference it makes just to keep on top of things."

Abhay sat down on the bed. He remembered how Chris had trouble keeping his homework organized in high school. He'd dropped out of college after a semester; he just wasn't interested. And then he spent what seemed like years bumming around, working here and there.

"My uncles give me a hard time because I'm still living at home." Chris sat down next to Abhay and peered at his fat hands. "But Mom and Dad don't mind. I take care of things around the house, and we have fun together."

"That's great, Chris," Abhay said. "You're being a good Indian son, living at home and taking care of your parents."

"Yeah. Too bad my uncles aren't Indian."

"So how'd you get into this?" Abhay waved his hand at all the boxes.

"I had a job for a while with an estate sale company. I got them started doing eBay sales, and then I went out on my own. Hey, what're you doing, Adios, now that you're home?"

Abhay wondered whether to ask Chris not to call him "Adios." He'd successfully left this nickname behind since he'd graduated from high school. He decided to let it pass.

"You looking for work?" Chris persisted.

"I'm temping now." Abhay didn't want to say that he'd just quit temping.

"I need someone to help take photos to post, and to pack stuff up to send out. You interested?"

"Um. Maybe." Abhay glanced at the shelf of figurines. "These are for sale?" Abhay picked up a little statue of a brown woman wearing a gold and blue sari blouse and loose pants, and sitting in lotus posture, palms in prayer position. "I had no idea there were yoga statues. What does this go for?"

"There's a whole set of them." Chris picked up another brown woman doing a backbend. "I'm selling them for $29.95 each, free shipping, but if you're interested I can make you a deal."

Abhay replaced the figurine. "No. That's okay. I'm good."

"Listen, now that you're home, you should come over to our weekly barbecues on Saturday nights. I grill up a bunch of things, Mom makes salad, Dad makes his famous cherry cheesecake, and we invite the neighbors. Remember Emily Cross from high school? She's Emily Nuttman now. She and her husband and kids come over."

"She has kids?"

"Three. They're five, four, and one."

"God."

"That's what I thought at first, but she's happy. So, come on over this Saturday. And on Sundays, a lot of times I get a group together to go bowling, or drive up to Cleveland to see a baseball game, or just go to a movie. Something to do. You have a standing invitation. You have a girlfriend or anything?" Chris was lying on his side, full length on the bed, his head propped up on his hand.

"Nah." Abhay crossed his legs on the bedspread. It was just like in high school, when they'd done their homework in Chris's room.

"Me neither, but I'm looking. Remember Michelle Tully? That girl you had a crush on in high school?"

Abhay tried to laugh. He didn't want to be reminded of his foolishness around women.

"Anyway, I saw her the other day over at that new upscale grocery store in Hudson. She was wearing a business suit, heels, nails polished, hair perfect. She tried to ignore me, as usual. She was always so full of herself, but I went up and acted all friendly. I found out she's a commercial real estate agent in Cleveland. Making a ton of money, I'm sure."

"Good for her," Abhay murmured.

"I don't know if I want to get married and all that yet," Chris said, "but I would like someone to hang out with, you know?" Chris rolled onto his back and slipped his hands under his head. "I haven't found anyone yet. Seems like a lot of girls want a guy with a fancy job. I'm thinking of expanding into organizing estate sales. I think the business has potential, but a lot of girls don't want potential. They want hard cash. So, what're you doing now?"

"I'm just here to regroup and think things through."

"Well, help me out then, while you're thinking." Chris rolled off the bed onto his feet. "Come down to the basement. I have so much stuff that needs organized. I'll pay you cash."

Abhay spent the rest of the evening sorting, labeling, and taking photos for Chris, and went home with thirty dollars in his pocket.

On Wednesday after work, instead of going straight home, Rasika headed toward the freeway and got onto I–76. She'd received Abhay's phone message, and she knew she shouldn't call him. She didn't want to go home yet. She'd just drive around a bit. She loved driving. Being alone in her car was one of the few places, outside of her bedroom, where she felt safe and invisible.

She punched through the radio stations she had programmed. She didn't want news or DJ banter. With one hand, she fed a CD into the CD player. The car was filled with Frank Sinatra's deep, smooth voice. She turned up the volume. Frank persuaded her to come fly with him.

She continued past Akron, exited at state Route 43, and drove until the highway turned into Main Street. Her heart was pounding, and her hands were sweaty on the steering wheel. She reached the intersection of Main and Lincoln. The light was green, so she couldn't stop. As she followed the line of cars ahead of her, she glanced around at the Starbucks, at the Fox and Hound, at the entrance to the university.

She saw no one she knew. She exhaled, realizing she'd been holding her breath. Frank crooned, and the muted trumpets chirruped cheerily.

At the next light she stopped, turned right, and circled back around campus. She drove slowly, looking at everyone passing on either side. She kept her eyes out for a slim, brown-skinned man. She knew it was crazy to be searching for Abhay on the streets when she wasn't willing to just pick up the phone and call him.

She'd been avoiding her parents since the fiasco with Viraj. She'd slept for the rest of Saturday. On Sunday, her mother refused to speak to her. Her father was in bed with a stomachache. She had wanted to take him a cup of tea and sit with him, like she normally did when he was sick. Instead, she had left the house. She felt terrible for abandoning her father, but she suspected that she was the cause of his illness. Maybe he preferred not to see her. So she drove around aimlessly for a while. She didn't want to go to a mall, because that would only remind her of her bad behavior. Jill wasn't answering her phone. She didn't want to call any of her other friends because none of them knew about her situation. She ended up at her gym and for once did her entire routine thoroughly: elliptical trainer, weights, abs, stretching. Then she took a long shower and spent an hour in the hot tub.

On Monday after work, she arranged to meet Jill for dinner, and on Tuesday she accepted her colleague Estelle's invitation to go with her to a Pampered Chef party. Rasika spent the entire time listening to Estelle's friends talk about their grandchildren, and watching a demonstration of something called "breakfast lasagna" being made—a concoction of hash browns, mushroom soup, bacon, sour cream, and cheese. She couldn't bring herself to try it once it came out of the oven. She thought about Abhay's mother and the sales parties she was trying to host. To be polite, she ordered something called a "pineapple wedger," which was supposed to peel and core a pineapple at the same time.

Tonight she was reduced to driving around Kent. On the sidewalk she saw no one dusky-skinned at all: only young white college students, many of them wearing as little clothing as possible.

She drove up to the Starbucks intersection via Lincoln this time. She veered left onto Main and then stopped in the turn lane, opposite the Starbucks parking lot, with her left blinker on, waiting for the cars to pass. She'd get a café mocha with whipped cream. It was her comfort drink, and she really needed one now. She drummed her fingers on the steering wheel. The cars continued rolling past in the oncoming lane. She inched forward, hoping someone would let her through. She'd order her coffee, take it to the upstairs dining area, and sit at one of those tables by the window, where she could look down on the street.

As she watched the line of cars coming toward her, she thought she spotted a shiny blue Hyundai. Oh, crap. Was that Subhash? She flicked her right blinker on and veered into traffic, causing the car behind her to brake. The driver honked and passed her in the right lane. She could see his angry face shouting at her through his window, but fortunately she couldn't hear what he said: her windows were rolled up, and her music was too loud.

As she zoomed back down the road toward the freeway, she

tried to laugh at her narrow escape. She was trembling, and her throat was dry. She wondered if Subhash had seen her car. Maybe it hadn't been Subhash at all. She turned off the CD player. The car was filled with an ominous silence. She turned it back on again. She really had to stop all this foolishness and get on with her life.

On Thursday evening, Abhay sat at his rickety desk with chipped corners, reading a book that advised him to allow his creative inner self to intuitively select his life's work. He wished the phone would ring. He vowed that if Rasika didn't call, he'd ask Shavonne out.

The book advised him to read one chapter every week and to do the exercises suggested, which involved things like breathing, writing, and asking specific questions of himself and others. He read this book like he read any other book: he inhaled it in one sitting with one part of his brain, the other part being occupied with taking off first Rasika's, and then Shavonne's, clothes. Did anyone actually limit themselves to one chapter per week?

By the time he finished skimming the book, he'd convinced himself that the advice in it was useless. The house was a jumble of low noises: faint drumming and wailing love songs from the radio in Seema's room, and from the family room, where his mother was reviewing one of her educational videos, a cheerful female voice asked, "What is the capital of Venezuela? Do you remember?" He felt hot and sticky in his bedroom, which was full of plastic: nylon carpeting, polyester curtains and bedspread, and the laminate top of his desk.

Why did he care about Rasika? Why was he bothering to pursue her? That was the question he couldn't quite answer. Yes, she was beautiful, but so were a lot of other women. He kept thinking about how she'd called his declarations "ridiculous" and "nonsense." Oddly, something about that appealed to him. She wasn't awed or struck dumb by his grand ideas. He liked the fact that she seemed to cut through all his words to the essence of—of something. Of course he didn't agree with her, but he wanted to keep talking to her. He was curious about what she'd say.

By Friday morning, Abhay's elation at almost being free from temping had dissipated. What was he doing with his life? He felt as if he were one big itch that couldn't be scratched. He called Rasika at lunchtime but hung up without leaving a message.

On Friday afternoon he told Shavonne it would be his last day at the office, and asked her to go out for a drink with him at the Fox and Hound after work. Her enthusiasm didn't lift his mood. Shavonne drove. Her car smelled of the pine air-freshener that hung over the rearview mirror.

He wasn't sure how to behave. She clearly liked him and hadn't acted put off by the fact that he had no car. They settled at a table near the door and ordered beers. He had no idea what to talk about. He looked at Shavonne's large silver hoop earrings, which tapped against her cheeks every time she turned her head. He looked at her long shiny nails, painted with tiny designs.

"What're you thinking about?" Shavonne leaned forward and reached out a hand, which jingled with bracelets, to stroke his hand lightly. Her fingers were cool and firm, her smile intimate.

"How did you decide to work in a dentists' office?" he asked.

"I just got the job." She shrugged and giggled. "Daloris is my aunt, and she told me there was an opening."

"So . . . you like working there?"

"For the most part. The benefits are good. Free dental care, too. Why are you leaving?"

"It's not right for me."

"What kind of job are you looking for?"

He didn't want to go over his whole life story with Shavonne. He wanted to escape from that for a while. "Tell me about yourself."

A waitress came by and deposited a basket of happy-hour popcorn on their table. Abhay helped himself to a handful of kernels. "Did you grow up around here?"

"Akron," Shavonne said. "I'm a Tiger."

This must be a reference to her high school mascot. "What kinds of things do you like to do for fun?" He wanted to find some connection with her, even if for only one evening, to take his mind off himself.

"I love to cook. And play with my cats. I sew. I made this blouse." She sat up straighter to display her work, and smiled proudly.

The blouse was purple with a V-neck and a spattering of purple blossoms sewn between the breasts. "Nice," he said. It did look good on her. "Did you make the flowers, too?" he asked.

She looked down and fingered one of the round posies. "You make them with the same fabric as the rest of the blouse. You cut out circles and gather them. I'd never done anything like this before."

"Cute." He couldn't care less. "So. What about your future? What are you thinking in that department?"

She laughed. "You sound like a job interviewer." She shrugged. "I guess I'll keep working. I want to get married, of course. And have kids eventually." She gave him a sly smile.

The waiter arrived with their beers. Abhay grasped the handle of his mug and concentrated on drinking.

"What about you?" Shavonne asked. "What do you want for your future?"

"I'm trying to decide what to do next. I want to make the right decision, and I keep getting tangled up in my thoughts."

"I've seen you reading those career books at work."

"Yeah, nothing seems to make sense. Everything's cloudy up here." He tapped his head.

"Maybe the problem is that you're trying to answer all your questions yourself. Do you believe in God?"

He stiffened. He didn't want to talk about God with Shavonne. "Have some popcorn." He pushed the basket closer to her.

"Maybe you need to let a higher power guide you."

"Thanks, but I'm not interested."

Her smile disappeared. "OK." She picked up a piece of popcorn and crushed it in her fingers. "I was only trying to help." Her lips trembled a little.

"I'm sorry." He felt terrible. As he tried to think of something more comforting to say, he became aware of Rasika at the doorway. He stood up so quickly that he upset the popcorn basket, spilling kernels over the table and floor. He waved, and Rasika saw him and Shavonne. Rasika turned and strolled out the door. He sat back down but couldn't take his eyes away from the door.

After several seconds, he realized Shavonne was staring at him.

"I'm sorry," he said. "Where were we?"

"Who was that?" Shavonne asked.

"Just an old family friend."

Shavonne brushed popcorn off her lap and stood up. "I saw the way you looked at her. You've seemed distracted all evening, and now I know why. I think it's time for me to go."

"I'm just . . . I'm sorry."

She dug a jangling bunch of keys out of her enormous handbag. "I'd offer you a ride, but I think you can take care of yourself."

He nodded and looked at his shoes as she and her keys and her bracelets jingled away from him. There was popcorn all over the table and the floor. He hoped Rasika would come back. He drank his beer slowly. Rasika did not return. He looked at Shavonne's beer, untouched. He left enough money for the drinks and tip, and started walking home.

He was soaked in sweat by the time he walked the few miles from the bar to his house. He felt somewhat better, as though his exertions made up for the way he had treated Shavonne. The house was quiet. His parents had gone to dinner at a friend's house, and Seema had a regular Friday-night babysitting job.

Without taking his shoes or backpack off, he picked up the phone extension in the kitchen, looked up Rasika's home number in the little address and phone book Mom kept in a kitchen drawer, and dialed. She answered on the first ring.

"Rasika, it's Abhay."

"I know. We have caller ID."

"Sorry about this evening. That woman . . . she was just someone from work. No one special."

No answer from Rasika's end.

"Why didn't you call me before?" he asked.

"I couldn't call you at your house. Your parents might answer."

"So?"

"You know the rules, Abhay. I'm not supposed to call men."

"Rasika, you're an adult."

A moment of silence. And then, coldly, "Do you want to see me or not?"

"Sure. Where?"

"Are your parents . . . ?"

"They're out for the evening."

"I'll pick you up in half an hour."

5

He showered and wore the purple shirt she had admired at the mall.

"Where are we going?" He settled into her spotlessly clean car.

"You'll see." She was wearing a silky dark blue dress that clung softly to her breasts. She held his gaze until he started to lose himself in those perfect half-moon eyes, and then she looked away.

She drove expertly, skimming in and out of lanes. They seemed to be heading for Cleveland, and he sat back to enjoy himself. The sky was dimming, and the rows of headlights and taillights up and down the freeway began to glow in the dusk. Lush classical piano music filled the car. He tried to place the composer, and had the urge, for a moment, to ask her for the details. He let it pass, and let the music wash over him. The road unfurled in front of them. The other cars and the people within them became mere curiosities, outside the scope of his world. He and Rasika were in a self-contained capsule heading into a future just as cool and comfortable as this car.

She stopped the car in front of a tall redbrick building. "Here we are."

"The Renaissance Hotel?"

She hopped out, handed her keys to the valet, and from the backseat of the car swung out a tapestry-covered suitcase. "Would you grab this, please?" She set the suitcase on the sidewalk and pulled up the handle for him.

He followed her, bewildered, into the lobby, rolling her very light suitcase behind him.

She stopped in the center of the lobby and looked up at the balconies. "I love the renovation they did on this place. I'm so glad they didn't let this wonderful building go to waste."

He was glad in a way, too. Now this hotel was on the National Trust for Historic Preservation's list of historic hotels. Certainly it was better to preserve than to destroy old, historic buildings. Yet he distrusted opulence. The lobby walls were done in a dull yellow, as though to suggest gold. A huge potted tree graced the center of the lobby, implying that nature, when tamed and brought inside, was so much better than when left to its own devices. Above the potted tree was an artificial sun: a yellow dome with a huge round light fixture in the center of it.

"Wait here." She strode off toward the check-in desk. Her dress was not at all revealing, but he couldn't take his eyes away from the way it swished around her legs as she walked. On her feet were navy blue Indian chappals.

He felt silly standing there, holding her suitcase. A part of him wanted to take on the traditional masculine role and be in charge of everything. Yet he certainly didn't have money for a room here, if that was what she was intending. He couldn't quite believe it. Had she done this before with other men? She seemed perfectly at home in this situation.

In a moment she was back holding a key-card. "Room seven forty-five," she murmured, leading the way to the elevator. Once

they were enclosed in the mirrored space, zooming upstairs, she
said, "I hope you don't mind that I've made these arrangements."

"Oh, no." He shook his head vigorously.

"Are you surprised?"

"Well, yeah. You tried so hard to get me to believe—"

"I'm a good liar. Just remember that." She arched her perfect
eyebrows at him.

He followed her down the long, carpeted hallway. The door
unlocked with a dull click, closed with a metallic thud, and they
were alone in the silent room. He set Rasika's suitcase in a corner and stood beside it, watching as she slipped off her chappals
and walked around the room, turning on bedside lamps, peeking
out the window at the view, opening the bathroom door. Like the
lobby, the room was painted gold. The king-size bed was covered
in a red velvet spread, and the carpeting was a textured royal blue.

She opened a minifridge under the television set and took out a
bottle of champagne. "Would you like some?"

He sprang into action, found a corkscrew on the dresser, and
twisted it firmly, carefully, into the cork. He didn't want to look
incompetent and leave part of the cork behind, or worse yet, be unable to extract it. He wrenched the cork out with a pop and poured
the pale liquid into two wineglasses, which were also on the dresser.
Rasika was on the loveseat near the window, and he carried the
glasses over there and sat down next to her.

"I love hotels." She sighed. She sat with her feet tucked under
her dress. "Don't you?"

Actually, he didn't like hotels very much, but he didn't think
this was the right time to bring it up. The whole atmosphere here
was of a minipalace, tightly sealed to guard against the outside
world seeping in. That was probably why the windows had sheer
curtains in front of them, so you didn't have to see the gory details

of real life going on outside, the traffic, the wires, the industrial flotsam on the tops of other buildings.

They clinked glasses and drank. She slipped one of her feet out from under her dress and laid it on his lap. He stroked her smooth sole. He wiggled her small, soft toes, and she giggled.

"Doesn't it seem like we're playing a game?" she asked. "Hiding from the rest of the world?"

"Where are your parents?"

"Out of town." She leaned back, holding her glass carefully. "They went to Pittsburgh to see some concert at the Hindu temple. They're staying with friends tonight. And Pramod is at his apartment. He said he had a lot of studying to do."

The mention of Pramod reminded Abhay that he was in a hotel room with the daughter of old family friends. How would he explain to his parents where he'd been for the night? He ought to come up with a good excuse and call them before it got too late.

Rasika removed her foot from his lap and set her glass on the end table. "I'm going to give you my cell number, so next time you can call me on that."

He was still marveling that there would be a "next time" when all thoughts went out of his head. Rasika took his glass away from him and put her hand on his chest, stroking him through his shirt. He touched her silky dress. She was warm and firm under his hands, and her softness pressed against him. They kissed, and she tasted of wine. He was enveloped in her scent, musky and floral at the same time. She pressed herself against him. He attempted to hold on to her and slide himself down to become more horizontal, but the seat was too short, and her dress was too slippery, and they both tipped onto the floor. She giggled and wrestled with him, rolling over and under him. He had the idea that they ought to get into the bed. She pulled his shirt out of his pants and unbuckled his belt. He was breathless with excitement. He ran his fingers over the back of her dress but couldn't figure out how it unfastened. Finally she pulled the dress over her head.

"Should we get in bed?" he whispered.

"Don't talk," she murmured. "I don't want to think."

Afterward they did get into bed and lay curled together under the covers.

"I can't believe this," he murmured.

"Shh." She kept her eyes closed as he stroked her. They snuggled together, dozed, and woke up hungry. They sat up in bed, and she looked rosy and rumpled. "Let's call out for room service!" She seemed as excited as a child. "Don't worry. It's totally on me."

They ordered fried calamari, bruschetta with chopped tomatoes, and carrots with an herb dressing. Before the food arrived Rasika opened her suitcase and wrapped herself in a pink fluffy robe. Abhay found a towel in the bathroom and draped it around his waist. They ate in bed, shoulders touching. She refilled their glasses.

"What happened with that guy you were supposed to marry?"

She stiffened. "I can't talk about that now." She shifted her body so she was no longer touching him. He put a hand on her arm, and she pushed him away. She had seemed so different this evening— alive and confident. He'd felt like he could talk to her about anything, yet now she was retreating back into her aloofness. After several minutes, she relaxed against him again.

"So what are you going to do with yourself?" she asked. "Now that you're home."

He thought it was safer to talk about himself than to talk about her situation, so he launched into a description of his problem. "I had the idea that I should allow myself to fully explore all options. But so far, I've just gotten more confused. Back in high school, I was sure I wanted to be a doctor. I thought it was noble to save lives, and of course Indian parents tend to pressure their kids to head in that direction." From the platter on the blanket between them, he brought a slice of bruschetta to his mouth and took a bite, being careful not to spill any of the chopped tomatoes. "Once I got into studying biology, I felt like it wasn't really about life. You kill fetal pigs so you can dissect them. And you classify plants and animals, into a human-made system."

She nodded, holding a napkin below her chin to catch any drips.

"It's not that I'm not willing to work. I do want to do something good for the world, but sometimes it just seems so pointless."

Her lips glistened with olive oil. He waited for her to give him advice, as she had at the campus memorial. That's what most people did when he talked about this stuff. They said things like: "You'll have to face reality someday."

Rasika patted her lips with the thick white napkin and considered the carrots, her fork poised above them. She carefully speared one carrot disk and held it up, examining its glossy surface flecked with dark green herbs. She chewed slowly. She swallowed. She picked up her champagne glass and drank. "Tell me more," she said.

"Aren't you annoyed by what I'm saying? I mean, most people don't want to hear me go on and on."

"It's your life. If you want to be confused, I guess that's your business."

"Does it make you feel nervous, or afraid, to hear me be so undecided about everything? About life itself?"

She shook her head. "Why should I be afraid?"

"I think a lot of people have thoughts like mine, but they don't want to admit it. They have their steady job, their benefits, their comfortable homes. And if they start questioning things, they're afraid they won't have anything."

"You're either having your midlife crisis really early or you don't want to grow up."

"That's what my dad thinks—that I don't want to grow up.

But that's not it. I want to figure it out. The other day, I went over to the KSU career center and did a couple of career and personality tests. And you know what? The counselor said I either had no strong interests or inclinations, or I was interested in just about everything. So that didn't help at all."

"You're so smart, you could choose almost anything and make it work." It was dark outside, and the bedside lamps threw a warm glow over her skin. He put out a hand and touched her cheek, ran his fingers along her jaw, feeling the hard bone beneath the skin. She looked at him.

"I had the impression for a minute that you weren't real." He smiled. "I can't believe I'm sitting here with you. On the one hand, I feel like I hardly know who you are. And then, I feel like I've known you forever."

"You have known me forever."

"Not like this. I never knew you were so uninhibited."

Her face grew hard again, as though something had closed. "I don't want to be like this," she whispered.

"Why not? I've never seen you so alive. I think you love being in charge. You love having your own money and spending it any way you choose. You love picking out the men you want to seduce. That's who you really are. Why not admit it?"

"Whenever I ask you about your life, you end up telling me what I should do with mine." She threw the napkin on the floor and kicked the covers off her legs. "I'm going to shower."

He stacked the plates and silverware on the tray and put it outside the door. He considered what she had said. Was it true that he didn't want to grow up? He straightened the sheets and blankets. He folded his clothes. It was ten o'clock. He called home and left a message that he'd decided to spend the night at a friend's house. He knew his mother would be worried, especially since he didn't leave a phone number. Oh, well. It couldn't be helped.

Rasika emerged from the bathroom wearing a pink nightgown, looking as fresh as Botticelli's Venus emerging from the sea. He watched her arrange her soap and shampoo in her suitcase.

"They have soap here, you know."

"I'm particular about what I put on my body." She smiled across the room at him as she toweled her hair dry. She sashayed over to him, sat down on the bed, and kissed him. "I don't have to tell you to keep all this to yourself."

He nodded and reached for her.

"We can meet every once in a while," she said in between kisses, "but only if I can completely trust you. I'll give you my e-mail at work."

He felt her hand traveling over his chest, and put his hand over hers to stop it. "I don't have e-mail."

"Why not?" She pulled her hand away. "You can't be opposed to e-mail. It saves paper."

"We didn't have personal e-mail addresses at Rising Star, and I just haven't signed myself up for anything yet. I thought I might as well keep myself out of that whole loop for a while. I don't want to be an electronic slave, constantly obsessing about checking my messages no matter where I am."

Rasika rolled her eyes.

"And more importantly," he continued, "what's the idea here? Are you going to keep pretending to your parents that you want an arranged marriage, and then see me on the sly?"

She crossed her arms over her chest. "I do want an arranged marriage. I'm not pretending."

"You've done this before with other men, haven't you? Lots of times." He saw her face close again, yet he kept talking. "I'm not interested in sneaking around with you. If you want to have a relationship with me, that's great. But I'm not going to play your game." He thought his words sounded fine and courageous. He also knew that if Rasika wanted to whisk him off to a hotel again, he'd let her.

"If I'm playing a silly game, then so are you. You pretend like you're so mature, but all you can talk about is that you don't know what to do with your life. You're only one person. You can't do everything all by yourself. Just pick something and start doing it. Get into the stream of things. How long are you going to wait to start living?"

He rubbed a hand over his hair. "I just need a break after the move home."

She pressed her fingers into the velvet bedspread, making light fingertip impressions. "That's how I look at it, too. When the time is right I'll get married, and I won't have to do this kind of thing anymore."

"So why don't you marry that guy? The one I saw you with the other day."

She kept pressing and rubbing away her finger-marks. "I ruined things. Everything was going well until I saw you. He was really angry, which made him look funny, and I couldn't help laughing." She laughed just thinking about it.

"He seemed like a complete jerk," Abhay said. "How could you even think about marrying him?"

"He fit all my criteria. I don't know why I went and ruined things."

"Maybe your subconscious knows what you really want and isn't willing to abandon you to an asshole."

"Maybe." Rasika crossed her ankles and tossed her wet hair over her shoulder. "So, Mr. Know-It-All. What does your subconscious want for you?"

"I don't know."

"Are you waiting for another clue? Like the dreams or signs you told me about?"

"I don't think that'll work anymore. I feel like I'm done with that phase of my life. I was naive to believe that I could run my life based on those kinds of signs. I want to try being logical. Try being reasonable. That's what my dad always told me to do."

Faint, tinny music sounded from a corner of the room. Rasika leaped up. "My phone. What did I do with it?"

"In your purse?"

"Where'd I put my purse?"

The music came from the area near the refrigerator/TV cabinet. Rasika stuck her arm between the cabinet and dresser, and pulled out a tiny black leather purse. The music stopped.

"Whoever it is will call back." Abhay leaned against the dresser. He wanted a dessert. Something creamy, like the key lime pie he'd seen on the menu, or maybe some cheesecake. Or even some ice cream. He wondered if he could order it up and pay for it himself, or if it would all go on the room bill. He wondered if Rasika wanted anything.

"It's probably my mother." Rasika opened the purse, took out the phone, and peered at it. "Yes, it was my mom. She'll definitely call back. She's probably already tried me at home. If I don't answer my cell phone the second time she calls, she'll start to panic."

The phone burst into life again. "Hello?" Rasika sat down on the edge of a chair.

Abhay threw himself back on the bed and examined the room-service dessert menu.

Rasika was saying something in Tamil. He had forgotten she was fluent in Tamil, which he didn't understand. He remembered that she had grown up in India until she was seven or eight. As she spoke with her mother, Rasika's voice became high and childlike, a pitch Abhay hadn't heard before. She sat with her legs together, her feet flat on the floor, as though to prove to her mother, by her unseen body language, that she hadn't been doing anything wrong.

He thought about going out into the hallway to find a vending machine. Or maybe there was a convenience store in the lobby where he could get something sweet. Besides, he didn't like hearing Rasika lie, even if it was in a language he didn't understand. He dressed quietly and left the room in his socks.

When he returned with two gourmet ice cream bars, Rasika was completely dressed in jeans and a blouse. "We gotta leave," she said. Her hair, still wet, was mussed. She was trying to lift the handle of her suitcase, but the suitcase kept rolling out from under her hand.

"What happened?"

"My parents are bringing another eligible bachelor home. Tomorrow." She yanked the handle up.

"So we can stay the night, can't we?"

"I can't. I have to get some distance from this."

"Rasika, sit down. You don't have to just follow your parents' lead." He tried to hand her an ice cream bar.

She strode over to the window and tugged the curtains open.

"Tell me what's going on."

"I told you." She flung back the covers of the bed. "I guess the people my parents are staying with have a relative who would be right for me. He's visiting them now, from Nebraska, and he's a doctor. So they're bringing him over." She kneeled on the floor and looked under the bed. Satisfied that nothing had been left, she pulled up the covers of the bed and smoothed them.

"What's the hurry?"

"The astrologer said I need to be married before twenty-six. Remember?" She went into the bathroom and opened the shower curtain.

"How do you feel about what we just did?"

"I'd like to give all this up. I'm not proud of myself for doing things like this."

"If you want to get married, fine. But that doesn't mean you have to let your parents push you around."

"I'm not. I really want to marry with their blessing." She looked under the sink.

"You're afraid to let your parents know who you really are."

"My dad would die if he knew about . . ."

"You just think he'd die. The more you let Indian parents boss you around, the more they try to control you. You might as well start gradually getting them used to the idea that you aren't the person they think you are. And you know what? They'll get used to it."

"You don't know my dad. He gets so upset over the littlest thing. I can't." She opened and shut each drawer of the dresser, even though they hadn't been in the room long enough for her to put anything into the drawers. She grabbed her suitcase handle. "If you want a ride home, you'd better come with me now." She pulled the suitcase toward the door. "I just wish it didn't look so bad. I'll have to sign for my credit card, and I'm sure the hotel clerk will guess what we've been doing. I can invent some excuse about a family emergency."

She bolted out the door while he shoved his feet into his sneakers. He caught up with her in front of the elevators, and they rode down in silence. She strode to the reception counter, and he stood by the tree under the false sun. He still held both ice cream bars in their cardboard boxes. Normally he refused to buy gourmet ice cream bars because they were so overpackaged, but tonight Rasika's love of luxury must have rubbed off on him. He tucked one box under his arm, pried open the other, and bit through the bittersweet chocolate coating into the melting vanilla.

He recognized a group of Indians clustered near the grand staircase. There were some short women—one in pants, one in a sari—an elderly man in dark pants and a light shirt, and a few slouching teenagers in jeans. What were they doing in a downtown Cleveland hotel at this time of night? He ought to get out of their line of sight in case he recognized anyone. As he moved around to the other side of the tree, the woman in pants raised her hand at him and started bustling toward him, and suddenly he remembered her name. This was Mita Auntie, a friend of his mother's, who had moved away from Cleveland about a year ago.

"We are here to attend Amisha Menon's wedding reception." Mita Auntie placed a hand on his arm. "You know wedding was in India last month, and Sunday is U.S. reception." Mita Auntie was short and round, and despite the fact that they were quite wealthy—her husband was a plastic surgeon—she was just as unsophisticated as his own mother.

"My mother mentioned it," he said. Slabs of chocolate coating threatened to fall off the ice cream bar, and he hurried to gather them into his mouth.

"Our plane landed so late. You are here to meet guests?"

"Just hanging out with friends," he said. "I didn't realize the reception was at this hotel."

"It is at party hall near the Menons' house. Kanchan likes to stay at these fancy hotels. Come say hello to everybody."

Abhay reluctantly walked with Mita Auntie back toward her group. Maybe he could send them on their way and they would avoid seeing Rasika, and avoid wondering why he had two ice cream bars.

By the time he joined their group by the stairs, Mita Auntie's husband, Kanchan Uncle, was heading toward them with Rasika beside him.

"Look who I found!" he exclaimed, and Abhay remembered that Mita Auntie's family was good friends with Rasika's parents.

"And, look who I found!" Mita Auntie grasped his upper arm in both of hers. "He is here with some friends." Mita Auntie's grip threatened to dislodge the other ice cream bar pinned under Abhay's arm.

"Drinking at the bar, I suppose?" Kanchan Uncle winked at Abhay. Uncle was more dashing than his wife, tall and trim, with thick salt-and-pepper hair. "And she was here having dinner at the restaurant."

Mita Auntie clasped her hands and looked from one to the other. "What a coincidence to see two old friends at same time."

Abhay was glad he wasn't holding Rasika's suitcase. She had abandoned it next to the registration desk. Mita Auntie seemed happy to assume that he and Rasika were there separately and by chance. The other woman, an elderly lady who was probably Mita Auntie's mother, because she was also short and round, glanced suspiciously from Rasika to Abhay and back. Abhay wasn't sure what Kanchan Uncle thought.

Rasika threw her wrist in the air and eyed her watch. "Oh my god! I had no idea it was so late. I have got to go. It was so nice seeing you."

"You will be at reception?" Mita Auntie called after her.

"Yes. I'll see you there!" Rasika waved and smiled and walked briskly toward the door, her tiny black purse dangling from one hand.

Abhay watched her get smaller and smaller as she walked across the vast reception area. He licked the last bit of vanilla from the ice cream stick. He felt something wet under his arm. The other ice cream bar had melted through its packaging and was oozing onto his shirt.

6

To make up for her dalliance with Abhay and for the misfortune of seeing Mita Auntie and Kanchan Uncle, Rasika woke up on Saturday determined to be on her very best behavior when her parents arrived home with the latest eligible bachelor.

Her mother called at eight in the morning.

"I can't hear you very well." Rasika was sitting up in bed.

"I am in the bathroom," Amma confessed. "I have turned the fan on, so no one will overhear. And maybe the signal is bad. This is the only place I can talk without others hearing. You know we are bringing them home with us in the car, so I can't even call you on the way home. I wanted to tell you that you don't need to wear a sari. One of your salvar kameez outfits should be fine. The boy is quite casual, and his parents are very nice people. He is the same age as you are, and he has not yet finished medical school."

As her mother talked, Rasika looked around her room for her robe and realized she had left it in the suitcase at the hotel. She was glad she had taken off the suitcase's identification tag before going to the hotel last night. There was no risk of the hotel calling her about it. But she had lost her favorite robe, not to mention her blue dress and the suitcase itself. She couldn't go back and retrieve it today, for fear of seeing Mita Auntie again.

"Is Pramod at home?" Without waiting for an answer, Amma continued, "I want you to send him out for some snacks. Tell him to get some nuts, chips, soda. And something sweet—cookies. Good quality cookies. Send him to the bakery at Acme."

"Amma. Shouldn't we check the horoscopes before I meet him?"

"There is no time for that. He is here now, and his family is from the same community. We will check horoscopes later. I only wish we had more time to prepare."

Rasika sprang into action. The housecleaner came on Tuesdays, and by the weekend the house always started to look a little shabby. She vacuumed the living room, wiped off the sink and counters in the downstairs bathroom, carried out the trash. She was glad to be busy, so she wouldn't have to dwell on the bad luck that had brought her into contact with Mita Auntie. She dusted the tables in the living room, and even ran a rag over the frames and glass of the photos on the walls.

First were black-and-white portraits of her grandparents, taken when they were middle-aged: proper photos in which the grand-mothers wore large round kumkums between their eyebrows, and had their hair pulled back severely. Her mother's mother had high cheekbones and beautiful skin, and was smiling faintly. Rasika loved her pati, and wanted Pati to be proud of her. Her father's mother, whom she called "Ammachi," glared out under heavy eye-brows and above her hooked nose. Rasika had always been afraid of Ammachi. She wanted to avoid her disapproval. Both grandmoth-ers had on large diamond earrings and diamond nose studs, in ad-dition to heavy gold wedding necklaces. That was all considered de rigueur back then.

In her parents' color wedding portrait, her mother stood draped in a pink sari richly decorated in gold. Her mother's kumkum was a sparkly pink teardrop. Her father, standing slightly behind her mother, wore a suit. The studio background featured a clean interior with pillars. Rasika had always thought her parents looked perfect in this photo: elegant, young, well-off.

The next photo had been taken just after she and Pramod and her mother had arrived in Ohio from India. They were all wearing Western clothes against a background of an American flag. Her father's hair was black, and he wore large, rectangular black-framed glasses which had been fashionable at some point, but which now looked ridiculous. Her mother had a young, bright-eyed look—not the hardened smile she so often wore now.

Soon Rasika's wedding portrait would grace this wall. She wanted her own picture to look as elegant and perfect as her parents', and she often wondered what kind of sari she'd wear, and what kind of pose would be best. Should she sit and have her husband stand? But then her sari would not drape so beautifully. Perhaps she ought to choose a pose just like her parents'. Of course the most important missing piece was the groom. In terms of looks, Viraj would have been perfect, if only he hadn't turned out to be such a complete jerk, as Abhay said.

Abhay. She stopped dusting. Her arms hung by her sides. She pictured Abhay beside her in a wedding portrait. He'd be smiling just as he had smiled when he'd seen her at the Fox and Hound the other day. He'd looked so delighted. Maybe he'd have his arm around her shoulders. Perhaps they would get a portrait showing just their heads and shoulders, so Abhay's lack of height would not be obvious. What would she have him wear?

The rag dropped to the floor. Why was she thinking about Abhay? She sank down onto the sofa. When she thought of Abhay, she felt a pull at her heart, a longing to be with him. Was that love? She'd never been in love before, and if she was in love with him, then what did that mean? In her view of the world, she had to marry her one true love. But she obviously couldn't marry Abhay. No matter what he wore and how the photo was posed, he would not be acceptable to anyone in her family. Pati would not approve; Ammachi would definitely not approve. Abhay would never fit into a portrait on this wall, and therefore, the logical conclusion was that she did not love him.

Her skin prickled with guilt at the thought of what had happened at the hotel. Abhay was right. She had to stop all this pretense, all this sneaking around, and bring her mind back to what she really wanted.

She thought about the young man who would be arriving soon. This prospective groom was just a twenty-five-year-old student. She'd wanted her husband to be older and more accomplished than she was. She didn't want to support him while he finished medical school and slogged through his residency.

She picked up her rag and finished touching up the living room. Since Pramod wasn't home, she drove to the store and selected a bouquet of flowers in addition to the cookies, nuts, chips, and soda. Her mother would see Mita Auntie at the reception tomorrow, and of course Mita Auntie would mention Rasika and Abhay in the same breath. Mita Auntie was so naive, Rasika knew she suspected nothing, but Rasika's mother was capable of reading evil doings into the most innocent encounter.

At two o'clock, her parents and the guests tromped through the garage door. Rasika stood at the stove with an apron over her clothes, boiling the tea bags and spices to make chai. She glanced quickly at the young man before being caught up in hand shaking and doing namaskar.

He looked like one of Pramod's friends, with his jeans and sweater. His face was round. He was just a boy. His parents were both short, round-faced, and smiling. His mother wore a pair of brown knit pants and a sweater with a yellow duck embroidered on it. His father said in English, "We have no idea we will find bride for Dilip on trip to Pittsburgh!" Dilip looked uncomfortable as everyone laughed. It was the Cute Family.

Rasika's mother stayed behind with her in the kitchen while Appa led the others into the living room. "Your father likes him very much," Amma whispered. "He is a little shy, but very friendly. He lives in Nebraska now. Don't make a fuss about that. Your Appa will use his connections to try to get him a residency in this area. We are doing the very best for you." Her face had taken on its "do what I say, or else" look. Amma untied Rasika's apron and patted Rasika's hair before turning to the stove to pour out the tea.

Rasika arranged the teacups on a tray. She couldn't marry this boy. She had to get out of it, although she didn't know how. At least for today, she'd play along. She took the tray into the living room. Her father was asking in English, "What medical specialty you will pursue?"

Dilip half-slouched on the sofa, one socked foot on top of the other. "Family practice," he mumbled. Rasika lowered the tray of teacups in front of him. His hand trembled as he lifted a cup and saucer.

Appa's hand hopped in his lap. "Family practice is not the best specialty. You cannot earn as much there. I am telling Pramod to choose surgery." His forehead twitched.

Dilip's father laughed. "Family practice is fine. We are glad he has gotten into medical school at all. We thought we will have to send him overseas, or to osteopathic college. Let us not put too much pressure."

Rasika set the tray on the coffee table, picked up her own cup, and sat down next to Appa to observe this young man with the less-than-stellar academic record. Her mother breezed in with a tray of cookies.

After tea, Rasika and Dilip were packed off to the mall. Rasika drove. She had to figure out a way to get this boy to dislike her. That was the only way out. If he chose not to marry her, she'd be off the hook. What could she do that would put him off without causing any blame to fall on her? He certainly did seem shy. He was silent all the way to the mall. Maybe if she talked a lot, teased him, and flirted noisily, he'd get scared away? It was her only chance.

Since they'd just had tea, she took him to a juice and smoothie bar, and ordered a bottle of water for herself. They sat at a table in the walkway. She was unscrewing the cap of her bottle when he started mumbling something.

"You seem like a really nice girl," he said into his strawberry-kiwi smoothie, "but I'm not ready to get married yet. Mom and Dad got all excited when they met your parents and found out we're from the same, you know, subcaste, or whatever. Your mom showed us your photo and told us all about you, and my parents thought you'd be good for me, because I'm quiet, just like you."

Rasika smiled. Her mother had probably painted a picture of a demure girl who loved to stay at home and cook all day.

"Your mom said you had to get married before you turned twenty-six, but I'll still be in school."

Rasika nodded and attempted to assume a disappointed look.

"I still like you," he said. "I mean, I don't know you. But I think I would like you, if we got to know each other. We could, you know, send e-mail or something. And then we could decide later. I mean, I'm sure I'll like you." His voice trembled during this speech.

Rasika didn't want to "send e-mail or something" with this boy, yet it was a small price to pay for delaying the wedding. She was sure she could figure out a way to delay the thing into oblivion.

"Sure," she said soothingly. "That sounds like a great idea."

* * *

So like Amisha's family, Rasika thought, sitting in a dark corner of a large banquet hall the next day. They invite a zillion people to the reception and then hold it in a dumpy party hall with no windows whatsoever, industrial heavy-traffic carpeting, and fluorescent lights that blinked off randomly. Someone had draped gold-colored cloths and strings of plastic mango leaves over a few of the walls, but these feeble attempts at decor couldn't disguise the overall low-rent quality of the place.

Amisha was a few years younger than Rasika. Her parents were old friends of Rasika's parents, although the families weren't particularly close. Amisha's family had money, but they tried to make it stretch too far and ended up doing things cheaply. They had just bought a huge new house. According to Rasika's mother, everything in it was bottom-of-the-line, low-quality stuff.

Of course, they spent enough money on Amisha's clothes and jewelry. Amisha, standing in line with the rest of the wedding party to serve herself at the buffet, was wearing gold cuffs on her upper arms and a wide gold belt over her heavy silk sari, in addition to the usual diamond earrings, gold bangles, and wedding necklace. They probably had to pay extra to get a belt large enough to go around Amisha's ample girth.

"Such a nice family," Mita Auntie said in English. She was sitting on the other side of Rasika's mother. Rasika was on pins and needles, waiting for Mita Auntie to bring up Abhay. He and his family were here, too, on the other side of the hall. Maybe by hiding in this dark corner, she could avoid him until it was time to leave.

Subhash and his parents, Balu Uncle and Deepti Auntie, wandered through the doorway at the far end of the room. Subhash towered over his very short, plump parents. Rasika's father waved them over, and they bustled toward them.

"Rasika!" Before Rasika could stand up, Deepti Auntie had enveloped her in a hug. Auntie's breasts pressed against Rasika's neck. Finally, Rasika managed to stand up.

"You look very nice," Auntie said in Tamil. "As usual."

Rasika wore a lavender salvar kameez with a matching gossamer scarf draped around her neck. "Thank you." She smiled down at Deepti Auntie, who was lifting Rasika's scarf to get a better look at the embroidery on her kameez. Rasika didn't mind. Unlike other relatives, Deepti Auntie never criticized.

"Where did you buy this?" Auntie asked. "At Saree Palace in Cleveland?"

"My pati got it stitched for me in India, and sent it with Ahalya Auntie. They just came back from India a couple of months ago."

"It fits very well. Your grandmother knows your size?"

"My mother sent an old outfit, and they used that as a pattern."

"The beading is well done." Deepti Auntie let go of the scarf. "Next weekend we are having pooja at the new office in Kent. Your parents will be coming. You must come, too."

Rasika nodded. "I'll definitely be there."

Deepti Auntie patted Rasika's cheek. "You are like a daughter to me," she said. Her voice thickened, as though she were about to cry. "I have only one son. So you must be my daughter."

Rasika wasn't sure what Auntie meant by this. Was this a reference to the fact that Subhash wanted to marry Rasika?

"You must come to our place for dinner," Auntie said. "We never see you. Come for dinner one Friday, and stay with us the whole weekend. We will rent all kinds of Hindi movies. Some of them have English subtitles."

As much as she liked Deepti Auntie, she didn't want to spend a whole weekend at their apartment in Cleveland, especially since she was now aware of Subhash's wishes. "Sure, I'll do that sometime," she said vaguely.

Subhash and his parents seated themselves at the table. Rasika sat back down. It seemed like every relationship in this room was a potential minefield. So far, Mita Auntie had not brought up Abhay at all. She had been happy to discuss the appropriateness of this marriage and of Amisha's family in general. "He seems like very nice boy," Mita Auntie was saying in English. Her mother tongue was Hindi, and so she spoke to Rasika's family in English. "So polite."

The groom had an overhanging brow and a bumpy nose, as though it had blisters all over it. Amisha, standing next to him, seemed oblivious to the fact that she had just yoked herself to a baboon. She seemed to be thinking of nothing except the food she was serving herself.

"And she has just been offered very good job," Mita Auntie gushed. "She will work for St. John's Hospital."

"Doing what?" Rasika's mother snapped. "She's not a doctor."

Rasika knew her mother was irritable today, although she'd taken the news about Dilip surprisingly well. A delay in plans was better than an end to them.

"In human resources," Mita Auntie said. "That is her degree, you know. She will be making very good salary."

"She will have to support him, I suppose." Amma said this to the air above Mita Auntie's head. She always spoke to the air when she was trying to pretend she wasn't being nasty. "It is difficult for people from India to get a job here."

"He has already had offers, I heard. He is very brilliant."

How did Amisha, of all people, end up marrying appropriately and thus surpassing Rasika? Amisha was so average, yet she always seemed happy flying under the radar. In high school she was one of those girls who were always getting involved with something, being the treasurer of the student council, helping to paint sets for the school play. She was never the leader, but this didn't seem to bother her. She not only didn't aspire to stardom, but she also seemed to imply, by her complacency, that her own role was after all the most important anyway, even if no one else realized it.

"Here comes Venika," Amma said.

Rasika's heart tightened as Abhay's mother walked toward them. At least Abhay was nowhere in sight at the moment.

"She has gotten involved with some new business," Amma continued. "She will tell you all about it."

"Oh, I almost forgot." Mita Auntie grinned conspiratorially at Rasika. "You will never guess where I met Rasika."

Venika Auntie was upon them. She had cut her hair recently and looked even younger than before. Except for the dark circles under her eyes, which had been there since Rasika remembered, she could pass for thirty. She bent down and put both hands on Mita Auntie's shoulders. "So nice to see you again!"

Mita Auntie looked up at Venika. "I was just telling Sujata— by chance, I saw Rasika and Abhay at hotel when we arrived."

Mita Auntie had a high, piercing voice, audible to anyone at the table. Rasika noticed that Subhash was looking at them from across the table.

The lights above the table blinked on. Rasika startled for a moment, and then smiled brightly. "It was really a coincidence, wasn't it? Seeing both you and Abhay there at the same time."

"Last night?" Amma's eyes narrowed. "It must have been someone else. Rasika was at home."

"We arrived Friday," Mita Auntie explained. "Our plane was late. We are standing in lobby waiting for Kanchan to finish registration, and I saw Abhay. He was just leaving. And then, Kanchan saw Rasika!"

Rasika kept on smiling. "I was so surprised! I was just finishing up dinner with a friend, and there was Kanchan Uncle!"

Venika Auntie smiled her sleepy smile. "Abhay told some time ago he saw you," she said.

The table grew silent. Subhash was still looking at them. Rasika forced a laugh. "I ran into him about a week ago at a restaurant, and then again at the hotel. We seem to keep bumping into each other."

"That is good you and Abhay are meeting. Maybe you can talk sense to him." Venika Auntie drew a business card out of her purse and handed it to Mita Auntie. "I am marketing representative for some really wonderful educational products. Your children are older, I know, but if you know someone else interested, please give me call."

Mita Auntie looked the card over. "We are so far away."

"I can sell anywhere. Any part of country. We will ship all over."

Mita Auntie nodded and smiled and kept looking at the card. Rasika was glad her mother had never tried to sell things to her friends. Venika Auntie drifted away to the next table. A uniformed server asked their table to go to the buffet, and Rasika leaped up to get away from her mother's icy glare.

Amma stood close behind Rasika in the line and whispered, "What is this about you and Abhay?"

"I just saw him a couple of times. It was by accident." Abhay's table was coming up to the buffet line. If she were unlucky, she'd end up facing him over the buffet. She'd just have to be as matter-of-fact as possible.

"It doesn't look good," Amma said. "I know you don't mean anything by it, but others will talk. He is nothing. He got good grades in school, but he has no sense. You don't want to ruin your chances now. What if the news got around to Dilip's family that you were seen with another boy?"

"I wasn't even with him. I can't help it if Mita Auntie saw us at the same place."

"And what were you doing out at some hotel? You told me you stayed home all evening. I don't know why you lie to me. We don't prevent you from having fun. If you want to go out with some girl-friends, why should I object? You have all the freedom you want. All I ask is that you stay away from boys."

Rasika listened, knowing that if she allowed her mother to scold without interruption, it would soon be over.

"Do you think I could move about like you do, at your age?" Amma hissed. "I was married. I had to ask my husband's permission before doing anything. And before marriage, I had to ask my father's permission. I didn't have my own car. I didn't have my own job. You have all of this, and still you lie. What is there to lie about? I don't know why you would bother. You cannot want to marry Abhay. And not just because of his caste. I can be open-minded if the boy is really special, but what has he done with himself? He has thrown away every opportunity. His wife will be supporting him."

"I'm not interested in him, Amma."

"We are strict with you for your own good. You don't want to turn out like Nita, do you?"

Nita was the daughter of an unconventional Indian couple in their community. Rasika shifted her eyes slightly to look at Nita's parents, standing and chatting at a table nearby. Rupal Auntie had short graying hair. Instead of a silk sari with a gold border, such as most of the other women were wearing, she wore a cotton sari with a pattern of small tie-dyed diamonds and dots. It was a cute, tribal sort of sari, but not appropriate for a wedding reception. Sri Uncle wore a dress shirt, but it looked wrinkled, as though he'd just gotten up from fixing a pipe—he owned a plumbing repair company, even though he was a trained engineer. Rasika was very familiar with their story, since her parents often used them as an example of what not to do. Theirs had not been an arranged marriage: she was from a Punjabi family, raised in Delhi, and he was a Tamilian boy who had somehow gone astray. They'd waited several years after marriage to produce a child. Nita had grown up without the usual restrictions placed by Indian parents: she had dated and participated as a dancer in school musicals wearing next to nothing, and had worked as a bartender during college. Now she lived in Alaska, of all places, working at some sort of hiking tour service. No, Rasika didn't want to turn out like Nita.

Abhay's family shuffled into the opposite line, and Rasika stepped back slightly in an attempt to get out of Abhay's line of sight.

"That family," Amma said. "They have so much potential. What do they do with it? His sister has no idea how to dress. If she would only smile, it might be okay."

Dark and skinny, Seema was the only female in the room not wearing Indian clothes. She was in a black ankle-length skirt and black sandals and a black T-shirt.

Rasika touched the gold and diamond necklace at her throat, picked up a plate, and waited while the person ahead of her selected a few flat, greasy pooris.

Abhay wished he hadn't agreed to come to this reception. His cab ride home from the hotel had cost him over a hundred dollars, and in the cab he'd vowed to himself never to see Rasika again.

Last night he'd gone over to Chris's house for the barbecue and had tried to enter into the casual cheerfulness of everyone there. Several friends from high school were there, and they all called him "Adios." He'd had trouble remembering some of their names. He'd eaten a hamburger, and Mrs. Haldorson's famous potato salad, and Mr. Haldorson's famous cheesecake, and had listened to Emily Nuttman's husband describe his job as a commemorative jewelry salesman. Abhay had come home with a stomachache, and had tried to persuade his mother that he was too sick to attend the reception.

His mom made him some fennel tea and urged him to make an appearance. Besides, he had to admit that, against his will, he was desperate to see Rasika again.

Now Rasika was pretending he didn't exist. What else did he expect? Yesterday, despite his efforts to distract himself, he'd been unable to think about anything except her. He was infatuated with her. He had tried, all day, to list in his mind her good qualities and faults, in order to bring some order and logic to his runaway feelings. On the one hand, he told himself, she was gorgeous, and even though she didn't see the world as he did, she was still curious and possessed some wisdom. He kept thinking about what she'd said in the hotel room—that he was waiting to start living. That was true. But how long was he going to go on like this, killing time because he couldn't make up his mind? Maybe it would be better to follow her advice, to pick something and just do it. If he were with her, maybe she could help him to see his path more clearly.

On the other hand, she was a liar and a cheat. There was no denying that. Yet he desperately wanted to be with her again. That's what she did to a lot of men, probably—messed up their heads and then left.

It was his turn to take a plate. Rasika was on the opposite side of the table. He glanced at her over the steaming chafing dishes, wondering how she would act. She was all dolled up in proper Indian clothes, with a sparkly kumkum on her forehead and the requisite gold jewelry.

She raised her eyebrows and smiled, as though surprised at his presence. "Hi, again. I was just telling Amma that I keep running into you." Her manner was casual and unconcerned. He had to admit, she was a terrific liar.

"How are you, Abhay?" Rasika's mother gave him one of her cool smiles. "What do you plan to do now that you are home?"

"I'm still exploring," he said.

His mother turned to Sujata. "Further studies he is thinking."

"In what field?" Sujata Auntie sifted through the pakodas with a pair of tongs. Most of them had already fallen apart, their onion or chili filling separated from the batter coating. "What is your background, exactly?" She selected one whole pakoda and dropped it onto her plate.

"Law we are telling him to look," his mother said. "Good background for law he has."

Abhay served himself some rice that wasn't too dried out. The buffet already looked unappetizing and picked over.

"Rasika, what about you?" his mother asked. "When you will invite me to your wedding?"

"We are very close to making the announcement," Sujata Auntie said.

A papadum slipped out of Abhay's hand to the floor. He bent down, retrieved the thin wafer, and took his time inspecting it for dirt. When he straightened, Rasika was smiling demurely at her plate. Sujata Auntie, head held high, pursed her lips, as though to prevent the good news from escaping prematurely. Was Rasika putting on an act, or had she really agreed to marry the guy she'd seen the day before?

She began to glow with a golden light. He blinked. Still she glowed, and appeared to be slowly expanding, filling up his vision with her presence. She was a goddess, and he was falling in love with her. What was he going to do about it? He stirred the mutter paneer to see if there were any pieces of cheese left and, finding none, poured a spoonful of peas onto his rice.

At the end of the buffet line Rasika turned and Abhay couldn't help but drift after her, like a leaf caught in a current. He balanced his plate and napkin in one hand and touched her shoulder through the golden glow. He was surprised to feel her solidness. She stopped and glared at him.

"I love you," he whispered.

Sujata Auntie, standing several feet away, stared at him. If she'd heard, he didn't care.

For an instant, Rasika looked at him with stunned eyes. Then she composed herself, crinkled her eyes, and gave a hollow laugh. "Very funny."

"Meet me tomorrow," he whispered. "After work, at the Fox and Hound."

She turned her back to her mother. "Only if you leave me completely alone today."

"Okay," he agreed. Anything to see her again.

Rasika turned away from Abhay and was walking back to her table when Kanchan Uncle appeared next to her. Her heart was pounding as a result of what Abhay had said. She forced herself to smile at Kanchan Uncle as they walked.

"I know what you were doing at the hotel with Abhay," he said quietly.

She stopped in her tracks. What was he implying?

"I saw you come out of the elevator with him, and with your suitcase," he continued. "Your hair was wet. I know what you were doing."

She stared.

"I want to make a suggestion." He was smiling slightly, balancing his plate piled high with a stack of pooris, mounds of rice and curries, and a large papadum crowning the whole thing. He kept his distance from her, as though they were just having a polite conversation. Other guests walked around them on their way to and from the buffet table.

"I want you to meet me at the hotel tomorrow," he said. "My family will be out visiting some friends. I will tell them I am not feeling well. You come and visit me."

Rasika was shocked. She'd never thought an Indian uncle was capable of making any kind of proposition like this. She furrowed her brow and glanced around her.

"I am going away on Tuesday," he said. "No one will know. I will be completely silent."

She laughed, as though she were finally getting the joke. "Very funny." She started walking away. He followed.

"I will tell Mita what I saw," he said, catching up to her. "And you know she cannot resist spreading good gossip."

"Go ahead and tell," Rasika said. "As if I care." She reached their empty table, settled into her seat, and spread her napkin over her lap.

In a moment everyone else returned to the table, and Kanchan Uncle paid no further attention to her. He sat on the other side of the table, showing his camera to her father. It was a big, black thing with a cylindrical protruding lens. It looked heavy. Appa's face seemed its usual mask of worry, with two dents above his eyebrows and his squinting blinks as he took the camera into his own hands and examined it. "We should get a digital camera like this one," Appa shouted across the table to Amma. "Single lens reflex. You can change lenses, so you can take a panorama, or a close-up from far away." He spoke half in English and half in Tamil. He held the camera up to his eye and aimed it at Rasika.

"This camera will produce a much higher quality image than the one you have." Kanchan waved his hand at the flat little silver box next to Rasika's father's plate. "I should have taken a picture with this when I saw Rasika at the hotel the other day." Kanchan winked at her.

Rasika had the urge to duck under the table. What would Appa do if he were to find out the truth about her? Rasika felt sick thinking about her father's distress and her mother's disappointment.

"Best Buy is having a sale," Amma said. "You go and look there."

"Kanchan says we will get the best price online. He is giving me Web site."

Kanchan scribbled something on a paper napkin. "And this comes with optical zoom."

"Kanchan loves to shop online," Mita Auntie shouted. "These days he will never enter any stores."

Rasika wondered if Abhay was right—that the United States was merely a place for her family to buy stuff. She looked around the windowless room. She recalled being in a very similar room a few years ago, when they went to North Carolina to visit Ahalya Auntie and their family. They had tagged along to someone's wedding reception, and although it had been in a different part of the country, with different people, it was much the same: a bland room with decorations brought from India, or made to look like something people remembered from India. The people in this room were perched here as if they had just landed temporarily. Everyone knew that their real home was India.

After lunch a DJ played cheesy Bollywood songs, American oldies, and top-forty hits, and the younger generation—those raised in the United States—danced lazily. The older women congregated at one another's tables. Everyone else at Rasika's table had wandered off, but Rasika thought she'd have better luck avoiding everyone if she just stayed put.

Subhash appeared at Rasika's side. "May I sit here?" he asked softly, putting a hand on the back of the chair next to hers. He wore a large white jubba over dress pants. There was a wet spot next to the buttons of his shirt, as though he'd spilled something on himself and then wiped it off with a wet napkin.

She pushed away her untouched kulfi. She'd never liked that extra-rich Indian ice cream. "Sure." It would be better to be seen talking to Subhash than to Abhay.

He sat awkwardly on the edge of his chair, leaning his arms on the table and drumming his fingers lightly. Finally he said, without looking at her, "You look really beautiful today." Although he had a fairly heavy Indian accent, he tried hard not to roll his r's.

"Thank you." She looked past him to the dance floor, and at the other tables. She didn't see Abhay anywhere.

"I am sorry to hear that things did not work out with Viraj," he continued. Rasika noticed sweat shining on his broad face. He had always been a serious, somewhat nervous boy. "Rasika, since we are cousins, I hope I can speak freely."

She looked at him in alarm. What was he going to bring up? They'd never "spoken freely" before in all the years she'd known him. In fact, they had hardly spoken at all. Mostly, when the families ate dinner together, Subhash ended up in front of the TV, clicking through channels, watching sports and news and sitcoms without showing any sign of emotional involvement with any of it.

Now he sat on the edge of his chair and slapped the stubby forefinger of his right hand onto the palm of his left hand. "Many men might be timid in a situation like this," he said. "They may wait for their parents to arrange things. My parents are reluctant to speak to your father, because of everything your father has done for us. They don't want to ask for more."

He was speaking to her knee. The forefinger moved up and down forcefully with each point. Rasika realized it looked like a machine—a typewriter spelling out the words, as though he had programmed himself to say what he was typing.

"Subhash. Let's not talk about this right—"

"But I have a different view," he continued, as though he hadn't even heard her. "In my business, I have learned the power of making a request."

His hands were still poised in the air. She leaned back, resigning herself to hearing him out.

"I am confident that I can offer you a very good life." The finger started pumping away again. "I know you must marry soon. I am also aware that people have been talking about you. This is very bad for a woman's reputation. I have heard from Viraj what happened. I have seen myself that you were with Abhay in Kent."

Rasika flinched inwardly every time his finger slammed down. She kept her face immobile, however.

"I cannot think you mean anything by it," he continued. "You were raised in this country, so you are not so familiar with Indian modesty. You do not realize that an unmarried girl should not be seen wandering about with men. Therefore, I am willing and able to offer you a good, safe life. Since I am just starting out at this new location, I can offer you a partnership. As my wife, you will be a full partner. You were raised in this country. You have an American accent. You are good with people. I think you will attract a wide range of customers." One last time, he dropped the rod of his forefinger into the claws of the other hand. Then he lowered his hands to his lap and looked down at them.

"I already have a job," she reminded him.

The hands were raised again. "You will be a full partner in the business," he repeated, talking to the table. "You will be an owner. This is better for you than working at a job where you can be let go at any moment."

She sat back to observe him. Was he really in love with her and didn't know how to express it? Or did he just think she'd be good for business?

"You see, I may not be able to offer this later," he said. "If too many rumors start about you, I will not be able to make this same proposal. But if you come in with me now, on the ground floor, and help me to build the business, then of course I would—"

"Subhash." She put both her hands over his hands, to stop his anxious movements.

He made eye contact, finally. His eyes were wide and his eyebrows were slightly raised. He looked scared—terrified, even. She realized this was more for him than a business proposition. Perhaps he was even in love with her. She didn't want to hurt his feelings.

She took her hands away from his. "I think we should let the elders deal with this," she suggested gently. "That's the Indian way, after all."

He bundled his hands together into one large fist between his knees. "I think my mother spoke with your mother. But my father is reluctant, as I said."

"My mother mentioned your interest, but my father is hesitant. He thinks we're too closely related. Maybe we should heed their wisdom."

Subhash sighed heavily. His broad shoulders seemed to deflate as he hunched over.

Rasika stood up. "Your offer is very sweet. But I don't think it's the right thing for me."

He looked up at her with his scared eyes. "Rasika, I do like you. I think you are very pretty. We are adults. We don't have to do just what our parents tell us."

"I'm not the right wife for you, Subhash," she said.

"Why not?" He was still looking up at her, and he seemed bewildered.

"For one thing, I'm not looking for a safe life."

His eyebrows knitted. He didn't seem to know what to say to this. She surprised herself by what she had said. She glanced around the room for a way to escape this conversation. "My parents are looking for a boy for me, and my marriage should be fixed quite soon."

"If you—if nothing works out for you, then—my offer still stands."

"Thank you, Subhash." Rasika didn't know what else to say to him. She fixed her eyes at a point across the room, smiled, and waved at an imaginary friend. "Excuse me." She made her way to the knot of women around Amisha Menon, and spent the rest of the reception with them, admiring Amisha's clothes, her accomplishments, and her job. In this way she managed to stay out of the way of Subhash, Abhay, Kanchan Uncle, and her mother.

At the end of the reception, while guests were milling around Amisha and her husband to congratulate them one last time, several girls took up a position near the doorway with baskets of favors. Rasika remained with Amisha until she saw both Abhay's family and Subhash's family leave. Mita Auntie and Kanchan Uncle were still talking to her parents. It appeared that the families would be walking out together.

Rasika drew near her mother, and away from Kanchan Uncle, as she walked toward the door. On the sidewalk in front of the party hall, in the darkness lit by car headlights and streetlights, she felt someone brush past her and press a piece of paper into her hand. As she glanced up, she saw Kanchan Uncle walking away from her. She crushed the paper in her fist and kept it hidden during the car ride home.

When she was safe in her bedroom, sitting on her bed in her Indian finery, she smoothed out the paper and read a time, 6 P.M., and a room number. Nothing else.

7

Raindrops pelted her windshield as Rasika drove to work the next morning. She flipped on her wipers. The sky was a heavy gray around her, and the familiar scenery outside dripped and smeared through her windows.

When she was growing up, all the Indian uncles—who weren't really her uncles, just her parents' friends—were men to be looked up to, intelligent men who'd graduated at the tops of their classes and who were thus able to attend graduate school or get medical training in the United States, and find jobs. Every once in a while, she'd hear a story about some uncle, not a close friend, who left his wife for someone else, or who verbally abused his children. Kanchan Uncle was within their own circle of friends. True, he'd moved away. Still, the idea of who he really was, what he had proposed . . . she felt dizzy and sick to her stomach, as though she had spun too fast in an amusement park ride.

Her office reflected the outside gloom. The windows and white walls all looked gray. As she stowed her purse in one of her drawers, her phone trilled. She didn't recognize the caller ID number on the display, so she let it go to voice mail.

The phone stopped. She realized she'd been holding her breath and let it out. Her heart was fluttering in her throat, and she still felt sick. She sat at her desk and opened a folder full of information about McMillan and Associates, a real estate development firm they were scheduled to meet with that afternoon. Kanchan Uncle would go back to Chicago tomorrow, and the whole thing would blow over. She flipped through the glossy brochures. The company was in the business of developing "a lifestyle of service, luxury, and convenience." She liked the photos: upscale brick apartment buildings with lots of windows. If she didn't live with her parents, she'd like to live in a building like that. She didn't pay much attention to the printouts of the financial data. Her role would be to charm the folks at McMillan and Associates into using her company's financial services.

The rain continued. She couldn't concentrate on work. She wandered into the kitchen for some coffee. Estelle, the grandmotherly receptionist, was rinsing out the coffeepot in the sink. She asked, "Did you get your message, honey?"

"No." Rasika decided not to wait for the coffee. She flipped the lever of the water dispenser, and water glugged into her mug.

"It sounded important." Estelle ripped open a package of coffee. Her upper-arm fat jiggled. "I put him through to your voice mail."

At her desk, she picked up the phone receiver and pushed the voice mail button. "Rasika," she heard, in a slow, cultured Indian accent. "Kanchan here. I have found out where you work. I am expecting you here at six. You will not want to disappoint me."

All morning Rasika told herself she could ignore Kanchan Uncle without any repercussions. And she wasn't going to meet Abhay at the Fox and Hound either. She'd go straight home and stay out of trouble.

At lunchtime she darted out in her car, picked up a salad and a cup of soup from a nearby restaurant, and ate at her desk. What if Kanchan Uncle spread scandalous stories about her, and what if her father became ill, or had a heart attack, as a result?

Late in the afternoon, after she'd assured the men of McMillan and Associates that her company would provide excellent service, she decided she'd better meet Kanchan Uncle for a short while. She'd be charming and chat with him, maybe have a drink, and pacify him enough to smooth things over. That's all he wanted—to spend a little time with a beautiful woman, since he was saddled for life with dumpy Mita Auntie. She was reading far more into this than was warranted.

After work she drove through the rain to the Renaissance Hotel. Her heart was beating in her throat. She kept reminding herself, "Don't worry. It's not what you think. He's an Indian uncle, after all. Indian uncles never do bad things." She gave her keys to the valet parking guy and ducked into the lobby. The glare of the lights hurt her eyes, and the noises—clicking of heels and rumbling of suitcase wheels on the hard floor—seemed too loud. A man in a gray jacket mopped rainwater off the floor. As the elevator car zoomed upward her heart plummeted. Her legs trembled. She wished she had worn a longer skirt today. This one just reached her knees. She pulled her jacket close around her. The elevator door slid open, and she strode down the thick carpeting. She'd considered asking him to meet her downstairs for a drink but thought it would be better if no one saw them together. She'd just chat with him up here for a short while, and then go home. It would be fine.

She knocked. The door opened immediately.

"Welcome," he whispered. He wore a long silk robe.

She didn't move. "I can't stay long." She clutched her purse to her chest. "My mother is expecting me home."

"Come in."

She thought about turning and running toward the elevator, but he took her by the hand and pulled her in. His touch was damp, and she wiped the back of her hand on her jacket. The door shut with a loud click. She was standing in the living area of a suite. She was aware of a dimly lit bedroom opening to her left.

"Make yourself comfortable." He ushered her to a sofa at the far end of the room. She sat on the edge of a cushion and studied the window, looking for an escape route. The curtains were closed. They were on the twelfth floor.

He handed her a glass of red wine. She set it on the table. Uncle sat down with his own glass of wine, and the silk robe flapped open, revealing white and black chest hairs. "Why don't you put your purse down and relax?"

She heard her phone ringing in her purse, and she clutched it tighter to her chest. It was probably her mother. What if Amma found out about this? She might think this was all Rasika's fault for agreeing to meet a man in his hotel room.

"Uncle." She stood up. "I really can't stay. I just came to talk to you for a minute." She took a step back.

He put his glass on the table carefully, and stood. Even though she was wearing heels, he was several inches taller than she was. He put his hand on her purse. She clutched it even tighter. He lowered his hand. "Come on." His voice was low and rumbly. "Relax. You don't have to worry about anything. We'll have a little fun, and then I'll go away. You'll never hear from me again. And your secret"— he looked pointedly at her—"will be completely safe."

Rasika turned and moved toward the door. Two hands gripped her shoulders. Without thinking, she screamed and kicked back at his legs with her heel. She rushed for the door and pulled the handle. It stopped. The safety latch was in place. Uncle was clenching her arm. She kicked him again, and he turned her and shoved her against the door. She aimed her nails at his eyes. He grabbed her wrist, dragged her into the bedroom, and pushed her down onto the bed.

"If you cooperated, I would not have to do this." His face was hard, his voice steely.

She couldn't believe what was happening. This scene was not supposed to be part of her life. She screamed and flailed at him with her nails and heels. His hands pressed down on her shoulders, and his knee was on her stomach. He had thrown her purse somewhere, and his damp hands were clutching at her blouse, trying to rip it open.

Suddenly, there was banging at the door. "What's going on in there?" someone shouted.

Kanchan put his hand over her mouth while she continued trying to kick him. The banging persisted. He leaped up and disappeared into the bathroom. She ran to the door, fumbled for the lock, and opened it to see a large black man in the gray jacket and cap of a bellhop. Rasika reached for him. "Get me out of here!" she screamed.

The bellman helped her find her purse. "Would you like to call the police, ma'am?" he asked.

"No." Rasika smoothed her hair and skirt with a shaking hand. "Thank you. I just need to go home."

Downstairs the bellhop called for her car, and Rasika hurried out to it. She was surprised she was able to drive home so competently—that she even remembered how to drive. She felt like she was in a flat movie background and would soon burst through to the other side, to her real life.

At home, her parents were finishing dinner. The air-conditioning chilled her.

"Come and eat, Rasika," Amma said. "Balu Uncle and Deepti Auntie are here. And Subhash. They are waiting to see you."

"I'm not hungry."

"Rasika, just sit with us then," Deepti Auntie called to her. "We never see you."

"I have a headache." She put her fingertips to her temples and hurried past the dining table. She could feel Subhash's eyes on her.

In her room, she took off her work clothes and lay in bed, waiting for the shivering to stop. She wished someone were there to comfort her, yet she knew she couldn't talk about this with anyone.

Then she thought of Abhay waiting for her at the Fox and Hound. He would never behave like Kanchan Uncle. He was a really good guy. Of course she couldn't marry him, but that didn't matter now. She just wanted to see him. She'd call him tomorrow and tell him everything. He'd comfort her.

On Monday evening Abhay stood outside the Fox and Hound in a drizzle of rain, waiting for Rasika. There was a disgusting splotch of something—pizza? dried vomit?—on the sidewalk, and he tried not to look at it. At six-fifteen, when Rasika still hadn't appeared, he went into the restaurant, found a pay phone, and called her cell phone. No answer. He decided to walk home. The rain wasn't too heavy, and he didn't mind getting a little wet. He had to forget about Rasika. He had to admit she wasn't interested in him. He needed to leave this tired town.

He entered his house in a black mood.

"Come and eat, Abhay," his mother called from the kitchen.

"Yeah, OK." He walked to his bedroom to dry off and change his clothes.

In the kitchen, his father and sister were in their usual places at the table. They always ate in the kitchen, Mom sitting nearest the stove, Seema next to her, Abhay near the back door, and his father next to him. These were the seats they had occupied as far back as Abhay could remember. When he returned home after a year away, it was apparent no one had thought to change anything.

Abhay took his usual seat and asked, "How is everyone?" Since he'd moved back, he'd been waging a one-man war against the usual silence at the dinner table.

His father grunted. His mother set a jar of spicy pickles on the table and said, "Seema, bring some ice water for Daddy."

Mom settled into her seat and began serving Dad first: a soft wheat roti, a steaming mound of white rice, ladlefuls of spinach dal and sweet-and-sour radish gojju, a spoonful of cucumber and coconut salad, a pile of crispy white sandige. She never served leftovers. Dad had always insisted on a fresh meal every evening.

Abhay was an adult before he realized his father was different from other Indian men. The stereotypical man from India was awkward and physically weak, although perhaps a genius in technical matters. His father, on the other hand, was commanding. He was tall, with a full head of pure white hair (it had turned white quite early in his life). His accent was more British than Indian. His movements were slow and deliberate. He picked up his water glass majestically and swept his eyes over the rest of them at the table.

"Chutney pudi you want?" Mom raised the jar of spice powder. She was much shorter than Dad, with a thin, girlish face and hesitant movements.

Dad drank slowly, put his glass down, and tore off a piece of roti. His nonanswer was taken as a "no," as it was meant to be. Mom pushed the rice container closer to Seema, who preferred to serve herself.

"So, Seema." Abhay looked at his skeletal sister mixing her rice with hot pickle. "In a few weeks you're starting the honors program at Kent State."

She seemed to flinch a little, as though the words had nicked her face.

"What're you going to study? Any more thoughts since we talked the other day?"

"Chemical engineering," she mumbled.

"Really. And how did you decide on that?"

"You can make fifty thousand dollars right out of college."

"Ah." He watched her swallowing and almost felt the burning pepper of the pickle make its way down her throat.

"She has done her research," Dad said. "She will do very well. She can go into biochemical engineering if she wants, and even on to medical school. It is a versatile degree."

"Abhay is also doing research," Mom put in. "He will be studying—what is it, Abhay? Environmental something. Good field it is supposed to be."

Abhay had recently mentioned to his mother that more and more colleges were offering an environmental science major, and Mom had leaped to the conclusion that he was going into this field.

"A good field according to whom?" Dad asked.

No one bothered to answer this, since it wasn't a question but a way of ending the discussion.

"Seema is the only one here with a head on her shoulders," Dad said. "Your mother is wasting her time and money on those games. And you, Abhay, are wasting your time chasing after an illusion. Universities should not be allowed to offer majors that lead to nothing. The administrators do not care. As long as they can convince people to pay for the classes, they will offer anything. It is nothing to them if the music majors will be working as cashiers afterward."

Abhay bit into a sandige and was startled by its loud crunch.

"If I were an American father I would say, get out. Go support yourself." Dad crushed a sandige and mixed bits of it into his rice. He finished chewing and swallowing before starting another sentence. "That is what the Americans do. But we Indians do not abandon our children. If you come home after your degree, without any job, and you want to live here, then this is your home. That is what we believe. I have tried to raise you with good sense. I do not know where I failed."

Abhay remembered what his mother had said about Dad getting angry when he felt worried. "Dad." Abhay's voice cracked. He cleared his throat and took a sip of water. "Dad, I really appreciate everything you've done for me." He shifted sideways so he could see his father better.

Dad grunted.

"Right now I'm exploring my options, and I'm glad to be able to stay here," Abhay continued.

"The time for exploring is past," Dad said. "You explored all during college, and came up with nothing."

"Did you always know what you wanted to do, Dad?" Abhay asked.

Dad mixed his rice and spinach dal so vigorously that his elbow knocked Abhay in the arm. "My father told me to study physics. According to him, that was the best way to pass the Indian Civil Service exam and get a good government job."

"What does physics have to do with civil service?"

"Nothing. But somehow, studying physics allowed people to pass the exam. At that time, those kind of government jobs were the highest paying, with complete job security."

"Did you take the exam?" Abhay had never heard this part of his father's story.

Dad finished chewing a large mouthful, and took a long drink of water. "I applied for further studies in this country, and never went back to take the exam. I am sure I would have been a poor government servant."

"Did you ever have any doubts about what to study?" Abhay asked.

"In this country, they allow you too many choices." Dad waved his fork in the air, as though lecturing to a class. "In India, you must decide what you want to do before entering college. There is nothing like 'general studies' there. You must decide, and apply, and then go wherever you get in. Here, there is too much freedom. You can complete your entire college degree and still not make any decision."

Abhay had heard this many times. Most Indians wanted their children to have the educational opportunities of the United States, but they were afraid of the freedom and choice. "Are you worried that I'll never decide, and you'll have to support me all your life?"

"I will support you as long as I can. Then I will die and you will have to support yourself. How, I do not know. In India, the son is supposed to support his mother, take care of his mother, when the father dies. How will you do that? What will happen to her?" Dad glared at Abhay.

Seema stood up and carried her plate to the sink, even though she hadn't finished her rice.

Mom looked from Seema to Abhay to Dad. Then she said, in a voice that sounded like she was choking, "I will take care of myself. Abhay should not worry." She glared at Dad. Abhay had never seen his mother glare at his father. "Always you criticize. Always you put down. It is not right. He is smart."

Dad was so surprised by this outburst that he stopped eating for a moment and just sat with his fork poised above his plate.

"Abhay never ask for money. Not once," Mom continued. "He works. All the time he works, and—"

"Enough," Dad growled. He picked up his water glass, then put it down without drinking. "I heard."

Mom bowed her head over her plate. Abhay saw a tear drop onto her rice. He wondered if silence at the dinner table was perhaps better than this.

* * *

The next morning was dry and overcast. Rasika left for work early, pulled into a gas station, and called Abhay at home. She didn't care if his parents found out she was contacting him. He had no cell phone, and she didn't know where he was working, so this was the only way to reach him. But he miraculously answered the phone himself.

"I'm sorry about last night," she said. "Something came up. I need to talk to you. Can you meet me tonight? Someplace private. Not that bar."

"I don't know," he said. "You stood me up."

"That's what I need to talk to you about."

There was a long pause on his end, and then he sighed. "How about Ledges?"

"What is that? A restaurant?"

"It's part of the Cuyahoga Valley National Park. It's beautiful. It'll be a nice evening, and we can have a private conversation."

She hesitated. How would she walk around the woods in her heels and panty hose? Then she said, "Okay." What did it matter, really? She just wanted to see him.

After work, she picked him up from his new job at the student bookstore in Kent. He got into the car holding a stack of books. The top one, with a white cover, was called *Happiness: A History*. She also noticed *The Analects of Confucius* and *Collected Poems of William Blake*. "Did you buy all these?" she asked.

"I get an employee discount." He placed his backpack, which also appeared to be bulging with books, between his feet.

They drove silently past miles of car sales lots, shopping centers, and housing developments. "Why don't people at least plant trees in parking lots?" Abhay asked. "I can see the heat radiating from all the asphalt."

Rasika turned up the air-conditioning in the car.

"You okay?" he asked. "You've got a death grip on that steering wheel."

She relaxed her fingers. The parking lots ended, and the road was lined with woods.

"We're entering the national park." Abhay opened the window. "You can feel the air is cooler here."

"I don't think I've ever been out this way," Rasika said.

Abhay directed her into the parking lot, and they started up the walkway next to the picnic shelter. The path was paved and surrounded by lawns. "We could sit here and talk." Rasika pointed to the picnic shelter.

"Let's go look at the ledges. They're up ahead."

The paved path, dappled with sunlight, turned into a pebble and dirt path, growing darker as the trees grew thicker.

"These are hemlocks." Abhay waved a hand at the trees around them. "You don't normally find hemlocks at this low elevation. This is a cool microclimate here."

The dark needles of pine trees prevented the sunlight from reaching the ground here. The lower branches of the trees were bare, and it was as though they were surrounded by a ghost forest.

They plunged down a short, steep path. Rasika's slick shoes slipped over the soil and rocks. Abhay held her hand as she scrambled down the path. At the bottom, they were surrounded by tall masses of rock, with patches of moss here and there, and ferns sprouting from cracks. The air was cool and still.

"Isn't this great?" Abhay asked.

They walked along the path beside the rock walls. Rasika's heels tottered, and she held out her arms stiffly to steady herself. She knew she looked ridiculous, walking in the woods in her office clothes, but she didn't care. Her back was sore from when Kanchan had gripped her shoulders and shoved her against the door. The door handle had caught her in the lower back and left a bruise.

"These were formed by glaciers." Abhay pointed up at the cliffs. "Look at the layers of the rock. Neat, don't you think?"

Far above them the green tree leaves rustled, and through the leaves peeked the pale sky. "I never knew about this place," she said. She felt safe here, insulated by the trees and rocks. "It's so quiet."

Abhay stopped and stood with his head tilted slightly back. "You can still hear the traffic."

She strained her ears and made out a faint whoosh of background noise. "Isn't that just the wind in the trees?"

Abhay shook his head. "It's from the highway. You can't get away from it, even in a beautiful place like this."

Abhay's smile had faded. He resumed walking. She stayed, listening to the distant hum of civilization. It wasn't a bad sound. Would she ever want to be so far away that she was completely cut off from the world? What would it be like, living out in a desert, or a deep forest, where the world as she knew it couldn't reach her? If she were alone, with no one else around her, it would be as if she were invisible, almost as if she didn't even exist. She hurried to catch up with Abhay, who had turned a corner ahead. The path curved abruptly, and she stumbled against him. He put a hand on her waist to steady her.

"Oh. Sorry." She stepped back. She didn't want to get drawn into anything physical with him.

Abhay sighed. "Here's icebox cave." He pointed to a rectangle of ground overhung by rock. They walked toward it, and the air dropped in temperature. They stepped into the mouth of the little cave and stood in the cold air.

Rasika wrinkled her nose. "It smells."

"Bats."

She backed out of the cave.

"I wonder if we can go farther?" Abhay peeked in and felt around with his hands.

"Don't, Abhay. What would I do if you got yourself stuck out here?"

He backed away, and they stepped out into the dappled sunlight of the path. "You want to talk?" Abhay asked. "Up ahead I think there are some rocks we can sit on."

Rasika suddenly didn't want to sit and talk. She didn't want to bring up last night here in this quiet, green, peaceful place. Abhay scrambled up to a flat boulder, kicked off his sandals, lifted his bare feet onto the rock, and wrapped his arms around his knees. She swallowed down the sick feeling in her throat and stomach and, after inspecting the boulder for dirt, carefully lowered herself onto it.

In front of them a full-grown tree rose out of the rocks, its roots exposed, as though it were trying to climb over the boulders.

"Amazing, isn't it?" Abhay said. "I don't know how these birches grow with hardly any soil."

She planted her heels on the earth and leaned back on one hand. She clutched her car keys in her other hand. She wished he would look at her. She didn't want to ask.

After a few moments, Abhay did look at her. "So. What's up?"

She pressed her fingers against the bruise on her lower back. "You won't believe what happened last night," she began. She told him the story quickly, in a monotone. A chipmunk scampered up and down the rock face in front of them. When she finished, Abhay looked thoughtful. He put his feet down and reached out a hand to her. She placed her hand in his.

"I'm sorry you had to go through that," he said.

"It just seems unbelievable." She shook her head. "I mean, an Indian uncle. They're all so—good."

"I know what you mean. When I was a kid I had the impression that Indian men were never interested in sex—only in providing for their families. I never really knew why they got married. I guess some only pretend to be good."

"My father is good," she said, and felt a catch in her throat. She instructed herself not to cry, but the next moment tears flooded out of her eyes and down her face. She didn't have a tissue. She'd left her purse in the car. She dabbed at her tears with the heel of her hand, smearing her eyeliner and foundation. She twisted her torso toward Abhay, threw her arms around him, and sobbed onto his shoulder. He put his arm around her waist and stroked her blouse.

After a few minutes she drew away from him and swiped at her eyes again with her palm. "It seems so unreal," she said. "I can't even believe it happened. Life isn't supposed to be like this. I feel like I'm in some kind of alternate universe."

"This is reality. This is what some people are really like, underneath the pretense."

She opened her hand in her lap and gazed at her keys. "I don't know what to think. Nothing fits into place anymore. My life is like one of those weird modern paintings, where people's limbs and heads don't quite fit together, and all the furniture is distorted."

"I have an idea." He held her hand and stroked her fingers. "I'm going to move away from here soon. To Portland. Why don't you come with me?"

"Maine?" She sniffed and rubbed at her nose with the heel of her other hand.

"Oregon."

"Why?"

"It's supposed to be the most environmental city in the U.S. At least, that's what the articles and tour books say."

"And . . . you think you'll figure out what to do with yourself there?"

"I'm not sure if Portland is the answer or not, but I've got to leave Ohio."

"What's wrong with Ohio?"

"If I stay, I'll get sucked into a life I don't want to lead. I'll get roped into hanging out with my old high school friends again, and it will be like nothing has changed. I've got to get away, so I may as well go to Portland as anywhere else. Portland's still a city, but they have a lot of bike paths and a good public transit system, and an urban growth boundary that preserves farmland near the city. I thought I'd give it a try."

"You don't sound all that excited about it."

"I'm trying to make this decision rationally, instead of relying on intuition, or wishful thinking, or whatever it is I relied on in the past. Portland might be a really good place. It could be a fresh start for both of us."

She pulled her hand away from his and wrapped her arms around herself. She was shivering in her light blouse. He slid an arm around her and held her close.

"You're trembling," he said.

"I must look awful," she said.

"Don't worry about what you look like. You're beautiful." He rubbed her bare, goose-fleshed arm.

She wiped around her eyes with a fingertip, but without a mirror, she was afraid she was making things worse. "When are you leaving?"

"Maybe in the spring. Come with me. We both need a change. They have banks in Portland. You'll find a job. You won't have to deal with your parents anymore, or the Indian community. You can be your own person, whoever you want to be."

"I don't know—" She almost said she didn't know who she wanted to be, but that sounded too much like something Abhay would say. She *did* know, after all—she wanted to be a high-class, married Indian-American woman. She pushed Abhay away with a realization. "I didn't obey my parents." Her right palm was streaked with gray from her eye makeup, and she rubbed her thumb over the marks to try to erase them. "I haven't been doing what they want me to do." This thought comforted her, oddly. The events of the past few days were beginning to fit into her view of the world. "That's why this happened," she said. "If Kanchan Uncle hadn't seen us at the hotel, he never would have started this whole thing. So it's my fault, really."

"You have to stop blaming yourself for being human, for having sexual feelings, for wanting to be in charge of your own destiny."

Rasika scooted farther from Abhay, irritated by his words. "I want to be the way they want me to be. I need more willpower."

"So you're going to forget that this whole thing happened and go on with your life as planned?"

"I'm going to send an e-mail to Dilip. He's the guy I met on Saturday. He seemed nice. I just need to try harder."

"Rasika." He braced himself with his hands on the rock on either side of him. "Why are you pretending?"

"I'm not."

"Yes. You've always tried to pretend. Pramod told me that in high school you cheated whenever you could. He said you'd sit next to the smartest kids in class and sneak looks at their tests. He said you were friends with this one unpopular smart girl just to get her to write your papers. You were trying to pretend you were smarter than you really were."

"That little snitch." She had only told Pramod about her techniques because she thought they might be useful for him, too. "I wasn't trying to be someone else, I was just trying to fit in. You know?"

"No. I don't know."

"I was in third grade when we moved to the U.S. I wore two long braids, and lacy dresses. I was so thrilled to be able to wear pretty dresses every day, because in India I had to wear a uniform. But then I noticed that I stood out. The other girls wore jeans and short hair, so I asked my mother to cut my hair and buy me some jeans."

"So you wanted to dress like the other kids. What does that have to do with copying other people's work?"

"We never had worksheets in India, so when I got a worksheet I looked at what the other kids wrote. We never had show-and-tell. I watched what the other kids brought in, and I did the same. I never brought in anything Indian. I imitated to learn to be American."

"And then, what—you just got used to copying?"

"My parents expected me to get good grades."

"Why didn't you just study and do the work? You act like you're not very smart, but I can tell you are. You could've gotten good grades if you'd studied."

"I didn't want to be the girl who slaved away at her homework. I didn't want to be like the other Indian girls. I wanted to be happy and carefree."

"You cheated so you could fit into an American ideal and an Indian ideal at the same time."

"I guess you could say that."

"Well, it's time to stop pretending."

"Why do you care?"

"I don't want you to give in, I guess." He grasped her hand again. "I meant what I said. I love you."

She looked at his trusting, boyish face, and smiled. "I'm not giving in. It's what I want to do."

"I don't believe it."

She shook her head. "We're too different, Abhay. You're only interested in me because you're rebounding from that other woman. The one from the commune."

"What are you talking about? I don't even think about her anymore."

She extracted her hand from his and stood up. "You're a good friend, Abhay. But you're not the right man for me." She was ready to get out of the woods, away from Abhay, and get on with her life. Her bruise would heal. And she would really, really be good from now on. "Come on," she called to him. She started walking back toward the parking lot. "Let's get home."

Abhay watched her teeter down the path in her silky skirt that draped around her hips and thighs, the fabric moving as she did. He was angry that she'd used him for sex and a sympathetic ear. He'd heard the same thing from other women—he was a pal, a friend; he was never *the one*.

She stopped. "Aren't you coming?"

He looked up at the sky. He wanted her to come back to him.

"I'm going to the car," she called. "I need to fix my face. I'll wait for you there."

He watched her until she turned a corner and was out of sight. He felt silly sitting there all by himself. He'd have to go back to the car and let her drive him home. It was too far to walk. He sat in the coolness and frowned at the path where Rasika had been.

He saw a low rock arch ahead of him and climbed up to investigate. He ducked through it and found himself in a narrow chasm, with the blue sky and lacy dark hemlock leaves above him. It reminded him of an aisle between library shelves. On the sandstone walls were carvings: a horse in full gallop, and three faces in profile. He ran his fingers over the horse's neck and back. How old were these? What an amazing little place. Did anyone else ever come here?

At the other end of the chasm he came across an answer: a pile of brown beer bottles. He picked up a bottle by its neck, and old beer gushed onto his sneaker. He flung the broken bottle down and fled back under the arch, back down the path toward the parking lot. He heard the grinding of machinery, metallic clanking and beeping. Someone was building something nearby.

Rasika was leaning back against her seat with closed eyes. He opened the door, heard the sounds of a string quartet from the CD player, and flung himself into the passenger seat. She opened her eyes. Her face was "fixed" and she was wearing her sunglasses, even though it wasn't particularly sunny. She looked cool, distant, beautiful.

"Let's go," he said.

They drove in silence. When Rasika dropped Abhay off at his house, she said, "Thanks for your help, Abhay. I hope someday you'll find what you're looking for."

He glared at her lovely, unattainable face. Then he clambered out of the car and slammed the door. As he entered the house, he heard her car zoom away.

As Abhay walked away from her, Rasika opened her window halfway. She felt the urge to call out to him. She knew she shouldn't. She had to forget about him. She zipped the window up, threw the shifter into reverse, and raced backward out of the driveway. Then she bolted down the road.

Once she turned the corner, she stopped and turned the car off. An elderly man walked a tiny dachshund past the car. Several lawn mowers were droning and whirring. Down the block, she saw a teenaged girl bouncing a basketball. The thump of the ball reached Rasika's ears after the ball was already on its way back to the girl's hands.

Rasika took off her sunglasses and tilted the rearview mirror down to look at herself. She wanted to make sure she was ready to face her parents at home. Her lipstick was a bit lopsided, so she dug around in her purse, found a tissue, and inched it along her lip. Then, in a fit of frustration and rage, she scrubbed all the lipstick off and threw the tissue onto the floor. Abhay didn't rely on artifices the way she did. And then a thought occurred to her: Abhay didn't approve of her. This realization made her feel incredibly sad. She tried to tell herself that she didn't care, but her throat felt tight, and then she was sobbing again. She let her forehead rest on the steering wheel. Her wails bounced off the closed walls of the car.

Finally she was able to catch her breath and stop herself. She almost never allowed herself to fall apart like this. As she lifted her head, she caught sight of her face again in the mirror: red, wild eyes and mussed hair. She used every tool in her purse to put herself together again.

As she combed and painted, she began to feel calm and washed clean. It would be okay. She would live through this. She had to go on as planned. She had no other choice.

8

On a cool, sunny Sunday in mid-September, Abhay sat on one of the concrete steps encircling the Ira Keller Fountain in Portland, Oregon, enjoying the sound of the waterfalls in the middle of a downtown city block. Not many people were at the fountain. A young man in dress slacks and a sweater was reading on a step below his.

Abhay had learned to say "*Ore*gun," accent on the first syllable, instead of "Ore*gawn*," and now, a few weeks after his arrival, he was beginning to feel at home. He was glad to be away from Ohio, away from his father's judgments, from Chris's job offers and barbecues, and from Rasika's craziness.

Even though he'd told Rasika he wasn't leaving until the spring, he'd made a decision to go right after their conversation at Ledges. He had no real job in Ohio, after all, and the only reason he was staying was for her. She was becoming the most important person for him there, and he felt himself falling into his usual unrequited-love despair. The best thing to do, in his experience, was to move on. Otherwise, he'd be in danger of brooding and depression.

A week before coming to Oregon, he'd called Rasika and left

a message on her phone, asking if she'd like to meet him before he left. In reply, she had sent him a short note—in an envelope with no return address—telling him that she had decided to take his advice: that she wanted to stop pretending and start living the honorable life she always intended. Therefore, they couldn't see each other again.

He had read this note several times. He had run his fingers over her pretty handwriting. Then he had ripped it up and stuffed it into the bag of to-be-recycled paper under his desk. She was right, of course. What they each wanted out of life was too different, and it was good that he was leaving.

While he was seen as bohemian in Ohio, in Portland he was quite straightlaced and entirely normal. He was perhaps on the conservative side, since he'd cut his tail of hair off for the temping jobs, and had gotten rid of the macramé necklace and leather bracelets he used to wear. Here, it seemed that everyone—mothers, office workers, grandfathers—was tattooed or pierced in odd places or wearing purple nail polish and bright green sneakers, along with their backpacks and jeans. Not that anyone was ostentatious. Everything was subtle in Portland.

The fountain he sat by was supposedly designed to imitate the movement of water in nature, although Abhay found amusing the prevalence of concrete, and the square and rectangular shapes that predominated. That part of it certainly wasn't natural. If he lifted his head he could see the green pine and maple trees surrounding the fountain and a tall, three-cornered building rising from behind the fountain. Abhay unzipped his backpack and pulled out the classifieds section of the Sunday newspaper. He tried to keep himself busy constantly, so he wouldn't think about Rasika. In order to stop thinking about Rasika, he ought to get involved with another woman, but he wasn't quite ready for another emotional roller coaster.

He shook open his newspaper, folded it to the employment ads, and dug around in his backpack for a pen. Over the past week he'd found work at Powell's bookstore, "the largest independent used and new bookstore in the world," according to their ads. As much as he liked Powell's, and the feeling of being surrounded by books, he didn't intend to spend his life as a store clerk.

Two young women descended the staircase to the left of the fountain and stepped over the concrete slabs to throw something— flowers, he thought—into the water. The woman with long red hair wore a bright dress, red swirls on a black background. Her breasts were small and high underneath the fabric. The brown-haired woman had on jeans and a sweatshirt.

They turned and walked toward him up the wide steps, and the red-haired one stopped on his step, her sandaled feet planted neatly together. She had traces of mud along the edges of her toenails, and a tattoo encircling one ankle, some sort of tribal design featuring spirals. She bent forward gracefully to throw a dandelion at his chest. The yellow bloom fell onto the step, and he immediately picked it up. He wasn't sure what to do with it. Her gesture made him uncomfortable. It reminded him of a priest in a Hindu temple throwing flowers at the idols.

"Hi." She smiled down at him.

Her friend had wandered away, maybe to throw blossoms at some other young man. He got to his feet and noticed with satisfaction that he was almost as tall as she was. Not that it mattered.

"Are you from India?" She had a rosy face and straight, even teeth. A thin ring glinted in one light-brown eyebrow.

"No." He didn't bother to enlighten her any further. It irritated him that this was often one of the first questions other people asked him.

"Oh." She looked down at her feet and brought her dandelions up to her nose to smell them. He noticed her fingertips were stained with mud, too, just like her toes. Her face seemed to flush even rosier. He thought she'd walk away, but she kept standing next to him.

"What's your name?" he asked.

She lowered the flowers. "Kianga."

He raised one eyebrow. "You make that up?" He was being flippant to hide the fact that he felt unsure and awkward.

She shook her head. "It's Swahili."

"Ah." He tried to put on a knowing smile. He wondered how a white girl had ended up with a Swahili name.

"I'm hungry," she announced. "Want to come over and have lunch?" She spoke slowly.

"I'm busy looking for a job." He held up his newspaper. "Thanks anyway."

"You have to eat, don't you?"

Kianga's friend rejoined them. She had a small stud in the side of her nose. "He's coming to have lunch with us," Kianga said.

"Okay." The friend smiled at him.

He figured he might as well go along with their plan. After all, he was hungry. He stuffed his newspaper into his backpack. "My bike's up there." He pointed to the sidewalk at the top of the steps. "How do we get to your place?"

"This way." Kianga led the way up the steps.

"I mean, do we have to take a bus, or something?"

"No." Kianga provided no more information, and Abhay wondered if he ought to press her for details on where, exactly, she lived and how they would get there.

Abhay walked behind the two of them, pushing his bike past a repair crew laying a new brick sidewalk, with orange cones and metal barriers around their work area; past parking lots and parking garages and a three-story, block-long brick building with no sign on it. They turned left into a strip of greenery: the campus of Portland State University. At the end of campus they crossed a bridge over a freeway, and right there—right next to the roar of the freeway—was Kianga's house. It was one of a row of houses built next to each other, with strips of grass in between. Kianga's was the ugliest of them all, a long narrow building with a garage underneath and a front door reached by a flight of stairs. Abhay locked his bike to a street sign.

In the living room there was almost no furniture—only a few hammock chairs hanging from hooks in the ceiling, and several large potted plants. The old, stained carpeting had been covered in places with what looked like printed tablecloths or bedspreads with colorful designs, florals and paisleys. The place smelled like incense.

Abhay slipped off his sandals inside the front door and followed Kianga and her friend into the kitchen, where they were taking things out of the fridge and cabinets.

"I'm going to make peanut butter and jelly sandwiches." Kianga's friend set a brown hunk of what looked like homemade bread on the cutting board on the island countertop, and started sawing off thick slices.

"What's your name?" Abhay asked the brown-haired woman.

"Ellen." She smiled at him as she scooped grainy peanut butter from a large tub printed with the faded words: NANCY'S LOWFAT YOGURT. "You want yours open-faced or closed?" She had a bit of a lisp. Her r's didn't come out right.

"Open-faced is fine."

Kianga went out the back door and came in with two large red tomatoes. "Feel them." She placed a tomato in each of Abhay's hands. They were heavy and warm from the sun and had a pungent tomato-leaf smell. Kianga took them from him, rinsed them in the sink, and sliced them onto a plate.

Ellen carefully wiped the crumbs off the counter before walking with the plate of sandwiches to the table in the small dining room, which was filled with light from the curtainless windows. Kianga placed her plate of tomatoes in the center of the table. Abhay made himself useful by filling up some water glasses, and they all sat down. They both smiled at him as they lifted their bread. He smiled back. He found it odd that neither of them seemed interested in his name. He wasn't sure he liked the anonymity of the whole thing. Did they do this every weekend—find a strange guy to invite home for peanut butter sandwiches?

"So. Uh. What do you do here in Portland?" He looked from one to the other.

"I sing," Kianga said.

"You're a music student?"

"I'm with a band."

"And you plan to make a living that way?" He felt like his father, grilling her about her moneymaking capacity.

"Singing keeps me alive."

"Ah." He wondered if she knew what he was asking and preferred not to answer, or whether she actually didn't have a clue. He looked over at Ellen.

She gave him a shy smile. "I'm studying health education," she said. "We both are."

"So you're going to be school nurses?"

"Something like that," Ellen said.

"Are you in the band, too?" he asked Ellen.

She blushed and shook her head so her curls covered part of her face.

They ate silently. It wasn't the same kind of silence as the dinners with his parents. It was more peaceful. Kianga looked out the window as she chewed, and Ellen seemed to be looking inside herself. Still, the silence made Abhay a little uncomfortable. He wondered who would be the first to speak. After slowly finishing the last bite of his bread, slowly eating several tomato slices, and drinking all his water, he asked, "Don't you want to know what my name is?"

Kianga looked at him and laughed. "Tell us, if you want us to know."

"Abhay," he said. "It's a Sanskrit name. It means 'fearless.'"

"uh-BYE." Kianga copied his pronunciation. "Fearless. That's wonderful."

"Why did you invite me over?"

"I thought you seemed lonely," Kianga said. "You were by yourself, so I thought you might like some company."

"Do you do this all the time? Invite strangers over for meals?"

"*She* does." Ellen tipped her head toward Kianga.

"Sometimes," Kianga said. "If I see someone I connect with." She gathered the dishes together in a stack. "Want to go out and look at our garden?"

They set the dishes in the sink and walked out the back screen door into the patch of fenced yard, most of which was taken over by a vegetable garden. This would explain the mud on her fingers and toes. She probably spent a lot of time digging in the soil. The ground was punctuated in several places by large greenish orange globes. "Pumpkins?" he asked. "You make a lot of pies?"

"I carve them for Halloween." Kianga sunk into a squat and grubbed out a few weeds. The hem of her dress trailed in the soil.

"That's a lot of jack-o'-lanterns," he commented.

Kianga stood up. "I line them up around the front yard. It looks amazing."

"Halloween's a really big holiday for Kianga." Ellen had her arms folded over her flat belly, holding her elbows with her opposite hands. "It's just about the only holiday her family celebrated."

"We did birthdays. And we did the solstices and equinoxes."

"No normal holidays, like Christmas or Easter," Ellen protested.

"My mom was raised Christian, and my dad was raised Jewish. They didn't like either religion. So they made up their own, I guess."

Back in the house, Abhay helped wash and dry the dishes, and then said he had to go. He didn't want to give them the impression that he was interested in either one of them romantically.

"Want to come and watch our rehearsal tomorrow?" Kianga asked. "It'll be here at the house." She leaned against the kitchen counter. Ellen seemed to have disappeared into some other part of the house.

"I don't know, I'll probably be busy."

She laughed at this. "You're funny. I have someone I want you to meet tomorrow. He's looking to hire someone to help him out, and I think you'd be a good fit."

His first thought was that Kianga couldn't possibly know what kind of job was right for him. But he reminded himself that he was keeping his options open. "Okay. Sure. I'll try to be here. What time?"

"About seven o'clock," she said.

She walked him to the front door and watched him put on his sandals. Then, before he could open the door, she placed her hands on his waist and kissed him on the cheek. He wasn't sure how to react to this gesture. What did such a kiss mean in Kianga's world? Did she kiss all the men she invited home for lunch?

She stood back with a smile, and he tried to say good-bye in a polite way as he opened the door. Walking his bike to the bridge across the highway, he wondered if Kianga was watching him go.

It was Sunday evening, and Rasika's parents had gone up to Cleveland for dinner and card playing with Deepti Auntie and Balu Uncle. Rasika had managed to stay home by pleading tiredness.

Pramod was at his apartment. She was alone in her room. Since Abhay had left, she'd been staying home as much as possible, to avoid getting tempted into any risky behavior.

The sky was growing dim outside her curtains. She'd been lying on her bed all afternoon, half-dozing. She didn't feel like doing anything. Her head throbbed. She'd been trying to ignore it, but finally the pain grew strong enough that she crawled off the bed, found some pain pills in the hall bathroom, and swallowed them.

Entering her room again, she decided to turn on the light and do something to distract herself until the pain subsided. She sat on the carpet in front of the low white bookshelf beside her bed. There were no books on these shelves. Instead, they displayed items from the various collections she had kept since she was a child. When she lived in India, she had begun collecting photos of female Bollywood stars. Although her mother would not let her see any of the movies, considering them too mature for a seven- or eight-year-old, Rasika had been intimately familiar with the actresses' names and pictures.

Once they moved to the United States, she had used scissors and far too much glue to make a collage of these photos, which was propped on a lower shelf of the bookshelf. She picked it up. The cardboard backing had yellowed over the years. The photos, so familiar, were stiff with glue. She shook dust off the collage and gazed again on the perky nose and oval face of Sridevi; the snub-nosed, round-cheeked face of Smita Patil; the large, toothy smile of Madhuri Dixit; the green eyes and shapely mouth of Mandakini. She was never interested in collecting photos of the male actors, although she remembered her mother and aunts swooning over the handsome features of Amitabh Bachchan. Who cared about men? It was the women she'd wanted to imitate. Her favorite actress, the one she considered most beautiful and elegant, was Rekha, whose photo was in the very center of the collage, larger than the others.

Rekha had fair skin, full lips, and high cheekbones. Her thick black hair flowed loose on either side of her heart-shaped face, and she wore a peach-colored sari.

Although Rasika grew to realize, as she got older, that these actresses' lives were often sordid or tragic, she preferred to still think about the fantasy lives implied by these beautiful photos. She wanted the glamorous, perfect, happily-ever-after life that should have accompanied such beautiful women.

She used to have a large framed photo of Princess Diana, with a small tiara on her fluffy hair, but that story grew so sad that Rasika could no longer pretend that there was a happy life associated with the picture. So she had thrown the picture away and given the empty frame to her mother.

As she looked at the photos in her hand, she wondered suddenly how Abhay would react if he saw this collage, which she had saved so carefully over the years. He'd probably think it was silly. He'd say she was chasing after a fantasy. And maybe she was. If she walked around an American street dressed like these Bollywood stars, with her midriff exposed and a kumkum on her forehead, she wouldn't look elegant and sophisticated. She'd just look weird. Yet if she walked around Kent dressed in a classic style like Jackie Onassis, she'd still look slightly out of place because of her dusky skin. Sometimes she felt it was impossible for her to be the sophisticated person she aspired to, because she just didn't fit anywhere, as Abhay had pointed out.

Fortunately, she didn't have to worry about his thoughts anymore, because he was out of her life. She crawled over to her dresser, pulled out an old T-shirt, and used it to wipe the dust off the bottom bookcase shelf, lifting and replacing other trinkets as she did so: little plastic statues of Krishna and Lakshmi, and Indian folk dolls dressed up to dance. She set the collage back in its place. The upper shelves were filled with her collection of Beanie Babies. Even in high school and college, she had been interested in collecting Beanie Babies. She remembered spending hours as a teen arranging and rearranging these toys. She had so many that the majority of them were in a box in a corner of her closet. Only her favorites lived on the shelf. Most of them were pink, since pink was always her favorite color.

Her headache was gone now. The sky was dark outside her window. She felt suddenly energized. She decided to go downstairs and make a batch of cookies. When she was in sixth grade, she used to love making a mint and chocolate cookie that involved two layers of dough, a light color and a chocolate color, rolled up together and sliced. She'd learned to make the cookies at a Girl Scout meeting. She hadn't baked those in a long time. Her father used to love those spiral cookies.

She found the recipe—a butter-stained, photocopied page tucked into her mother's almost untouched copy of *Joy of Cooking.* Amma rarely fixed Western food, and used the cookbook only for an occasional cake or pan of brownies. Rasika drove to the store for ingredients. In the kitchen again, she set out flour, butter, sugar, eggs, cocoa powder, and mint flavoring. She felt happy to be mixing and rolling. She wondered if she ought to learn to sew, or make lace, or get involved with stenciling, or something. Her problem, perhaps, was simply that she lacked a hobby, now that she had stopped collecting Beanie Babies.

After work the next day Abhay returned to his apartment, which he shared with another guy who seemed to spend most of his time at his girlfriend's place, heated up some minestrone soup from a can, ate handfuls of cheese crackers out of the box, drank a glass of milk, and biked over to Kianga's place. He was a bit early. The sun was descending behind Kianga's house, but the sky was still light.

Kianga sat in a lawn chair in the tiny front yard, with a heavy book open on her lap and a highlighter in her hand. She was concentrating so hard, she didn't notice him as he locked his bike and walked up to her.

"Hi," he said.

She looked up, startled. Then her face grew rosy and she smiled. "Abhay! I'm so glad you're here!"

He was surprised she could pronounce his name, after only hearing it once. She was very pretty, with her cheerful smile and blue-green eyes.

She closed her book and stood up. "I'll get another chair."

"No, let me." He put out his hands, as if to prevent her from exerting herself on his behalf.

"It's fine," she said. "Have a seat. I'll be right back." She was wearing jeans shorts and a sleeveless top, and her limbs were long and fit. She trotted up the stairs into the house. In a moment she came back down with another lawn chair. "Ellen's inside," she explained as she unfolded the chair and sat down. "She can't study outside. She says it's too distracting." Kianga had to shout over the noise of the traffic from the freeway. "Listen, the guy I wanted you to meet tonight couldn't show up. But he says you should come by his office tomorrow for an interview."

Abhay sat down in the chair she had vacated. "What kind of job is it?"

"My friend Justin is using inheritance money to start a new environmental organization in town. I know him from Green Party meetings. He's a good guy. Really intellectual. You reminded me of him, so I thought you two might be a good match. He needs help with just about everything. You'll get to learn all about running a nonprofit organization."

This was starting to sound good—better than he'd expected. "What's the organization?"

"It's called HOPE. It stands for Humans Off of Planet Earth.

It's a population organization. He asks people to sign voluntary pledges to get sterilized. The idea is, humans need to stop taking over the planet."

Abhay laughed. "It sounds kind of ridiculous."

"I thought so, too, at first. But I can see the appeal of something like this. The organization takes a logical point to an extreme, and that can be helpful sometimes to wake people up and help them consider all their choices. Childlessness is certainly a valid environmental choice, although personally, I think humans are part of the plan."

"What plan?"

"The plan of existence." She held out her hand, palm up, and waved it in a slow arc in front of her. "God has put us on this earth for some reason. Or if you're not comfortable with the word *God*, think of it this way. Humans evolved on Earth for a reason. Mother Nature created us. Life created us. We're here."

"God didn't ask us to destroy things," he said. "Mother Nature can't be happy that humans are polluting the water and air, and burying nuclear waste in the earth. Even most humans didn't ask for so much of Earth to be paved. It was a few industrialists who made those decisions for all of us."

"I knew you'd be great for this job! You totally get it. Justin will love you. Listen, I've just got to finish this chapter before rehearsal."

Abhay sat silently while Kianga read. The sky was starting to dim. He shifted his chair so he faced away from the highway, and looked over the tops of the houses to the wispy clouds drifting slowly across the sky. After several minutes, a long-haired guy with a guitar case slung over his back walked up the sidewalk and over the lawn to where they were sitting. "Hey, cutie," he said, and leaned over to kiss Kianga on the lips. This must be her boyfriend.

"Abhay, this is Preview," Kianga said.

"Preview?" Abhay must have looked puzzled because the guy said, "I made it up to remind myself you always have another chance. Even this life isn't the final life. So if I think of my whole life as a preview, it helps keep me cool." He smoothed the air with a flattened hand.

Preview's long brown hair was matted in places. It didn't look like he'd combed it in ages. Perhaps he was in the middle of an attempt to create dreadlocks.

"We met Abhay at the fountain yesterday." Kianga stood up and folded her chair. Abhay did the same, and they all went inside, where several stools had been set up in the living room. Preview perched on a stool, balanced his guitar on his thigh, and started strumming. A man arrived with a set of bongo drums draped around his neck. He was brown, with short stubs of hair all over his head. He kissed Kianga, who was sitting on a stool shuffling through pages of music.

Abhay backed away. He felt like a fifth wheel. He wondered if Kianga invited all men to kiss her. Ellen appeared behind him and whispered, "Sit down here." She had set up two chairs in the dining room, so they could look into the living room and be out of the way.

The rehearsal was irritating. Kianga and the two guys seemed unsure about whether they were a folk group, a reggae group, or a rock-and-roll band. Kianga had a beautiful voice: clear, true to the note, and unaffected. But her melodies were often drowned out by frantic drumming or guitar riffs.

Every so often Abhay glanced at Ellen, and noticed her gaze on him. She smiled, and he smiled back. As the sky grew dark outside the windows, Abhay wondered what this job with HOPE would be like.

The next day, during his lunch break from the bookstore, he rode his bike west, crossing over Interstate 405. The address turned out to be an old apartment building. Abhay wondered if he was in the wrong place, but he locked his bike, changed his shirt so he wouldn't be too sweaty, climbed the stairs, and rang the doorbell.

A white man in his forties or fifties, slim and bald, opened the door. His face was creased, as though it had been folded up for a long while. He neither smiled nor held out a hand. "I'm Justin Time," he said. "Come on in."

Justin Time. Was the man serious?

Messy stacks of papers covered every available surface: a large round table in the middle of the room, a lone filing cabinet, smaller tables lining the walls, and the floor. Not what Abhay expected from an innovative, new environmental group.

"As you can see, I need a lot of help. Sit down here." Justin moved a stack of papers off a chair. "What we're doing now is cataloging the damage that has been done to Earth because of the human population explosion. There is so much information out there, and people are just blind to it. Blind."

Abhay nodded. "I agree." He was glad to meet someone in alignment with his own point of view. A large cobweb hung in the corner near the window, which let in a bit of light around the closed venetian blinds. He tried to push away the suspicion that Justin was not quite all there mentally. Maybe he was merely a bit eccentric.

"I've been collecting policy proposals, newspaper articles, magazine articles for years. And now I'm ready to launch my organization. My goal is to persuade all the males of our species to undergo a voluntary vasectomy. Women are included, too, but mainly I focus on men, because one man can do a lot of damage. Once people realize the destruction we're causing, I think this solution will become self-evident." Justin had a strange, clipped way of talking, and he didn't seem to like making eye contact. "Anyway, I thought I'd start you off with this." He lifted a stack of booklets from his side of the table and handed them to Abhay. "This organization does a book every year of planetary health indicators. Every one of the negative indicators can be tied directly to humans overrunning the planet. I want you to look through these and figure out how to organize it for the Web site."

Abhay realized this wasn't an interview. He had apparently already been hired.

"I'll pay you in cash at the end of every week," Justin said. "I don't see that we need to get the government involved with this—do you?" Justin raised an eyebrow at him.

Abhay was startled. That was *his* gesture, raising an eyebrow when he wanted to make a point. Was he going to end up like Justin someday? "I can't stay right now," he said. "I've got to get back to my other job."

"When can you come over?"

Abhay wasn't sure he wanted to get involved with Justin and his strange organization. He hadn't imagined working in someone's messy apartment. Yet, Abhay loved to read, and he was sure to learn something. "What are you planning to do once you get everything summarized and organized?"

"I want you to help me write grants. Publicize the Web site. Set up radio interviews. Write articles. You're getting in on the ground floor."

Abhay nodded. The goal of the organization was odd. And yet, when Abhay thought about it, it made sense. People needed to stop breeding. It was such a simple solution. A population decline would mean fewer farms turning into housing developments. And those farms in turn could then be restored to their original habitat: prairie, forest, wetland.

"Did you get a vasectomy?" Abhay asked.

"Absolutely. After my son was born twelve years ago, I realized what I had done. I saw that I had caused another being to enter the planet, which would result in more pesticides being applied to the soil and water. More rain forests felled to graze cows so my son could eat at McDonald's. And if he has children of his own—which I hope he does not—I will have created a self-perpetuating cycle of destruction."

"So you don't think anyone should have any children at all?"

"No. Do you?"

Abhay shifted in his seat. "I don't know."

"Incremental change hasn't made a dent," Justin declared. "We need to do something drastic now. Here." He pushed over to Abhay a piece of paper that looked like a certificate, with a scalloped edge and embossed decorations. "This is the pledge."

Abhay read silently:

> I, _____, pledge not to have any (more) children to add to the earth's burden. I volunteer to become sterilized in order to prevent further destruction of the earth's fragile web of life.

"You can keep that," Justin said.

"Do I have to sign it before I start working?"

Justin hesitated. "I don't want you to feel coerced. Once you learn what's really going on, you'll sign it on your own."

As Abhay biked back to the bookstore, he decided to go ahead and work with Justin, at least for the time being. Even though the man seemed odd, and even though Abhay recoiled from the thought of working in that dusty, dim apartment, no one else had articulated so clearly Abhay's own point of view about the world. He'd always heard that it was good to get in on the ground floor of something, and here was his chance. It made sense to take it.

9

It was a Saturday afternoon in early October, and Rasika was in her car on her way home to change her clothes. She didn't want to face her parents, who were waiting at home to show her photos of eligible bachelors sent via e-mail by a matrimonial agent in India. They wanted to take her to India and marry her off this winter. To keep herself out of her parents' clutches, she had agreed to meet Benito, her gym trainer, at his apartment for dinner.

Since meeting Dilip in August, she had dutifully exchanged e-mails with him. He seemed nice enough. He wanted to come and visit her again, but she had discouraged him, saying that she was very busy.

Then, a few weeks ago, against her mother's wishes, her father had sent Dilip's and Rasika's horoscopes off to India. Three mornings ago Appa had received an e-mail from the astrologer stating that it wasn't a good match, but if the two wanted to get married, they should send $200 for a special pooja to compensate for the unlucky star positions.

Her father spent a few days pacing and twitching, while Rasika acted disappointed. Her mother had wanted to go ahead and send the money. "How long are we going to wait to get her married?" she demanded. "Let's get this pooja done and get it over with."

"No," her father had said, shaking his head and jerking his shoulders. "If it is not in the horoscope, better not to risk it. She is our only daughter. Let us make the best match for her."

India was their last hope.

Rasika had escaped early in the morning, before they could catch her. She'd gone to her gym, where she'd agreed to the date with Benito, and had brunch with Jill, and then they both had wandered around a mall. Now she hoped she could sneak quietly into the house without her parents noticing.

She hadn't so much as flirted with any men since Abhay. Oddly, one reason she had been keeping away from men was that she wanted Abhay to be proud of her. She wanted him to know that she was following her chosen path in a mature, honest way. She'd get married soon to someone appropriate, Abhay would be a wedding guest, and she wanted to be able to look at him with clear eyes and have him know that she really was the person she always wanted to be. So she'd been plodding along, dutifully going to work, coming home, and helping her mother with the cooking. She'd bought a couple of craft magazines but hadn't decided what craft she wanted to learn. Her days passed in a gray fog. Once, last Saturday, she had driven by the bookstore in Kent where Abhay used to work. It was silly, she knew, but somehow she felt better after seeing a place where he'd been.

But today she just couldn't be dutiful anymore. She was desperate for some excitement. Benito had been interested in her for months. She thought he was gorgeous but held back from flirting. She'd been remarkably demure. But she just had to get away from her parents tonight. Anyway, she and Benito didn't have to end up in bed tonight. She had some self-control, after all. She was just going over to his place to relax and have a little fun. No one had to know.

Unfortunately, as she drove up to her house, she saw that both her parents were at home: Amma's car was in the garage, and Appa's was in the driveway. She opened the door to the house as quietly as possible and slipped off her shoes.

"Rasika?" Her mother's voice shouted down to her.

"I'm just here for a minute. I'm going out with Jill tonight."

"Come here." Amma appeared on the upstairs landing as Rasika tried to sneak up to her room. Amma's hair was messed up. It was held back in its usual ponytail, but one side was sticking out in a puff. "We talked with Prabhu Uncle last night about arranging for some meetings once we get to India. Your appa was up all night, on the phone to India. You must look at these photos and select."

"I don't have time now. We're seeing a movie, and it starts really soon." At the top of the stairs she tried to slip past her mother and into her room, but Amma gripped Rasika's upper arm.

"You are not going anywhere. You will look at these photos now. We are trying our best to get you married before the deadline. Before your birthday in January."

Her father emerged from his office. He had pouches under his eyes, and his hand trembled as he reached an arm toward her.

"Come on, raja." He put his hand on her back and guided her to a chair placed next to his.

"Show her the best one first." Amma stood behind Appa with her hands on the back of his chair.

"We will get to that." Appa clicked, and Rasika saw a smiling brown man with a mustache.

"That one is too short," Amma said.

Appa scrolled to the next: a long-faced man who looked as though he'd just eaten a lemon.

"I don't know why they don't smile for their photos," Amma said. "Although this fellow is so ugly, it wouldn't matter."

"He is an IIT graduate," Appa reminded her. "No one is looking at his photo."

"Maybe he has bad teeth," Amma suggested, "and he is trying to hide his teeth by keeping his lips like that. I am not giving Rasika to someone who already has bad teeth. As if she needs that headache."

"We don't know if he has bad teeth," Appa said. He scrolled to the next photo. Rasika waited for their comments. They were both silent. She saw a somewhat puffy-faced smiling man. His teeth looked OK. Was this the "best one"?

Amma said, "He has a brother in this country. He will already be somewhat Westernized, Rasika."

"Just because his brother lives here?"

"His brother will be talking about this country, sending things home. This fellow will be familiar with the U.S. You won't have to worry about someone who is—how do you say? FBI?"

"FOB," Rasika said. "Fresh Off the Boat."

"This one is no FBO. He is Westernized. And living in Bangalore, how can he not be? Bangalore is a world-class city. At least that is what they say nowadays. Twenty years ago no one paid any attention to Bangalore. Now all the high-tech companies are there."

"It may be a high-tech city, but I still don't think I could marry someone who grew up in India." Rasika stood up.

"But he is so handsome!" Her mother put her hand on Rasika's shoulder and pushed her back down on the chair. "Just look!"

Rasika looked. He was light-skinned for an Indian, which for Amma meant handsome.

"His field is biomechanical engineering," Appa said. "A very promising area."

"That goes without saying," Amma remarked. "All these fellows are in promising fields. We would not bother showing Rasika someone who is just an arts graduate, after all. Appa has called the travel agent about tickets. We will go in December. The matrimonial agent will send some more photos later on today."

"Amma." Rasika stood up again. "I am not marrying someone who grew up in India."

"What is wrong with India? You are Indian!"

"I'm Indian-American. I don't think I could get along with someone raised in India."

"Look at this girl!" Amma raised her eyebrows in disbelief. "You were born in India. You lived there for eight years. Your own parents were raised in India. Don't you get along with us? Anyway, you will be bringing him back here with you. No one is asking you to live in India."

"What about horoscopes? Aren't you going to check the horoscopes of these guys first?"

"Once we find some good prospects, then we will check. It will all take time. That is why we must hurry."

"I need to go." Rasika ducked away from her mother's outstretched arm and fled to her room.

"You come straight home after that movie!" Amma called. "We must look at the next batch of photos and make some decisions!"

The dinner with Benito was lovely. He had a cute tortilla press that made round circles out of balls of dough. It would be so handy for making rotis, since whenever Rasika tried to roll rotis they always ended up lopsided, or thick in some spots and paper thin in others. Benito had the sweetest little gas grill on the balcony of his apartment, and he expertly tossed on the beef strips and vegetables he had marinated earlier in the day. He served her a wonderful, fruity sangria.

Now Rasika was on Benito's oversize recliner with her arms

around him and her eyes closed, allowing him to nuzzle her neck. She could stop things whenever she wanted. She just hadn't chosen to yet.

She heard, faintly, her phone melody. Benito pressed closer to her. The phone continued to ring. It stopped and started, over and over again.

She pushed Benito away gently. "I have to get that." She wandered into the kitchen, found her purse on the counter, dug out her phone, and opened it.

"Where are you?" her mother's voice demanded. "We are sitting here waiting for the princess to come home. They have sent more pictures. There are one or two very good prospects."

"I'm out with Jill." At times like this, she was glad she could speak to her mother in Tamil.

"Isn't that movie finished yet?"

"We just went out to a café. I'll look at the pictures tomorrow."

"You tell Jill this is an emergency. Everyone has been working around the clock for you. Is this how you show your gratitude? It is morning now in India. If you make some decisions, they can book the meetings. The boy might have to travel, too, you know. One is in Delhi. One is in Singapore. Not everyone is sitting there just waiting for you to show up. These boys are well educated and they are not going to last long. If we delay, who knows?"

"Rasika," Benito called from the other room. "Come back."

"The waitress is here," Rasika said. "I need to order now."

"Why don't you bring Jill home? I have not seen her in so long. She can look at the pictures too and help you decide."

"No. I can't. We're too far away."

"Where are you, then? How far away could you be?"

"Jill's going through a hard time now. You know Jared? The man she's been living with? He's left." That was true, although Jill had wanted him to go. "I'm comforting her."

"That is what these American men are like," Amma said. "Any difficulty arises, and they leave. Poor Jill. She should never have agreed to live with him without marriage. That is why we are looking for an Indian husband for you, Rasika. You say you don't want a man from India. If he is raised in India he will have the right values. He will not be thinking of divorce when the first thing goes wrong."

Benito wandered into the kitchen.

"You bring Jill here. I will make her some chai. She will feel better."

Benito hugged Rasika from behind. "Amma, I'll be home soon." She pressed the "off" button while her mother was still talking, then shoved her phone to the bottom of her purse.

She turned toward Benito, and he gave her a long, slow kiss. "Benny." She halfheartedly extracted herself from his grip. "I can't do this. I'm not ready."

"Hmm." He hugged her tighter. "You seem ready to me."

"I gotta go." She pushed at him a little harder. "That was my mom. There's been an emergency at home."

He let her go with a sigh. She picked up her purse and, without looking at him, slipped on her shoes and was out the door before she could change her mind.

A week later, on a bright and cool Sunday morning in October, Rasika and her father were on the golf course at their country club. As Appa went through his usual routine before teeing off at the first hole, Rasika gazed over the smooth green lawn dipping and rolling, and the wide crisscross plaid patterns made by the lawn mowers. She loved the trees posed around the course, the blue-green and black-green of the spruces displaying their feathery branches, the bright red and yellow of the trees in the distance.

Appa loved golf. He was completely relaxed and focused on the course. It was like meditation for him. Now he stood behind his ball, ruminating on the shot he was about to take. His hair ruffled in the breeze, and his face was calm.

Years ago he had tried to get Rasika and Pramod interested, paying for expensive lessons when they were preteens. Pramod declared the whole thing a bore and refused to play. Rasika had tried to please her father by joining him sometimes. The game was not bad, she thought. But her father would get so agitated at her grip, her stance, her choice of golf clubs, that her playing actually seemed to ruin the experience for him.

So she gave up playing but sometimes just came with him. When she was thirteen or fourteen, she had been thrilled to be allowed to drive the golf cart, bumping and puttering around the course. As she had grown older, she grew to appreciate the beauty of the course itself—the way the trees were placed, the glint of sunshine off the mirror of the water trap in the distance, and the feeling of being insulated from the rest of the noisy, cluttered world in this quiet oasis. She preferred nature like this to the dark and wild park she'd visited with Abhay, where the trees looked like they were trying to climb around on their bare roots.

"This will be a very good thing for you," Appa said as they walked to the fairway. "We know the family. They are respectable, well educated. All the sons are in top fields—medicine, computers, business. And your horoscopes have matched very well."

He was referring to Yuvan, the most promising of the eligible bachelors. He had not come through the matrimonial agent. He was the son of Rasika's aunt's husband's sister—he was Rasika's cousin's cousin. He was quite handsome, even Rasika had to admit, with a mustache, small goatee, and thick hair. She had first seen his photo last Saturday, after her dinner with Benito. His height was adequate, and he had an advanced computer degree. Rasika's parents were impressed by the fact that he had won a lot of awards in school. His interests were old film songs, watching cricket, traveling, and exercising.

Her parents had immediately procured the boy's e-mail address and had begun corresponding with him and his parents. Over the past week they had even talked to them a few times over the phone and arranged for the horoscope evaluation. Rasika had thus far refused to have anything to do with him, which was why her father had invited her to join him this morning. Even though she knew her father's goal was to persuade her to meet this guy, she had nevertheless accompanied Appa out here.

They had reached her father's ball. Instead of considering his next shot, he led her to a bench, and they sat down. After what seemed like an eternity of silence, Appa came out with, "You are a good girl, Rasika. You have been living at home. You have not wanted to date. We are glad"—Appa's shoulder twitched—"*very* glad to have raised such an obedient daughter."

Rasika's face burned.

"Since you have been raised outside of India, I know it is difficult for you to understand why we want to get you married in this way. You see, in India there are almost no divorces. Why is that? There is something about the Indian marriage system that works. We do not just rely on the inclinations of youngsters. We look for someone of a similar background, someone from a good family. Then we match the horoscopes. In that way, we get God involved. God knows better than anyone, is it not?"

Rasika nodded. She didn't like to think too much about God, because what she had been doing was obviously not in line with what God wanted. At least, not the God her parents believed in. After she was safely married, she could think about God all she wanted.

"What are your objections to meeting Yuvan?" Appa asked. Before she could answer, he continued, "Is it just that he lives in India? You must keep an open mind. You may like him. No one is asking you to live in India. After all, he is saying he is eager to come here. Your mother is very anxious to see your marriage take place. I was really astonished at how well the horoscopes matched. Why don't you at least agree to speak to him over the phone?"

She wanted to believe her father, and to move on with her life. She didn't want to keep living at home as a single woman and being tempted by every random male. She'd never think of actually marrying someone like Benito—a gym trainer who'd never graduated from college—even if he were Indian. So what was she playing at? What was she waiting for?

"I am wondering"—Appa's voice became ragged, and he cleared his throat—"if you might have someone you are already interested in."

Rasika bit her lip and glanced at her father. "What do you mean?"

"Balu Uncle called the other day."

Subhash's father. Rasika's heart gave a sick leap.

"We were talking about this and that, and I mentioned the latest batch of photos we received. He said, you know, these girls raised in the U.S., they want to find someone of their own. I told him, Rasika is not like that. And then he told me that he thought you were interested in"—her father's cheek twitched—"Abhay."

"No, Appa." She let out her breath.

"Subhash says he has seen you with Abhay, here and there."

"It was just an accident, Appa. I wasn't really with him. We just happened to be in the same place at the same time." She had repeated this so many times, she was starting to believe it herself.

"Abhay is a good boy, I am sure." Appa blinked rapidly. "But I cannot accept, and my mother will not accept. You know, Rasika, his family is of a different caste. We are Brahmins. They are not."

"Appa, I don't even know why you're talking about this. He's not my type at all. Caste has nothing to do with it."

"Of course, caste does not matter when it comes to job opportunities, and socializing." Her father seemed not to have heard her. "I am not so backward."

"Appa, I'm not interested in Abhay. He's just a boy, Pramod's friend."

Her father continued, still oblivious to what she had said. "But when it comes to marriage, we cannot allow. When you have children, the blood will be mixed. That is not our way."

"I don't understand why we even still follow the caste system, Appa. Brahmins are supposed to be priests, and we're not priests." Rasika used to ask these questions as a child, and she'd never received a satisfactory answer.

"It is not just a question of profession." Appa clasped his hands tightly, yet they were still shaking. "Nowadays science has discovered genes. In olden days, no one knew about genes, so we had the caste system. Brahmins are the highest caste for that reason."

"What are you saying? You really believe Brahmins are genetically superior?"

"The story says Brahmins are created from the face of God. The other castes are from other, lower body parts. The Kshatriyas are from the arms, Vaishyas from the thighs, and Shudras from the feet." Appa seemed calmer now, pointing to each body part as he mentioned it. "Of course, everyone has equal opportunity now in India. In fact, the government bends over for the backward castes. They have so many reserved seats at the best colleges for the tribals and lower castes. Sometimes smart Brahmins cannot even get into those colleges."

"I don't want to hear about all that again, Appa. Anyway, not all Indians care about caste the way you do. And what about sub-caste? Why is that important?"

"You see, India is a very diverse country." Appa slung one knee over the other. Rasika realized she was in for a long lecture. "In America, we are friends with Indians from all over. We are even friends with people from Pakistan, Bangladesh, Sri Lanka, Nepal. We see them all as part of the same general culture. But you must understand that everyone's traditions are different. We are Tamilians. We want to hold on to our culture." Appa held up a hand and folded a finger down with each point. "We speak Tamil at home. Not all Indians insist on their mother tongue as we do. We have not taken up Western habits like drinking and meat eating. We believe in marrying within the subcaste because that is our tradition. It is tradition all over India, but so many people are becoming Westernized these days, dating and having love marriages. That is why there are so many divorces now. You see, even among our own friends, Shanti Auntie and Raghu Uncle have gotten divorced, after forty years of marriage." He lowered his hands to his lap.

"But they had an arranged marriage," Rasika said.

"The point is, they have become Westernized. In our family, we believe in holding on to our traditions for the sake of family stability. . . ."

Rasika stopped listening to the lecture. On the hill below them, a young couple in matching lime green jackets stood discussing the course. Leaves rustled in the breeze, and the faint tok of a golf ball being hit sounded from the distance. Rasika didn't belong to the country club anymore, though she had enjoyed the club thoroughly as a child. She'd loved swimming in the bright turquoise pool, lying on her back with her ears underwater and looking up at the sky; jumping off the diving board again and again; crunching into onion rings and slurping up slushees. As a teenager she had sworn off onion rings and had enjoyed showing off her body in a swimsuit as revealing as her mother would allow her to wear, which wasn't saying much, since she had not been allowed a bikini.

She could imagine joining a club such as this one after she got married. She and her husband would perhaps play golf together, or tennis. She wasn't terrible at tennis, plus she liked wearing tennis skirts. They would have friends, other club members, and they'd all eat dinner together sometimes at the club restaurant with their children.

As her father droned on, she realized it was too hard to fight against her parents. She couldn't let her father think she'd throw herself away on someone like Abhay. Anyway, everyone—her relatives, her parents' friends—would be very impressed with her if she married a guy from India. It might not be so bad. She had cousins in India who were as sophisticated as she wanted. Maybe this guy would be similar.

Her father put out a trembling hand and rested it on her knee. "You may like Yuvan. You will never know until you try."

"OK," she agreed. "Maybe I can call him tonight."

Appa's forehead was damp with sweat, maybe from the exertion of trying to convince her. He patted her knee. "Your mother will be very pleased."

Rasika talked with Yuvan, she e-mailed with him, and when she couldn't really find anything to object to about him, when things seemed inevitably to point to her marriage with him, she agreed to go to India to meet him. He seemed like a polite, cultured young man. He was soft-spoken yet not shy. It's true they didn't speak for long on the phone, but after all it was international long-distance. It's true they didn't spend hours chatting on the computer. Still, he seemed everything she had hoped for in a husband.

Her mother, frantic with excitement, insisted that Rasika buy a few silk saris at the Cleveland sari shop, and get some outfits stitched by a local Indian seamstress. Amma suggested that, in addition to salvar kameez outfits, Rasika order a pants set, which was apparently a new fashion: flared pants with a hip-length top and scarf, done up in a dark purple silk with decorative silver borders. "You will be meeting the boy as soon as you arrive," Amma pointed out. "We won't have time to shop before you meet." Rasika went along with everything, even allowing her mother to choose a bright red, heavily embroidered salvar set as one of the outfits.

Amma spent days shopping for gifts for Yuvan and his family, even though the engagement wasn't final. Rasika helped her pick out some nice knit polo shirts for Yuvan and his younger brothers. Appa consulted with several friends and read innumerable articles before purchasing one of the new iPhones for Yuvan, which allowed the user to connect to the Internet from the phone itself. "Everything is available in India now," Appa noted. "But we want to bring him something from the U.S."

Appa had also arranged, just in case, for Rasika to meet a few other eligible bachelors whose horoscopes had been fairly good matches. Her parents were determined to get her married on this trip—to Yuvan or to someone else.

Amma was busy calling all of their relatives in the United States and India, telling them about the planned wedding. She talked to her mother and sister in Bangalore and her sister in Durham, North Carolina; as well as Appa's mother, brothers, and sister, all in Bangalore. Amma had already found out, from the astrologer, the best dates and times for a wedding between Rasika and Yuvan, and she spent a lot of time on the phone discussing wedding halls and cooks for hire. "It will have to be a small wedding," Amma apologized. "Just our relatives and friends. Maybe a hundred people. We can't get a big wedding hall on such short notice. And if by chance you choose another man, we may have to move the date. But don't worry. We'll get it done on this trip." Amma made the whole thing sound like a surgical procedure that had to be done before Rasika's health failed.

Rasika went through her days in a fog. She removed her summer clothing from her closets and dresser. Yuvan would be staying with her in this room until they found a house. She recoiled at the idea of a strange man invading her beautiful room. As she sat on the carpet in front of her bookshelf, packing away her Beanie Babies in a paper grocery sack, she tried to remind herself that the man would not be strange, he would be her husband. She slid the Bollywood stars collage down the side of the sack, and carried the whole thing down to the basement.

"If all else fails, there is still Subhash," Amma said one Saturday as they were driving home from the mall. "They will be coming to India for the wedding."

The trees on either side of the wide roadway had lost most of their leaves by now, and the bare brown branches rose against a dull white sky. Rasika tightened her grip on the steering wheel. "Amma, I can't marry Subhash. You haven't had the horoscopes matched."

"We sent them to the astrologer last week. It's not a very good match, but it would be a last resort only."

"I won't marry him." She veered into their development, realized she was driving a little too fast, and jammed on the brake.

"Then you had better make up your mind to accept Yuvan," Amma retorted, bracing herself with a hand on the dashboard.

The next day, Sunday morning, Rasika showed up at Jill's place unannounced.

"So you're actually going through with this wedding," Jill said. She was on the sofa in a white robe and bare feet, toweling dry her wet dark hair. She had always been beautiful—tall, high cheekbones, and effortlessly thin (she never exercised, as far as Rasika could tell)—but she was casual about her beauty, unlike Rasika, who spent hours putting together outfits, tweezing her eyebrows, and applying makeup. If Jill wore so much as lipstick, you knew she was going somewhere special.

Jill's apartment held a few comfortable pieces of expensive furniture: a tan Italian leather sofa and armchair and two solid maple end tables, set on an expanse of off-white carpet. The other furniture—the bookshelves, the entertainment center, the floor lamps—had been taken by Jared when he moved out.

"Are you happy?" Jill tossed her towel onto the carpet, ran her fingers through her damp hair, stretching her legs over the sofa cushions.

"I think so." Rasika was in the leather armchair, holding a steaming cup of coffee. She had been feeling so sleepy recently and relied on coffee just to keep herself functioning.

"What's he like? Was it love at first sight?"

"I haven't met him yet. I don't know."

Jill threw her legs onto the floor and strode to the bedroom, from which she emerged with a wide-toothed comb. She sat down again and began untangling her hair. "I'm never going to get married. I'll never live with another guy, either. They take you for granted when you're around all the time. Jared turned into a baby once he moved in. I had to nag him to pay his share of the rent and utilities. And you think he'd ever bother to make a meal for the two of us? I was like the mommy who was supposed to take care of everything for him, clean up after him, pay his bills."

"You'll find another guy," Rasika consoled.

"I'm going to find lots of other guys. I'm never going to limit myself to just one. Guys are for having fun with. They're not for living with." Jill tossed her comb onto the side table. "I'll make my own money, live my own way, do my own thing, and pick up whatever man I want."

Jill's robe had become loose, and Rasika could see a bright blue sports bra with red trim. She said, "You look like Wonder Woman in that bra."

Jill cast off her robe and planted her feet apart on the empty carpet in front of the sofa. Her panties were also bright blue. "I am Wonder Woman!" She flung her arms out.

Rasika tried to laugh and managed a stiff smile. "I wish I could be Wonder Woman," she said, a bit sadly.

"Well, why can't you? We'll be twin Wonder Women. It'll be great! You can get an apartment just like mine, and we'll entice men to do our bidding."

Rasika knew Jill had never really understood family ties. Jill's father had abandoned the family when she was a small child. Jill had never seen him again. Her mother had remarried, and then divorced, and now lived alone nearby. Jill had no siblings and no cousins, at least none whom she cared to keep in touch with. Jill would never make life decisions based on whether or not her relatives would approve.

Jill picked up her robe, put it on, and sat down. "Rasika, you're disappearing. You're wearing a tan shirt and brown pants. It's like camouflage. You hardly smile. You look like you're about to go to sleep."

"I'm OK." She sat up straighter and made an effort to open her eyes wider.

"How about we run away together? We can quit our jobs, take all our savings, and go somewhere new. Someplace exciting. We'll get jobs and start over. How about Hawaii? Or Miami? I want to go where I can live in my bathing suit. I only stayed in Ohio because I was in a serious relationship. Now I'm free. So what do you say?"

Rasika smiled. "You know I can't."

"What's stopping you? We're not kids anymore. You're not going to get grounded if you do something your parents don't approve of. You're not going to have your allowance taken away. Why are you still trying to please them?"

"Because, Jill. They're my parents. You don't understand. My dad's so happy about this marriage. He's been walking around whistling. He never whistles. He said now he doesn't have to worry about disappointing his mother."

"His mother? Your grandmother?"

"Yeah. She never wanted him to live in this country. He's her youngest child. After medical school in India, he came to the U.S. against her wishes. She kept asking him to come home and get married. She was so afraid he'd marry a foreigner. So finally, after he turned thirty, he did go home and agree to get married."

"I can't believe your mother agreed to have an arranged marriage. She's so modern, so classy."

"Everyone had arranged marriages back then, Jill. Most people in India still do."

"Your mom's really educated, isn't she? I mean, she used to work at a college, right?"

"She has a master's degree in biology. There are only girls in her family, and her father wanted all of them to be well educated."

"So they got married, and they lived in India for a long time, right? Because, you were born there. Did she work in India? I don't remember if you ever told me that." Jill was sitting with her elbows on her knees and a puzzled dent on her forehead.

Rasika took a sip of coffee and tried to be as clear as she could. "After my mom got married, she pretty much had me and my brother right away. My dad tried to settle down in India, but he got so upset about the dirty condition of the hospitals in India, the lack of equipment, and the corruption. So he came back to the U.S., and my mother raised us in India for a while, and she didn't work then.

And when we all came here, she worked for a while as a temporary lecturer at Akron U."

"That's right! I remember that! Why'd she quit?"

"I think the low status of the job got to her. She didn't feel like she had to do that kind of work, when she was a mother and a wife of a doctor. So she never really worked after that."

"It's hard for me to understand someone like your mother. She's so educated, but she had an arranged marriage. Do you think your parents were in love when they got married?"

"That's not the point, Jill. No one expected them to be in love."

"Do they love each other now?"

"Of course. They're married. They're my parents."

"So you think that'll happen to you, too? You'll get married to this person, and then later on, you'll love him?"

Rasika closed her eyes. She didn't want to think about her parents' relationship. That had nothing to do with her own marriage. "I like him already."

"Well, it's your tradition." Jill sat back and waved her hand in the air. "If you understand it, I guess that's good enough for me."

"The way we're doing it is really quite modern, Jill. If you want tradition, my dad's mother is very traditional. She only went to school through eighth grade, and she got married at fourteen. She wasn't even allowed to see her husband before they got married."

"God. I never knew that."

"I guess I never told you much about my family in India."

"I remember hearing about your cousins, but you never told me about your grandmother, that's for sure."

"All my grandmother's other children stayed in India; my dad is the only one who left. She doesn't want her grandchildren marrying foreigners. So now, my dad feels like he'll be satisfying her, because I won't be marrying a foreigner."

"Well, this guy might not be a foreigner to your grandmother, but isn't he sort of a stranger to you? I remember when you started third grade. You had just come from India. You were Indian then. Now you're American."

"To my parents, I'm still one hundred percent Indian."

"You've been so good, Rasika. You've always tried so hard to please your parents. You live at home, you don't stay out late, you help your mother when she has parties."

"But I have this whole secret life that I feel really awful about."

"Your parents can't expect to know about your sex life."

"I'm not supposed to have a sex life at all, Jill. The life of an unmarried Indian woman should be a completely open book."

"That's crazy. Does anyone actually manage to live like that?"

"I'm sure my cousins do."

"I don't believe it."

"Girls are a lot more supervised in India."

"So you've had a few flings. That's nothing."

"More than a few flings."

Jill's eyebrows went up. "What're you hiding from me?"

Rasika shook her head. Jill knew about almost all of Rasika's encounters. For Jill, what seemed like "a few" seemed to Rasika a never-ending, revolving list of sins and transgressions. "I'm ashamed of the way I've acted, Jill. My parents see things differently. Even if it had been only one man, my parents would think I was a whore."

"Come on, Rasika. You're twenty-five! What do they expect?"

"They expect me to have an arranged marriage to someone they pick out."

"Are you agreeing to marry this guy just to please your grandmother?"

"This is the way we do things in our family, and I want to fit in."

"What about your cousins in North Carolina? Have they gone off to India for arranged marriages?"

"All my cousins on my dad's side have had arranged marriages. They're all in India and all older than me. I'm the oldest cousin on my mom's side. No one else is married yet. I'm supposed to set the good example."

"So, the pressure's on."

Rasika had already received congratulatory phone calls from some of her aunts and uncles, and the praise felt good. "You are doing the right thing," Ahalya Auntie had told her from North Carolina. "Happiness comes from obeying your parents."

"What if you left with me?" Jill persisted. "What would happen then?"

"How, Jill? What would I do with my car? What about all my things? I can't just abandon my clothes, and my bedroom furniture."

"Why not? They have clothes in Hawaii. They have furniture wherever we'll go."

"Are you serious?"

"Absolutely."

"I can't, Jill. You don't know my parents; they'll track me down. They'll fly out to see me. My mother will cry. My father—I can't even imagine what he'd do. He'd be so disappointed in me. Maybe he'd fall ill from the stress of it all. And then all the relatives will find out about it, and they'll feel sorry for my parents."

"What about your brother? Doesn't he have a girlfriend? Aren't your parents worried about that?"

Pramod had been dating a fellow student, Hannah, for the past several months. Rasika had met them for dinner once. She was a thin, intense white woman who seemed to study a lot. "My parents don't know about her. Anyway, once Pramod is finished with his education, I guess they'll work on finding a girl for him, too."

"You think he'll go for it?"

Rasika shrugged. "He's going to be a doctor. They're really

happy about that. My dad wanted someone to follow in his foot-steps, and it clearly wasn't going to be me. So, if Pramod wanted to marry someone of his own choice . . . I don't know . . . my parents might get over it."

"Wouldn't they get over it with you, too? Eventually?"

"I'm the only daughter. I'm the oldest. I have to do this."

"Well, I still don't get it."

Jill couldn't understand. Rasika was reluctant to even articulate her fear that if she, her father's beloved daughter, were to align her-self with someone her parents didn't approve of, her father would no longer be able to love her.

10

Abhay stopped by Kianga's house occasionally after work. He knew that in order to quiet his constant thoughts of Rasika he had to keep himself busy and occupied with other people. Alone, he started to brood about Rasika.

He didn't have many friends in Portland yet. His coworkers at the bookstore already had their own partners and friends. And his work with Justin Time was mostly solitary. Justin wasn't always present. Abhay spent what seemed like hours alone in Justin's dim apartment. He summarized articles and books, and added them to the online database he had created. He felt like a centipede, crawling among the tomes of paper.

The work was frustrating, mostly. Everything he read pointed to the fact that Justin was right, yet Abhay wasn't sure that compiling all this information was really going to convince anyone to do anything. Justin promised that, soon, they would start working on events and publicity.

Kianga and Ellen always seemed happy to see him. He couldn't quite figure out the situation at their house. There were often several other people around, and some of them seemed to live in various rooms of the house.

One Tuesday evening in late October, he went over to help Kianga carve her pumpkins. Abhay's job was to cut out the stems and scoop out the seeds, and to haul the pumpkins outside after Kianga finished carving. Kianga had a set of special, thin knives, and she took the pumpkins very seriously, drawing her designs on the orange globes first before cutting. Her pumpkin faces were beautiful and ethereal, full of swirling eyebrows and smiles. They created a row on either side of the driveway. Kianga planned to put the candles in the next day—Halloween.

They ordered in Chinese food for dinner. Abhay walked to the corner store to get some beer. After dinner, Ellen went to her room, and Kianga gave Abhay an intimate glance with her beautiful, cool eyes, and invited him out to the backyard, where there was a hammock on the tiny back patio. They lay side by side on the swinging hammock in the chilly night. Abhay could still smell the sweet vegetably scent of pumpkin on his hands.

"How's it going with Justin?" Kianga asked.

"Okay, I guess. I can see this work is really important, and I'm the only one doing it in the entire world, as far as I can tell." Abhay felt something soft and fluffy on his chest. He held it up.

"What's that?" Kianga asked.

"A dust bunny. I think. Sometimes I feel like I'm turning into dust, working in that messy apartment." He dropped the fluff over the side of the hammock.

"Justin's always been kind of a pack rat. We had him keep our records for the Green Party, because we knew he'd never get rid of anything." She laughed. "Maybe you can clean up the place for him."

"He doesn't want me messing with his stuff. He's really particular about it."

"I was afraid of that. I was hoping this organization would bring him out of his shell."

"I don't think he wants to come out of his shell," Abhay said.

"Well, don't give up yet. I've always thought he had interesting ideas. I think he just needs someone to help him connect his ideas to the real world."

"He does have good ideas," Abhay agreed.

The traffic from the freeway had died down somewhat and was less apparent in the back of the house. Abhay wondered why Kianga was so interested in helping Justin. He was quite a bit older than she, and somewhat musty smelling. He couldn't imagine she had romantic ideas about him.

After several moments, Kianga reached for his fingers and held them lightly. "Do you want to tell me about your parents? And your childhood?"

"I'll tell you if you care."

"I do. I'm always interested in knowing where my friends come from."

As they swayed in the hammock, he told her about how his father had gotten his Ph.D. in the United States and had then gone back to India to marry his mother. He told her about living in a little dying rural town near Kent, and how he had run with a pack of other kids who lived in the same town-house complex. "It was great," he recalled. "There were these woods surrounding the town houses, and we'd explore in there, and pick wild blueberries. There was this little muddy pond we'd go to. We skipped rocks and caught toads. In the summer we'd go into whoever's house was nearby, and make sandwiches, and eat our lunches outside. My parents never knew anything about this. Dad was too busy with work to pay attention to what I did, and Mom was too busy with housework and my baby sister, I guess."

He told her about the move to Kent when he was twelve, how he had trouble making friends in junior high school, how he had developed a crush on a beautiful girl, much taller than he, and how other kids had somehow found out about it and teased him the entire year.

"Hm." Kianga pressed his fingers in sympathy.

He looked up at the dark gray sky through the branches of a tree. There were lights all around them, from living room windows and yard lamps, and he could see Kianga's face glowing in the dimness. He told her about all the silent family dinners he had endured, about his trouble deciding on a college major, about living at Rising Star. He turned his head against the rough ropes of the hammock to see her smiling gently on him, and he felt she could see right into him.

"Do you still keep in touch with any of the folks from the commune?" Kianga asked.

"No," he said. "I had a bad experience there with a woman that I'm trying to forget about. And it's hard to correspond privately with anyone at Rising Star. No one has their own personal phone or e-mail address, and the mail is sorted centrally, so if I contact anyone, the entire community'll know."

"Don't you miss that lifestyle?"

He thought about this. "When I first got there, I was so full of hope. So sure it was the right thing for me. I think I miss that feeling more than anything. By the time I left I was sick of the place."

When a member left, it was never a happy occasion at the community, never a time for a party or sharing food or dancing. He had packed on his own, the treasurer had solemnly handed him $100 in exit cash, and the woman in charge of the communal cars had driven him to the bus station. And that was that.

"In fact, now that I'm telling you about my childhood, I'm realizing something," Abhay said. "I'm wondering if my quest to live in a commune was an attempt to recapture something from my childhood."

"What d'you mean?"

"I had this wonderful communal experience as a child, sharing food, sharing adventures. And when that all ended, I was shoved into an environment where my vulnerabilities were exposed and mocked. So I wonder if through the commune I was trying to get back to that happy time of my childhood."

"I think you're overanalyzing," Kianga said. "Communal living makes sense: it's cheaper and it's more energy efficient. There doesn't have to be any deep psychological reason for it. Isn't that how people in India live, in families all together?"

He thought about his summer trips to Bangalore as a child. "Yeah, I guess I never realized that. My grandparents and my uncle and his family all lived in the same house, and when we went it was like a party every day. I remember one time sleeping with a whole bunch of cousins on the floor of the living room. I was maybe seven or eight, and the house was full of people. Relatives had come to Bangalore for someone's wedding—I can't remember whose—and it was like a big slumber party. My cousins and I ran around the house and yard, playing hide-and-seek, marbles, cricket."

"So maybe communal living reminds you of the way your family in India lives."

"Yeah. Maybe. I never thought of that until just now. And out there in Ohio, we've been all by ourselves."

"When were you in India last?"

"It's been years. As I got older I found it boring to spend my entire summer in Bangalore. I couldn't ride my bike because there was too much traffic, and there weren't any public libraries, and my cousins were usually at school all day when we went because their school vacations were different. My parents and my sister went when I was seventeen, and I just stayed home."

A nearby light was shut off, and he and Kianga were now lying in a pleasant grayness. She rolled onto her side, lifted an arm, and let it drift down onto his chest, where it lay warm and solid. He stroked her forearm, and soon was stroking more of her. He was melding into her warm body, and his breath was mixing with hers. He was part of the night air, part of the hammock, part of her, and she was part of him.

The next morning he woke up alone in Kianga's bedroom. She had a loft bed. He sat up and looked down at the room below, at her desk near the window with its stack of textbooks, a few large crystals, and a potted plant trailing dark green leaves. The closed white curtains let the sunlight in. The flowered dress she had worn yesterday was on the carpet below him. She had let it fall from the loft bed last night. He remembered its softness, and liked seeing it lie there in disarray. The room smelled faintly of incense, sweeter and different from what his mother used at home during her pooja. He smiled to himself. Kianga was definitely the type of woman to fit his life. How could he have possibly gotten so attached to Rasika, who was completely unlike him?

He climbed down from the loft and put on his clothes. He needed to get back to his place to get ready for work. This morning he had a meeting with Justin, and in the afternoon he had a shift at the bookstore. And in the evening, perhaps he'd be back here, making dinner with Kianga, swaying in the hammock again, eventually drifting to her room.

In the hallway, he almost ran into Ellen as she exited the bathroom. She was holding her toothbrush and towel. "Hi!" he said cheerfully.

"Sorry." She darted around him, peering at the floor. He was a little taken aback at her unfriendliness.

He finished in the bathroom and floated down the hall to look for Kianga. He imagined wrapping his arms around her and continuing their blissful connection of the night before.

In the kitchen, Kianga was at the stove, stirring a pot of something. She called, without turning around to face him, "You want raisins?"

"I don't know," he answered. "What're you making?" And through the window above the sink he heard a male voice say, "Yeah."

Kianga turned to Abhay and smiled. Preview stepped through the back door, holding a cucumber and a bell pepper. He nodded to Abhay, washed the vegetables at the sink, and started slicing them at the island counter.

Abhay felt useless standing in the middle of the kitchen. He'd thought he was going to gaze into Kianga's eyes while they ate a private breakfast.

"You got here early," Abhay said as Preview arranged cucumber slices on a plate.

"I live here." Preview scratched his head of matted hair.

Kianga was spooning oatmeal with raisins into four bowls. "Abhay, go ahead and put on some water for tea," she instructed. He thought about walking out the door, but he had to eat breakfast anyway. He just needed to be cool about the situation—whatever it was. He strolled over to the sink and filled the teapot. By this time Ellen was in the kitchen. She stood on a stool next to him, took several boxes of tea bags out from a high cabinet, and set them on the counter. After he turned on the stove he picked up the boxes of tea bags and took them into the dining room. Ellen was setting out spoons next to the bowls of oatmeal. "Would you bring the honey?" Ellen asked softly. "It's next to the stove." He found a jar of honey and a spoon and brought them out.

Then, not knowing what else to do, he stood near the doorway between the kitchen and dining room. Preview set out bottles of olive oil, vinegar, and herbs on the counter in front of him.

"So, Preview," Abhay said. "What do you do for work?"

"Well, right now I'm kinda between jobs." He splashed olive oil and vinegar into an empty jelly jar. "Kianga got me a temporary gig helping a disabled woman who's making this film about disabled street performers. I carry her equipment and help set it up." He added generous pinches of herbs with his fingers, capped the jelly jar, and shook it vigorously.

Kianga came in the back door holding stems of bright red tubular flowers, which she set into a drinking glass filled with water and brought into the dining room. "I needed to thin these plants anyway," she explained to Abhay. "They grow like crazy. The hummingbirds love them."

Preview set his plate of vegetables, drizzled with dressing, on the table. Abhay thought about slipping out without eating, and perhaps never coming back to this house again. Ellen smiled at him and said, "Come and sit down." So he sat next to Ellen and across from Preview, who was next to Kianga. Preview laid a hand on Kianga's bare shoulder and massaged it carefully. Kianga and Preview exchanged a long glance. Abhay noticed Ellen gazing at him in the same way. He gobbled down his oatmeal as fast as he could.

Abhay stayed away from Kianga's place for the rest of the week. On Friday evening he went with his roommate, Victor, and Victor's girlfriend, Tiffany, to see a movie called *Sicko,* about everything wrong with the American health care system.

"Our country's going to hell," Victor said when they exited the theater. He had his arms around Tiffany, and she was nuzzling his neck. "Canada's got a way better system than we have, so does France, even Cuba's better off than us. Those governments take care of their people. We spend our money on wars and shipping arms to dictators." Victor gave Tiffany a sloppy kiss. Abhay looked away.

Victor and Tiffany took off for her place. As Abhay walked in the other direction, he could hear the two of them laughing. Why was it that Victor, and so many people like him, could see a disturbing movie like that, and complain about the country, yet continue to be apparently happy with their lives? Abhay, on the other hand, brooded.

In the apartment kitchen were dirty bowls, plates, glasses, and pans in the sink, which Victor and Tiffany had failed to wash. Abhay noticed a large black bug squeeze itself into a crack between the countertop and wall. He walked past it all to fall into bed with his clothes still on.

Saturday morning dawned dull and overcast. The greasy popcorn from last night still sat heavily in his stomach. He showered, dressed, washed his dishes, and then sat at his kitchen table looking out at the gray sky. He thought about calling Rasika.

The phone rang. It was his mother. She called every week or so, worried about his low-paying job as a bookstore clerk, and worried that the job with Justin Time didn't really count as decent work.

"How are you?" she asked dolefully.

"Great!" He tried to make his voice full of pep. "Things are going really well here. How are you, Mom? How's your business going?"

Mom clicked her tongue. "Remember big sale I made? Last month?"

"To that home-schooling group?"

"So much work it was. So many times I met with them. Then they bought lot of books, so I am happy. I think, it is all worth it. Finally I receive my check. Hardly anything it is. All people above me have taken so much."

"That's the way it is with these pyramid schemes, Mom."

"Your father is angry. I did not even earn enough to pay for all samples I bought. They did not tell all this. In those meetings they just told how much money we will make."

"I'm sorry to hear that it didn't work out, Mom."

"So I will not do this work anymore. I gave samples to my friend Linda. I don't know what I will do now."

"Well—do you feel like you learned something from this?" He watched a black water bug march boldly across the floor. "You were running your own business, after all. Maybe some of those skills are transferable. You could start another small business."

"What business? What I know to do? I can cook. I can take care of children. I can type and answer phone. What business I can start?"

"What about catering? Or a small day care? Or, I don't know, maybe a typing service or answering service?"

"Right now I have too many worries. I cannot think about anything new."

He flung himself back in his chair and looked at a stain on the ceiling in the shape of a dog's head. "What worries?"

"I want you to talk to Seema."

"Why? What's going on? I thought she was doing great in her classes."

"I think she has—boyfriend," Mom choked out. "Black boy, I think."

"Oh?" Abhay focused on one of the dog's ears, hoping that his mother's comment wasn't as bigoted as it sounded.

"Some Pan-Africa group she is involved in now. One freshman class is about multicultural something. I thought they will be learning about different countries. But she is spending lot of time with these black students."

"How do you know she has a boyfriend?"

"I can tell. One day she came home wearing new dress, some kind of loose African thing. She said her friend gave it. What friend,

I said. And she told this boy's name. He must be black boy, if he is giving African dress."

Good for her, Abhay thought. He sat up straighter and placed his elbows on the table.

"I cannot tell your father," Mom said. "So upset he will be. I want you to talk to her. I will go and give her phone."

In a moment Seema's quiet monotone was on the line. Abhay had no intention of discouraging Seema from dating anyone she wanted, so he just chatted with her about her classes. But Seema brought up the subject herself.

"Mom doesn't want me to get involved with the Pan-African Studies department," she said. "When I told her there were a lot of black people in my class, I thought she'd be happy that it was, you know, more ethnically diverse. But instead she said, 'I didn't know so many blacks went to college.' I never realized Mom and Dad were prejudiced."

"I don't get it either. How can one group of brown people look down on another group of brown people?"

"It's crazy," Seema agreed. "I feel at home when I visit the Pan-African Studies department. Their offices are in the basement of Ritchie Hall. It's cozy and colorful, and they welcome everyone. They're not like Indian people, who look you over and want to make sure you're good enough for them."

"That's great, Seema. Are you thinking of changing your major?" Maybe she'd come to her senses and would choose something that really mattered.

"I'm still in engineering. But I'm going to sign up for a class called the Black Experience next semester. My friend Jawad suggested it. He said it would be a good introduction for me."

Jawad was obviously the boyfriend. Abhay was delighted and amused. He wondered how his father would react to Seema's defection from the role of obedient Indian child.

He said good-bye to Seema and sat for several minutes, staring at the phone in his hand. He wondered what Rasika was doing at that moment. It was about noon in Ohio. Was she happy? She'd said she wanted to live an honest life. He wanted her to be true to herself, yet he still wanted her truth to include him.

To prevent himself from calling Rasika he dialed Chris Haldorson's phone number instead.

"Hey, Adios! How goes it in Portland?"

"It's going OK. I have a job. Not too many friends yet, though."

"I imagine it's tough moving to a new place. You get lonely."

At these words, Abhay realized that his heart did feel empty. "Yeah, I have been kind of lonely."

"Don't worry about it. You'll find some friends soon. What about women? You looking for a girlfriend?"

"Yeah. I guess I kind of have a girlfriend here. Maybe."

"That's great, Adios. What's she like?"

He told Chris briefly about Kianga. Chris talked about his business, and about his father's continuing ill health. "He just got out of the hospital," Chris said.

"So he's fine now?"

"He's home," was all Chris would say, and Abhay felt guilty for not having called Chris since he arrived in Portland. Chris was being a good son, and Abhay could tell the situation at home was stressful.

After inviting Chris to call him anytime, Abhay pushed the "off" button and sat with his elbows on his knees, staring unseeing at the floor. Chris was right. He was lonely and virtually friendless in a strange city. What was he going to do about it? He sat up and, holding his breath, quickly dialed Rasika's cell phone. It rang six times, and Rasika's voice informed him that she was not available to take his call. He turned off the phone, stood up, and flung it away from him. It skidded down the hallway, and the battery popped out. He sat with his head in his hands for a moment before walking over to retrieve it and put it back together again.

He didn't want to be in love with Rasika. She'd made her choice clear and he wasn't it. He set the phone into its holder near the refrigerator. He should forget about her and try again with Kianga. He'd told Chris that she was his girlfriend, and maybe she ought to be. He just needed to figure out the situation there.

He rode his bike to Kianga's. She was leaving the house with a few shopping bags over her shoulder, on her way to the farmers' market. "You want to come?" she asked Abhay.

They headed toward campus, where, on the long green park space between the buildings, a field of white-topped shelters had sprouted, like mushrooms after a rain. He wandered with Kianga from one stall to the next, tasting chèvre spread on minicrackers, and roasted hazelnuts, various flavors of pesto, and a tiny spoonful of lavender-blueberry jam.

"I need to stop by the peace booth," she said. "They've got this beautiful button I want."

"Kianga!" a gruff voice called. "Kianga, honey!"

Kianga stopped in the midst of the shoppers streaming by. A heavy white woman, half-drunk it seemed, wavered toward them through the crowd.

"Hi, sweetie." Kianga gave the woman a long hug. Abhay stood behind them, holding the bags, and wondered what he was doing here. Kianga gathered around her people who needed help in one way or another. Ellen, for example: they'd met at school, and Kianga had helped Ellen when she was going through a hard time, something about an alcoholic and manipulative mother. Preview was another. Kianga had met him when she volunteered for some sort of peer counseling group, and he had shown up with suicidal urges. Abhay wasn't interested in Ellen, or Preview, or this strange woman who was now dominating Kianga's attention.

He began to realize that Justin was probably also one of Kianga's "projects." She had probably gotten Abhay the job with Justin because she felt sorry for Justin and wanted to help him out. And maybe Abhay himself was nothing more to Kianga than her latest project: she wanted to rescue a lonely, confused young man.

After the woman had invited Kianga to some event, and after Kianga had agreed to attend, the woman staggered away, and Kianga led Abhay toward the peace table, where she bantered with the folks while sorting through the pile of pin-on buttons on the table.

"Maybe you guys ought to make up some buttons," Kianga said to him. She held up a button that said MAKE ART, NOT WAR.

"What d'you mean?"

"HOPE. Your organization. You could have buttons saying VASECTOMIES WILL SAVE THE EARTH."

"HOPE is not my organization."

She picked up a button of a penguin with a peace sign on its belly. "This is so cute!" She added it to the handful she had already collected. "You should suggest it to Justin. He doesn't get out much." She took out her wallet, extracted a five-dollar bill, and stuffed it into the donation jar.

On the way back to her house, Abhay held her bags bulging with bread, cheese, jam, mushrooms, apples, peaches, and flower bulbs. He carried them into the house and was about to deposit them on the counter, when he noticed it was covered in crumbs.

"Just put the bags on the floor." Kianga set a large pot on the stove. "I'm going to make some hot spiced apple cider. There's some couscous left over from last night."

She handed him a wet sponge before grabbing a broom in the corner and starting to sweep the floor. Preview wandered in and opened the fridge door.

Abhay dutifully wiped off the counter. "Unfortunately, I have to leave for work in a minute."

She bumped him lightly with her hip as she swept. Preview slapped a bagel on the still-wet counter and began sawing it in half, creating more crumbs.

"I want to take you somewhere tomorrow." She replaced the broom in its corner and pulled out a jug of apple cider from a bag on the floor.

He rinsed out the sponge. "Where?"

"It's a surprise." Right behind Preview's back, she gave him a noisy kiss. "Meet me here tomorrow morning at eight-thirty. Wear something nice."

On Sunday morning, Abhay wore a dress shirt and pants, and took the streetcar to Kianga's place. She was wearing a flowing yellow skirt and a lacy white blouse. They borrowed Ellen's car—a heap of junk that smelled of cat pee—and drove to a nondescript two-story brown brick building on a side street somewhere in the suburbs of Portland.

In the parking lot, Kianga took his hand and led him into the building vestibule, where they were greeted by the scent of incense. He and Kianga took their shoes off, lined them up neatly on a shelf, and hung their jackets on a coat rack, before entering the main room, which was carpeted and bare of furniture. At the other end of the room was an altar on a raised platform draped in white cloth, and on top of the cloth was a large framed color photo of a long-haired, dark-skinned man wearing a garland—some sort of Hindu saint, Abhay guessed. The altar was decorated with silver vases of yellow and white flowers, white candles, and a stick of incense. On the wall above the altar were religious symbols: om, a cross, a Jewish Star of David, a Muslim crescent and star.

"What is this place?" he whispered. It seemed like a Hindu temple, with the incense and the altar and the removal of shoes, yet he didn't see any Indian faces. Also, it was much too quiet and orderly for a Hindu temple. People dressed in white and yellow were filing in silently to sit in neat rows on the carpet.

"It's the Premananda Temple," Kianga whispered. She picked up a couple of printed handouts from a basket near the door, and led him to sit down in the center of the room, just behind a full row of people. "Have you heard of it?"

He shook his head. A short, smiling white woman slipped something into his hand. It was a brochure with the same long-haired, dark-skinned man on the front. He opened the brochure and read that Premananda was a Hindu saint who had come to the United States at the beginning of the twentieth century, for the purpose of spreading brotherly love throughout the Western world. Before he could read more, the room was filled with the sound of everyone chanting "om" as loudly as possible. Startled, he looked up. Everyone had their eyes closed and mouths open, including Kianga.

He tossed the brochure onto the carpet. He didn't want to participate in this farce. Religious rituals were nothing but a way to manipulate people. He wasn't going to surrender his mind to God, or eternity, or any kind of crazy group where the members all dressed alike. In the past, he had based certain life decisions on a vision or a dream, but they were *his* visions, *his* dreams, not something imposed from the outside. In any case, he wasn't sure anymore that there was value in his visions or dreams.

He scanned the room for a way out. He was trapped, hemmed in on all sides by this sea of white and yellow. He clutched his hands together and hunched down to endure the ordeal. He could, if necessary, simply step over all these people and head for the door, but at the moment he preferred not to draw attention to himself. He decided to stay put. He wondered if this was how people got sucked into cults. They were polite, they went along with things, they didn't make a fuss. He looked at his watch: almost a quarter after nine. He'd give this thing until ten, and if it wasn't over by then he'd make a break for it, walk out, find a bus, get himself back to real life.

After everyone had finished "oming," someone lit a small fire in a metal bowl on the altar, and everyone repeated a few prayers in unison—one in English, one in Sanskrit. Then everyone grew silent, with their eyes closed.

He looked around at all the people meditating. Some of the women wore Indian-style clothing, and a few of them even had round red kumkums on their foreheads. Here was this group of Westerners practicing what they believed to be Hindu rituals, following a Hindu guru, and yet they were doing it in an American way. The altar was clean, orderly, and symmetrical. There were no oily deepas or cracked coconuts or idols draped in silk and jewels, as in a Hindu temple. Hindu rituals never used printed handouts like the one he held in his hand. Instead, the priest mumbled whatever prayers were required, or a participant would start singing whatever song came to her mind, and the others followed along as best they could. Here, some of the devotees who sat along the wall were stretching their feet out in front of them, toward the altar. No Hindu would ever dare to show the soles of the feet to the altar.

This temple was not as extreme as, say, the Hare Krishnas, where all the white women wore saris, and all the men shaved their heads. It wasn't as crazy as the Rajneeshees, that Oregon commune from the 1980s where everyone wore red and engaged in frenetic, exhausting exercise, which they called "meditations." These folks were calm and measured and quiet.

After the meditation, a tall, gray-haired white woman stood up next to the altar and talked in a singsong voice about the war in Iraq and loving one's enemies and world peace. Just before Abhay's ten o'clock deadline, the whole thing was over, and everyone filed up to the front of the room, where a large tray of prasada, food supposedly blessed by God, was on a table near the altar. The devotees picked up the tan balls of prasada with their right or left hands—not only with the right hand. As a child, Abhay had had this important Hindu rule drilled into him: you accept and give things with the right hand only.

As Kianga and Abhay ate their prasada—peanut butter and dried apricot balls, not something he'd eaten at any Hindu ritual he'd ever attended—the gray-haired woman minister approached them.

"This is my friend Abhay," Kianga said, and he shook hands with the minister. "He's interested in communal living, and his family is from India, so I thought he'd like to come here."

The minister nodded. "Some of us live upstairs. Swami Premananda taught that living together in a spiritual community is the best way to practice brotherly love. We try to share at least one weekly meal with the entire congregation, even those who don't live in the building. Our congregation comes from all over the area." She spoke softly and slowly. "We also have daily meditation every morning, and anyone is welcome to join us for that. And, of course, the weekly Sunday service, which you've just seen."

Kianga must have thought his Hindu upbringing and his interest in communal living would come together in this community. The minister was now explaining something about the guru of Swami Premananda back in India, and how the swami had come to the United States, and how she herself was initiated by a direct disciple of Swami Premananda. Abhay tried to look politely interested.

By the time Abhay and Kianga were back in the car on their way home, it was drizzling. The windshield wipers squeaked.

"Whad'ya think?" Kianga pulled out of the parking lot.

"I'm not that interested in religion." He tried to keep his voice bland, and not reveal all the frustration he felt about the morning.

"This is a community based on your tradition. I thought you'd like it."

"What happened in that room has very little to do with my tradition. And even if it did"— he let out a huff of air in frustration— "just because I'm brown and my parents happen to be from India, doesn't mean I'm into everything else that happens to be connected to India or Hinduism."

Kianga pulled onto the freeway. "This isn't about any particular religion. It's about spirituality."

"What's the difference?"

"Religion is when you tell people they have to believe in a certain manifestation of God, and do certain rituals. Religion is about hating people who believe in a different religion, or trying to convert them to your religion. Spirituality is totally different. It's about connecting with God at a fundamental level, connecting with the eternal, working toward enlightenment. You can do that through traditional religious methods like prayer or meditation, or you can do that by being out in nature, for example."

He frowned out the windshield and watched the wipers slap back and forth.

She put a hand over his. "I get that you're not interested in everything from India, but have you ever heard of Auroville? It's an intentional community in India."

"I've heard the name, but I don't know anything about it. Isn't it some kind of religious retreat?"

"A friend of mine is moving there. I looked up their Web site. It seems really amazing. People from all over the world live there. It's devoted to peace and connecting with the earth. I thought you might know more, since you're interested in communal living."

He shook his head. "I'm sorry, I don't."

"Well, I'm thinking of visiting there, in December. Maybe you should come with me." She glanced at him and gave him an encouraging smile. "You said you haven't been to India in years. So—maybe now's the time. Maybe Auroville will be the place for you."

"When I go to India, I don't hang out at intentional communities. I'm stuck in Bangalore with my relatives."

"Auroville isn't that far from Bangalore. It's just south of Chennai."

Abhay didn't want to try to explain to Kianga his complicated feelings about India, so he said nothing.

At Kianga's house, the sun was out again. "Want to come in? Ellen's at home, too."

As they got out of the car, Ellen stepped out the door of the house and stood at the top of the stairs, her slim shoulders sloping slightly toward her chest as usual. She was wearing a pair of bell-bottom jeans with ragged hems. She waved to him, and he waved back.

"I've got some work to do," he lied.

Kianga slipped her arms around his waist and pulled him into a tight hug. He felt embarrassed to be hugging Kianga as Ellen watched. Kianga rubbed his back. She felt soft and warm, yet his face burned, and he gently pulled himself away. He walked fast over the bridge above the freeway, and once he was sure they couldn't see him, he broke into a run to the streetcar stop.

At home he plugged in and turned on his laptop, changed out of his nice clothes, and sent an e-mail to Rasika's work address, inviting her to visit him in Portland. He didn't think she'd take him up on it. Then, on impulse, he searched the Web, using the key phrase "organic flowers," found a company that delivered pesticide-free bouquets, and ordered a vase of white lilies to be sent to Rasika's office on Monday morning.

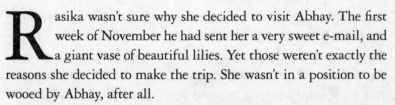

Rasika wasn't sure why she decided to visit Abhay. The first week of November he had sent her a very sweet e-mail, and a giant vase of beautiful lilies. Yet those weren't exactly the reasons she decided to make the trip. She wasn't in a position to be wooed by Abhay, after all.

As soon as she read Abhay's note, she'd called and made her plane reservations for the coming weekend. She'd never made travel plans at the last minute, like this. She told her parents she was going to California with Jill, to visit an old school friend of theirs. Part of this was true. Jill was going to visit Amanda in Los Angeles. Her mother made a fuss because Rasika was buying the ticket so late. "When did Jill decide to go?" Amma demanded. "Why didn't you book your ticket so you could get the two-week advance fare?" Amma also worried that Rasika's boss wouldn't like her taking time off on such short notice.

"I'll just be missing work on Thursday and Friday," Rasika said. "I'm flying back on Sunday."

"Why so short?" Amma then demanded. "If you are going all

the way to California, why not stay longer? You must plan in advance, raja."

Appa was the one who smoothed things over. "Let her go," he said. "She has worked hard. It is her own money. Let her have some fun."

Her father's words made Rasika feel guilty. If he knew what she was really going to do, he wouldn't have been so calm about it. Still, she pushed ahead with her plan, arranging her plane ticket so she was leaving on the same day but somewhat later than Jill. She even allowed her parents to drive her to the Cleveland airport, where they met Jill near the ticket counter. Her parents then left, and once she was sure they were out of sight, she rolled her luggage over to a different ticket counter.

As she waited in the check-in line, she told herself that this trip was entirely justified. She just wanted to have a little fun before getting married. She didn't intend to sleep with Abhay, and to prove it she had booked herself into a hotel suggested by him. She had been very good since agreeing to go to India. She had even switched to a different gym to avoid Benito. She felt extremely virtuous. She deserved a little vacation.

Waiting in the gate area after clearing security, she realized this was the first time she had traveled anywhere alone. She clutched her purse on her lap and observed the other waiting passengers. A young couple dressed in shabby jeans was sitting across from her, sharing a messy plastic tray of French fries and ketchup. A mother nursed her toddler in a sling, while another little girl sat beside her, sucking her thumb. The mother had three large plastic bags stuffed with clothes and toys around her feet. How would she navigate herself, the two kids, and the bags onto the plane?

There were a few people who seemed to be traveling alone: a man in a business suit was tapping away on his laptop, and a fat woman wearing a shirt that read BABY DOLL in sparkly letters was holding a cell phone to her ear.

Rasika didn't have a virtual companion like a computer, and she didn't feel like talking to anyone on her phone. She walked casually over to one of the shops and bought a *House Beautiful* magazine. She might as well think about how to decorate her future home. Yet she didn't really want to read about "Five Big Paint Color Trends" or "Thanksgiving Table Setting Ideas." She kept checking her ticket for the time of her flight, and peering at the board above the check-in counter to make sure she had the right gate.

Once she boarded, Rasika grew increasingly relaxed the farther she got from Ohio. At first she kept busy looking through the airplane catalog of expensive items that the well-heeled passenger might want: a robotic vacuum cleaner, a restaurant-quality frozen margarita maker. She considered whether she might want to order a pair of golf-ball-finding glasses for her father. The catalog slid off her lap and under the seat in front of her. She didn't want any of it. She just wanted to rest. She pushed her seat back and closed her eyes and slept.

Abhay met her at the airport that evening. He almost couldn't believe she was really here, that she was close enough to touch. He was always surprised when he saw Rasika anew. She was never the static beauty he pictured. He had remembered her as fragile and glassy. Today she looked sweet and pliable, like a child who'd just woken up from a nap. Her hair was a bit tangled, and the side of her face was imprinted with the woven pattern of the seat where she must have pressed her cheek. He held out his hands to her, and she placed her tapered fingers in his.

"Your hands are so cold!" He wanted to pull her close to him right away but didn't think she'd appreciate that in public.

"It was freezing on that plane." Rasika pulled her hands away. "You look tired. Washed-out. Maybe you've been working too hard."

He ignored this remark. After they collected her suitcase she asked, "Should we take a cab? I assume you don't have a car."

"We'll take the train." He pulled her suitcase behind him out the baggage claim doors.

On the MAX platform, a train was waiting. "This is so convenient!" She sank into one of the molded plastic seats and closed her eyes. Her long black lashes lay in delicate fans on her cheeks. Abhay smiled at her beauty. He was elated that she'd agreed to come see him. She had told him over the phone that she was going to India in December to get married, and she insisted that she was just coming out to visit him as a friend. Yet she must love him, just as he loved her. How could he make her see this? He put a hand over the cold fingers on her lap.

When the train pulled out, Rasika opened her eyes and looked out the large picture windows with interest. She curled her fingers around his. "How can they do this?" she asked. "How can the train be on the road?"

"It can go wherever they put down tracks." He was again surprised and moved by her almost childlike curiosity and naïveté.

The next thing she observed was, "Portland is just like Ohio, except the trees haven't lost their leaves yet."

He was irritated at this statement, although he realized she was right in a way. They were passing the usual warehouses, parking garages, office buildings, and billboards. The scenery from every freeway in America probably looked just like this one.

"It'll get better," he reassured her.

As they approached the Steel Bridge across the Willamette River, she clutched Abhay's arm. "Oh my god."

"What?"

"I hope we're not going over that big black thing."

"You don't like bridges?"

"It looks like a huge roller coaster."

He laughed. "It's a drawbridge. It opens up to let boats through. That's why it has those tall sections."

Once in the city, Rasika said, "This is a really big city. I didn't realize the buildings would be so tall." She ducked her head and peered up through the window.

"It isn't that big, actually. It's nothing like New York City or Boston. You'll see, when we get out."

"I've never been to New York City or Boston."

"Really? Your parents never took you there?" Abhay's parents made it a point to take him and Seema to all the important tourist destinations in the United States. His father believed in the educational value of travel.

"My father doesn't like driving in a big city. It makes him nervous. He won't even drive into downtown Cleveland. The airport is as far as he'll go."

"Where did you go on vacation, then?"

"Mostly to India. Almost every summer my parents took us to Bangalore. Other times we'd drive down to North Carolina to visit my mom's sister."

"I guess your dad doesn't drive in India? That would make him even more nervous."

"My uncles drive. One of my uncles usually has a driver, from his job. Or we take a taxi or autorickshaw."

When they arrived in front of Rasika's hotel, she looked dismayed. "Is it safe to stay here?"

"This is a neat hotel. It's a hundred-year-old converted apartment building."

"There's a parking garage across the street. And what's that building? The one with the sign."

Abhay shrugged at the windowless wall of a building with a

huge painted sign advertising Oriental rugs. "You said you wanted something inexpensive," he reminded her.

"I didn't want to be extravagant with money, but this place is so old and shabby!"

"I didn't want you to stay way out in the suburbs," Abhay said, "since I don't have a car. This is a nice place. The bookstore where I work is just around the corner, and it's on the streetcar line."

He dragged her suitcase in, and they got her settled in her room, which was clean and basic; nothing opulent like the hotel she'd taken him to in Cleveland.

"You can see Powell's from here," he said, standing at the window. "Come on, I'll show you."

Rasika collapsed on the bed in a fetal position and closed her eyes.

"You're not tired, are you?" Abhay asked. "I'm taking you to a really nice restaurant for dinner. You'll like it. Don't sleep now."

She sat up. "I need to call my parents."

He looked out the window while she talked to her mother in Tamil, in that same high-pitched voice he remembered from the last time they were in a hotel room together.

"Everything OK?" he asked when she turned off her phone and threw it back into her purse.

"They think I'm in Los Angeles with my friend Jill. I had to make up some stuff about how nice the weather is."

"What're you going to do when your parents find out the truth about you?"

"They'll never find out." She stood up and pulled her fingers through her mussed hair. "After I get married, everything'll be fine."

"You're really going to go through with this marriage? To the guy in India?"

"Of course."

"But you're here now. With me."

"I just wanted a break from all the stress at home." She picked up her purse and walked into the bathroom. When she came out, her hair was smooth and her face newly painted. "OK. Let's go."

They ate at a stylish Vietnamese place, decorated in black and white, with huge cylindrical glass vases of bamboo and orchids strewn about. They ordered mango daiquiris. Rasika giggled as she wrapped one of the tiny fried spring rolls in a lettuce leaf, along with a sprig of mint and some pickled daikon. "I've never had Vietnamese food before."

"Do your parents mind that you eat meat and drink alcohol?" Abhay asked.

"They don't know." Rasika dipped her roll into the bowl of soy-vinegar.

"So they'd mind?"

"I think so. My dad more than my mom."

Abhay's parents didn't exactly approve of his meat eating and alcohol drinking, but those were minor issues compared to his total lack of a lucrative profession. "You have to hide a lot from your parents. Doesn't that bother you?" He bit into the hot, crunchy spring roll.

"I don't want to make them unhappy."

"They're happy with someone who doesn't exist. You are not the person they think you are."

She held her hand up to her full mouth and rolled her eyes at him.

Then he thought of something. "Hey. I never asked how you're doing after Kanchan—you know—what you told me at Ledges." Abhay couldn't even get the words out.

"I don't have any post-traumatic stress, if that's what you're asking. Mostly I'm angry that he ruined the Renaissance Hotel for me. I can never go there again."

Abhay nodded. "I'm really sorry."

"I'm fine. I really am. I'm just going on with my life."

He wasn't sure if this was true. Her face, when she insisted she was fine, had become pinched and sad. Yet she obviously didn't want to talk about it anymore, so he let it pass.

When they got back to her hotel room, Rasika stopped with a halt just inside the door. "I've never slept in a hotel all by myself."

"I can stay."

"No. I'll be OK." She threw her purse on the bed, pulled the curtains closed, and opened her suitcase. He sat on the edge of the bed, hands clasped between his legs, assuming she just needed a few moments to invite him to stay. She lifted her pajamas from the suitcase and said, "You need to leave. I'll see you tomorrow." She planted her feet firmly on the carpet and pointed at the door.

As soon as he stepped out, she closed the door, and he heard the metallic swish of the chain-latch slide into place. Then he heard a thump, and the door rattled in its frame—as though she'd dropped to the floor and slammed her back against the door.

The next morning, Abhay walked in the misty air to Rasika's hotel. She met him in the lobby, near the reception desk. She was sitting on the edge of a chair, dressed neatly in jeans, a pink sweater, and a gray jacket. She wore no makeup as far as he could tell, and her hair was in a ponytail. Even though her clothing was casual, it was so crisp and new that she looked dressed up.

"Very cute," he said, looking at her pink sneakers. "I thought we could go somewhere and talk."

"Why?" She stood up, and in her flat shoes she was only a few inches taller than he.

"I want to know more about what you're thinking, why you're here. Have you had breakfast? We can go to a coffee place if you want."

She hung her purse, a gray pouch kind of thing, over a shoulder. "I told you, I just came out here to have some fun." She spoke softly and stepped away from the reception desk.

He stayed put and declared, "Most people don't run off to see other men right before they're about to get married."

"Come on." She headed toward the outside door. "Let's not make a scene. I've already had breakfast. Let's just go see something."

At the streetcar stop in front of the building, Abhay tried again. "You're really serious about marrying this guy?"

Rasika slipped sunglasses over her eyes. "I haven't met him in person, yet. We've talked over the phone. I think I'll like him." She turned away from him so her shoulder and purse were between herself and him.

"Yeah. You're so excited about marrying him that you flew all the way across the country to see scruffy old me."

She ran her black lenses over him from head to toe. He wore a pair of faded jeans and an old green fleece jacket. "You don't have to be scruffy if you don't want to."

"That's not the issue. Why are you here?"

A middle-aged, square-shaped woman holding a large tan shopping bag stopped right in front of them to look at the streetcar schedule.

"You invited me," Rasika hissed. "Why did you invite me?"

"I invited you because I love you."

"Oh, please." She turned her back to him again.

The streetcar pulled up with a faint squeak of its wheels against the track, and he decided to give up figuring her out for the time being. "Let's go to the library," he suggested as they hung on to the streetcar straps and swayed down the street. "I want you to meet someone." Justin Time spent hours at the public library, finding and photocopying new materials to bring to Abhay.

On the sidewalk in front of the library, they gazed at the grand building. "I love the fact that this building, which is free and open to the public, is more imposing than the Portland Art Museum," he told her.

She followed his gaze to the beautiful tall arched windows, the broad steps from the street to three arched doorways, the bronze lamps on either side of the stairs. They climbed the steps and entered the lobby, with rows of pink marble pillars and a black grand stairway ahead of them.

"It looks like a ballroom, or something." She pulled off her glasses and tucked them into her purse.

"Yeah and it's for all of us. Take a look at these stairs." He led her to the black staircase, heavily embossed with garden imagery. "You can see shapes hidden in the design. Here's a bird. There's a crocodile, I think."

"It's like finding the hidden pictures in one of those children's magazines." They clambered around the staircase. She was giggling with pleasure, putting her hands down to feel the shapes.

On the second and third floors, she admired the rose-patterned carpet. There were more pillars, beautiful light fixtures, heavy wooden doorways leading to rooms with rows of bookshelves, and tables of people reading or using computers. "I don't think I've been in a library since I was in college," she said.

"Where do you get your books?" Abhay asked.

"I buy magazines. Sometimes I borrow a book from Jill or a friend at work, but I can't even remember the last book I read."

Justin Time generally occupied a far table on the third floor. As Abhay led the way, he could see Justin's bald head bent over a pile of papers.

"Justin," he whispered, and the man startled.

At that moment, Abhay saw Justin as Rasika was likely seeing him: a humorless middle-aged man in rumpled clothes. He felt embarrassed to be introducing this glowing woman to this lifeless man. But Justin was waiting expectantly, so Abhay finished the introductions. Rasika held out a clean, elegant hand, and Justin grasped it in his ink-stained one. Abhay said a few sentences to Rasika about the important goals of the organization. Justin seemed impatient to get back to his research, so they left him and walked out of the library.

Outside, they sat on a stone bench. "That guy gave me the creeps," Rasika said.

"He's a little eccentric."

"He's like a zombie or something. There's nothing there. What is it you guys are trying to do?"

Abhay explained HOPE again to Rasika. Her eyes grew larger, and she burst into laughter. "You've got to be kidding. That's the most ridiculous thing I've ever heard."

"Do you know that the world's population will top nine billion by 2050? That's about eight billion more people than can live a comfortable, enjoyable life on this planet. And do you realize that each person born in America will produce millions of pounds of trash, and lead to the consumption of thousands of barrels of oil?"

"Do you really think you can get everyone on the planet to stop having children?" She shook her finger at him, and he realized she was imitating his gesture to her. In fact, his hand was still up in the air, ready to make his next point.

He put his hand down. "That's a goal." He tried to make his voice less strident. "You have to have a goal, so you know what you're aiming for."

"It's not a goal. It's a delusion."

She looked so funny, with her eyes wide open and her eyebrows raised, that he had to laugh. "He is kind of a strange guy, I admit. And the organization is unusual. I'm just doing this for a while, until I figure out what I really want to do."

"Are you getting closer?"

"Maybe. I'm realizing at least that I like the research I'm doing for Justin. I love libraries, and I love books. I miss being in school."

"You could become a professor. Then you could be in school all the time."

"I think what I really want is to be a perpetual student!" He laughed.

"Sometimes I wish I could permanently be eleven years old," she said.

"Why? What's so great about eleven?"

"I wasn't conflicted then. I wanted the same things for myself that my parents wanted for me. I made cookies. I was a Girl Scout. I collected Beanie Babies. Boys had cooties, and I stayed away from them."

"I thought you still wanted the same things your parents want."

"I do. But—it's just different now."

"Rasika, if you'd just admit that you don't want the same things as your parents—"

"Abhay, if you'd just admit that you're refusing to grow up—" She held up both hands, palms parallel, as though handing him a large box of her thoughts.

He realized she was imitating his gesture again. He dropped his hands. "I guess we should stop trying to fix each other."

"Good idea."

A woman with a wrinkled face and gray hair walked a bike slowly past them. Blue sky and sun peeked out from among the clouds. The misty air of the morning was gone.

"Everyone seems so casual," Rasika said. "I guess it's casual Friday?"

"People in Portland are always like this. No one dresses up."

Two men in dress shirts and ties approached. As they passed by, one of them revealed a backpack, and the other sported a ponytail.

"What should we do now?" Abhay asked.

"Let's have some fun! Isn't that why you moved all the way out here? Because you thought it would be more fun?"

"I moved out here to find meaningful work in a community that cares about the fate of the planet."

"That sounds so serious."

"Well, what do you want to do, then?"

"I love water." Rasika sighed. "I just want to see something flowing."

They took a bus down to the riverfront and rented bikes. "The city tore down a freeway in order to reclaim this green space," he explained to Rasika as they stood on the lawn next to the bike path. "On the other side there's even a floating path to ride on." He had to shout when talking to her, because although the city had torn down one freeway, there was another one on the other side of the river, roaring with traffic.

"Look at the bridges." He pointed to the series of arches spanning the river. "They're so massive, and all so different. Like giant sculptures." One bridge was made up of a series of green arched trusses above the roadway, and another had gray trusses underneath. "They're so big, so industrial. I mean, I prefer nature, but this is amazing. I sometimes wonder what this river was like when Lewis and Clark arrived. It's hard to even imagine what it looked like then."

Rasika dangled her purse on a handlebar, and they rode along the path by the Willamette River. "I haven't been on a bike since I was a kid!" she shouted, wobbling her way down the asphalt. As they approached the black trusses of one of the bridges, Rasika stopped and straddled her bike. "I'm supposed to ride on that thing?"

"The bike path is lower down, so we won't be up there with the traffic. But if you're afraid, we can just keep riding on this side of the river."

She boosted herself onto her seat again. "I'm here for adventure, so let's do it. But you go first."

On the other side, Abhay stopped and looked back at her. "You OK?"

She smiled breathlessly. "Good thing I'm not afraid of heights."

"I thought it was kind of scary, too, the first time I did it."

They rode on. The path widened into a small plaza with benches. They parked their bikes and stood next to the handrail. Rasika gazed down at the steel-blue water rippling past, while Abhay gazed at Rasika. She had gathered the end of her ponytail into one fist to keep it from blowing in the breeze. Her sunglasses were perched on top of her head, and her eyelashes dipped over her eyes as she glanced from the water below to the shoreline across the river. Behind her head a faint glow appeared and brightened.

"What are you thinking about?" he asked softly.

"Nothing."

"No, really."

She took a deep breath and let out a long, slow exhalation. "I really wasn't thinking about anything. Or—I guess I was just enjoying the idea of flowing, like the river. Just going, and not caring. You're so lucky, Abhay, to be living out here, away from everyone. You can do anything you want."

"You can live out here and do anything you want, too."

She leaned her back against the handrail. "No. It's different for me. Indian parents expect more obedience from their daughters." She settled her glasses over her eyes again.

"Seema has a boyfriend," he said.

Rasika's forehead dented.

"My sister," Abhay repeated. "Remember?"

"I know who Seema is." She removed her ponytail band and shook out her hair.

"She isn't letting my parents stop her from living her own life." Rasika shrugged. "Seema is very different from me."

"That's true," Abhay said. Gulls swooped overhead, screeching to one another. A crowd of children swarmed onto the plaza, clambering on the benches, crowding against the railing. A few adults strolled after them. Rasika scooted closer to Abhay along the railing. "Do you come out here a lot?" she asked.

"Not since I first moved out here. I've been really busy."

"With what?"

"Work. I'm scheduled for thirty hours a week at the bookstore, and I put in thirty hours with Justin."

"Why? Is it that expensive to live here that you need to work all the time?"

"I don't have much else to do, so I figured I might as well earn money. I've got a lot saved up now, and it feels good. I have more money in the bank than I've ever had before. I don't even know what to do with it."

"Abhay." She lifted her glasses and looked at him reproachfully. "You're being silly. You've got this amazing city to play in, and all you do is hole up with books and papers. Is that why you moved out here? To slog away in a bookstore, and to organize papers for a creepy man who smells funny?"

"I moved out here partly to get away from you. I figured if I worked hard enough, I'd forget; I'd be able to move on. But, it's not working."

"You shouldn't have invited me, then."

"Are you sorry you're here?"

"I don't want to think about that." She twisted several strands of hair tightly around her fingers.

He untangled her fingers and kissed her fingertips. "What do you want to do now?"

She was motionless for a few moments. A gull sailed down and landed on the ground near her. She shook his hand away and re-gathered her hair into a ponytail. "Let's get lunch."

12

They ended up at a casual Pan-Asian place not too far from his neighborhood. He still couldn't figure out his bearings with her. During lunch she asked him all sorts of questions about his life in Portland and his friends in town. He carefully avoided mentioning Kianga and Ellen. He wasn't sure how Rasika would react to the idea that he had women friends.

When they exited the café, he had an inspiration. "I'm going to show you some beautiful old houses in this neighborhood."

She had her arms wrapped around herself as she walked. They turned up a side street and stopped outside the iron fence of a large powder-green house amid the apartment buildings and cafés. Two columns of bay windows went up all three floors of the house on either side of the wide stairs leading up to the pillared porch and double doors. An intricate wrought iron fence bordered the yard.

"Take a look at how far back this house goes." Abhay stepped along the sidewalk until he could see the side of the house. "It looks like they have a greenhouse back here." He pointed to a glassed-in porch at the back of the house, with large houseplant leaves against the windows. "Maybe they have a separate library room downstairs.

And maybe there's an artist's studio on the top floor. Wouldn't you like to live in a house like this?"

Rasika lifted her sunglasses to the top of her head. "I never thought about living in an old house, although it's very pretty."

"I like the plaster decorations between the bay windows," he said. "And the flower baskets hanging from the porch roof."

She stood with her hands pulled into the sleeves of her jacket. "It's right up against everything else. There's a print shop on the other side, it looks like."

"That's what's great about it. You have this wonderful house, and you can step out your door and go out to eat or see a movie, without even having to get in a car. There are a bunch of big houses around this neighborhood. I like to walk around and look for them."

"I'd want to live away from everyone."

"Like on some kind of English manor? That's what the new expensive housing developments are trying to imitate, with their huge lawns and the houses set so far back. They want everyone to feel like they're on their own private little estate. What would you do, away from everyone?"

"I'd invite people over, I guess."

Abhay laughed. "You'd live far away from everyone so you could invite them over and have them admire your secluded mansion?"

She rolled her eyes at him.

He took a step closer to her and put an arm around her waist. "What would it be like if the two of us lived in this house? If we were married?"

She nudged him away. "I can't marry you, Abhay."

"Why not?"

"Because you're not the kind of man I want. You're too young, for one thing."

"I'm only a year younger than you."

"Well, you act like a boy. If I were as smart as you, I'd go back to school and get a degree so I could have a really great job. It's not just about making a lot of money. You could get a job where you'd be someone in the world, and make an impact. I don't understand why you're letting yourself work at these menial jobs. It's like— you're not grown-up, Abhay. You're still playing around."

"When I was a kid, my mom would give me my allowance and then take me over to the discount store, but I could never choose anything until Mom threatened to leave. And then I'd always feel sad in the car, with my toy, because I couldn't have all the other toys, too." He laughed at this memory.

"You're still being like that. Except your mom's not here to threaten you, so you haven't chosen anything yet. If you don't pick something, you'll never get anywhere. That's why I'm going to get married. I know I can't have every man in the world. I can only have one."

"So if I pick a good career, then you'd marry me?"

"Why do you keep talking about marrying me?"

"I love you. You love me. It makes sense."

"I don't love you."

"Rasika, you came all the way out here to see me. You've never traveled anywhere alone before."

"I just needed a break from my life."

"Then why did you choose to come out here? You could have gone anywhere." He unwrapped one of her arms and placed her hand against his heart. "If you want to get away from your life, why don't you stay here for a while? Portland's full of interesting things to do. Maybe you'd like to get involved with watercolor painting, or beading, or self-defense. We have movies, music, lectures. You can take all sorts of exercise classes. You can learn Japanese flower-arranging, and how to read tarot cards. You can even go shopping every day, if that's what turns you on. And then we can decide later about our future. I know your freedom is really important to you.

Just let yourself be free for once." He slipped his fingers into her coat sleeve and stroked her wrist and forearm.

"I've got enough freedom as it is."

"You've spent your life trying to fit into an impossible situation, being Indian in America. Just come out here, and figure out what you really want."

"You sound like my friend Jill. She wants us to run away to some tropical island together. But my parents would never leave me alone."

"You have to train them to leave you alone. Don't answer their phone calls for a while. They'll get the idea."

She pulled her hand away. "I can't. They'd be on my case all the time if I were single and living on my own. And I could never marry you. My father—"

"He'll get over it."

"No." She stamped her foot like a child. "Let me finish. You're from a different caste. My father is very proud to be a Brahmin, and he says he could never accept it if I married someone who isn't." She looked down.

"You don't agree with your father?"

She shook her head. "I don't know what caste you are, and I don't care."

"I personally don't think of myself as belonging to any caste." He spoke gently, hoping to soothe her. "My parents consider themselves Vaishyas, the traditional caste of business and trade. It's the caste Mahatma Gandhi belonged to, and that's pretty much all I know. Anyway, even in India, things are changing. Lots of people are marrying outside of their caste. One of my uncles married someone from college who was of a completely different caste, and everyone's been fine with it."

"Not in my family. Things are different for me. That's why I've decided to go ahead and get married the way they want me to." Rasika's hands were inside her jacket sleeves again.

Abhay put his hands in his pockets and leaned back against the wrought iron fence. Down the street, a hairy man in athletic shorts and hiking boots clumped closer and closer. Rasika stared at the man as he tramped past.

"This is why I can't stay in Portland." She jabbed a finger at the man's receding back. "I'd forget how to dress and wind up in faded jeans and hiking boots all the time."

He smiled. "Come on. I'll show you the bookstore where I work, and then we'll get some bubble tea. I bet you've never had that before."

"I'm so tired." Rasika sank onto one of the rows of brick steps surrounding the open, empty oval space. She felt a pleasant ache all over her body. She was content to sit and rest. "We must have gone all over this city in one day. What is this place, anyway?"

"It's just a community space." Abhay sat on the step beside her. "There's the courthouse on that side." He pointed to a large gray building across the way, with two wings and what looked like a little bell tower in the middle of the roof. "They have different events and fairs here."

Right now the place was almost deserted. Dusk gathered around them. A few people sat on the steps across the courtyard, reading or just sitting in the fading light. To her left down below was a small circular pond with a bridge across it leading to a set of glass doors. "Is that the entrance to a store?" Rasika asked.

"That's the TriMet office," Abhay said. "You can get public transportation passes and maps there. Stuff like that."

She looked away from the promising glass doors, which now held nothing of interest.

"You look like a picture," Abhay said. "Or a statue. You're so still."

She sat with her elbow on a knee, hand supporting her chin. He slid closer to her on the step and put an arm around her. She leaned against him. She felt empty and light, as though the weight of her life had dropped away.

Nearby, at the bottom of the steps, a bearded man lifted a violin out of its case. He tucked it under his chin, closed his eyes, put the bow to the strings, and drew out a melody that sounded melancholy and happy at the same time.

Abhay stood up and held out a hand to Rasika. "Let's dance."

"Not right now." She stayed put on the step. "There's no one else dancing. People will look at us."

"So what? Come on. No one knows us here." He pulled her up, and they descended to the vast brick-floored space. He put a hand at her waist and took her right hand in his left. Rasika tried to make her pink sneakers follow his sandals, but they kept stumbling over each other. She giggled quietly and glanced over at the violin player, who still had his eyes closed.

"I think it's an Eastern European tune," Abhay said. He put his arms all the way around her, and they managed to sway together, hugging and standing in one place.

Rasika closed her eyes and relaxed against Abhay. He was surprisingly sturdy, despite his short stature. The violin music seemed to penetrate her, the strings vibrating inside of her. She was hollow, as though she were a reed instrument being played by someone else. She could allow herself to float along in Abhay's arms.

After the song ended on a long, high note, the violin player immediately launched into a fast, bouncy tune. Abhay stepped back and looked at her, and then leaned forward and kissed her. She didn't resist.

Abhay dug in his pocket for a few dollars, tossed them into the violin case, and led Rasika by the hand up the stairs. They walked silently back to her hotel with their arms around each other. At one point, her phone rang.

"You gonna get that?" Abhay asked.

"I'll just let it go to voice mail."

The melody stopped, then started again. She slipped her hand into her purse and turned the phone off by feel. She was so far away from anyone who might be calling her that she didn't even care. She wasn't even aware of where they were going. She just floated along. Up in her room, when Abhay pressed her close to him and kissed her, she allowed everything. It all seemed fine and right and perfect.

The next morning, when she opened her eyes, she saw Abhay sitting in an armchair, hunched over a folded-up section of newspaper.

"You're up already?"

"I've been awake for a while. I took a shower and went downstairs to buy a newspaper."

She stretched under the covers and closed her eyes, allowing herself to drift in pleasant relaxation. It was funny to be out here with Abhay. She was supposed to be in Los Angeles. Well, really, she was supposed to be at home, preparing for her wedding. The thought made her giggle.

"What're you laughing about?"

She wriggled herself upright on the bed, holding the sheet over her front. "It's just strange. I'm not supposed to be here."

He flung aside his newspaper and crawled onto the bed. "Sure you are." He slid a hand under the sheet. "This is exactly where you're supposed to be, because you made the decision to come here. You're in charge of your own destiny."

"You're freezing." She gasped, yet didn't push him away. She shivered and giggled as his cold hands stroked her. She helped him shed his clothes. Soon she grew warm in the tangle of sheets. There was nothing in the world except her and Abhay, moving together in the pale morning sunlight. They dozed again, and when she woke up, the sun was bright and high, streaming into the room.

Once they were dressed and outside on the sidewalk, Abhay asked, "What should we do today?"

She squinted in the bright light as they stepped onto the sidewalk. She thought about putting on her sunglasses but decided not to bother. She felt so light, as if she could drift along like a leaf without caring where she went.

He took her out to a fancy brunch at a nearby hotel. They filled their heavy china plates at a long, gleaming bar stocked with marinated asparagus, herbed potatoes, mini-omelets, scones, and a fruit salad with glistening berries, orange sections, and melon slices. They sat at a table covered with a thick white cloth and ate looking out the window at a patio and garden.

Rasika enjoyed the taste of everything. She felt empty of worries, and full of—something. Happiness? No, not exactly. Just full of being here with Abhay. He was so funny. It was adorable how he had tried to dance with her the evening before. But *her* husband had to be sophisticated, accomplished, important, and both older and taller than she. Abhay was none of these things.

They split the bill and stepped out to the sidewalk. "Let's go to the Japanese garden," Abhay suggested. He took her hand and they walked, swinging arms, to the MAX station.

"This garden is one of my favorite places in Portland," he said as he paid for both of them. They passed along the stone-slab path among the trees to the pavilion. "Sometimes they hold receptions here," Abhay said. They stood on the wooden porch and leaned over the railing to look at the Zen garden of gravel raked into a complicated pattern of circles and swirls.

"I wonder how long it took them to do this," Abhay said.

They walked around to the other side of the pavilion, where the ground sloped down and away. From this height they had a view of downtown Portland, and past the linear forms of the buildings in the distance, against the pale blue sky, floated the pale gray form of Mount Hood. "I love seeing this scene from the city," Abhay said. "It looks like the mountain's nearby when actually it's about fifty miles away."

Rasika took in a deep breath and let it out slowly. The mountain was like a vision from heaven.

They continued along the paths, not looking at the few other visitors who walked past them. The garden was cool, green, tranquil, balanced. When they got to an arched bridge over a pond, Abhay said, "How about I take a picture of you? I can stand over there." He pointed across the pond.

She turned in alarm. "Did you bring a camera?"

He shook his head. "No, I figured you had one, though."

"I don't want to have any record of this trip."

He left her on the bridge and walked along the path until he was on the opposite side of the water. She saw him standing there, observing her. After a few moments, he motioned for her to join him, and she walked off the bridge and down the path toward him.

He picked up her hand and kissed the palm. "You were framed by this weeping willow, and you looked like a flower yourself, in your yellow sweater."

They wandered under the trees, among the ferns. The path took them over a little creek. They stepped over and around the flowing water, balancing on the flat stones. Rasika squatted down and dabbled her fingers in the trickle. She wanted to stay here forever. They descended to a little hut enclosure with a bench, in a quiet, dark corner of the garden. They sat. No one else was within view. They looked out at the gray slender tree trunks among the layers of leaves in front of them, the light green of the maples, the darker pines beyond. Birds twittered and chirped. Water trickled over rocks somewhere nearby. From a distance came the dull roar of traffic.

She closed her eyes. "I wish it could always be like this." She took a deep breath.

"It can." He slid closer to her on the bench, and put his arm around her shoulders.

She opened her eyes. The sun peeked around the rim of the roof above them. Tomorrow at this time she'd be on a plane home. She needed to put herself back together, get herself into shape for her upcoming wedding. Since last night she had forgotten her goals. It was as if she'd forgotten to get dressed, and she hadn't even cared. She needed to clothe herself again. She pushed Abhay away. "It wouldn't be like this even if I lived here. I'd be stressed-out and my parents would be angry and I'd never be able to relax. Right now, no one knows I'm here. I'm hidden."

They heard voices, and another couple emerged from the path. Abhay stood up. Rasika didn't want to move, but she knew the other couple would want a moment of privacy. She pushed herself up, and her body felt heavy as she followed Abhay along the narrow path ahead.

They were back in the central area, near the little gift shop, which Rasika entered. Abhay followed and stood with his hands in his jacket pockets. After a few moments, he pushed open the door. "I'll just be sitting on that bench. Take your time."

Rasika picked up tea cups and pots, packets of origami paper, cherry blossom bath beads, enameled butterfly earrings, silk scarves, carp kites. She wanted to buy something to represent her tranquil time in this garden with Abhay. Finally, she settled on just one thing, which she paid for with two quarters. Its simplicity would remind her. She held it in her hand and walked out to where Abhay was sitting on the bench.

He rose. "You get anything?"

She opened her fingers and displayed a smooth black pebble on her palm. "They have these rocks all around the trees," she explained. "I like them."

He picked it up and rubbed it. "What'll you do with just one?"

"When I look at it, I'll think of Portland." She took the pebble back.

"Why can't you stay?" he asked gently. "If you like it so much."

Her throat felt tight, but she refused to cry in public. It was too messy, too inelegant. She swallowed down her tears, blinked her eyes, and was able to look at him steadily. "I don't know anyone here," she said.

"You know me."

She opened her mouth to respond, and then shut it. Instead she shook her head. "I can't stay here because—" She couldn't think of a reason. She stepped closer to Abhay, he opened his arms, and she leaned against him and gave way to her sobbing. She was still clutching her stone in one palm. She felt as if all the water of Portland—the river, the little creek here in the Japanese Garden—were all flowing through her, and she allowed herself to be swept along. She felt Abhay working, slowly, on untangling the strands of her hair. She heard footsteps coming through the entrance gate, and voices. It was all background noise, like the breeze through the branches.

Rasika managed to control her sobbing, and stepped away from Abhay's embrace to find a tissue in her purse. She knew she looked terrible: wet face, mussed hair. At least she hadn't put on any makeup this morning. As she was mopping her face, she was aware that some people had stopped to say hello to Abhay. She didn't feel like being introduced to anyone, so she continued to pretend to rummage through her bag.

"Rasika," Abhay called.

She ran her fingers through her hair and turned around. Standing next to Abhay were two pretty young women: one had long reddish hair, and the other, short brown hair. They were smiling at her with interest. She felt a jolt of jealousy. Abhay stepped over to Rasika, grasped her hand, and pulled her into the little triangle.

"Rasika, I want you to meet my friends, Kianga and Ellen."

She managed, as graciously as possible, to shake hands with both of them. This is what she'd turn into if she stayed in Portland. She'd wear baggy, old clothes and wouldn't bother with makeup or manicures.

Abhay was talking fast, filling in his friends on how he knew Rasika, and what they'd been doing in Portland.

"You should have told us you were having a friend visit," Kianga said. "We could've had you over."

Rasika said, "You didn't tell me you had women friends in Portland." She realized she was showing a lot of teeth when she smiled, the way her mother did when she was trying to hide negative feelings. "He pretends he works all the time."

Kianga and Ellen both laughed. "He does work a lot," Ellen agreed. "But he comes over pretty often."

"By the way, can you come to my birthday party next Saturday?" Kianga asked Abhay. "I want to ask you about India. I'm leaving right after Thanksgiving."

Rasika was shot through with jealousy. She knew it was completely irrational. Why should she care if two hippies happened to like Abhay, and if he happened to like them? In order to control her feelings, she excused herself, pulled her hand from Abhay's, and walked away toward the gate. She stood sideways, half-looking at Abhay, and half at the driveway and trees outside the gate.

The two girls were saying their good-byes and Abhay was backing away from them, waving. The brown-haired one skipped over to him and pecked him on the cheek.

Rasika whipped her sunglasses out of her purse and shielded

her eyes. She planted herself with her back to Abhay and crossed her arms over her chest. When he joined her, she felt him place a hand on her elbow. She shook him off.

"It's not what you think," he said.

"I don't know what you're talking about." She marched down the driveway.

"I mean—I hope you're not jealous."

"Of course not. Why would I be?"

"It seems like you're angry." He placed a hand on her lower back, and she elbowed him away. "They're just some people I met. Nobody special. That's why I didn't even bother mentioning them."

"I don't know why you think I care." She swept ahead of him down to the bus stop. When the bus arrived, she tucked herself into a corner of the seat and, still with her black lenses on, kept her face toward the window.

They got off the bus in front of a long white building with rows of windows. "Where are we?" she asked.

"I thought you might like to go shopping. This is a mall downtown."

"You hate malls."

"But you like them." He reached for her hand, and she crossed her arms again. "I'm really, really sorry about what just happened."

"You have nothing to apologize for."

Inside the mall, she stopped in the bathroom, combed her hair, and gathered it into a ponytail. Then she wandered from floor to floor, from shop to shop. Thankfully, Abhay had planted himself on a bench on the first floor. On the top floor of the mall, she circumambulated the balcony and felt she was regaining herself. She consciously held herself tall as she walked. She didn't purchase anything but drifted past the store windows, absorbing all the things she might want to buy once she was married.

Suddenly, she remembered her phone. She dug around in her

purse, fished it out, and checked to see who'd called. Oh, god. Her mother, of course. Sixteen times. And Jill, three times. And even Benito. She speed-dialed her mother's cell phone.

"Where have you been?" Amma demanded.

"Amma, I'm sorry. My phone got turned off. I didn't realize it."

"I called Jill. She kept telling me you were taking a shower. How many showers do you need?"

"Sorry, Amma."

"I don't know where you are, or what you are doing. Some man named Benito called the house. He seems very friendly with you. We have been giving you too much freedom to go and come as you please. At least you will be safely married soon. We will not have to control you anymore. That will be your husband's responsibility, and what he will do—"

Rasika held the phone away from her ear for a moment. Then she shouted, "Amma, you're breaking up. I can't hear you."

"Hello? Hello?" her mother shouted, very clearly.

"Amma, I can't hear you. I'll hang up now." She pushed the "off" button and shoved the phone into her purse. She leaned back against the balcony railing and covered her face with her hands. She just wanted to disappear. Why did she think she could run away from her life? Her parents could always track her down. And why had she even bothered to visit Abhay? She didn't want a life like Abhay's. She didn't care about him. Her jealousy of those two girls had jolted her back to reality. She had to go through with what she had planned. She had to make the whole thing work, because there was no real alternative, after all.

Outside the mall, as Abhay walked Rasika back to her hotel, he tried to reason with her. "It's not like you think."

"Abhay, it doesn't matter."

He persisted, "You don't know what they're like. They have all sorts of people living at their house, and I don't even know who's sleeping with who. It's kind of strange."

"I thought you liked that kind of thing—everyone living together and all that."

"I don't like sleeping around."

"How do you know about the situation at their house? You must have participated."

Abhay ran a finger over his upper lip. How was he going to get out of this? "We're just friends. I mean—Kianga and I—we got together once, but she has a lot of other boyfriends."

"I don't want to know." She covered her ears. "It's none of my business."

A saxophonist had set up on the street corner, with his case open in front of him. He was playing a bouncy rendition of "Good Morning, Heartache."

Outside her hotel he said, "I'll come by tomorrow to ride out to the airport with you."

"Don't bother."

"I want to."

She pulled open the glass door so hard it flew out of her hand. She rushed through without saying good-bye.

Early the next morning, Abhay hurried to her hotel. He saw as he strode down the hall to her room that the door was open. Inside, a uniformed maid was stripping the bed. He went down to the front desk and found that Rasika had checked out half an hour before.

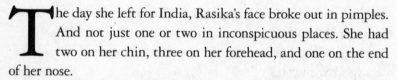

The day she left for India, Rasika's face broke out in pimples. And not just one or two in inconspicuous places. She had two on her chin, three on her forehead, and one on the end of her nose.

Ever since her trip to Portland a month ago, Rasika had been on her best behavior at home. She hadn't contacted Abhay at all, even though he'd e-mailed and called her several times. She'd come home right after work, had kept to a rigid schedule in terms of exercising, and had limited her caffeine intake. Just yesterday she'd gotten a manicure and pedicure, and had her arms and legs waxed. Why pimples? And why now?

Her mother was in such a rush that she didn't notice them until they were on the plane to New York. "Since high school, you haven't had pimples like this!" she said. "Don't you have any cream?"

Rasika shook her head. When they got to the New York airport, her mother's mission was to find some acne cream. She commanded Pramod to scour one corridor while she frantically inquired at stores along another corridor. No one carried any kind of acne cream. So her mother could do nothing but inspect Rasika's face at frequent intervals. "Couldn't you have waited until after the wedding?" As if Rasika had broken out on purpose.

They arrived in India after midnight, and after a short nap, Rasika woke up. She was sharing the bedroom with her cousin Mayuri, who worked nights at a call center.

Rasika sat up in bed. She knew her mother wanted her to have a good, long nap so she'd be fresh when Yuvan and his parents arrived that evening, but Rasika was wide awake. Her senses were alert and her heart was pounding, as though she were facing a grave danger. She put her hand over her heart to try to steady it, closed her eyes, and attempted to breathe calmness into herself.

In the evening, Rasika bathed and changed into a heavy silk sari in her mother's family home. Only after she was dressed did she realize how ugly the sari was: wide stripes of black, olive green, and maroon, with a gold border. "Mridula Auntie has given you this sari," Amma said. Mridula Auntie was Rasika's aunt—her mother's younger sister—and also she was Yuvan's aunt. She was the one who had originally sent Yuvan's information to them.

Mridula Auntie smeared Rasika's face with foundation cream, and patted on some powder, which was the wrong shade—far too light.

Rasika's grandmother, who was still tall and graceful, appeared in the doorway. "Ayyo, why are you putting so much on? You are hiding a beautiful face."

"She has pimples." Mridula Auntie kept working.

"The sari is not good," Pati said. "She needs something delicate—not dark like that."

"This is the latest style, Amma." Mridula Auntie stepped back to examine Rasika, and adjusted the palloo of the sari over her blouse.

Rasika submitted to everything. She didn't really care what she looked like.

When Yuvan and his parents arrived, Rasika was seated in the corner of the living room with the palloo of her sari wrapped demurely around her shoulders. She had always loved this elegant space of her mother's family home. Because there were no brothers in the family, Mridula Auntie and her husband stayed here with Rasika's grandparents. Mridula Auntie liked to look through magazines for decorating ideas. One wall of the long room was made up of glass doors, which could be opened to the courtyard to create extra entertaining space. The lightbulbs were covered with actual shades—unusual in Indian houses. The furniture was appropriate for a tropical Indian home: thick embroidered cushions placed on solid teak furniture. At that moment, however, Rasika did not much care about the beauty of this room.

She stood up and put her palms together in a namaskar to Yuvan's mother, who had a friendly face. Then she turned to Yuvan's father, and was startled. He was slim, with a thick head of graying hair. He was handsome. In fact, he looked like Kanchan Uncle. Of course, not exactly. His eyes seemed kinder, and he was shorter. Still, her heart began to race, and her throat felt dry. She could barely whisper, "Namaskar."

Yuvan calmly shook her hand and seated himself next to her. He didn't seem to notice her agitation. She took a few deep breaths to calm down. He spoke slowly and softly, in English, just as he had over the phone. His manner was very cultured and cool. He didn't smile. He didn't seem in awe of her beauty. Of course, she wasn't much to look at today with her pimples and face powder and ugly sari. He asked her about the plane ride. "I'm sorry we had to insist on meeting you right away," he said. "It's just that you are here for only a short while."

"It's fine. I understand." She tried to smile. Her face felt stiff and dry.

He clasped his hands on one knee, cleared his throat, and

launched into a description of his career. He wanted to work on artificial intelligence. "The field is broad enough to keep me interested," he said. "Cognitive science comprises not just computer science but also philosophy, linguistics, neurobiology, and other subjects. I tend to get bored of a single subject. And the career possibilities are very good."

Her mother and Yuvan's mother were chatting with animation, and Rasika was shocked to see Yuvan's mother reach out and take Amma's hand. Had things progressed so far? Maybe Yuvan's mother was just naturally affectionate. Her father's face was calm, and his hands were still as he sat next to Yuvan's father. Pramod was talking to Yuvan's brother, whose name she couldn't remember.

Suddenly the electricity went out, and the room was plunged into darkness. "It is because of the road construction," Mridula Auntie said. The elders were all speaking in Tamil.

"They are constructing an underpass for the new airport road," Prabhu Uncle said. "Right on the next street. When I take my morning walk, I go that way and watch."

"Every day, five or six times a day, they cut the current," Pati said.

Mridula Auntie left the room and returned with two bright lanterns, one of which she placed right next to Rasika and Yuvan. Rasika didn't even want to think about how she looked in the glare of the lantern.

"You do not have this problem in the U.S., I think," Yuvan's mother remarked.

"In the U.S., when the electricity goes out we don't even know what to do," Amma said. "We don't even remember where we put our flashlights or candles."

Amma and Mridula Auntie carried a lantern into the kitchen and came back with cups of juice and plates of crunchy murukkus. No one spoke for a long time. It was like eating in the beam of car headlights. Rasika tried to choke down some food. This was not how she'd pictured her first meeting with Mr. Right. She could hear him crunching and sipping next to her. He apparently didn't feel the need to say anything, and she couldn't think of what to say to him.

The next day, Yuvan was scheduled to take her out for lunch. This time she did her own makeup and chose a simple pale yellow tunic, embroidered all over with blue flowers, worn over matching yellow straight-legged pants. Yuvan arrived in an autorickshaw. Again, he was very polite. He made sure to say hello to her parents, and to sit in the living room chatting with the relatives for a few moments. Yet he was distant. He didn't smile at her or look at her.

As they left the house he said, "There's a fairly good restaurant nearby. We'll walk. The traffic is very bad." He didn't seem to care what she would prefer.

Whenever she was out in a Bangalore street, Rasika felt the pollution depositing a layer of grime on her skin. Nevertheless, she had always loved this particular street, with tall trees on either side forming a green canopy. They strolled past the decorative gates of two-story middle-class houses whose courtyards overflowed with bushes and potted plants. The grinding of the machinery from the road construction nearby, combined with the usual traffic noise, made talking difficult.

The restaurant was nothing special—just a brightly lit, noisy neighborhood place. They entered the air-conditioned section and ordered different kinds of chaat, and when Yuvan received his plate of six tiny pooris filled with potatoes, he carefully lifted half of them onto her plate. Rasika normally loved crunchy, spicy chaat, with piquant tamarind and yogurt sauces, but today she didn't have much appetite. She lifted her plate of bhel puri and spooned most of her puffed-rice-and-onion concoction onto his plate.

Yuvan seemed content to eat without speaking. Rasika couldn't think of anything else she wanted to know about him. The table next to them was occupied by a love-struck young couple who stared into each other's eyes. The young woman had a plate of mini pooris, and she was placing them, one by one, into the mouth of her beloved.

Desperate to break the silence, she pointed to the pimples on her chin. "My mother acted like I sprouted these on purpose."

He raised his eyes from his plate. "Yes, I noticed you had a problem with your skin."

For the first time, Rasika began to wonder if Yuvan might actually refuse to marry her, perhaps because she wasn't beautiful enough. Her beauty was always the one thing she could be sure about. "I normally have very good skin," she said.

"While you are in India, you should see an ayurvedic physician. Our mutual cousin, Mayuri, used to have the same trouble."

Mayuri was Mridula Auntie's daughter and Yuvan's cousin.

"Her mother took her to an ayurvedic physician," Yuvan continued, "and he prescribed a diet and some ointment. Her skin is quite clear now."

Rasika felt humiliated to receive beauty advice from a man.

Yuvan seemed unaware of her discomfort. He pushed his plate away, leaned back in his chair, and began discussing American job possibilities. It became clear that, if they got married, they might not be able to remain in northeastern Ohio. He preferred a job that involved a lot of research, either at a university or a corporation, and it really depended on where the openings were. "I know you have a good job already, but I am sure it will be easy for you to find another one. You are in a flourishing field."

By the time the saffron and pistachio ice creams arrived, Rasika felt thoroughly confused. She put her spoon down. Yuvan was socially adept, poised, handsome, and had the potential to make a good living. He didn't talk too much, and he didn't insist that she quit her job. Yet he was not terribly friendly. She hadn't thought friendliness mattered all that much, but could she stand to be married to the perfect man if he didn't love her or even like her very much?

She thought about Abhay, and how much fun they'd had together in Portland. He'd been calling her and sending her e-mails. She'd virtuously deleted all his messages without listening to or reading them. Now she pushed thoughts of him out of her mind. She was just going to have to steel herself and go through with this.

In mid-December, on his first morning in India, Abhay stepped out of the front bedroom of his father's family home, stood under the portrait of his late grandfather hung above the front door, and eased open the metal bolts on the wooden door. He could hear murmuring in Kannada from the kitchen, but didn't understand the language.

"Abhay? Where you are going?" His aunt yelled in English from the kitchen.

"Just for a walk."

His aunt, a small, perpetually cheerful woman, hurried through the living room, holding a stainless steel bowl full of cilantro stems and leaves. "Why so early? Have coffee first."

"I don't drink coffee."

"Don't walk all by yourself. You may get lost. Stay and I will send Mahesh with you."

Mahesh was Abhay's cousin. "Thank you, but I'll be okay. I just want to be alone."

"Later on you must tell us where it is you want to go. Pondicherry, you said?"

"Auroville. It's ten kilometers north of Pondicherry."

"You can take bus from here straight to Pondicherry. Guru Uncle will book for you."

"It's okay. I can do it myself."

"We will do for you." She laughed. "For so many years you have not been here. We will take care of you now. Anyway, it is good you will be gone next week, because we are having the bore well drilled. It will be very noisy."

"Bore well?" he asked. "So you'll have a better water supply?"

"We are selling the house and land!" she said happily. "We will have eight apartments built. One is for us and your granny. Mahesh, when he marries, he will have one. Another will be for your parents when they come to India. The others will be rented out. For that we must have a bore well drilled."

Abhay was stunned. He hadn't realized his own relatives would be participating in the transformation of the neighborhood from single-family homes to apartments. "But it's so cozy with everyone living in the same house!" he blurted out.

"It is cozy for the children, but it is difficult for women to share a kitchen. My daughter-in-law will want her own kitchen."

Abhay was amused that Auntie was speaking of a daughter-in-law as though she already existed.

"We will still all be here in this compound. We are not going anywhere." His aunt bustled away. "Guru!" she called as she entered a bedroom.

Abhay walked out the door, past the motor scooters parked between the house and compound wall, and unlatched the gate. There he turned back and stood, looking at the house. It was a typical Indian house—one story, with a flat roof and plaster walls. If his father hadn't moved to the United States, this is probably where Abhay and Seema would have grown up. His father was the oldest son, who was expected to live in the family home and take care of his parents. But since he didn't stay in India, the second son—Mahesh's father—took on those duties instead.

Abhay felt sick about the idea of tearing down the house and putting up apartments. This was the house where he'd had his first experiences with communal living: three or four generations of relatives living together in one household. When he'd visited this house as a child he'd loved waking up in the morning and having his grandmother give him a cup of warm milk to drink, and his aunt reminding him to take a bath, and his uncle driving him and his cousins out to Cubbon Park for a picnic. He'd loved having more people to interact with every day than just his parents and sister.

Now the household would be cut up into small apartments, with every family living on their own. There was nothing he could do about it. He closed the gate behind him and stepped carefully along the bumpy granite sidewalk. Being in India after so many years was eye opening. Why had he ever thought India dull as a teenager? If anything, the country was overstimulating. The traffic itself was an amazing sight. He could hardly even cross the street in front of his grandmother's house, there was so much activity from early morning until late at night. There were no crosswalks, no stop signs, and very few stoplights. Vehicles paid no attention to lane markings. The buses, cars, autorickshaws, and motorbikes simply maneuvered into any space that could fit a wheel or a portion of bumper. If there was space in the oncoming lane, people casually drove along that lane until they encountered a wave of traffic surging toward them, and then, just as casually, horn honking, they veered back into their own overcrowded lane. If there was a suggestion of a pause in the traffic, pedestrians would insert themselves into the mix, calmly strolling across the vehicle-choked road.

Abhay generally avoided the main road on his early morning walks. Now he turned off the main road and walked down a side street. He moved carefully along the roadway—there was no sidewalk on this narrow street—to avoid running into anyone who happened to be wheeling a motorbike out from a compound gate, and to escape being hit by any cars that happened to be lumbering along. He made his way around women stooping in front of their gates to sprinkle rangoli powder in pretty patterns on the ground. He barely avoided being splashed by a bucket of water being dumped from a second-floor balcony. The traffic from the main road was already starting to surge, with cars, motorbikes, and autorickshaws roaring and beeping along.

In mid-November, a week after Rasika had left him, Abhay had mentioned to his mother that he was thinking he might go to India in December. She had immediately bought him a plane ticket and telephoned the relatives. His parents even insisted on paying his plane fare. Maybe they wanted to make sure at least one of their children identified with India, since Seema was so enamored of African-American culture.

He was here in a last-ditch quest to see Rasika. Mom had run into Sujata Auntie at the Indian grocery store near Cleveland, and had heard about the eligible bachelor Rasika planned to marry. Apparently Sujata Auntie had even shown Mom a photo of this guy. "Very handsome," Mom had informed Abhay, rolling the *r* in *very* extra-long, to emphasize his good looks. "And so intelligent, they say. No trouble he will have to find job in U.S. Beautiful children they will have."

Abhay had pretended to be completely uninterested, although he felt like he might explode with anger and frustration at Rasika's stupid choices. He'd tried to contact her several times after she left Portland. He knew Rasika's relatives lived somewhere in Bangalore, but he didn't know where. It was insane to think he was somehow going to run into her here, but he felt compelled to see if it might happen. Of course he wouldn't see her, and that, he hoped, would be enough of a sign for him to forget about her once and for all.

Anyway, he had public reasons for visiting India, too—to reunite with family and to check out Auroville.

He had decided to come to India right after Kianga's birthday party. Kianga said Auroville was started by a group of people who had reclaimed a desert by planting two million trees, and that she was going to volunteer there at an organic farm. She invited anyone interested to visit her in India. With these words, she gave Abhay a long look.

The night after the party, he'd done an Internet search on Auroville. At first he was put off because it seemed to have a religious foundation; the place was started by some sort of Hindu guru, and the Web site spoke of a "divine consciousness." Nevertheless, the Auroville home page insisted that they followed no religion and wanted only to unify people. They experimented with rammed-earth buildings, creative ways of educating children, all sorts of healing therapies. The place was quite large, with almost two thousand residents. Could this be the community he'd been searching for? He planned to go and see Kianga in about a week, after spending a polite amount of time with his relatives.

Abhay turned left and passed a construction site, with piles of sand and stacks of bricks. The scaffolding was made of straight branches. As he approached the railroad tracks he could smell something burning, and soon came across a small trash fire. People stepped over the rails, seemingly oblivious to the litter strewn around: juice boxes, potato chip bags, banana peels, random shreds of plastic and rags. This was one of the things Abhay disliked most about India—the way the trash dispersed itself on the ground in certain public places. As he stepped over the tracks he encountered, on the other side, a few people picking through a mound of rubbish.

He looked up at every house he passed, wondering in spite of himself if Rasika might be behind the walls. At the end of one narrow street he stumbled upon a rectangular neighborhood park, about two blocks long. He walked along bricked paths among the formal arrangements of low shrubs with yellow or red leaves. The place was immaculate, with women workers in saris and men in their skirtlike lungis sweeping and clipping hedges.

He sat on a bench and gazed at the scene. Next to the park was a row of three-story apartment buildings, with laundry hung over the balcony railings. Many of the older single-family houses in the neighborhood were being torn down to create these small apartment complexes. The colors were pastel: light yellow with blue trim, light peach with a dull red trim. On one balcony, a slim woman in a long blue nightgown was shaking out her hair, bending over at the waist as her long black hair fell over the railing. She straightened up, flung her hair back, and started combing it. She reminded him of Rasika. A small naked child toddled out onto the balcony and clung to the woman's nightgown as she combed.

Had Rasika met her intended already? For all he knew, she was married and on her honeymoon.

The woman on the balcony picked up the baby and went inside. Abhay raised his eyes to what was happening behind the low apartments. Looming over everything were the gray skeletons of twenty-story apartment buildings under construction. Who would live there? How would the residents even maneuver all their cars along the roads? What was happening to the Bangalore he knew? Abhay tilted his head back and looked up at massive yellow cranes moving slowly against the blue sky. He could hear faint clanging sounds from that direction. There were no branches for scaffolding on this monstrosity.

Bangalore was growing like crazy. He'd heard his parents talk about it, and now he could see for himself. Since the Indian economy opened up in 1990 to foreign investments, many multinational companies had set up operations in major Indian cities. Bangalore had been one of the early targets of this, because of its relatively mild climate.

Now that Abhay was being confronted with the polluted, crowded, and often incomprehensible reality of this rampantly developing country, he wondered whether he was crazy to even be checking out an intentional community in India.

After Rasika's lunch with Yuvan, things came to a standstill for a few days. His mother called and said they were going to do some sort of pooja before making a final decision. Oddly, during this time Rasika herself was almost ignored. No one seemed to think it necessary to consult with her or pay her any special attention, although Mridula Auntie did take Rasika to the ayurvedic doctor who had helped Mayuri. Rasika came home with a yellow skin cream and some bitter herbal tea.

Every day her mother and aunt inspected her skin, supervised the application of her ointment, and brewed the herbal tea for her. Everyone was pleased that the pimples were disappearing. Yet no one noticed that Rasika had hardly eaten since arriving in India and that she was having trouble sleeping, which was unusual for her. Sleep was generally the one thing she could count on to take her away from her problems.

Rasika spent time with her grandmother, helping her gather jasmine blossoms in the garden and tying the blossoms into short garlands. Pati had taught her this skill many years ago, and Rasika found it soothing to sit in the sunshine and loop and knot pairs of flowers by the stems. Then Pati would hand around these garlands so the women of the household could pin them into their hair.

"What was it like when you got married, Pati?" Rasika asked one morning. They sat on a bench in the backyard, their heads shaded by a crape myrtle tree. Rasika stretched her bare feet into the warm sunshine. They were somewhat insulated by the house and yard from the usual sounds of the city: traffic beeping and rumbling, someone's radio broadcasting a male voice, and a female chorus singing a rhythmic Hindi movie song.

"I was very keen to get married." Pati chuckled. "The wedding was an excuse to get dressed up for three days in a row. Back then weddings used to go on for three days, but nowadays no one has the patience for all that." Pati spoke in Tamil, slowly and calmly, as though she had all the time in the world.

"You were only sixteen," Rasika said.

"I was born in 1940, and married in 1956. At that time, among our people, girls were married at fifteen or sixteen. If you reached eighteen and you were unmarried, you were considered old for a bride. We thought we were very modern because we did not believe in child marriage. The girls finished schooling before marriage, after all. We started school early in those days. By the age of four I was in school, so by fifteen I was finished with tenth standard. No one thought of college for girls in those days."

Rasika knew that her other grandmother, her father's mother, hadn't even been allowed to finish tenth grade—the end of high school in India—before getting married. "What about Ammachi?" she asked. "She was only fourteen."

"She is quite a bit older to me," Pati said. "From her time to my time, things changed for women."

"Was it difficult to decide which man to marry?" Rasika picked two more blossoms from the basket between them. The maidservant exited the back door of the house with a basket of wet clothes from the washing machine, and began pinning the garments to the clothesline.

"No one asked me. My parents chose. Maybe it was difficult for them. I don't know." Pati held the blossoms deftly in her left hand. Her right hand made a loop of the cotton thread and pulled it tightly around the stems. Her fingers were still supple. "One day they told me that I was going to marry so-and-so. I had never seen him. Nowadays, girls have much more say. You go here and there with the boys, even before engagement. In those days, we didn't have any choice at all. Only after marriage did we go about with our husbands."

"Were you afraid to marry someone you didn't know?"

"I didn't even know what marriage was. I just thought about the wedding—being the center of attention. I was considered quite beautiful then. Everyone talked about my beauty, and it went to my head."

"You are still very beautiful, Pati," Rasika said.

Pati smiled. "I was very interested in saris and jewelry." Pati held up a string of flowers and considered its length. "I would always be thinking about what sari I wanted to ask my father to buy for me. If anyone wore new jewelry, I would inspect it carefully."

"Really?" Since Rasika had known her, Pati had seemed most interested in cooking and chanting prayers. She could hardly imagine Pati as a teenager obsessed with clothes. "What was it like after you got married?"

"My mother-in-law was very particular. She was not a bad woman, but I had to do exactly as she wished. She told me when to get up in the morning, how to cut the vegetables, what prayers to say, when to wash my hair. That was all fine. I did not mind working and following orders." Pati knotted her thread, snapped it off the spool, and set the flowers in the basket. "But she also told me what to wear and not wear. That was the difficult part for me. She bought me so much jewelry—heavy gold necklaces." Pati mimed the width of the necklaces against her collarbone. "Thick bangles. I wanted something light and delicate. She bought me heavy silk saris in dull colors with lots of gold embroidery, but I wanted something bright." Pati picked up the spool and measured out another length of thread against her arm.

"Pati, you mean you never chose your own clothes?" Rasika was horrified.

"My mother-in-law bought all the clothes for me. I had many saris."

"You didn't choose anything for yourself?" Rasika asked again in disbelief.

"After all, we must not think about clothes all the time. I became a mother, and then I stopped worrying about my saris, finally."

Rasika had been so absorbed in this story that she'd only managed to connect a total of six flowers. She picked up two more flowers from the basket, and then rested her hands on her lap. She felt a weight around her heart at the thought of what her grandmother had had to go through. Pati had to give up even her smallest inclinations and desires once she was married.

Nowadays—was it better? After marriage, Rasika would have her own job, her own money, her own clothes. Yet she was not completely free. Her parents had let her meet a few eligible bachelors, but in effect, they too had told her that she was going to marry so-and-so. And she had agreed. In fact, her biggest worry now was that Mr. So-and-So would reject her.

When Yuvan's acceptance was conveyed through his father, Rasika was so relieved that she exclaimed, "Tell them I also accept."

"Don't worry, we have already told them," her mother said.

Two days later, the engagement ceremony took place at the

house. All the furniture was moved out of the living room and bedsheets were spread over the floor for people to sit on.

Again, her aunt dressed Rasika and applied too much makeup. It seemed to Rasika that she was a doll they were playing with in their game of "the perfect wedding." Although it was supposed to be a small gathering, all sorts of relatives crowded into the house to observe the ceremony: Appa's siblings and their families, Amma's distant cousins. Subhash and his family were there, too.

Rasika tried not to look at Yuvan's father. She knew, intellectually, that he was not really Kanchan, but whenever she saw his face, her mind flashed to that evening in the hotel, and she felt panic and the urge to run away. During the ceremony, as she sat on the wooden platform at one end of the room, she kept her eyes down, as a modest bride should.

After the engagement ceremony, as Yuvan and Rasika stood at one end of the room accepting blessings and greetings, the crowd parted. Appa's mother was being led toward them. Thin and bent, gripping a walker in her clawlike hands, she thumped slowly toward them, with Balu Uncle pressing the crowd back from her. When she stood in front of Rasika, Amma said, "Do namaskar to Ammachi," and Rasika and Yuvan both obediently kneeled in front of the old woman and touched their foreheads to the floor. Ammachi blessed them by sprinkling raw turmeric-colored rice over them. When Rasika rose from the floor, her grandmother gripped Rasika's hand in her claw, and stood there for several seconds, her hand shaking, her lips working. Finally she said, "You have come home to marry. Now I can die in peace."

As the old woman hauled herself away, Amma whispered, "She always says things like that. Don't worry."

That evening, Rasika stayed at home with a headache. Everyone else in the house went out to the ISKCON temple, which, her uncle informed them, was the largest Hare Krishna temple in the world. She didn't want to endure a long car ride and then jostle among thousands of other tourists.

In the room she was sharing with Mayuri, she swallowed a couple of painkillers and then sat up in bed, sipping water from a steel cup. The window was open, and a soft evening breeze wafted into the room, bringing with it sounds of street vendors calling out their wares, the grinding of traffic, and whiffs of smell: the acrid scent of burning trash, and the oniony smell of fried food. As the headache faded, she was surprised to discover that tears were running down her face.

"What is it?" Pati had appeared at the side of her bed. "Why are you crying, raja?" Pati sat down next to her, put her strong fingers against Rasika's temples, and massaged firmly.

"I thought you went with them." Rasika took another sip of water.

"I have already seen that temple. Lie down. You are exhausted." Pati took the cup away from Rasika and patted Rasika's shoulder. "Go to sleep now."

Rasika obediently lay down. "Pati, stay with me." She rolled onto her side and grasped her grandmother's hand. "I feel so sad."

"Sometimes it happens like that after a lot of excitement. You will feel better in the morning."

"I don't know if I made the right decision, Pati."

Pati began massaging Rasika's head with her free hand. "We pray to God, and make the best decisions we can."

"What if—what if I'm marrying the wrong boy?" Rasika said this almost to herself.

"What other boy is there? Hm?" Pati's fingers worked on the nape of Rasika's neck. "Don't worry. One boy is just as good as another. Tomorrow you will feel better."

Rasika closed her eyes and tried to relax, but her mind kept racing. She felt as if all the guests at the ceremony were swarming toward her, led by her crippled grandmother. "What if there is another boy?" she asked softly.

Pati's fingers stopped. "What are you saying?" she asked gently. "Is there someone else you want to marry?"

Rasika put both hands up to cover her face. "I don't know."

Pati grasped Rasika's wrists and pulled the hands away from her face. Her sharp eyes penetrated into Rasika's eyes. "If there is someone else, you must speak up now."

"But they won't approve." Rasika closed her eyes. She couldn't look at Pati.

Pati let go of Rasika's wrists. "Listen to me. Sit up, open your eyes, and listen to me."

Rasika sat up. She opened her eyes but kept them focused down on her hands in her lap. For the engagement ceremony, Mayuri had decorated Rasika's palms with intricate henna designs. She concentrated on following the spirals and flowers Mayuri had drawn.

Pati put both hands on either side of Rasika's head and turned the head so Rasika had to look at Pati. "Now is the time to speak. If you don't speak, you must not speak after marriage."

Rasika nodded.

"Is there someone else?" Pati demanded softly.

Rasika looked into Pati's eyes. What would Pati say if she knew about Rasika's life? She would be shocked. Rasika couldn't let everyone down now, after she had come so far. "No," she whispered. She shook her head, with Pati's hands still on either side of her face. "No."

During the engagement ceremony, Yuvan's parents had given Rasika thousands of rupees as a gift. "We wanted to give you something, but we want you to select your own gifts, so you will use them," Yuvan's mother said, and everyone agreed this was very sensible.

The next day, Rasika was sent shopping with Mayuri, who would help Rasika select only the most fashionable outfits. They attempted to walk along the narrow sidewalk on Commercial Street, which most of the time was blocked by merchandise displayed outside of shops, or by A-frame sidewalk signs advertising the wares of a shop. She and Mayuri jostled among all the other shoppers and tried to stay out of the way of the cars and motor scooters that attempted to squeeze their way down the narrow street.

"You're so lucky, Rasika." They carefully stepped past a shop bursting with frilly little girls' dresses. "You've fallen in love with a man who is acceptable to your parents."

"I haven't really fallen in love with him," Rasika said. "I'm not even sure he likes me."

"He has agreed to marry you! Of course he likes you. He is not a very emotional person, but I don't think he would agree to marry someone he didn't like. Everyone is talking about what a great match it is. You're very lucky."

Rasika and Mayuri were accosted by a young man holding a wooden snake in his hand. "Snake, madam?" he asked politely. On Commercial Street, even the pavement peddlers spoke in English.

"Go away," Mayuri said.

Undaunted, the peddler walked along with them, holding the snake by the tail and demonstrating how it could sway in the air because of its jointed construction. "Three hundred rupees," he said. He was dressed in a nice plaid woven shirt and long pants, with sandals on his feet.

"Go," Mayuri commanded.

"Chess set?" The young man produced a travel-size wooden chess set. He opened its tiny drawers to reveal the minute chess pieces.

Rasika couldn't help laughing. He looked like he was about sixteen years old, with a hint of a mustache on his upper lip. They escaped him only by entering a random store, where they pretended to look at shelves of men's polo shirts.

"Rasika, I must tell you something." Mayuri unfolded a shirt, held it up in front of her face, and said softly, from behind the shirt, "My misfortune is that I have fallen in love with the wrong man. He is the most honest, caring person I have ever met. And he is extremely smart. He didn't do well in school because he is not good at memorizing. He is more of a big-picture person. He has a great business sense. He will be very wealthy someday. But I will never be allowed to marry him, only because he is a Muslim." Mayuri said all this in a rush, although her voice continued to be quiet.

Rasika was surprised Mayuri would talk about her personal life in public like this. There were no other customers in the small, air-conditioned shop, and the four or five employees were standing around, looking attentive. Unlike stores in the United States, where it was often difficult to find anyone to help you, in India the sales-clerks were everywhere. This shop even had someone just to open the door for customers.

"How did you meet him?" Rasika asked softly.

"He works with me." Mayuri lowered the shirt and stepped closer to Rasika. "He was my trainer. He was so gentle and patient, Rasika. I started to love him from the first day of training."

"Will you marry him anyway?" Rasika asked. She wondered how Mridula Auntie would react to her oldest daughter marrying not just out of their caste, but out of their religion altogether.

"I don't know what to do. His family will also disapprove. He is afraid to ask their permission."

Rasika looked out the glass doors of the shop. The young ped-dler was nowhere in sight. "Shall we go?"

Mayuri clutched a shirt to her chest. "I want you to meet him. I want someone in my family to understand. He is so beautiful, I cannot live without him."

All the male salesclerks were gazing at them with interest. Rasika hustled Mayuri out of the store.

As they were sorting through the kurtis at the Stylish Shop, which, despite its silly name, was one of Rasika's favorite stores in Bangalore, Mayuri told her all sorts of things about Khaleel: how he planned to start his own outsourcing business, but he didn't know exactly in what field yet; how he had secretly bought her a necklace—he had a cousin in the jewelry business. She tugged a chain out from under her blouse. "I don't dare wear it at home, in case Amma asks me about it."

Rasika placed her fingertips politely under the pendant, a small square of gold set with a minuscule diamond. "Very nice. Couldn't you tell your mother you bought it yourself?"

Mayuri tucked the necklace away again. "I don't like to lie." She shoved a line of blouses down the bar and eased out a hanger.

Rasika threw another blouse over the pile of clothes already on her arm. She didn't like to lie either, and now that she was going to be Yuvan's wife, at least she would never again be compelled to utter an untruth.

"He lives near the Lalbagh gardens." Mayuri held up a patterned brown top and made a face at it. "Who would buy such an ugly thing, without any sparkle?" She attempted to squeeze the blouse back onto the rack, but someone else had shoved all the clothes down in their direction, so Mayuri flung the blouse underneath the rack. "Anyway, sometimes I arrange to meet a friend at Lalbagh, and he walks over, and I see him that way." Mayuri pushed her way through the crowd to another rack of clothes. "I will take you to meet him one day."

As soon as they left the shop with their bulging bags, they heard a voice: "Madam, just one hundred rupees for snake. Please look, madam." The boy followed them, holding out his chess set, lowering his price to fifty rupees as they attempted to maneuver through the crowd. At the corner, they leaped into a newly vacated autorickshaw, giggling at their escape. "MG Road," Mayuri shouted to the driver, and then sat back, cradling her bag on her lap. "There's a nice restaurant there. We'll get juice or ice cream or something, and then go home."

As they buzzed and bumped along, Rasika heard the melody of her cell phone. She'd managed to get an Indian SIM card inserted into her phone. She looked at the display, and her heart sank. It was Yuvan. She hurried to answer. "Hello?"

"My meeting was canceled," he said. "Where are you?"

Since they'd agreed to be married, Yuvan called her every day, although they often didn't have much to say to each other. Rasika got the impression that Yuvan was determined to do the appropriate thing by her, but she didn't sense much enthusiasm. Perhaps he was never particularly excited.

"We're going to MG Road," she shouted. "I don't know where exactly. To a restaurant."

"Call me when you get there. I'm catching an auto now."

She made herself smile brightly as she told Mayuri that Yuvan would be meeting them. She'd hoped to have a whole day away from him, free of having to be on her best behavior.

Once they reached the restaurant she dutifully called Yuvan, who as it turned out was not too far away. They stood on the sidewalk—a wide, walkable sidewalk—and waited. Rasika looked around with eyes shaded by her sunglasses. There were many white Westerners strolling along MG Road, and many well-dressed Indians. This was a more expensive part of town. Every other store advertised "foreign exchange" services.

She noticed a young man walking toward them along the sidewalk, reading a paperback. He wore knee-length shorts and a T-shirt imprinted with the words CARPE DIEM. She saw, without really noticing, the title of the book: *The Upanishads*. Her face flushed and her whole body began tingling.

"Abhay?" she asked.

"Rasika!" He stopped abruptly and lowered his book.

"What're you doing here?" She tried to keep her voice light.

"I was at the bookstore. Gangaram's." He pointed to a three-story gray building behind him. "I can't believe I'm actually seeing you!"

"But, what're you doing in India? In Bangalore?"

"I—well. I haven't been here for a long time. I wanted to see my relatives."

Rasika collected herself. "This is my cousin Mayuri," she said.

Mayuri smiled and shook his hand.

Yuvan appeared at Rasika's side. "Yuvan, this is Abhay." She spoke as calmly as she could. "Abhay is the son of old family friends from Ohio."

Yuvan shook hands with Abhay. "I am Rasika's fiancé. We're just going to have a bite to eat. Why don't you join us?"

Abhay glanced from Yuvan to Rasika. She shook her head slightly at him. He cleared his throat. "I think my aunt might be expecting me home."

"Please join us," Mayuri invited. "You can keep me company while the two of them talk."

Abhay stood motionless, as though not sure which way to move. Rasika sighed. He was just a friend, after all. "Come on, then."

After the waiter delivered their juices and a tray of vegetable pakodas, Abhay tried to catch Rasika's eye. She ignored him. She was sitting on the other side of the table, beside Yuvan and as far away from Abhay as she could get. She wore a red and orange blouse that was too bright for her wan face. Her lipstick had strayed to the corners of her mouth. She'd lost weight, and her eyes seemed glassy. She was leaning toward Yuvan and whispering under her breath, but he answered so the whole table could hear, recounting details of his morning at work.

Yuvan was handsome, just as Abhay's mother had said. Abhay could see that Rasika wasn't crazy about him, although she was putting on a good show by keeping her eyes on him and responding enthusiastically to his words.

Abhay's heart was racing. He'd tried to convince himself that he'd never see Rasika in this city of six million people, yet here she was, sitting across the table from him. He brought a pakoda to his lips but realized he couldn't eat. He was too nervous. Mayuri was talking to him, and he gathered that she worked at a call center, providing customer service for an American airline company.

"The dollar is going down against the rupee," she said, "which is hard for companies like ours, since we depend on dollars." She was wearing jeans and a sleeveless knit blouse.

He noticed that if he turned to face Mayuri, he had a good view of Rasika from the corner of his eyes. She was pretending to eat her pakoda, nibbling at its edges. "Are you getting paid less?" he asked Mayuri.

"The employees are not affected. Not yet. Anyway, I'm sure the dollar will go back up again. I'm not worried."

He struggled to keep his mind on the conversation. "You must work nights, then. Your family doesn't mind?"

"The company bus comes to pick me up at my door, and drops me off in the morning." Mayuri moved her shoulders and hands in a free, fluid way as she spoke. "They provide food and health care." She seemed so Westernized. Many Indian women held their bodies more still as they talked.

Mayuri flung herself back on her chair and ran her fingers through her hair. "Of course, my parents want me to get married and settle down soon, but until then, it's OK. A lot of women work at the call centers." Mayuri yawned behind her hand. "It's difficult after my nights off. I don't have the motivation to sleep during the day."

Yuvan was working away at the pakodas, carefully selecting each one and dipping it into the spicy sauce. As Rasika spooned some green chutney onto her plate, her hand shook, and she spilled some onto her blouse. She rubbed the spot with her cloth napkin and excused herself from the table. Abhay's gaze traveled with her as she walked to the back of the restaurant. At one point, she stumbled briefly, and he startled, ready to leap up to help her, but she continued on her way.

When he turned back to the table, Mayuri was tilting her head questioningly. He sipped his fizzy limeade to calm himself.

Yuvan rubbed his hands free of crumbs. "Abhay, how do you find Bangalore now, after so many years away?"

"There aren't any more movie billboards," Abhay said.

"What do you mean?" Mayuri wrinkled her forehead at him.

"Last time I was here, there were all sorts of giant billboards advertising Hindi movies." Abhay remembered the dark-eyed Indian beauties and rakish, mustached heroes overlooking the streets.

"I don't remember that," Mayuri said.

"Now the billboards advertise mobile phones, jewelry stores, high-rise apartment complexes, mutual funds," Abhay said. "I guess enough Indians have enough money now so they don't have to fantasize through the movies about living someone else's glamorous life. They can actually live that life themselves."

"Things are really changing in India." Mayuri extended a hand and rubbed her fingertips over her glittering rings. "You can't believe how much money is coming into India nowadays. My friend Khaleel says Indian companies have more money than they know what to do with. He says the stock market is going through the roof."

Rasika returned to the table. Her lipstick was fixed. Abhay tried to catch her eye and was aware of Mayuri gazing from him to Rasika.

Yuvan didn't even glance at Rasika. He asked Abhay, "What are your plans in India? Just visiting the relatives?"

"I'm going to check out a place called Auroville. Have you heard of it?"

"You mean the Aurobindo Ashram? I've been there long back, I think. When I was a kid." Yuvan turned his attention back to the tray of pakodas.

"No, not the ashram." Many Indians confused Auroville with the hermitage in Pondicherry founded by Sri Aurobindo, a Hindu saint, in the early 1900s. "Auroville is about ten kilometers north of Pondicherry. Have you heard of a French woman who became the chief disciple of Sri Aurobindo? She is called the Mother."

"Yes, yes," nodded Yuvan. "I have heard of the Mother."

"After Aurobindo's death, she thought up the idea of forming Auroville as an international intentional community. "

"What do you mean by 'intentional' community?" Yuvan asked.

"It's a place where people decide to live intentionally, and not just by chance."

"So . . ." Mayuri picked up the conversation. "It is sort of an offshoot of the ashram?"

"In my understanding, Auroville is much more free and loose than the ashram. There is a spiritual aspect, but I'm not sure how important that is. It's a place where thousands of people from all over the world have come together to try to create a better life, a community more in tune with nature."

At the table next to theirs, the host seated a couple of business-men in dress shirts and dark pants.

"Are you thinking of moving there?" Rasika asked.

"I'll have to see it first." Abhay held her eyes for a moment. "What would you think if I did?"

She shrugged. "Your choices are irrelevant to me." The last word caught in her throat, and she began coughing into her napkin.

"You'd really think about moving to India from the U.S.?" Yuvan asked. "So many people from here want to go to the U.S. And here you are, coming from America, reading the Upanishads and visiting ashrams."

"I never want to leave India," Mayuri said. "More and more jobs are opening up in Bangalore itself, so why should anyone leave? Rasika tells me India has everything that's available in the U.S. The latest computer equipment, cameras, mobile phones—you can buy everything here now." She fluttered her hands in the air, as if to conjure the myriad goods that India now had. "We have microwave ovens, washing machines, toasters. So I don't see any reason to go to the U.S. and have to suffer with all that cold weather, and have to do my own housework."

Rasika was still coughing. Yuvan didn't seem to notice. Her eyes watered, and she caught her breath and took a sip of limeade.

"Is India going to just imitate the West, and start overconsuming?" Abhay felt his hands under the table curl into fists. He opened his fingers and consciously tried to relax them. "What about India's own wisdom and traditions? What about creating India as a world innovator in some way, instead of an imitator of Western ideas and values?"

"Indians are just as materialistic as anyone else." Yuvan picked up his fork and tapped the handle on the table. "If you give us a chance, we will buy everything we can afford."

Rasika patted her eyes and upper lip with her napkin. She seemed out of breath.

"I notice more people have air conditioners now," Abhay said. "And along the road near the golf course they're cutting down all those big trees to widen the road. That's going to make the city even hotter, and you're going to need even more air conditioners."

The waiter deposited their bill on the table, and Yuvan put his hand on it. "That is the way life is." Yuvan stood up. "I will take care of this."

Abhay pulled out his wallet. "Let me at least contribute."

"No, no. Don't worry." Yuvan headed toward the cash register near the door.

Mayuri excused herself and walked toward the bathroom. Yuvan was in the lobby, waiting his turn at the cash register, leaning over and peering at the glass case of desserts. Abhay and Rasika were alone at the table.

"You're not really going to marry him, are you?" Abhay asked.

"Shh." Rasika stood up.

"Give me your phone number."

"Stop it, Abhay." She gathered her purse.

"I'll send you an e-mail, then." He stepped in front of her so she couldn't just walk away. "I need to talk to you. In private."

"No." She attempted to squeeze between him and the next table.

"I came to India to find you. I didn't think I would. It's a miracle. I think it means something."

"Everyone ends up on MG Road at one time or another. It's no miracle."

"When's the wedding?"

"None of your business."

Abhay sensed someone looking their way, and saw Mayuri approaching, her eyebrows raised, and her lips pursed. He backed away from Rasika, and she stepped out and walked toward the front of the restaurant. Yuvan was waiting for them by the front door. Abhay wondered, as he strolled out beside Mayuri, if Rasika had said anything about him.

On the sidewalk, Abhay watched as the three of them hailed autos. "Which way are you headed?" Yuvan shouted to Abhay as a couple of vehicles stopped.

"I don't know," he replied. He stood with the strap of his backpack slung over one shoulder, hands in pockets, as Rasika and Mayuri climbed into one of the autos. Abhay watched as it sputtered away. Yuvan left in the next.

Abhay remained on the sidewalk as tourists and wealthy Indians milled past. He didn't know what to do now. Another auto pulled up to the curb, and the driver gestured to him. Abhay shook his head, and the auto veered away. He felt rooted to the spot. This is where he'd found Rasika. Now what? She was gone again into the mass of humanity in Bangalore.

15

Two days later, Abhay boarded a luxury bus early in the morning from Bangalore to Pondicherry. He'd sent Rasika an e-mail from a little Internet browsing place—fifteen rupees per hour—near his grandmother's house. She hadn't responded. He was starting to feel like a stalker. He was beginning to think he had to finally move on.

He turned his attention to the book in his hand. He had found, in Gangaram's bookstore, a book about the new Indian economy. However, it proved almost impossible to read on the bumpy bus ride, along a narrow, rutted path that everyone pretended was a two-lane road. He gave up and looked out the window. From his high, plush seat he saw scrubby meadows, groves of coconut palms, fields of tall grasslike plants with feathery purplish heads. Every once in a while the bus barreled through a village with low houses, the streets choked with people, bicycles, and vehicles. Between villages, the road was shaded by rows of squat, gnarled trees. He loved this Indian practice of planting trees along almost every roadway. How long before these trees were also cut down to widen the road?

They drove by an outdoor market in one village: mounds of flowers, pyramids of fruit, neat rows of leather chappals for sale. What would it be like to live all one's life in one of these small, crowded, anonymous towns? From the high bus window he could see all sorts of people busily selling things, buying things, going places. They all seemed reasonably content with their lives. Why was he alone unable to find something to keep himself satisfied, some way to get involved with the world?

Eight hours later, the bus finally pulled into Pondicherry. Like Bangalore, Pondicherry was full of trees and plants, but was not nearly so crowded with people. At the bus station he arranged to hire a taxi to drive him the ten kilometers to Auroville.

Once they were out of town, the car turned off the busy main road onto a smooth black ribbon of asphalt, with red dirt on either side and green trees all around. These must be some of the two million trees planted by the Aurovillians. It really was beautiful and peaceful, and perhaps this place would be what he had been seeking for so many years. Soon the cab turned onto a red dirt road and dropped him off inside the Auroville gate at a large, clean, tree-shaded courtyard.

He wanted to enjoy his first impression of this international community. He hoisted on his camping backpack and spent a few minutes reading the series of white placards at the entrance, which explained that "Auroville wants to be a universal town where men and women of all countries are able to live in peace and progressive harmony above all creeds, all politics and all nationalities. The purpose of Auroville is to realise human unity." He liked that statement. He saw various people strolling around: a plump Indian woman in jeans, a few white women in gold-bordered skirts, Indian men in pants and polo shirts, one woman who looked like she might be Japanese wearing a salvar kameez outfit, and some slim, dark-skinned Indian women in saris. Were these all Aurovillians, or just tourists like himself? There did not seem to be any kind of religious uniform or a rigid standard of dress.

He walked over the paving stones to the visitors' center ahead, a low white building in a sort of Frank Lloyd Wright style. A slim, elegant, very dark brown Indian woman in a sari walked out onto the porch and closed the door behind her.

"Excuse me." He held up a hand. "I'm looking for—"

The woman turned the key in the lock. "We are closed for the day."

"Yes, but I just got here. I'm staying at the—"

"You will have to go to the restaurant." She pointed across the courtyard at a tan brick complex with a series of arched entrance-ways under the palm trees. She strolled away, her sari palloo sway-ing as she walked.

He stood there feeling lost and angry and exhausted. He didn't have any way of contacting Kianga. She'd said she would get hold of him through his guesthouse. He unzipped his waist pack and pulled out a ragged sheet of paper on which he had written im-portant phone numbers. He scanned the list and found the Cen-tral Guest House, where Kianga said she had booked a room for him, and then, holding the list in one hand, he proceeded down the pathway and under the arches to what looked like the restaurant. There was a cluster of outdoor tables on a patio. Many of the patrons were white. He heard what sounded like French, and perhaps Ger-man, or maybe Dutch, being spoken. No one looked his way. He gazed around for some sort of helper or waiter, and seeing none, ap-proached the counter of the restaurant, where there were cakes and cookies displayed in the glass case. Behind the counter an Indian man and a blond woman were busy putting desserts on plates.

"Is there a phone here?" he asked tentatively.

The Indian man looked up. "Is it a local call?" he asked in what sounded like British English.

"I need to reach the Central Guest House," he said.

"Come round this way," the man instructed, and Abhay went around the corner to the cashier's table, where there was a telephone.

Although he reached someone at the guesthouse, and although she confirmed his reservation, she was not able to help him get to his room. "You will have to walk," she informed him. He couldn't quite place her accent. Maybe Italian? Spanish? "It is not far. Half a kilometer."

"Isn't there a bus or something?" He had no idea where he was heading.

"No. We have no buses. See you soon." And she hung up.

So he was still stuck in this very pretty visitors' complex at Auroville. He walked to the entrance gates, where he remembered seeing some sort of information booth. His back was feeling the effects of the bumpy bus ride, and he just wanted to get to his room, take off his backpack, and lie down. Of course now there was no one in the booth.

"Where you want to go?" someone asked from behind, and he saw, to his relief, an Indian man approaching him. This must be the entrance guard, and he would undoubtedly have a map.

"The Central Guest House," Abhay said. "Do you know where it is?"

"That way." The man gestured vaguely down the road. "Three kilometers."

"I was told it was only half a kilometer."

"Three kilometers. I will take you. Only one hundred rupees." The man pointed to an autorickshaw sitting outside the entrance gate.

This man was not the guard, but an enterprising auto driver. Abhay had now been in India long enough to be outraged at this price. "A hundred rupees to go three kilometers?"

"I come from Pondicherry. You will not find auto here."

Abhay stood there fuming. How could Auroville realize human unity if they wouldn't even help people get into the place? He slipped his arms out of his backpack and thumped it to the ground.

"Eighty rupees," the man said. "I will take you." He reached for the backpack.

Abhay waved him away. "I'll walk," he declared, slung on his backpack again, and stepped out onto the dirt road. Probably if he kept walking, he'd come across a sign. His sneakers padded over the soft red dirt. The trees all looked alike, a tangled forest of thin trunks along the sides of the path, and it felt like he was just walking in place instead of proceeding to his goal. He could see no signs of any sort, and there was no one ahead of him to ask. Should he go back to the courtyard? At least there were people there. He might have a chance of getting some help, if he kept asking. Out here, he was all alone.

He heard a motor puttering toward him, and turned in relief. Maybe the autorickshaw driver had followed him. He was now willing to consider paying whatever it took to get to his room.

It wasn't the autorickshaw, but a motor scooter. Instead of passing him, the scooter stopped. "Can I help you?" The driver was a plump, light-skinned Indian man, with a fringe of graying hair around his bald crown, wearing a dress shirt and sandals. He looked as if he might be traveling to his office.

"I need to get to the Central Guest House." Abhay tried not to appear too desperate. "Do you know where it is?"

"Please sit," the man offered, pointing to the back of his seat. Enormously relieved, Abhay perched behind him and clung to the bottom of the seat with both hands, trying not to topple over with his heavy backpack as the scooter buzzed and tilted along the road. Within a few minutes the man stopped amid a cluster of low buildings. "This is Central Guest House," he said, and Abhay eased himself off the bike. The man motored away before Abhay could thank him.

The next morning Abhay opened his eyes and gazed at the wood struts of the roof above him. Birds trilled and twittered outside. His room was small and clean, with a fan hung from the middle of the ceiling. The climate here was much more humid than in Bangalore, and during the night he'd felt chilled by the dampness and hadn't slept well.

He wondered what the day would bring. At the guesthouse office last evening, he'd been given a message from Kianga. He'd called her back from the phone outside the office, and she'd given him directions to reach her farm, called "Guidance," this morning.

Last night the manager of this guesthouse, Paloma, had given him a map and lent him her copy of an Auroville handbook, on the cover of which was a photo of the gold globe of the Matrimandir—the shrine or temple in the center of the community. It looked like some sort of extraterrestrial spaceship that had only temporarily landed on the red earth. Paloma had also given him detailed instructions as to how he could manage to gain entry into the Matrimandir grounds, as well as the temple itself. He wasn't sure he would bother with the whole to-do, yet Paloma seemed to assume that the main purpose of his trip was to see the Matrimandir. He was starting to fear that religion, or spirituality, was far more important in Auroville than he had envisioned.

Before going to bed he had pored over the Auroville handbook, attempting to absorb all the details of Auroville's history and its hundreds of communities and businesses. He read about the health care services available to Aurovillians; libraries within the community; language classes; community schools. There was a whole section on alternative energy experiments. He discovered a list of about a dozen organic farms, including the one Kianga worked on. The information was overwhelming and exciting.

He read far into the night, and now, in the morning, the booklet lay on the mattress next to him. He began to hear sounds of dishes clattering in the dining hall, so he got out of bed and bathed in the little adobe bathhouse, in which a large metal pot of water had been heated with a wood fire underneath, so the whole place was warm, toasty, and smoky-smelling. When he exited the bathhouse into the cool damp morning air, something hopped away from his foot. He startled, and then realized with relief that it was only a squat toad.

Relaxed, he made his way under the trees to the dining hall. Ferns and other plants grew alongside the bricked paths. A black stone bowl, filled with water, displayed floating red and orange chrysanthemum blossoms. Decorative shaded lanterns graced the outdoor seating area. Near the reception hut was a small statue of dancing Shiva, in front of which someone had lit a stick of incense that perfumed the morning air.

The line for breakfast snaked out the dining hall door. Abhay glanced at the bulletin board covering the outside wall of the dining hall. In the middle of the board was a poem:

Light, my light, the world-filling light, the eye-kissing light,
heart-sweetening light!

Ah, the light dances, my darling, at the centre of my life; the
light strikes, my darling, the chords of my love; the sky
opens, the wind runs wild, laughter passes over the earth.

The butterflies spread their sails on the sea of light. Lilies and
jasmines surge up on the crest of the waves of light.

The light is shattered into gold on every cloud, my darling, and
it scatters gems in profusion.

Mirth spreads from leaf to leaf, my darling, and gladness
without measure. The heaven's river has drowned its banks
and the flood of joy is abroad.

Abhay didn't normally pay much attention to poetry yet found himself scanning the words over and over again.

"You like the poem?" It was Paloma, the office manager, standing in front of him. "Every week I put a different poem on the bulletin board."

"Who wrote it?'

"This is from the *Gitanjali,* by Rabindranath Tagore. You must be familiar with his work."

Abhay was familiar with the name of the famous Bengali poet but had never read any of his poems. He liked this one. It was full of joy and seemed to fit so well in the calm beauty of the morning. Before he stepped into the door of the dining hall, Abhay read the lines one last time.

After he'd filled his plate with buttered bread and fruits, Abhay took his plate and cup of tea to a table and sat down. At the next table, also alone, was seated the plump, balding, middle-aged Indian man who had given him a motor scooter ride the day before. Abhay stepped over and held out his hand. "I'm Abhay. I didn't have a chance to thank you for the ride."

The man held out a small, delicate-fingered hand. "Nandan," he said. "Please, sit down,"

Abhay transferred his plate and cup to Nandan's table.

"How do you like Auroville?" Nandan asked.

"So far, so good."

"I have been coming here annually for years," Nandan said. "I am a physician in Chennai. My life is full of stress, noise, crowds." He spoke slowly, reclining comfortably in his chair. "I come to Auroville for a rest. It is so peaceful here. My wife and my children find it dull, but I love the quiet."

Abhay was surprised. Didn't Nandan realize that Auroville was not some sort of retreat or resort? But maybe to Nandan, Auroville was just a place with a lot of trees and fresh air.

"Tell me about yourself," Nandan invited. "Where are you from? How did you decide to visit Auroville?" He leaned forward and clasped his hands on the table, looking expectantly at Abhay, as though his only concern in the world was Abhay's life.

There was something so calm and friendly about his eyes that Abhay started talking, and soon he was telling him everything— growing up in Ohio, his parents' expectations of him, his time at Rising Star, his move to Portland, and now the visit to Auroville.

"I just want to find a place to fit in." Abhay frowned up at the blue sky through the leaves above his head.

"And you see that every place has its faults."

"I'm not expecting perfection."

"You want to belong someplace, and you find yourself always an outsider. You are like an oyster."

"An oyster?"

Nandan curved his hands into two closed shells. "You have a pearl inside, but you do not know it. You are searching every- where for something that you already have, but you do not want to open up."

Abhay had no idea what Nandan was talking about. He wasn't reluctant to open up. He was trying everything. Nandan was ap- parently like so many Indians—eager to give advice to strangers.

After breakfast, Abhay rented a bicycle at the shed near the reception hut to go see Kianga. The bicycle turned out to be a rusty, one-speed vehicle. It was better than nothing. He hopped on and started out slowly over the earth road.

Immediately, he was lost. He hadn't remembered such a plenitude of red roads the night before. According to his map, he was to connect up with the main road and circle around to the other side of the Matrimandir grounds, where he'd pick up another path to Kianga's farm. He had no idea how to reach the main road. There were paths meandering everywhere through the trees, with no road signs anywhere. He struck out along one track and encountered no one at all for several minutes. He was already sweating in the humidity. He saw someone walking along—a dark Indian man bent under a load of sticks on his back—and he shouted, "How do I get to the main road?"

The man looked at him quizzically. Maybe he didn't speak English.

"Matrimandir," Abhay tried.

The man pointed back the way Abhay had come, so Abhay turned around and tried again. After a few more false starts, he reached the main road and saw the shining gold globe of the Matrimandir in the distance. He kept this on his right and pedaled around the road surrounding the walled grounds of the temple. At the next crossroads he saw a series of road signs. Abhay followed the arrow for "Guidance" and kept pedaling and pedaling among the trees. He didn't see any more signs, nor the landmarks Kianga had mentioned. He approached a hut along the side of the road, with a rooster tied by the leg to one of the support poles. A woman in a sari sat in the doorway of the hut with a baby on her lap. He wondered if these were Aurovillians, or a village enclave in the middle of Auroville.

"Guidance?" he asked.

The woman inclined her head in the direction he was going,

so he continued. In this way, by pedaling into the unknown and asking anyone he came across, he rode into a clearing with a brown barnlike structure and a wide brick-sided well. He pushed down the kickstand of his bike and looked for Kianga. No one was around. In a field nearby were a cow and two calves. Auroville was so different from the rest of India. There were so few people, and many of the people who were here were Europeans. The place was not exactly desolate. Not lonely. Full of solitude, maybe.

As he stood there, wondering how he might find Kianga, she appeared along a path under some small trees with umbrellalike leaves. She was tanned and muscled, wearing a pair of shorts and a faded tank top. Her hair was pulled back into a ponytail, and one of her calves was smeared with mud.

She walked over to him silently and gave him a hug and kiss. She smelled musky with sweat, and felt warm and firm.

"How do you like Auroville?" She spoke quietly, stepping back and observing him.

"I'm not sure yet. It's so much bigger than I thought it would be. How do you like it?"

"Wonderful." She passed her gaze over the landscape. "It's a magical place. People are really committed to experimenting in all sorts of ways." She headed closer to the well, and he followed. Water glimmered far down the brick sides. "This fills up after the monsoon, and we use the water all year for irrigation."

"There aren't too many people here," Abhay remarked. "I thought a farm would be full of workers."

"It's Sunday morning," Kianga reminded him. "Tomorrow it'll be a lot busier."

They walked between rows of papaya trees—those were the ones with the umbrellalike leaves—and small banana trees with their huge rectangular leaves. The earth here was dark, amended with compost, probably. "We interplant the trees with crops." She pointed out rows of low plants. "Right now we have lettuce, basil, and pineapples." He had always thought pineapples grew on tall palm trees. Here he saw low circular structures of spiky leaves, like a yucca or cactus, in the centers of which appeared small reddish pineapples.

They walked slowly in single file. He was behind her, and he gazed at the symmetrical, delicate tattoo draped over her shoulders and upper back. The air was still and warm. Black and green butterflies flitted past. Abhay and Kianga stopped to watch, holding still, trying to see if the insects would land so they could get a better look at their beauty.

Another field was filled with cream-colored flowers with a dark red center. "This is a kind of hibiscus," Kianga explained. "We make a jam out of the fruit." She plucked what looked like an orange bud, pulled off a fleshy petal, and gave him one. It tasted sour and fruity. He started to feel a calmness seeping into him, from the dark earth and the penetrating heat of the sun.

As they wandered among the plants on the brown paths, he didn't see anyone else on the farm at all. It was like a Garden of Eden, with the blue sky, the rich earth, the green plants. It was so strange to be in this Indian place, in this humid, tropical climate, without the culture of Indians around him—no aunties and grandmothers cajoling him to eat more, no uncles disapproving of his lack of career, no pushy crowds, no noisy temple rituals.

"We have about eighteen acres here," Kianga said. "We keep cows for the milk and manure. In the corporate farming structure, animals are raised miles away from crops. On the animal farms, no one knows what to do with the manure, and on the cropland, they have to use artificial fertilizers for the soil."

In the next field, past a gnarled, spreading tamarind tree, she dug up, with her bare fingers, the root of some plant. "This is jicama, from Mexico." She held up the bulbous tan root. "Devi, the manager of the farm, likes to try different plants from around the world, to see what'll do well here. The plant produces a kind of bean, and we use those for a natural pesticide." She brushed the soil off the tuber, pulled a penknife out of her pocket, and peeled and sliced off a section of white root for him.

"So, you think you'll stay here?" He chewed the fresh, juicy jicama. "Seems like you feel really at home already."

Kianga squatted down next to some low plants with heart-shaped leaves. "I do feel at home. These are sweet potatoes." She reached under the spreading dark-green leaves and pulled out a few weeds. "I only heard about Auroville a few months ago, but I felt so pulled to visit." She stood up and gazed over the green and brown fields. "Now I love it here."

"Have you finished your degree?" He tossed the rest of his jicama root onto the soil and slid his hands into the pockets of his shorts.

"I haven't graduated, if that's what you're asking. But I'm realizing how limited that training was. There's so much more to health than the physical. I can learn about holistic health right here."

"Sounds like you would like to stay here."

"I have to get the logistics worked out. If I want to live here, I'd have to be able to pay for a year's stay, and find my own housing. That's the rule for newcomers. I could probably keep staying here. I'm living in a hut with Nick. A year's worth of expenses would only be about fifteen hundred dollars. I'm sure my folks would send that to me, if I asked them."

"Is Nick—he's your boyfriend?"

"Not really. There's a housing shortage, and Nick said I could stay with him. We dated in high school, and then we had a stupid fight. He was jealous because I paid attention to his friend. So we broke up. When he e-mailed me about Auroville that was the first I'd heard from him in years. We've both matured a lot. He understands that I need to be able to love anyone I choose."

Under the umbrella of a papaya tree, she slid an arm around him. He put his arm around her waist, feeling the motion of her hip under his hand as they walked. He tried to imagine himself living in Auroville near Kianga. Immediately, he thought of Rasika. What would she think of a place like this? Would her curiosity allow her to appreciate it?

When they reached the well, where Abhay had left his bike, Kianga led him past it to a little shelter—it looked like an outdoor kitchen—where she filled a tall glass of water for him. "It's filtered," she reassured him. He drained the glass and set it into the sink. She sliced open a yellowish green papaya to reveal its orange flesh and cache of black, glistening seeds. She handed him a spear. They consumed the sweet, juicy, slightly bitter flesh, and threw the peels to the cows.

"Do you have your pass for the Matrimandir?" she asked.

He shook his head. "I don't know if I want to bother with that."

"You should. It's the soul of the community. You can't understand Auroville if you don't visit the Matrimandir."

"I read in the guidebook that there are no ceremonies there. No one is required to visit the temple, or meditate, or do anything."

Kianga wiped the counter. "The Mother didn't want the Auroville experiment to become a religion. There are no rituals in the Matrimandir, no flowers, no incense. The Matrimandir is not a temple; it's a shrine to the universe's feminine energy. It's a place you can use to help raise your consciousness. It's about each person's own inner enlightenment and transformation, not about any of the other stuff that usually goes along with religion."

"How can it be the soul of the community if nothing in particular happens there?"

She stood in front of him and took his hands in hers. Her palms and fingers were tough and calloused. "A lot of the people who live in Auroville have been drawn here by the Mother's words. When Nick first e-mailed me, he sent me a quote of hers." Kianga paused and closed her eyes. Sunlight glinted off her eyebrow ring and brushed over her pale eyelashes. "'Humanity is not the last rung of the terrestrial creation. Evolution continues and man will be surpassed. It is for each individual to know whether he wants to participate in the advent of this new species.'" Her lids lifted again. "That was so exciting, to be part of this divine evolution. Even though the Mother is no longer inhabiting a body on earth, I felt like she was speaking to me personally. And when I first visited the Matrimandir, it was like her words were around me. They had taken form."

The Mother's quote was odd. It reminded Abhay of the introverted French socialist Charles Fourier, who inspired a series of short-lived American communities in the 1800s. Fourier also believed that his communities would cause humans to evolve: they would grow to seven feet tall, live for 144 years, and would develop a tail with a small hand at the end of it.

Abhay dropped her hands. "I feel like you're trying to convert me."

She laughed. Her eyes crinkled and her face grew pink. "Come on. Just experience what you experience."

After Kianga had changed into a skirt and braided her hair, they pedaled in the heat to the visitors' center and got two passes for the Matrimandir gardens for later that afternoon. They had lunch at the outdoor restaurant where Abhay had made his phone call the day before. After lunch, they got on their bikes and started again down the dusty path. Kianga took him through the back gates of the Matrimandir grounds. Almost the first thing they encountered was a giant yellow backhoe rumbling around. The ground sloped away from their path toward the shrine. Abhay could see scaffold-ing over one part of the globe, which was as yet empty of the golden scales, which covered the rest of the structure. Far down a path, on a cart, he could see a stack of the glinting disks. Abhay heard sounds of sawing and clanging. "I didn't realize the place wasn't finished," he said lightly. It seemed odd that Kianga hadn't mentioned this.

"It will be finished in time for the fortieth anniversary celebra-tion next month."

They sat down on some blocks of stone near the path, which gave them a good view of the entire scene. Kianga was gazing at the shrine. "It's been a real challenge to translate the Mother's ideas into reality. She had repeated visions about what the inner chamber should look like. She worked with an architect to design the outside of the sphere, and the gardens. She died in 1973, and since then people have been working on making this a reality. The gold disks were a problem. It's turned out to be difficult to put the ethereal vision of the Mother into reality. They first applied gold leaf to glass disks, but the foil got damaged by birds. Then they designed a way to sandwich the gold foil between two glass disks. Now it's really dazzling, isn't it?"

The shrine was not a perfect sphere. It was somewhat flattened, wider around the equator, like an egg laid by some giant, extrater-restrial creature.

"The gold globe symbolizes the sun breaking out of the earth," Kianga said. "You see the twelve meditation chambers?"

He noticed, low to the ground, a series of sloping rectangular structures surrounding the globe, as if cradling it.

"The sun is breaking through, opening up the earth, bring-ing light and consciousness to humanity. In those sections of earth that are upturned, we have twelve meditation chambers. Each one embodies a different quality. Each one is painted a different color on the inside."

"Are those finished?" He stood up and strolled over the grass to a tree nearby, where he leaned and looked away from the structure that so captivated Kianga's attention. She seemed to him to be wearing her spirituality conspicuously, and it bothered him.

She didn't answer his question. Instead, after a pause, she turned her gaze on him. "The most important thing, according to the Mother, is the inner chamber of the Matrimandir, especially the sunlight coming in through the top. Inside is the largest crystal ball in the world. That took some effort to manufacture."

As she talked, Abhay's attention was diverted by a figure he saw in the distance: a tan woman with long hair, wearing what looked like a white pantsuit. She was walking toward him slowly. He stared at the figure.

"What're you looking at?" Kianga joined him at the tree, and placed her hand on his lower back.

He leaned his head against the rough bark. "That woman reminds me of—someone I love."

"Is it the woman we saw you with at the Japanese garden?"

He lifted his head. "How did you know?"

"Just a guess. Does she love you back?"

"I think she does. But she's determined to have an arranged marriage, to please her parents. She's in India now. She might even be married by now. I feel like we're meant to be together. She doesn't see it that way."

Kianga removed her hand from his back. "Why don't you ask the Mother for help tomorrow, when you go inside the Matrimandir."

Late the next afternoon, Abhay joined other tourists sitting at the concrete picnic tables on the Matrimandir grounds. They were all waiting for the tour into the shrine to begin. The other tourists included middle-class Indians dressed in saris and button-down shirts, and white tourists in shorts and sandals.

A slim Indian man walked over to the group and said, "The tour will begin now." As they gathered around him on the broad red earth path, under the bright sun, he began telling them, in soft Indian-accented English, that Auroville was inaugurated in 1968 and soil from every Indian state and 124 countries was placed in an urn on what was to become the Matrimandir grounds. "The gold dome is as tall as a ten-story building, and the inner meditation chamber is as tall as a five-story building," he said. Abhay looked across the brilliant green grass and red earth at the egglike structure, and found it hard to believe it was so tall.

The guide stressed that, once on the path leading to the shrine, they were to observe absolute silence. Within the "concentration chamber," as the inner crystal chamber was called, they were to be silent, choose a cushion, and sit down. "The Mother said the inner chamber is 'a place for trying to find one's consciousness,'" the guide explained. "We don't have any prescribed meditations. It is for every individual to find their own way."

The group started down the path, and as Abhay descended with the others between two of the meditation chamber "petals," the walls of the chambers rose on either side of him, so that his whole field of vision was directed toward the now-enormous "sun" ahead. He had to admit that the whole Matrimandir experience had been perfectly engineered to provoke some sort of reaction of awe.

They were directed to leave their shoes at the bottom of the path, and they climbed the stone stairs to enter. Inside, Abhay was in a low-ceilinged white space, with the rose-gold curving walls of the dome around them, and a large pillar in the center. Two workers silently handed white socks to each tourist. They were to wear these socks to keep the red earth off the white carpeting in the crystal chamber. Then everyone was directed through a small doorway and up a wide, white curved staircase between white marble walls, to another chamber, a huge white empty space, also round, with a pair of spiral ramps leading up. Abhay ascended one of these ramps with the group. He felt more and more as if he were in some sort of science-fiction setting.

At the top of the spiral ramp they entered the dim "concentration chamber." This space was also all white, including white carpeting, but appeared gray and shadowy because the lights were off. In the center, under the round skylight at the top of the globe, stood the largest crystal ball in the world, about twenty-eight inches in diameter, according to the guide. The crystal was supported on a golden stand, and a beam of sunlight was directed precisely down through the center of the glass ball, making a small splash of light under and around the ball. Apparently a computerized system of mirrors was used to position the sunlight at the correct angle at all times, and on cloudy days or at night, an artificial light was used to create the same effect. Abhay was amused that, in a shrine to the Universal Mother, it was found necessary to keep out most of nature—no dirt, no windows—and to strictly manage the nature— sunlight—that was permitted in.

Abhay walked slowly around the room, considering the large square white cushions that had been set out at precise intervals in three concentric circles around the chamber. He seated himself on a cushion next to one of the twelve columns surrounding the crystal ball.

The doors were shut softly, and they were left to their individual fifteen-minute meditation. Abhay didn't know how to meditate. For a while he gazed at the light in the crystal ball, but since it didn't move, he grew bored and closed his eyes. The place was cool, but not quiet. The room magnified any small sound, so that whenever anyone moved or cleared a throat, it was like a small burst of thunder rolling through the room. Abhay now became aware of a slight tickling in his throat. He swallowed. He'd been required to leave his water bottle at the entrance check stand. He wished he had chosen a cushion near the door so he could exit easily in case of a coughing fit. Now, looking around the room, he couldn't even make out where the doorways were. The walls of the room were evenly smooth and shadowy.

. He spent the next fifteen minutes concentrating on his throat and trying not to cough. As he sat there, perspiring in his effort, he realized that he felt disappointed not to be having any sort of out-of-the-ordinary experience, after all the buildup to this place. He realized he had hoped, semiconsciously, that the Matrimandir might give him some answers to his never-ending questions. Instead, all he was doing was trying to suppress a cough. He couldn't imagine how anyone could have a spiritual experience in a place with so many rules.

He decided to take Kianga's advice and see if he could come to any conclusion about Rasika. Why had he so often seen a glow around her? Why had she come to visit him in Portland? Why had he run into her just a few days before in Bangalore? Were they all meaningless coincidences?

He tried to calm his mind, to allow the presence of whatever spiritual power might be here to help him. As he thought about Rasika, he came to a realization: perhaps she was merely a distraction from his quest to figure out what to do with his life. Maybe he only thought he was in love with her in order to give himself some certainty in his uncertainty. After all, they were so different. In the shadowy grayness, these thoughts became clear to him.

The doors were opened, and everyone filed out of the room, down the ramp and staircase, and outside. After slipping on his sandals he proceeded, still in silence, toward the banyan tree nearby that marked the exact center of Auroville. This had been one of the only trees growing when Auroville first acquired their land. It was beautiful but not huge, as banyans go, although it did of course have its share of root-trunks descending from the spreading branches. Abhay saw some of the Indian women from his group approach the central thick trunk of the tree and press their cheeks against it.

Sitting on one of the benches around the tree, observing the others wandering around among the thin columns of the root-trunks, Abhay reflected that the Matrimandir fit a Western idea of a spiritual place—a place of sensory deprivation. Most Hindus, on the other hand, wanted noise, food, crowds, incense, dogs, monkeys, flowers, and hawkers of all kinds at their temples and religious places.

Kianga joined Abhay on his last evening in Auroville for an un-usual dinner at his guesthouse consisting of eggplant parmigiana, garbanzo bean curry, and papaya. After dinner, they sat under the trees, drinking herbal tea. The sky was dark, and the courtyard was lit by shaded lanterns hung from the tree branches. Abhay had changed into long pants and socks for protection against the mosquitoes that arrived every evening. Kianga didn't seem to be bothered by the insects: she wore a faded, flowing sleeveless dress. She had worked all day at the farm, and she still faintly emanated the scent of manure, perhaps from her sandals.

"What do you think of Auroville now?" Kianga asked.

"Interesting." Abhay slapped at a mosquito poised on his fore-arm. "Fascinating, actually. But I could never live here."

"In terms of ecology and community, Auroville is just about as perfect as it gets."

"I'm not looking for perfection."

"I think you are looking for your own variety of perfection," Kianga insisted. "What's wrong with Auroville that you could nev-er live here?"

He could tell that Kianga was growing frustrated with him, and he didn't blame her. He took a few sips of his woody, aromatic tea to buy some time. "I like it here, and I can see why you love it. But for me, it's too spiritually focused, in a confusing way. I don't understand the Mother's words that everyone quotes. 'Supramental.' 'Divine anarchy.'"

Kianga stirred her tea a little too vigorously. "They're not meant to be understood. You just allow the words into your consciousness, and they can provide you with a certain insight, a kind of opening into another world. A strong spiritual force holds this place together, which is the force of the Mother. Not just that particular woman who was a disciple of Sri Aurobindo, but the elemental Mother. I think there is something really supercharged, superenergized, about this place."

"To me, that explanation is just as confusing."

Kianga closed her eyes, took a deep breath, and let it out in a slow exhale. "You're thinking too much. Just let go, and see." She leaned back in her chair and gazed up at the dark sky. "The Mother said, 'Auroville wants to shelter people happy to be in Auroville. Those who are dissatisfied ought to return to the world where they can do what they want and where there is place for everybody.'"

Abhay reached up to a branch hanging low over the table, pulled off a leaf, and rolled it into a cylinder. "I feel like I'm a foreigner no matter where I go."

"What're you going to do after this trip?"

He shook his head. "I don't really want to work with Justin anymore, even though things have been kind of successful. I've booked him on some AM radio talk shows, and the hosts think he's a joke, but maybe about forty people actually signed the sterilization pledge on our Web site." Abhay began tearing the leaf into even strips. "It's not the right job for me, but I've organized things well enough that someone else can take over."

"Oh, well. Poor Justin. I'll get Ellen to help him out. I think they kind of like each other, actually. And listen, I'm not giving up on you yet. A friend of mine back in Portland wants to start a community radio station in her garage. I think you met her that one time when you went with me to the farmers' market. Since you have some radio experience now, maybe you could—"

"Don't worry about me, Kianga. I'm not even sure I'll stay in Portland much longer. Maybe I don't belong there either." His leaf was now in shreds, and he pulled off another leaf and began ripping. "Being in Auroville actually has helped. I agree that this place is just about as perfect as a community could be, and if I don't feel like I fit here, then I'll probably always be an outsider no matter where I go. And for the first time, I'm wondering if that might actually be a good thing."

He reached up for another leaf. Kianga put her hand on his forearm. "Stop it already with the leaves," she said.

"What?"

"You're acting like everything's fine, but you're ripping these leaves to shreds." She pointed to the bits of green scattered over the table. He looked down, surprised. He hadn't realized what he was doing.

"Just because you're ripping apart Auroville, and Portland, and Justin, and your relationship with this woman, that doesn't mean you should harass this tree," Kianga continued.

Abhay clutched his hands together on the table, and took a deep breath. "I'm not trying to rip everything apart."

"What are you trying to do, then?"

"I'm realizing something about myself. I'm interested in societies. I seem to want to figure out what makes them tick. So maybe I ought to take advantage of my alienated feelings."

Kianga tilted her head at him inquisitively.

"For example, I could study societies from the perspective of an outsider. I could be a professor." He was surprised at his own words. In Portland, Rasika had mentioned that he should be a professor.

"Hm." She wrapped both hands around her tea mug. "If that's what you want."

"I don't know if it's what I want. In some ways, it's exactly not what I want. I don't want to end up a stuffy professor at some low-ranked state university, trying to impress students by mentioning the few obscure papers I've managed to publish." He brushed the shredded leaves off the table.

She took his hand in hers. "Listen, Abhay." She seemed to be searching for words. "Would it help if I taught you a very simple meditation technique? This is something that can help ground you and also help you be open to God's guidance. Maybe you just need to relax and forget about yourself."

The hotness of her skin irritated him. He pulled his hands away and stood up. His metal chair tipped over with a crash. He picked it back up and set it carefully back on its feet. "I don't think so, Kianga. I just need to be alone."

She gathered up her mug and his. They walked out of the circle of lantern light and down the sidewalk to the dining hall door. It was locked. Kianga placed the cups on the flagstone floor outside the door and then kissed Abhay lightly on the cheek. He watched her walk away, toward her bike, adjusting the strap of a headlamp around her head. A sudden flash of light appeared as she switched on the lamp, and then she turned away, the light disappeared, and the squeak of her pedals faded as she left.

The next morning, Abhay opened his eyes and tried to sit up in bed. Pain shot from the side of his neck through his right shoulder and upper arm. He eased himself up and massaged his shoulder with his left hand. He must have slept funny. Carefully, he inched off the bed, gathered his towel and soap, and made his way to the bathroom. A warm bath should help. Yet by the time he was standing in line for breakfast, he could still hardly move his right arm.

He slid his plate along the counter, clumsily serving himself tea and scrambled eggs with his left hand.

Last night, after his conversation with Kianga, he'd had a strange dream. He was standing at a doorway, and he could see the white door frame—a square frame, luminescent in the darkness around him—but he couldn't make out anything through the door. It was black outside. He had the sense that he was supposed to walk through the door. But he wanted to be able to see where he was going. He strained his eyes. Nothing materialized out of the gloom.

"What happened to you?" Paloma was at his elbow, watching as he tried awkwardly to spread butter on his bread with the knife in his left hand.

"My shoulder hurts. I think I slept on it wrong."

"Why don't you get a massage?" Paloma pointed to a flyer on the wall near the telephone, which advertised "Thai Yoga Massage with Jerome." "You sign up here." Paloma tapped a chart at the bottom of the flyer. "I get this massage every week. You keep your clothes on. It is like someone else is doing the yoga for you, and you just relax."

The price was eight hundred rupees. About twenty dollars. He didn't have much else to do that morning, before taking a taxi to Pondicherry in the late afternoon. He planned to catch the night bus to Bangalore. With his left hand, he grasped the pen hanging on a string near the flyer and printed his name in block letters in the 10:00 A.M. slot.

The massage took place in a small, empty white room in the guesthouse complex. The windows let in the sunshine, yet the place was shaded by high trees, so the room was bright but not stuffy.

Jerome was a short, athletic Frenchman who gently stretched and twisted Abhay's limbs as Abhay lay on a thin futon mattress. Abhay was tense at first, fearing his arm would be hurt with the stretches. As the minutes passed and he experienced no pain, he began to relax into the mattress. A light, spicy floral scent wafted throughout the room. Outside everything was silent, except for the wind rustling in the leaves, and sometimes muffled voices in the distance.

Abhay had the sensation that his body was dissolving. It was not a frightening feeling—it was somewhat comforting. Jerome gently lifted and stretched his limbs. Abhay's body felt almost transparent. Its parts were starting to fade into the atmosphere. He knew, intellectually, that matter is made up mostly of empty space, since atoms are over 99 percent empty. So logically it followed that his own body was also mostly empty. He'd never before experienced it as such. Now he saw himself as though he were a constellation in a dark night sky, a random collection of pricks of light, with arbitrary lines drawn to suggest a human. The lines delineating his form were fading, and his atoms of empty space were dispersing through the emptiness of the universe.

As Jerome supported and pushed Abhay's right shoulder and arm into a stretch, Abhay felt no pain, yet he started to cry. It wasn't a wrenching kind of sobbing, just a gentle release of tears. He was embarrassed. He couldn't wipe away his tears without changing the position of his body, so he let them come. Jerome continued to work on his arms, then his hips, lifting and bending and leaning on his legs. The crying subsided and was replaced by a feeling of calm. Abhay heard the words: "It doesn't matter."

"What?" he said.

Jerome was silently working on Abhay's feet. The voice had come from near his shoulder—the painful one—so it couldn't have been Jerome's voice. Abhay heard it again. This time the voice seemed to say: "It isn't matter." The voice was clear and soft—he couldn't tell if it was a woman's or a man's. Abhay realized these words were answers to the questions that had been hammering away in his mind.

Lying there in the warm sunshine, Abhay felt his mind about to bristle with more questions: Who, or what, was providing these answers? How could it not matter? Or if he had misheard the first time, what did the voice mean by the words "it isn't matter"?

Almost as soon as these questions began forming, he was flooded with the realization: God. Existence. His guardian angels. And himself. It wasn't matter. It didn't matter. And he knew.

16

The next morning, Mahesh, Abhay's cousin, picked him up from the bus station. "The house is a mess," Mahesh explained as he stowed Abhay's backpack in the trunk of the car. "The bore well drilling was supposed to be finished by the time you returned, but unfortunately it started only this morning." Mahesh removed his glasses, rubbed the lenses with the bottom of his polo shirt, and set them back on. "I think the dust has entered the car, too."

Abhay didn't care about the dust in the car, or the noisiness of the city. He was glowing, calm, and blissful from his experience during the massage. He still didn't know what to do with his life, but strangely, he felt almost thrilled with his uncertainty.

"Looks like you had a good time," Mahesh remarked. "You have been smiling since I picked you up."

"It was beautiful," Abhay said.

As they approached the house, Abhay saw that the gate was wide open, with a truck parked in the driveway. A sea of mud escaped from the yard and into the roadway. Mahesh parked the car outside the compound wall. In the yard, they stepped over the mud and past the rumbling truck, which had a long cranelike attachment at its back—probably the drilling apparatus. The noise, the machinery, the mess—none of it bothered Abhay. He looked at it with interested detachment. He wondered how far down the bore well would have to be drilled.

The noise was loud even inside the house. Abhay deposited his backpack in the room he was sharing with Mahesh.

"Let's go out somewhere!" Mahesh shouted. They got back into the car. "I'll take you to see Electronics City," Mahesh yelled. "You'll see office buildings just like in America, and houses just like in America."

Abhay had heard about this, a new section of town called Electronics City. Could it possibly be just like America?

They drove for about an hour through traffic, to the outskirts of Bangalore. Despite the massage, Abhay's neck, shoulder, and right arm still hurt, although his range of motion was much wider. During the drive he kept tilting his head to the left to stretch his neck. Even the pain seemed delicious to him now.

"Here it is," Mahesh said.

From the roadway, Abhay saw giant glassy office buildings proclaiming "Hewlett-Packard" and "Wipro" and "3M India." The buildings themselves looked very Western, it was true—just like innumerable office buildings to be seen from any freeway in the United States. Abhay was amused to see that next to and in between the flashing buildings were browsing cows and corrugated-roof shacks.

"This is one of the largest industrial parks in India," Mahesh said. "Over a hundred companies on one-point-three square kilometers of land."

"What was here before?" Abhay asked.

"A couple of villages." Mahesh waved his hand in dismissal.

Abhay was surprised that he felt no anger at the idea of villages being destroyed for the sake of this industrial complex. It was the cosmic cycle—the destruction of Shiva, the creation of Brahma, the protection of Vishnu.

"Each of these buildings you see is like a campus. If you go inside the gates, it is so clean and beautiful, with gardens, fountains, places to eat, bookstores. Everything you will find there."

"Can we look at one of them?" Abhay asked.

"No. You must have a security pass. One of my friends took me in once. I am interviewing for jobs at several of the places here, so next time you come to India, I may be able to show you. Let's go see some houses."

They drove toward a high-walled complex and stopped inside the gate at the guard stand. As his cousin spoke with the black-uniformed guard, Abhay gazed down either side of the clean, empty roadway at two-story Indian-style houses, with the typical flat roofs and rectangular shapes. However, unlike other Indian neighborhoods, these houses were not walled off from each other but were placed on green lawns, with cement sidewalks running along the street.

"One of my friend's bosses lives there," Mahesh said. "These houses go for the equivalent of a million dollars. A lot of the residents are ex-pats—people who've come from the U.S. to work in Electronics City for a few years. Inside the complex they have a swimming pool, tennis courts, a clubhouse. Everything just like in America."

"Would you like to live there?" Abhay asked.

"Of course! Who wouldn't like to live there?"

They were not allowed to enter the complex—the guards turned them back, since they didn't have an invitation from any resident—and so they had to reenter the dusty, noisy traffic of the main road.

Just as they turned onto the main road, they were stopped in

traffic. A boy in drab shorts and shirt, holding a bucket and a squee-
gee, approached the car, offering to wash the windshield. Mahesh
shouted and waved his hand, and the boy wove his way through the
traffic to another car. Abhay looked back to find him, and could see
only a sea of cars, their roofs glinting in the sunlight.

"Doesn't it bother you that millionaires from abroad live in that
complex, while these boys in rags try to make money by washing
windshields?" Abhay asked this not with anger, but with curiosity.

Traffic started moving again. Mahesh veered into the oncoming
lane to pass a slow truck, and then veered back just before encoun-
tering a bus barreling toward them.

"I hear you have beggars in your country, too," Mahesh said.
"Does that prevent you from living where you want to live?"

Mahesh was right. Abhay didn't sleep on the sidewalk with the
homeless people in Portland.

Mahesh waved his hand. "That is the way it is. Will our worry
feed all these beggars? Of course not. So why worry?"

Traffic had stalled again. Cars sat like glowering animals,
honking and growling at one another. A truck just behind them
began its yodeling horn. After several minutes, they began inching
forward, and the honking subsided.

Abhay didn't know how to help the beggar boy, but he also
realized that he did not blame himself for not knowing.

Later that day, to escape the commotion at home, Abhay wandered
around the back streets near his grandmother's house. His euphoria
was starting to dissipate. Instead, he felt a deep satisfaction. He
was reminded of Nandan's words. He did feel as if he had found a
glowing pearl within himself. He passed a tiny motorcycle dealership with shiny vehicles displayed on the sidewalk. He walked past
new three-story apartment buildings, and past a cow shed tucked
between the houses. He nodded and smiled at everyone he saw.

On almost every block were piles of sand or dirt, and stacks of brick, for new construction. On one street Abhay saw a boy worker—perhaps ten or eleven years old—standing outside the compound wall of a half-finished house. He was wearing shorts, a colorful button-down shirt, and sandals. Abhay watched from across the street as the boy used a small scoop to shovel from a pile of red earth and pour the soil through a large screen, set on the ground and tilted at an angle, so the sieved earth fell into a shallow pan below. The boy looked up and caught Abhay's eyes, and Abhay had an odd sense that the boy was himself, that he was that boy worker who perhaps did not get a chance to go to school.

In a second the boy's eyes traveled past Abhay, and he pointed and smiled silently. Abhay turned his head, and on the compound wall behind him, partly hidden by the trunk of a tree, was a large gray-furred monkey sitting on its haunches. Its body and face were perfect, beautiful. Its black eyes looked at Abhay, and Abhay, holding as still as he could, looked back at the monkey. In a moment, the monkey pulled its body onto the branch overhanging the compound wall and glided silently up into the leafy canopy until it was invisible.

The boy worker, still smiling, began gesturing and letting out a stream of words at Abhay. "Hanuman" was the only word Abhay caught. Maybe the boy thought the monkey was a representation of the divine monkey who had helped Rama in his quest to save his wife Sita. Perhaps the boy believed that Hanuman watched over him as he worked.

The boy turned once more to his scooping and pouring, and Abhay was flooded with gratitude. God had given him the life he had. He had been educated. He had been blessed with shelter and food, and caring parents.

Abhay continued on his walk and came across an Internet browsing place next to what looked like an open-air workingmen's café of sorts, with men in pants or dhotis drinking tea and eating idlis while standing at high tables. He ducked into the low doorway of the Internet place and settled into a plastic chair. The computer whirred. He scanned his messages, deleting the junk: several messages from Chris about the latest eBay items for sale, notices about home-based business opportunities, and movie offers from Netflix.

His breath caught in his throat. There was something from Rasika. He clicked on her name with a trembling hand. She wrote:

> Can you meet us in Lalbagh? My cousin Mayuri wants me to meet her boyfriend, and Mayuri thought it would be better if there was another man with us, so it wouldn't look like we were there only with Khaleel. I don't want to get Yuvan involved. He might not understand.

Abhay took a deep breath and let it flow out. Although he realized Rasika was inviting him as a sort of decoy, he didn't care. At least she didn't seem to be married yet, and he would be seeing her again the next day. He wrote down Rasika's cell phone number. He'd call her as soon as he got back to his grandmother's house.

He had the nagging feeling there was something else he ought to be doing here at the computer. Abhay remembered how, in Portland, Rasika had praised his intelligence and advised him to make an impact on the world. She'd said, "If you don't pick something, you'll never get anywhere." A line of pain burned down from his neck to his fingertips, and almost as if they had intelligence of their own, his fingers clicked open a new message and typed in the address of his old mentor at Kent State—the professor who had gotten him interested in utopian communities in the first place.

In his e-mail, Abhay updated Dr. Ben-Aharon on his departure from Rising Star and his visit to Auroville, and asked about graduate school possibilities. "I want to study different kinds of communities and societies, and find out what is satisfying to people about various ways of organizing life," he wrote. "Would this be anthropology? Or sociology? And could I get into a graduate program in either of those fields, given that my undergraduate degree is in general studies?" He didn't know if he really wanted to be a professor or not, but figured it couldn't hurt to explore this avenue.

After lunch the next day, a Saturday, he took an autorickshaw to Lalbagh, where he met up with Rasika, Mayuri, and Khaleel as they stood on the grassy strip next to the small parking lot. The day was hot, and Rasika wore a pretty sleeveless white embroidered top over jeans. Her hair was gathered into a large barrette at the nape of her neck, and she wore her usual sunglasses. As soon as Abhay saw her, he knew his love for her was no distraction, no mistake. She barely acknowledged his greeting, and in fact stepped away from him, to the other side of Mayuri and Khaleel.

They walked up a slanted expanse of bare rock, on top of which was one of the Kempe Gowda watchtowers, which looked from a distance like a small temple with a white carved dome on top.

"There are four such towers in Bangalore," Khaleel said. "They were built in the sixteenth century by Bangalore's ruler, Kempe Gowda, to mark the four corners of the city."

Khaleel apparently thought of himself as a travel guide. Abhay knew all about the Kempe Gowda towers. Of course now Bangalore sprawled for miles beyond these watchtowers.

At the top of the rock, next to the tower, a dark man squatted on the ground, roasting corn over coals in a shallow pan. Khaleel took out his wallet and said something to the man, who began to shuck ears of corn from the pile next to him.

"I don't want one," Rasika said.

"Come on. My treat," Khaleel insisted. Abhay sensed that he wanted to impress Rasika.

"They're very tasty with the salt and masala." Mayuri smacked her lips.

"Just a small one," Khaleel suggested.

As the man rotated four ears of corn over the coals, Abhay inched closer to Rasika, who was standing with her back to the pan, gazing at the scene below. The gray rock sloped down and away from them. Layers of Lalbagh trees in various shades of green appeared below them, and past that was the busy intersection outside the park entrance. "Those look like toy cars, don't they?" he remarked.

"What do you mean?" She gave him a small smile. He couldn't see her eyes behind the black lenses.

"You can't really hear the traffic or smell the exhaust, so it all looks really calm down on the street, like something a kid would play with."

Khaleel handed around the hot corn, wrapped in husks and smeared with red spices. Abhay bit into his. Indian corn tended to be tough, for some reason, yet he enjoyed gnawing on the scorched, mealy kernels. The spices made his lips burn.

Mayuri and Khaleel wandered down the slope, and Abhay and Rasika were left to each other. Rasika held her corn carefully in one hand. Her forearm trembled slightly. She didn't eat any of it. At the bottom of the rock, they reached a shaded dirt path among the trees.

"How was your trip?" she asked.

"I had an amazing experience."

She stumbled on the sandy path. He put a hand on her elbow to steady her, and she shrugged him away.

"Are you going to move there?" Her voice was low and hard.

"No, but I'm thinking of applying to graduate school. Maybe I'll even get a Ph.D."

She turned her face to him. He smiled. He wished he could see her eyes. She looked away and sighed deeply. "Of course you will. You're so smart. You'll be a great professor."

He felt an outpouring of love for her. He wanted to look into her eyes, to touch the twinkling diamonds in her earlobes, the wisps of hair escaping her barrette. On her upper arm were several dime-size bumps. "Mosquito bites?" He brushed a fingertip against them.

"Don't touch me," she murmured.

"You're way too thin," he said. "Your hand is trembling. You're a mess."

"Leave me alone."

"Why'd you invite me out here?"

"I just wanted to help Mayuri."

"So it had nothing to do with me?"

Rasika bit her lip. They walked along a path through the grass. On their right was a strip of colorful flowers; on their left, a grove of trees. Mayuri and Khaleel were several yards ahead. As Abhay and Rasika passed a trashcan, she calmly tipped her corn into it and brushed her palms together.

"When's the wedding?"

"Next Friday. January fourth."

"And your birthday is, when?"

"End of January. So we'll be fine."

"You're really going through with it?"

She pressed her lips together and watched her sandaled feet taking one step after the other.

"I don't think you like him," Abhay said. "Do you have to marry him?"

"Everything's been arranged. The guests have been invited. I've bought my saris and jewelry."

"Does anyone care that you don't actually want to spend your life with this man?"

"How do you know what I want?"

"It was completely obvious when I saw the two of you together. I don't understand why you're doing this to yourself. You look completely lifeless."

Rasika cleared her throat. "I'm just kind of stressed-out because I'm dreading all the Hindu rituals—sitting in front of that hot fire, and changing my sari halfway through, and chanting all those prayers." Her voice quavered. She cleared her throat again. "That's all. After the wedding's over, everything'll be fine."

"Stop." Abhay stood still and put a hand on her shoulder. "You're running blind. You need to open your eyes. Listen. We've both been looking for an ideal. You think your life will be perfect if only you can be the kind of person your parents seem to want. I thought my life would be perfect if only I could find a place on earth that matched the utopia in my imagination. We're both searching for something we've built in our own brains."

While he was talking, Rasika stopped, but she seemed to be looking past him, at something in the distance above his ear. He stopped talking, and she walked ahead. He trailed behind her. They came upon a pond, shining blue water edged with greenery. No one stopped to look. Mayuri and Khaleel seemed deep in conversation, and Rasika just kept walking. They passed benches from which people were selling cucumber slices, newspaper cones full of peanuts, sliced guavas smeared with chili paste.

They passed a small garden of bushes clipped into animal and cartoon shapes, and reached a clearing with a huge tree. Its roots climbed out of the ground, and its branches rayed out just above the roots. The whole thing, roots and trunk, seemed to have a diameter as broad as a bus. They all stopped near the tree, and Rasika strayed a few steps away from the group. Abhay noticed her remove her sunglasses and dab carefully at her eyes with a hankie.

"This is the largest tree in Lalbagh," Khaleel said.

The tree was obviously a photo opportunity: women in bright saris, boys in shorts, and girls in dresses were crawling all over its roots to find places to sit, before smiling for the camera.

"Mayuri, you and Rasika stand near the tree. I will take a photo." Khaleel held up his cell phone. The sun dappled the ground around them.

"I'll take the picture," Abhay offered, holding out his hand. "You go stand with Mayuri and Rasika."

Mayuri stepped toward Rasika to bring her into the picture. Rasika was now blinking her eyes and trying to smile brightly. Suddenly, Mayuri clutched at Rasika's arm. "My cousin is here," she whispered.

Abhay looked in the direction of Mayuri's frightened gaze. A group of young men strolled toward them over the sandy earth, holding newspaper cones and tossing peanuts into their mouths.

Mayuri turned and walked swiftly away in the direction of the tree. Abhay, Khaleel, and Rasika stood around awkwardly. Mayuri disappeared behind the tree. Khaleel slipped his phone into his pocket.

"Do you come here often?" Rasika asked Khaleel, smiling at him.

"Yes, I do," Khaleel answered, grinning and playing along.

The young men had stopped to watch. Rasika and Khaleel kept up their silly banter. Abhay wandered a few steps away. The young men were now whispering to each other.

Rasika called cheerfully, "Abhay, come on. Let's get our picture taken." Khaleel was displaying his phone again. She hooked an arm through Abhay's— he winced in pain as his arm was jerked—and

marched him over to the tree. He was surprised at her willing-
ness to touch him in public. He obliged by slipping an arm around
her shoulders. She held her sunglasses in the fingertips of her other
hand. As Khaleel held out his phone to frame them, one of the
young men from the cousin group seemed to be aiming his cell
phone at Rasika. Abhay glanced at Rasika to see if she noticed.
She wasn't looking at the men. She was beaming determinedly at
Khaleel.

The men walked away. Khaleel pocketed his phone.

"We should leave," Rasika said as she and Abhay joined Khaleel.

"Yes," Khaleel agreed. He continued to look at the tree.

"You go first," Rasika said. "We'll find Mayuri and walk in a
different direction."

Khaleel put his phone back in his pocket and walked away,
still gazing sideways at the tree. He gave a surreptitious wave and a
quick smile, after which his pace quickened.

Mayuri and Rasika gave Abhay a ride back home. Mayuri had
use of the family car for the day. No one spoke of Mayuri's narrow escape, and she herself seemed fairly calm. She wove comfortably through the traffic, accelerating aggressively whenever anyone
threatened to cut her off.

As they dropped Abhay off at the gate of his grandmother's
house, Rasika said, "You're not far from our place."

"We could walk home from here," Mayuri said.

"It might be faster," Rasika agreed, and they looked at each
other and giggled.

Abhay, unlatching the gate and stepping into the compound,
still heard their laughter from the car. He rubbed his sore neck and
shoulder. As the car pulled away from the curb, Abhay looked back
at Rasika and discovered her eyes on him. She turned away as soon
as she saw him looking, and the car moved off.

* * *

"How do you know Abhay?" Mayuri asked casually. "You seem on very good terms with him."

Rasika and Mayuri sat on the flat rooftop in the evening, eating slices of cucumber and talking. Rasika felt exhilarated, as she often did when she flirted with the life she wasn't supposed to live. In this case, she was experiencing it vicariously, through Mayuri's narrow escape that afternoon.

"He's just an old family friend. Nobody, really." Rasika laughed.

Mayuri dabbed her cucumber slice in the small pile of salt on her plate. "I wondered if you had ever dated him. I wondered how your parents would feel if you were in the same situation I am in."

Rasika glanced at Mayuri's pretty face. She felt a connection with Mayuri, since she had helped her cousin in a way Jill and other friends had always helped her. "I have dated," she said quietly. "Not much. And my parents don't know."

"You never wanted to marry anyone else?" Mayuri's eyes looked eager.

Rasika felt that Mayuri would understand her own predicament. As the sky grew darker, Rasika began to reveal more and more about her own life. She started out cautiously, talking merely about being "friends" with men in college. When Mayuri didn't seem shocked, Rasika told her about her friendship with Abhay. She left out the part about the Renaissance Hotel, but mentioned that she had visited him in Portland. She felt more relaxed now than she'd ever been on this trip. It was a relief to confess to someone who cared.

"You have experience with men, but you have not fallen in love like I have." Mayuri covered her face with her hands. "I don't know what I should do."

Rasika laid a hand on Mayuri's shoulder. "It's hard for us. We have a little more freedom than our mothers did, but just enough to get ourselves in trouble. They still expect us to do what they tell us."

"You are the only one who understands me," Mayuri said.

"Now you know what I'm going through. I don't know if Yuvan is really the right person for me, but time is running out, and everyone wants me to do this. So I'm going to go through with it. This is what we have to do."

Mayuri looked up and nodded sadly. "I don't know if I'll be able to be like you, Rasika. I'm afraid for myself."

Rasika held Mayuri's hand in silence. All that mattered now, in the darkness, was that Mayuri understood her—that an Indian woman, someone in her own family, was aware of what she was sacrificing in order to sustain the structure of tradition. In some way this almost made up for what Rasika was going to have to go through.

17

Early the next morning, while Abhay's uncle was still sitting in the living room in his dhoti, watching the dawn pooja from Tirupati on television, the doorbell screeched through the house. His grandmother was taking her bath, and his aunt was in the kitchen grinding something in the blender, so Abhay answered the door. Rasika stood on the doorstep. She looked terrible. Her eyes were wild, her hair was uncombed, and she had on a pair of jeans, a baggy T-shirt, and unmatched sandals—one brown, one black.

"What're you doing here?" He stepped out of the house and pulled the wood door shut behind him. The bore well drilling was finished, but the yard was still muddy.

"They found out," Rasika gasped.

"Found out what?"

Rasika appeared not to know how to answer this question. Her eyes darted around, as if trying to see the answer in the air. Then she closed her eyes, shuddered, and opened them again. She looked like she'd been deflated. Her eyes were sad and distant now. "The wedding's off," she said in a monotone.

"Why?"

Rasika held a palm up to her face and peered at it. She rubbed it with the thumb of the other hand, as though trying to wipe off some dirt. Abhay remembered that gesture—she had done the same thing at Ledges, although then she had been wiping off mascara. Now, her palm seemed clean.

It was awkward trying to talk in the muddy yard. His cousin's motor scooter was parked on the narrow pathway between the house and the compound wall, and his uncle's car was in the driveway.

"Let's take a walk." He ducked inside and slipped on a pair of sandals. When he returned, Rasika was still standing in the same position, still rubbing her palm.

"Come on." He headed toward the gate. When she didn't move, he grabbed her by the elbow and steered her out with him. It was so early that the traffic hadn't really started yet. He led her around the corner to a little high-walled park tucked between the houses. It was filled with trees and a formal arrangement of greenery, a bricked path going around in a square, and several concrete benches. No one was here at this hour. This park was too small to be useful for the fast-paced morning walking that many Indians seemed to engage in. Abhay dropped onto the bench closest to the entrance. He knew from experience that the far corners of the park smelled distinctly of urine.

Rasika sank down beside him. She looked crumpled.

"Tell me everything," he said.

"The wedding's off," she repeated. "Yuvan saw us." She looked up at him plaintively. "You shouldn't have put your arm around me."

"What? When?" He tried to think when he had last had his arm around her, and remembered the big tree at Lalbagh. In order to play along, he had put his arm around her as Khaleel was taking the photo. "How could . . . was Yuvan at Lalbagh?"

"His brother showed him a picture. They took a picture."

He remembered the group of young men, Mayuri's cousin and friends. One of them had taken a photo. "Mayuri's cousin?" he asked.

She nodded, and sat up straighter. "Yuvan is Mayuri's cousin. On her father's side." Her eyes were clear and hard now. "His brother was at the park."

"Didn't you recognize him?"

She shook her head. "I've only seen him once, when Yuvan and I first met. I didn't recognize him yesterday. I wasn't really paying attention, I was so busy wanting to protect Mayuri."

"Well, you can explain, can't you? I mean, you were only flirting to draw attention away from Mayuri. Just tell the truth."

Rasika looked at him, and her eyes gradually grew dull. "No." She shook her head. "I couldn't do that to Mayuri."

"Well, Mayuri will have to tell the truth, then."

"She's backing them up."

"What?"

"She's telling everyone that I asked her to drive me to Lalbagh so I could meet you there."

"That's insane!" Abhay was outraged that Mayuri would drag his name into her sordid affair. "You've got to set things straight."

Rasika shook her head sadly.

"Why not?"

"I just . . . don't want to stoop that low."

"It's not stooping, it's standing up for yourself."

"I don't want to point fingers at Mayuri. I'm not that kind of person. I've lied in the past, but only to protect myself. I don't tattle. I've never done anything to get anyone else into trouble. Anyway, I don't know if anyone would believe me. Even my mother has bought into the whole thing. Yuvan's father called this morning to tell us their decision, and Amma woke me up by screaming at me. That's why I had to leave the house. I think she's always suspected me. Remember when Mita Auntie saw us at that hotel in Cleveland, and told everyone?"

Abhay nodded. That seemed so long ago now. He was proud of Rasika's integrity toward her cousin. "So Yuvan believes Mayuri?"

"I don't know what he believes. He didn't call, his father did. His family's already involved. It's a mess." She turned her eyes toward him, and they seemed soft and open. Her mask had dropped away.

"I would think Yuvan would at least give you the benefit of the doubt and listen to your side of things."

"What can I say that would convince him? I'm not innocent."

"You mean you're not innocent because we've had a relationship?"

Rasika nodded. "Mayuri knows about that. Last night we stayed up late talking. I felt like she understood me. And now she's telling all the details to everyone." Rasika covered her face with her hands. "I can't go back." She was still for a moment, and he realized she was crying. At first she seemed to be trying to control herself, holding her breath and wiping at her eyes, and then she let go. It sounded like the tears were ripping out of her.

There was something wild about her now, something true, and he loved that. When she stopped shaking with emotion, he said, "At least you're free now. You never wanted to marry him anyway."

She took her hands from her face and looked at him, and he felt he could see into her soul.

Then her tear-filled eyes narrowed and turned sharp. "You could marry me." Her voice had a rasping quality.

"What?"

"Everyone thinks we're together anyway. You could marry me. Everything's all ready for a wedding next week. You could fill in and be the groom." She looked up at him with pleading eyes, yet the mask was there again.

He stood up, as a way to gain more control over the situation. "Of course, I'll marry you. But not like this. I don't want to marry you as a substitute." He paced in front of the bench. "In a way, it's good this happened. You didn't even want to marry that guy. Now you can be who you really are. You don't need to pretend anymore. Now you can decide what you really want to do." Abhay stopped pacing and let out a deep breath. Rasika wasn't even looking at him. Her eyes were narrowed, and she was gazing off to the side, as if thinking of something else.

"You don't understand me," she said. "No one understands me."

Crows screeched and cawed in the dark branches overhead. The quacking beeps of a motor scooter passed by outside the walls of the garden. Various smells reached them on the morning breeze— snacks being fried in oil, cow dung, a whiff of roasting coffee.

Rasika stood up.

"You ready to go home?" Abhay put a hand on her elbow. "I know you can be strong. They'll get over this."

Abhay took her hands and looked into her eyes. They seemed cold and distant. What might happen after she stood up to her parents? They might be together. He pressed her fingers in his. "I think it'll work out fine," he whispered.

She suddenly pulled her hands from his, snatched her purse up from the bench, and peered into its depths.

"What's wrong?"

"I'm—I don't have any money." She let the purse drop to the ground. "I spent it all. This morning I had enough to pay for the auto to your house. That's all."

Abhay pulled out his wallet and offered several hundred-rupee notes. She hesitated, and then put out a hand. He picked up her purse and handed it to her.

"I'll give you the phone number at my grandmother's house." He scribbled on a scrap of paper.

Abhay led her out of the park and up to the main road, where he put up an arm to hail an autorickshaw. When a vehicle veered toward them and stopped, the engine muttering softly, she did not get in. Instead, she clung to him. "Come with me," she said.

"You want me to come home with you? Won't your mother—"

"Let's just get away. Let's go somewhere." She was trembling against him.

"Rasika." He stepped away from her and took her by the shoulders. "I think it would be best if you went home to explain. Your family will be worried sick." He had to shout over the rumble and roar of traffic.

She nodded. She was still shaking.

The autorickshaw driver shouted something to them in a language Abhay didn't understand; clearly, the man was impatient. "If you want me to come home with you, I can," Abhay said. "Just for support."

"No," she said firmly. "You don't understand."

"Call me as soon as you talk to your folks. I'll be waiting."

She threw her arms around him and gave him a fierce hug. "I love you," she said gruffly. Then she flung herself into the waiting autorickshaw.

The autorickshaw driver pumped his starter and jerked away from the intersection. "Where to, ma'am?" he asked in Kannada. She understood that much but didn't answer, because she didn't know what to say. He brought the autorickshaw to a puttering halt along the side of the road, and glowered at her.

Her mind was in a fog. She felt as if she had a swarm of ants crawling around inside her head, in front of her eyes. She shook her head, and wiped her hair from her face. She could see the dusty street, and she could see the driver's bare brown feet in flip-flops. She could see the stub of incense stick in front of the tiny photo of

Ganesha behind the driver's handlebars. But she couldn't see what she should do next.

The driver said something to her in a harsh tone. She didn't quite understand the words, but she knew she had to figure out where she wanted to go. She couldn't sit here motionless forever.

A thought arose out of the muddle of her mind. Yes, that might work. It would mean swallowing her pride, but it was her only option now. Over the roar of the traffic, she shouted out the name of a neighborhood bordering the area in which her grandparents lived, and the vehicle was off again.

She clutched her almost-empty purse. She had to escape, and for that she needed money. But she had none, except for the rupees Abhay gave her, which would flow through her fingers in minutes. She couldn't buy a plane ticket with this money. She couldn't even stay in a decent hotel for this amount of money.

She'd spent all the thousands of rupees her father had given her, and also the thousands Yuvan's parents had given her. She'd bought silk clothes, cotton clothes, gold jewelry, corals, hundreds of cheap glass and metal bangles in every color to match all her outfits, several pairs of sandals, batik wall hangings, sandalwood carvings, brass deepas, idli pans and chapati boxes and spice boxes and a pressure cooker and a special dosa batter grinder. All of these purchases were packed in suitcases, bags, and boxes at her mother's family home, waiting for her to get married and carry them back to Ohio with her.

She wanted to be honorable. She loved Abhay. He was a very good man. She wanted to make him proud of her. She wanted to make her parents proud of her. This was really the only thing she could do.

Rasika exited the autorickshaw in front of a small house. She stepped through the gate, threaded her way through a clutter of motorbikes and bicycles in the paved front yard, and rang the doorbell.

Shouts and laughter sounded inside the house, but no one came to the door. She rang again, and finally the door was hauled open by a small child who took one look at her and then ran shouting through the house, "Some woman is here." Eventually, an elderly man appeared at the doorway and looked at her quizzically.

"Is this where Balakrishna stays?" she asked in Tamil.

He nodded and held the door open. She entered and slipped off her mismatched sandals in the front hallway. He disappeared through the doorway curtain, calling, "Balu! Someone is here to see you!"

In the moment she was alone, she combed through her hair with her fingers to try to bring some order to it.

Balu Uncle appeared through the curtain. He wore a white dhoti wrapped around his waist and legs, a button-down shirt, and a cloth folded neatly over one shoulder: the typical at-home outfit of an Indian man. When he saw her, he halted for a moment. Then he said quietly, "Please sit down." He held a hand out to a chair right there in the front hallway, and she sat. He placed himself on a bench opposite and crossed his legs on the seat, one ankle over the other knee, tucking his dhoti neatly around his legs.

It seemed odd to her that he didn't take her into the living room and offer her some tea. Perhaps it was because she had arrived so early, and so unexpectedly.

They sat without talking for several moments. The house resounded with thumping footsteps and children's high-pitched shrieks. She wondered how many people stayed in this small house.

Finally he asked in Tamil, "What is it, dear?"

She felt faint and nauseated, but she gulped down some air, sat up straight, and squared her shoulders. She had to do this. "I came here—Subhash—I know he would like to marry me," she blurted out. "And it is fine with me now."

Balu Uncle grasped the ankle of his top leg and leaned back against the wall. His gaze rested on her face for several moments before wandering up the wall behind her. "We have heard about what happened," he said finally. "This morning your father called us."

She waited for him to go on. Somewhere in the house, a toilet flushed with a gurgle and whoosh of water.

"A few days ago we arranged Subhash's marriage with a girl raised in India," Balu Uncle said. "We realized it would be best for him to marry someone with good values—the values of our family."

Good values. She had *better* values than Subhash and his family, because she also had grace, beauty, and appropriateness. But now she couldn't say any of this. She wouldn't stoop to defend herself.

"Did you come here on your own?" Uncle asked.

"Yes," she answered.

"No one brought you?"

She shook her head.

"They should not be allowing you to go about on your own," he murmured.

She stood up and saw black, as the blood drained from her head suddenly. She put a hand on the chair to steady herself. She felt sick to her stomach. In a moment her head cleared, her vision returned. "I'll go now," she said.

"Your father has been so good to us." He shook his head slowly, and patted his forehead with the cloth folded over his shoulder. "He helped us come to your country. He loaned me the money for our business. Subhash always liked you. He wanted to marry you, but we discouraged him. At that time, we did not think our son was good enough for you. We thought, how can we ask for the hand of a girl whose father is so wealthy, and has already been so generous?

But now—I don't know what will happen to you. I feel very bad for your father." Balu Uncle's mouth twisted with pity.

He felt bad for her father. Did no one care about her any longer? She found her sandals and opened the door.

"Let me send someone with you." Balu Uncle stood up. "My brother's son can take you home on his motorbike."

"No." She opened the door. "I'm leaving now." She stepped out the door and shut it behind her before Balu Uncle could make any other arrangements.

She had failed. She had failed herself, and she had failed Abhay. She could no longer go home and expect to be a respected part of the family. She could no longer face Abhay. She walked a block to the nearest main road, hailed another autorickshaw, climbed in, and shouted out the first destination that came to her mind: "Commercial Street." The autorickshaw started grinding and weaving through the traffic.

Abhay waited at home for several hours, but Rasika didn't call. He hesitated to call her cell phone. He didn't want to bother her during her important mission. He tried to assume that everything was fine, since she didn't show up at his place again. He knew how these blow-ups went. He'd certainly experienced enough of them at his own house. Her parents would rage for a while, and then they'd calm down, look at the situation realistically, and see that things weren't so bad.

After lunch, instead of waiting at home by the phone, he thought he'd take a walk to the Internet place and send her an e-mail. That way, she could answer whenever she got a chance.

He settled into the plastic chair in the tiny computer room and opened his e-mail. Right away, he saw a message from Dr. Ben-Aharon, his former professor at Kent State. He was nervous to open it. Would Dr. Ben-Aharon tell Abhay that he had no hope of getting into graduate school?

Abhay composed a short message to Rasika expressing his concern and inviting her to call him soon. Then he looked at a message from his mother, a long complaint having to do with Seema, the fact that she was planning to go on a trip with her boyfriend (they were driving up to Cleveland for New Year's Eve), and how upset Abhay's father was. Abhay didn't know what to say to his mother, so he closed that message. He'd think of something later. He wrote a short note of support to Seema.

He went through and deleted the spam: investment opportunities, stuff from the alumni association at his college, sales pitches from office supply stores, advertisements for cheap drugs. He filled out his name and address in a petition from a pro-Tibet group.

Finally, he opened the message from Dr. Ben-Aharon, scanned it, and let out a long breath. His professor had written a warm reply urging Abhay to apply to the best sociology and anthropology graduate programs, and had provided a list of such schools. "There is quite a bit of overlap between sociology and anthropology. If I were you, I'd take a look at each school and see which one offers you the closest match to what you want to do. Given your outstanding senior honors thesis at Kent State, and the fact that you have, in effect, conducted personal field research, you would be an ideal candidate for graduate school." Dr. Ben-Aharon went on to express his eagerness to write letters of recommendation for Abhay.

In one small part of his mind, Abhay was telling himself that he didn't really want to be a professor. He always thought he'd do something more unique with his life. His father was a professor, after all. Lots of people were professors. Abhay didn't want to grow rigid and jaded and resigned, as he'd seen so many people become once they'd settled into their careers.

Yet as Abhay sat there, rereading the e-mail, he felt an enormous knot in his forehead untie itself. He felt the clenching in his stomach unravel. He felt his heart blossom with love for everything around him: the photos of Ganesha and Lakshmi observing him benevolently from the shelf next to his computer; bright sunshine pouring through the window, and the steel plates and cups rattling at the outdoor café next door.

He didn't want to reply to Dr. Ben-Aharon yet. He was too full of emotion. He signed off from the computer, paid his fifteen rupees, and walked out onto the hot street again.

The nearby shopping district was crawling with customers as usual. As he approached a fruit stall, he saw the barefooted proprietor, one foot propped on the bottom tier of his display, catching papayas tossed to him from the back of a truck parked at the curb. After receiving each papaya, the man arranged it on an upper tier of the display, and turned to catch the next. Abhay watched as the driver tossed and the fruit man caught maybe fifty large papayas and arranged them in neat rows. Abhay kept expecting at least one of the melon-size fruits to end up in an orange and black splatter on the sidewalk, yet none did. The two men had a steady rhythm, tossing the weighty fruit across the sidewalk despite the people milling around.

Abhay felt astonished. None of the other customers seemed to take any notice, and probably this same scene, this same miracle, repeated itself at fruit stalls all over India. This fruit vendor was happy with his life, tending his little stall day after day, catching fruits, arranging them in beautiful rows and pyramids, haggling over prices.

Abhay walked past a store that sold batteries and plugs, past glass cases displaying trays of white, pink, and silver sweets. People worked in all of these places and were apparently happy with their lives, and Abhay was going to join them. He was going to be happy with his life. He was going to choose one path now and leave the others behind because, after all, there would be passages up ahead, leading out from that first path, and he would never encounter those further ways unless he started forward.

Abhay rotated his shoulder—the pain was gone. He lifted his arms and tilted his head back and forth. He had a full range of motion.

He strolled past a sewing machine on the sidewalk, powered by the thin dark foot of the man who sat behind it. A plump woman was settled on the granite slab of sidewalk next to the machine, ripping the seam out of a piece of clothing. A metal cabinet behind them apparently held all their supplies. As Abhay passed, he heard the man humming while he worked.

Toward evening, he made his way back to his grandmother's house. His aunt let him in and whispered, "Someone is here to see you."

Rasika. She'd come back to him.

When he entered the living room he saw not Rasika, but her brother Pramod, who stood up and held out a hand. Abhay hadn't seen Pramod in months—probably not since Amisha Menon's reception—and hadn't really talked to him in years. Pramod looked solemn and asked if there were any private place to talk. It would be getting dark soon, so the walled garden would be closing. Abhay suggested a restaurant. Pramod shook his head. "I don't feel like being in public."

There was no private place in the house or in the yard. Abhay led Pramod outside the gate, where they stood under the glaring streetlight as cars and autorickshaws and buses rumbled and honked and rattled past.

"Is Rasika OK?" Abhay asked over the jangle of traffic.

"No." Pramod rubbed a hand over his face. "She's had an accident. It's a miracle we even found her. She fell out of an autorickshaw near Commercial Street. She banged her head on the sidewalk"—

Pramod knocked his knuckles against the side of his head to indicate the site of injury—"and became unconscious."

Abhay felt as if his own head had been smashed. He pressed his hands to the sides of his head. "Oh my god. How did you find her?"

"A street vendor saw the whole thing. Someone tried to contact an ambulance, but the ambulance services are private, and I don't know how they can even get through the traffic. So this street vendor flagged down a car, and the driver of that car took her to a nearby hospital. This man looked through Rasika's purse, found her cell phone, and saw our phone number. He called us."

His head throbbed in response to Rasika's injury. "I didn't know—"

"She left the house this morning," Pramod shouted over the traffic. "My mother was having one of her usual fits, and Rasika left. We figured she'd be back, so when she didn't return in a few hours, we tried calling her. There was no answer. Then my mother sent me out to look for her. How do you find one person in this gigantic maze of a city?"

"She came to see me this morning." Abhay still clutched his head. "We talked. I thought I had convinced her to go home and face her parents." He put his hands down. "I didn't know she was so distraught when she left. I should have—"

"Yuvan's brother came over today and showed us the photo of you and Rasika. I didn't know you were even in India. I contacted your parents in Ohio and found out where you were staying. My cousin is telling everyone that Rasika had a relationship with you and that she's in love with you."

"I do love her." A particularly noisy truck rattled past. Abhay stepped closer to Pramod to be heard. "And, I believe she loves me. I came to India to see her. We ran into each other on MG Road one day. She asked me to meet her at Lalbagh. Mayuri was going to see her boyfriend there, and they wanted another man around."

"I suspected Mayuri had something to hide." Pramod scowled.

"Where is Rasika now?" Abhay asked. "What hospital?"

"We transferred her to Aarogya Hospital, which is one of the best in the city. People from the U.S. come there for surgery. I've been very impressed."

"Is she going to be OK?"

Pramod shook his head slowly. "It's hard to tell. The problem is, she was unattended for maybe an hour or more. With brain injuries, it's important to get treatment right away." Pramod's face had taken on a look of professional competence. "As I said, I've been very impressed with the hospital," Pramod continued. "They controlled the brain swelling; they got her a CT scan and an MRI. Right now she's awake, which is a good sign, and she sometimes responds to commands. She knows her own name, and she seems to recognize us, at least part of the time. So far she hasn't been speaking much at all, which my father's really worried about."

"I need to see her."

"It's too late now."

"Tomorrow—"

"I don't think that's a good idea. My mother doesn't leave Rasika's side, and we're having a hard enough time keeping Amma calm. If you show up, who knows what she'll do."

The traffic screeched and rumbled past. Across the street, a plump woman wearing a blue sari and carrying a briefcase inserted herself into the mix and calmly walked toward them, as cars and autos and scooters veered past her.

"I need to get back," Pramod said.

Abhay stood with Pramod until he flagged down an autorickshaw. Abhay felt nauseated. After Pramod left, Abhay lay on his bed in the darkness. Through the open window a temple bell clanged, over and over, above the rumble of traffic. His heart was beating so hard that it felt like the bell was resounding inside his chest.

How had Rasika fallen out of the autorickshaw? Although the autos had open sides, once you were seated inside you were fairly well enclosed. Had she actually—jumped out? Or maybe she had changed her mind about where she was going and tried to get out of the moving autorickshaw? Drivers sometimes didn't pay much attention to whether their passengers were fully out or in before they jerked up their starting handle and rattled off.

As everyone went to bed and the house quieted down, Abhay's mind continued to turn the situation over and over.

The next morning, Abhay couldn't decide what to do with himself. He wanted to see Rasika, yet he didn't want to cause more trouble for her. He didn't know how to reach Pramod. He made his way back to the little secluded garden where he'd had his last conversation with Rasika. The garden was deserted. He stood near the bench where she had sat. Should he have agreed to marry her on the spot? It was only yesterday morning. It seemed like a lifetime ago.

His eyes were drawn to the wall behind the bench. A flowering vine spilled over the concrete, with unusual flowers, like little ears, or like funnels. He stepped behind the bench and touched the yellow and brick-red petals. Four long white structures, two pairs curving to meet each other at the top, nestled inside the petals. The flowers hung in chains down the wall, among the glossy long leaves.

There were so many flowers in India. Every day something new burst into bloom: rows of small purple blossoms along shrub stems, or bells of bright orange bedecking a tree. In sunny areas he'd seen profusions of the low-growing "touch-me-not," with pink puff-ball flowers and delicate fernlike leaves that folded closed when you touched them.

An image flashed into his consciousness—Rasika on the bridge in the Japanese garden in Portland. She'd looked like a flower in her yellow sweater, under the hanging branches of the tree.

He plucked one of the firm blossoms, and then another, and placed them on his palm. He needed something to carry them. He walked out of the garden to one of the little shops lining the street opposite, bought the first cloth bag he could find—a tan sack imprinted with ICICI BANK—came back to the garden, and filled the bag with the blossoms. Then, on the main road again, he hailed an autorickshaw and shouted, "Aarogya Hospital."

Abhay carried his bag of flowers into the hospital. The lobby was lit by large windows. The walls were plain white, the floor shiny gray cement. The women at the front desk wore matching green saris. They directed him to the third floor. "Ultradeluxe room," one of them murmured. He climbed the wide stairs. His heart was beating wildly, and his palms were sweaty. At room 310 he paused. He could see, through the partly open door, that the room was full of people—Rasika's relatives, no doubt. They were sitting in chairs and on a couple of sofas in one corner. He had expected a stark, plain room, like the rest of the hospital, but this one was paneled in wood, with curtains at the windows and blue carpeting. Ultradeluxe. He inched his way through the doorway. No one saw him yet.

Rasika was sitting up in bed. She wore a scarf around her head. He couldn't see her hair. Maybe it had been cut short or shaved off. Her face looked blank. Her mother sat on a high stool next to the bed, holding a spoon in front of Rasika's mouth. "You must eat, raja," her mother said. Rasika wasn't opening her lips.

Abhay grasped the handle of his bag firmly and strode through the crowd. All eyes turned to him. Rasika's father stood in the far corner next to her bed, plucking at something on the wall with a fingernail. Pramod looked up from the magazine he was reading. Abhay approached the bed and stood next to Rasika's mother.

"What?" Sujata Auntie dropped the spoon and stood up. "Get out!"

Rasika's face was bruised, but in her eyes he seemed to see a flicker of recognition. He spilled the flowers out onto the blanket, and she put out a hand and touched a blossom.

"Get him out!" Sujata Auntie shouted. "Take him away!" A couple of rough hands grabbed Abhay's arms.

"Yes," Rasika said, very clearly, looking straight at Abhay.

Her mother put a hand on Rasika's cheek. "What is it, raja?"

Rasika stared at Abhay, holding out a bloom in her cupped hands, like an offering. One of her hands had an IV taped to the back. Rasika opened her mouth and said, "Yes, I want to marry you."

The room fell into stunned silence. Pramod cleared his throat and stood up. His magazine splashed onto the floor. "This is a very good sign," he explained. "She remembers. She spoke a full sentence."

Rasika's face glowed with light. Abhay stepped toward her. Sujata Auntie held up a hand, palm outward, at Abhay. "Get out," she said. She leaned over and, with both hands, slapped at the flowers strewn on the bed. Rasika grasped at several more blossoms and hugged them to her chest.

The hands pulled at Abhay. He shook them off. He didn't want to create even more of a scene and disturb Rasika. He leaned toward her and whispered, "I'll be back tomorrow," and strode out before he was physically removed from the premises.

Rasika watched Abhay grow smaller and then disappear as he stepped out the door. She was still holding the blossoms. She felt open and free, as though she had finally turned to the sun and bloomed.

Amma said to Appa, "She did not mean it. She does not know what she is saying. She is not in her right mind."

"I'm here," Rasika said in Tamil. "I know. Let me eat. Where's the food?" She set the flowers on the blanket beside her.

Her father put a spoon in her hand, and she ate rice, dal, and yogurt. She asked, "Where am I?"

"We are in Bangalore," Appa said. "You are in a hospital. You have had an accident."

"I thought I was in Portland," she said. She told them about her trip. Amma shouted. Appa sat by her bed and held her hand and listened.

"Why am I in Bangalore?" she asked.

"Don't you remember?" Amma asked. "We came here to get you married. And you had to go and ruin everything."

Appa put a finger to his lips and said, "Shh."

"But why would I come to India to get married? I'm going to marry Abhay."

Amma threw up her hands and retreated to a chair on the other side of the room. Appa put his hand on her forehead. "You rest now. We will talk about all that later."

She saw her brother standing near the window. "Pramod. Are we really in Bangalore?"

He stepped over to the bed. "Yeah."

"Then I want you to do something for me." She tugged at his sleeve until he leaned over, and she whispered her task into his ear.

It was so simple, now, to know what she should do. Why had she been so mixed up before?

The next day Abhay came back, carrying a garland of jasmine flowers. He wasn't sure he'd be able to enter the room. However, Rasika's father himself ushered Abhay to Rasika's bedside. "She has been talking about you," he murmured to Abhay. "I have explained to Sujata that you are helping her to recover."

Rasika's mother barely acknowledged Abhay's presence. When she saw the flowers she said, "You don't need to bring a garland.

You are not marrying her yet." But her father helped Abhay put the garland around her neck.

"It feels soft. And cool." Rasika lifted the garland to her nose and took a deep breath. "I love jasmine."

Her father placed a chair near her bed for Abhay. He sat down. He could feel everyone in the room looking at him: Pramod, Rasika's parents, and an elderly woman sitting in a chair in one corner of the room, who looked like an older version of Sujata Auntie. She was knitting something, wrapping and pulling the yarn quickly and rhythmically, while keeping her eyes on Abhay.

"How're you doing?" Abhay asked softly.

"Better, I think," Rasika said. "I'm remembering more, and the doctors say that's a really good sign for my brain. I remember our trip to India, and seeing you at Lalbagh. And talking to you in that little garden."

"So you remember everything, it sounds like."

"I can't remember how I got hurt, though. I went—after I left you—I'm ashamed to tell you—I went—" She put her hands up to cover her face.

"Don't worry about it," Abhay soothed. He rubbed her upper arm, and she took her hands away and looked at him with a clear face. "Do you know what day it is today?" he asked.

"No. What day is it?"

"New Year's Day. The first day of 2008. The first full day of our engagement."

Rasika smiled. "I'm new now, too. I feel like I've been born again." Rasika looked at her grandmother. "Pati," she called, and the old woman set her knitting aside and strode over to the other side of Rasika's bed. Rasika put her arms around her grandmother's neck and whispered something in her ear. The grandmother smiled, and then held out both hands across the bed. Abhay grasped her hands, which were warm and strong. "God bless you," the grand-mother said in English. She gazed at him a moment longer, then let go and retreated back to her knitting.

"What did you say to her?" Abhay asked.

"I told her that you were the other boy."

"What does that mean?"

Rasika smiled. "I'll tell you later. Now I want to give you some-thing." From under her blanket she drew out a flat package and placed it on his lap.

"Your face is lit up with a huge smile," he said.

"I'm happy because we're going to be together. Open it."

Pramod and Rasika's father stood near the bed. Pati observed from her seat. Sujata Auntie, sitting on a sofa, held a handkerchief to her mouth and stared out the window.

Abhay removed the tape from the package and pulled out an embroidered silk jubba. "It's beautiful. I love the color." He held it up to the light from the window behind him. "Usually these kinds of shirts are white. Is it blue? Or green?"

"It's two colors in one," she said. "Looks different, depending on the angle. There's a word for it. I can't remember."

"Iridescent," said Pramod.

"Iridescent," she repeated.

"How did you manage to go shopping from the hospital?" Ab-hay asked.

Pramod said, "My sister'll figure out a way to shop no matter what."

Everyone laughed, except Sujata Auntie.

"Actually, she sent me out to bring back a bunch of shirts from a little place we know about, and she picked this one," Pramod said.

Abhay refolded the shirt and laid it in his lap. It was the first gift Rasika had ever given him. He tried to swallow down the lump in his throat. It was no use. He accepted a hanky from Pramod, dabbed at his eyes, and cleared his throat. "So you're really feeling better?" he asked Rasika.

"She's making a remarkable recovery, really," Pramod said. "Her speech is improving so fast. The physical therapists are amazed at her progress."

"I'm going to stay in India with you until you're ready to leave," Abhay said.

"Why?" Rasika asked. "You have important work to do. Go home, and I'll get better and come to see you."

"I'll study for my GRE right here and I can apply to graduate schools online. I won't lose any time. I just want to be with you."

"What about your parents? They'll be expecting you at home."

"I just talked to my mom and dad. They were shocked to find out about your accident, but they're thrilled that we're getting married. They've always liked you."

"I'm so happy that I'll be their daughter-in-law."

"They're also really happy that I'm going to graduate school. They give you all the credit for the fact that I've come to my senses."

Rasika smiled and pressed his hands in hers.

"My parents will work out a new airline ticket for me," he said. "They agree that I should stay with you. They want you to get better."

Rasika's father and Pramod were still clustered around them. Her mother had approached, as well, and was standing like a sentinel on the other side of the bed. Abhay leaned close and whispered into Rasika's ear, "I love you."

She laughed and declared, loud enough for everyone to hear, "I love you, too."

Epilogue

It has turned out beautifully." Mita patted Sujata's arm and glanced around the airy room, with French doors revealing the greenery outside. Wedding guests in Indian finery milled around the room as waitstaff cleared away the lunch plates. Rasika, wearing a gold-embroidered pale pink long skirt, blouse, and scarf, and Abhay, in a knee-length maroon embroidered kurta over calf-hugging pants, strolled hand in hand among the guests. A tall white and silver wedding cake graced one corner of the room.

"We had so much trouble with this wedding. You won't believe." Sujata pulled her cell phone from her waist, where it was clipped to her sari. "What could it be now? The ceremony is over. The reception is almost over." She glanced at the screen and re-clipped the phone. "My sister in India. Her daughter has run away with some Muslim boy. So my sister is calling me every day, crying. I always told her she was giving Mayuri too much freedom. We raised Rasika so she understood that she must choose a Hindu."

Mita smiled sympathetically and pressed Sujata's hand in both of hers. "Yes. She has chosen a Hindu, at least. Abhay—what is he going to do now?"

"As a matter of fact, he has gotten a full fellowship to the University of California at Berkeley."

"Oh. Berkeley. Very good school. I thought he was—"

"What people think has nothing to do with reality." Sujata touched the diamonds gracing her earlobes, and put a palm over her heart. "He has been so good to her, Mita. He stayed with us in India until we left, and then he moved back to this area—you know he was in Oregon—but he came back, just for Rasika."

"Life is hard sometimes." Mita patted her eyes with a hanky. "She is completely well now?"

"That is what the doctors say, thank God." Sujata cleared her throat. "Rasika wanted an outdoor wedding. She has been through so much, so I didn't insist on a temple wedding, but this was not easy to arrange."

"You did wonderful job. It is too bad Kanchan could not come. He had important meeting, he said. To look at her, no one would know all trouble she has been through. Her hair is short, but still she is beautiful."

"Where is she now?" Sujata's eyes raked the room. "We will cut the cake in a few minutes." Sujata's husband was standing in a dark corner, discussing something with the videographer. Her gaze passed over Amisha Menon Nayar, who had gained even more weight since her own wedding, and who was feeding her very fat baby with a bottle. At the next table Subhash sat with his new wife, a thin, shy girl with an enormous belly—she was about seven months pregnant. Deepti brought a bowl of rice payasam and set it on the table next to the girl, but the girl shook her head.

Past tables of Abhay's and Rasika's college friends, Sujata's eyes fell on the couple making their way toward the wedding cake, where Abhay's mother was hovering. Sujata glanced at her watch. "I hope the icing has not melted."

"It will be fine, I am sure. The air-conditioning is so cold." Mita wrapped the palloo of her sari around her shoulders.

"Balu had to drive the priest here," Sujata continued. "We had to pay the maintenance people here to put together the mantapa. At first they did not want us to put up our own structure, but I said, it's just a temporary canopy. We must have this for a traditional Hindu wedding. And then of course there was the question of lighting the fire. At first the director of the garden said, absolutely not. But how can we have a Hindu wedding without the fire god as witness? I had to bring in an aluminum tray and show him how small the fire would be—hardly more than a couple of candles. Still they wanted extra for insurance."

"They let you bring Indian food in?"

"We had to pay for their food, even though we didn't need it. And we had to bring in our own food. I thought I would have to pay twice, but Venika said she would do it, as her contribution to the wedding. She has gotten into catering, you know."

"Venika made cake, too?"

"She ordered it. She does not make Western desserts, but she decorated the top of each layer with silver leaf, so it looks more Indian."

Mita nodded her head. "Very beautiful."

Sujata shot a glance toward the far corner. "I must tell the videographer to be ready for the cake cutting." She strode off, leaving Mita standing alone.

Rasika and Abhay, at the opposite side of the hall, were talking to his mother.

"Mom, the food was amazing," Abhay said.

"Rice was little overcooked," his mother said.

"No, it was great," Rasika insisted. "You worked so hard. You must be exhausted. We are so grateful."

"Thank you so much, Mom," Abhay added.

Venika grasped Rasika's and Abhay's hands. "No need to thank. I am mother of groom. I am used to cooking. We are just glad, so glad things work out for both of you." She let go of their hands and stroked their cheeks. "Now you both be happy together, and have good life."

Sujata arrived with the videographer. "Don't go too far," she warned Abhay and Rasika. "We'll cut the cake in five minutes."

They strolled over to Jill's table.

"You look so tan!" Rasika said. "Hawaii's been good to you."

"I don't know why it took me so long to get there." Jill stood up and put out a hand to touch Rasika's gold wedding necklace. "Is this a significant symbol?" She fingered the pendant.

"Normally, you have caste symbols on your wedding necklace," Rasika said. "But since Abhay and I don't care about caste, we decided to choose an om on a lotus."

A couple of little girls, wearing long silk skirts and Indian jewelry, raced past. The room was clamorous with loud adult voices and children's shouts. The gentle plinking of the veena music, piped through the speakers, could be heard only at moments when the noise subsided somewhat.

"I love the translation of your wedding vows." Jill opened her copy of the program.

Abhay took it from her. "I had no idea there was a translation. I just repeated whatever the priest told me to say." He read out loud, " 'With these seven steps we have become friends. I am blessed with your friendship. I shall always be with you. You shall always be with me. We shall live together. We shall combine our minds in our thoughts. We shall combine our hands in our actions.' "

"That's so great," Jill said. "I thought maybe the two of you made up those vows."

Rasika grasped the program and scanned the lines. "This was a very traditional wedding—or at least as traditional as my mother could make it. But the meaning is really so modern, isn't it? Abhay, we should get someone to write this out in calligraphy, in Sanskrit and English, and have it framed."

"Go for it. You're better than I am at decorating." He put an arm around her waist and strolled to the next table, where Chris Haldorson and his mother were seated.

"What a beautiful wedding," Mrs. Haldorson said. Tears were shining in her eyes. "Your mother must be just beside herself."

Chris gave him a bear hug. "I'm so happy for you, Adios!"

"Adios?" Rasika furrowed her brow at Abhay.

"It's a long story," Abhay said.

Chris shook hands with Rasika. "Watch out for this guy." He nudged Abhay, then sat down and began mopping up some tamarind sauce with the last portion of his samosa. "Hey, this food is great."

"It must be hard without your dad." Abhay set a hand on Chris's shoulder.

"It was his time." Chris grasped his mother's hand with his free hand. "So now it's just me and Mom in the house."

Mrs. Haldorson dabbed her eyes with a napkin. "You'll find someone of your own soon, just like Adios here," she said. "You'll have a place of your own."

"Mom, I'll stay with you as long as you'll have me." He shrugged at Abhay. "I'm being a good Indian son, right?"

Abhay laughed. "Better than me, I'm sure."

Rasika and Abhay stepped out onto the sunny patio to talk with Seema and Jawad. Abhay waved to Dr. Ben-Aharon, sitting at a patio table gesturing to Abhay's father, who seemed to be listening intently.

"This is a dramatic outfit." Rasika fingered the hem of Seema's purple spaghetti-strap top, worn over a matching slim long skirt with a slit up one leg. "It feels like silk. And the hat is great."

Seema put a hand up to her purple head wrap. "Jawad bought the whole set for me." She smiled at Jawad, who said, "I don't know anything about fabric. I just like how she looks in it."

Leaves rustled in the breeze. Rasika glistened in the sunlight.

"So I hear you two are moving to Berkeley," Jawad said.

"We went out last month and found an apartment," Rasika said. "And I put in applications at about a dozen banks."

"She's already had three phone interviews," Abhay said proudly.

"Where are you going for your honeymoon again?" Seema asked.

"Point Reyes National Seashore," Rasika said. "It's near Berkeley, and of course near the ocean. I have to be near water."

"She claims she's going to camp with me." Abhay raised an eyebrow in mock disbelief.

Rasika laughed at him. "I want to save money. My parents have spent so much on the wedding and my medical treatment. I can deal with a few nights of camping."

Pramod leaned out the door. "Amma says we're going to do the cake now."

Guests streamed into the room and toward the cake. Rasika lingered behind. "Something smells lovely." She lifted her face to the air. "I wonder what that's from." She walked away from the doorway, toward the urns of flowers at the edge of the patio, and bent over a stalk of white bell-shaped flowers.

"Come in." Abhay followed after her and grasped her hand.

"Stay with me a minute." She pulled him close. "Smell these."

He bent down and sniffed. "Nice. Come on, everyone's waiting."

"I don't want to go in yet. I don't want this day to end."

They stood quietly, facing away from the wedding hall. The air was very warm. Surrounding them was the low hum of insects, changing tone every so often, becoming lower and softer, or higher and louder. Above that hum, birds burbled and chirruped. Tiny insects flitted white in the sunlight, and disappeared into the shade.

"Look up," Rasika said. They both tipped their heads back and gazed at the maple leaves above them, some dappled in shade, and some glowing pure green in the sunlight.

"Everything is so beautiful." Rasika sighed. "I just want to hold on to this moment. Can anything ever be this beautiful again?"

"We'll have lots more wonderful moments." Abhay slipped an arm around her and pulled her close.

She pressed her palms together and touched her index fingers to her chin. "For all these months I've been so focused on getting better and planning the wedding. And now we're married. What happens next?"

"You mean, you're worried because there's nothing more to plan? You just have to step through that door and eat some cake!"

She smiled. "After that, I mean. Part of me wishes I could plan our future the way I planned this wedding."

"We can't know what's in store for us." Abhay took her hands in his. "We have to proceed anyway, and the path will appear as we go."

She touched his cheek and smiled. "I always knew you were wise." She readjusted her gold and pink scarf over her shoulders. "I'm ready. Let's go."

Hand in hand, they walked through the doorway to the rest of their lives.

Acknowledgments

This novel was inspired by *The House of Mirth* by Edith Wharton. I have always been fascinated and frustrated by the character of Lily Bart in Wharton's novel. Her situation—the need she felt to fit into her society by marrying the right kind of person—seemed so similar to the situation faced by many Indian-Americans, who feel pressure to enter into an arranged marriage. So, I wanted to explore a Lily-type character who is a modern-day Indian-American woman.

The character of Lawrence Selden in *The House of Mirth* represents an alternative to Lily's gilded-cage society. Selden's world is about art and music and has a bit more freedom in terms of behavior. Yet Selden always seemed too sure of himself, leading me to wonder: did he ever have any doubts about his own choices? I wanted to explore this question by creating a Selden-type character who is seeking his place in the world, who has a vision of what a perfect society would be like, but who is not able to find it.

My friend Sally Kearney was the first person to read a draft of this novel, and her enthusiasm for the story gave me confidence.

My agent, Jenni Ferrari-Adler with Brick House Literary Agents, was able to see the potential of this novel and worked hard to help me realize it. Her guidance and good judgment have been invaluable. Also at Brick House, Sally Wofford-Girand, Melissa

Sarver, and Miya Dunets provided valuable feedback and suggestions.

My editor, Maya Ziv, has been tireless with her perceptive questions and suggestions. She has helped me smoothly navigate the journey to a published book. Mary Sasso, Maggie Oberrender, and Jennifer Hart in the HarperCollins marketing department were early, enthusiastic supporters. Emin Mancheril designed an evocative cover, and Shelly Perron did a thorough job copyediting.

I would like to thank my family for their general love and support, as well as for their enthusiasm for this novel and their suggestions: my husband, Mark Winstein; my parents, Vimala and V.V. Sreenivasan; and my brother, Sharad Sreenivasan. My two sons provide lots of fun and help me keep life in perspective.

I have benefited greatly, in my life and my writing, from classes I've taken through Landmark Education, and meditation techniques I've learned through Swami Nithyananda's Life Bliss Foundation. I would like to thank both organizations for their contributions to my life.

Jyotsna Sreenivasan

JYOTSNA SREENIVASAN, the daughter of Indian immigrants, was born and raised in Ohio. She earned an M.A. in English literature from the University of Michigan. Her short fiction has appeared in numerous literary magazines, and she has received literature grants from the Washington, DC Commission on the Arts and Humanities. The author of several nonfiction books published by academic presses, and the creator of the online Gender Equality Bookstore, she lives in Moscow, Idaho, with her family. This is her first novel.